PANDORA'S
PLEASURE

USA Today Bestselling Author
VANESSA FEWINGS

Cover created by: Karen Hulseman
Cover concept: Liz Fewings

Cover Photo: Shutterstock: Art of Life

Formatted by: Champagne Book Design
Editor: Debbie Kuhn

ISBN: 9781733774253

For

My wonderful editor Debbie Kuhn

and for

Karen Hulseman, Lauren Luman, Susie Steinle, Hazel Godwin,
Heather Amber Pollock, Paramita Patra, Stacey Ryan Blake,
Lupita Gonzalez,
Melanie Moreland, Kay Hutcherson, Pam Stack, Barbara Danks,
SueBee Crue, and Ava Harrison.

"She was powerful not because she wasn't scared but because she went on so strongly, despite the fear."
—Atticus

PANDORA'S
PLEASURE

CHAPTER
ONE

Pandora

I failed to escape.

A blur of movement caught my attention as someone stormed toward the BMW. The driver's side door was flung open and Carter Godman dragged me out, pulling so violently I knew there'd be bruises later. My heart pounded and I felt heady from the rush of fear.

Soon, everyone would know I'd tried to leave.

Struggling with Carter would only make things worse. Maybe I could talk him out of telling my parents.

They were here, somewhere, mingling with the other distinguished guests in the ballroom—drinking the Godmans' champagne, eating their canapés, and working the room along with the rest of Washington's elite.

Carter's decision to steal away for a smoke break out back had been badly timed—he'd caught me attempting to drive off in his brother's car.

There were no words exchanged between us; not when a member of the valet staff could be the eyes and ears of the tabloids.

My future brother-in-law was just as cruel as the rest of his family. No doubt he'd suffer no repercussions for treating me like this. With an ironclad grip on my forearm, he hauled me back inside his family's manor.

I teetered on high heels, tripping on the hem of my beaded pink tulle gown as I tried to keep up. Feeling humiliated, I prayed we'd not encounter any of their staff along the way. Only a Godman would dare treat a Bardot in this fashion.

We finally made it to the private sitting room, where Carter caged me between his body and the wall, gripping my throat. A trickle of sweat snaked down my spine.

Carter stared down at me, his expression furious. "Just where do you think you were going?"

I'd known they would try to talk me out of leaving if I was caught, but I hadn't expected *this*. Now I realized what they really thought of me.

"Nowhere."

"I don't believe you." His pupils were dilated, proving he was garnering pleasure from threatening me.

This was what privilege looked like; all wrath and revenge with no fear of any consequences. Carter was the youngest son of a trillion-dollar banking tycoon. But his cockiness prevented him from advancing in his daddy's business—his temperament was too unstable to trust with any kind of responsibility.

His father, Gregor Godman, had wealth that was beyond comprehension...the kind of new money that allowed him to own islands. He was a man destined to sit in the most distinguished seat in the Oval Office in less than thirty days—if all went well and no one fucked up. Unfortunately, that included *me*.

Six months ago, when I was still a naïve nineteen-year-old, I'd met Gregor's oldest son, Damien. It had not been by chance. We'd been unaware at the time that our relationship had been arranged by our parents.

I'd hardly seen Damien Godman over the last few months. When our paths did cross, he was dismissive and rude. Clearly, the realization of what we really were to each other—a fusing of two dynasties—had been just as devastating for him.

I'd been purposefully caught in the crosshairs of his family's empire and ambition and there was no getting out of this alliance.

And now Carter and I were alone in one of this ostentatious mansion's thirty rooms, where he could do whatever he wanted to me and get away with it.

I tried to wriggle free. "Your brother—"

"Isn't standing here."

"You're hurting me."

He relaxed his grip on my throat slightly. "We expected more from you, Pandora," he said in a low sinister tone.

"Damien will wonder where I am," I insisted.

"Wait until I tell your fiancé that you were ready to walk out on him on the very night of the big announcement."

I swallowed hard at the thought.

"It isn't what it looks like."

He made a harsh noise like a game show buzzer. "Wrong answer. Explain to me what you were doing trying to drive off in my brother's car."

Looking over his shoulder, I saw the plush couch where I'd sat a few weeks ago while having high tea with the matriarch of their family. We'd swapped pleasantries to pass the time and I'd tried my best to impress her, sharing details of my elite schooling in Switzerland. I'd proudly told Mrs. Godman about my flair for learning foreign languages, competing in sports and refining my culinary skills, and that I also had a natural aptitude for computer science.

"You won't have any use for that sort of thing," Mrs. Godman had told me, her words striking hard. I'd always imagined I would be more than just someone's wife. After that meeting, I realized what marrying into this family would truly mean for me. I would lose my freedom, my independence…and my self-respect.

"Look at me when I'm talking to you." Carter towered over my petite frame, his tuxedo camouflaging the animal inside of him.

I felt powerless against his strength. Tension as thick as the smoke radiating from the nearby black marble fireplace settled over us. Resting upon the mantelpiece was a doomsday clock that ticked away the minutes. Soon the official announcement of my engagement would be made to the hundreds of guests who'd gathered in the ballroom. The press would be notified and then the wedding frenzy would be set into motion. I'd be counting down the hours until my miserable day of reckoning when I'd finally become Mrs. Damien Godman.

"You're scaring me," I whispered.

"You remember who my father is, right?" Carter asked, sneering.

A voice boomed from the doorway, "That's hardly any way to treat my fiancée."

Carter's older brother walked into the room—the man who used to make my heart soar whenever I saw him…right up until the day he'd made it clear he didn't actually like me.

Carter glared at Damien. "I stopped her from leaving. You're welcome."

Damien shot a look of disapproval my way. "I see."

He was a tall, ruggedly handsome man of thirty-two. The epitome of what a gentleman from the ruling class should be—all new money and decadence.

I'd once found Damien's confident jaw, dark intelligent eyes, and full, sensual mouth incredibly appealing, back when I'd watched him from afar and before we'd been formally introduced. I'd flown too close to the solar glare of a man whose aggressive tactics intimidated all who came close to him.

Damien Godman was his father's son.

My affection for him was fading. I'd been in love with the idea of him. The idea of an *us*.

"She thinks nothing of embarrassing this family," said Carter.

"Tell him to let me go," I pleaded as my hand snapped to Carter's wrist, trying to ease the pressure of his grip.

Damien eased his hands into his pockets. "Carter, you're being very rude."

"I'm not done with her." Carter looked at his brother defiantly.

The fact he hadn't pulled his brother off of me was my punishment for trying to leave. I saw that now. He had probably found out about my escape attempt from a member of the staff. Or perhaps Carter had sent him a text before dragging me back in here.

Damien's dangerous expression intensified. "I'll take it from here."

Carter clenched his jaw and released me, stepping back. "The Bardots will regret the day they handed you over to us."

"I don't belong to anyone," I snapped, caressing my throat. I hoped his aggression wouldn't leave a bruise.

"Why do you insist on insulting us, Pandora?" Carter replied. "Our guests want to meet you."

Damien smirked. "Sweetheart, it appears you've been very naughty."

Carter glared at him. "Make sure she doesn't embarrass us any further."

"I'll handle her," Damien said darkly.

The way Carter looked at me caused the hairs on my nape to prickle.

"Out." Damien's tone was severe.

With a final glare of contempt, Carter turned and marched out the door, proving he was just as wary of Damien as the rest of us.

The air was saturated with a coldness that I shouldn't have felt—not with a fire ablaze nearby. I could smell the scent of burning logs and hear the torrid crackling.

Orange flames reflected in Damien's chestnut brown irises... eyes that had once looked upon me with kindness. His devastatingly attractive face rarely smiled now, reminding me that he was a Godman.

I'd heard a rumor that Damien was set to follow in his father's ambitious footsteps and one day rule the nation from the Oval Office. Such ambitions had to be the reason he always looked past me, like I was a frivolous distraction to be tolerated when present.

My own father insisted the Godmans could turn around the damage inflicted by the current administration and the incumbent President's selfish agenda. My parents had reassured me that marrying into this family would benefit everyone. Including my father's own political aspirations; he wanted a place in Godman's Cabinet.

"I sent the staff to find you," Damien said tersely, running a hand through his raven hair. "Now I know why they couldn't."

His name made me think of that old movie, *The Omen*—his parents had chosen it well. Damien might as well be the Devil's son. His family's hunger for power was never sated.

At first, I'd believed that what we had together could become special. Even after he began ghosting me, I'd refused to let go of the illusion I had of him—the man I'd secretly fallen for as a teenager from afar while reading stories of him in *GQ*.

I'd turned twenty in August, and that birthday had become a milestone occasion—the beginning of the countdown to my loss of freedom.

"Where were you going?" Damien's tone was almost kind.

"Getting some fresh air."

"Right." He stepped closer until he towered over me. "How am I meant to protect you if you run off like that?"

Even now his nearness sent a thrill through me. "Sorry."

His eyes darkened. "I have a reputation to live up to. If I appear to have no control over you, others will take advantage."

"No one noticed."

"Oh, they noticed."

"I'll go back to the party."

"Yes, you will. You'll smile at everyone's conversations, laugh at their jokes. You'll hang on my arm and be the pretty young thing you are meant to be while you entertain our guests. You will make my father—" He gritted his teeth. "Look good."

I hated all of these self-entitled assholes.

I glanced at the clock.

"Are you even listening, Pandora?"

"At least let me visit the restroom." My tone sounded calmer than I expected.

His eyes narrowed and his gaze fell on my lips. "Of course, darling. I'll escort you."

"Thank you." I was starved for any sign of kindness from him, no matter how fleeting.

He weaved his fingers through mine and led me out of the room and along the sprawling hallway, his palm hot against mine, possessively controlling our pace.

"I'll make you proud," I said softly, trying to appease him. "I promise."

"You have a lot to make up for."

I shouldn't have been shocked when he preceded me into the bathroom, intending not to give me any privacy. He locked the door behind us and then leaned against the sink, his dark eyes following my every move.

Damien dragged his teeth along his bottom lip. "Hurry up."

My nostrils flared with annoyance at being rushed, but I turned and lifted my hem, pulling down my panties to sit on the toilet. "I can't go with you watching."

He stepped closer until he was looming over me. "I think you should get used to this."

I avoided his stare.

"You're my trophy, Pandora."

I didn't want to believe the elite private finishing school I'd attended had been all about preparing me to be his wife and nothing more. But our relationship had come about so two American families could forge a powerful alliance through marriage, hijacking all the power in Washington through this allegiance.

Mine and his.

I had flown into this gilded cage. At first, I'd entered willingly because I didn't know this man. The papers painted Damien Godman as a modern-day hero. A man who fought for social justice. A senator's son who was willing to dedicate his time to those trapped in poverty, to see them lifted out of it.

They didn't know him like I did.

"Damien, please step back."

He rested his palm on my head as though anointing me. "Do you want me to run the tap for you? Help you pee?"

I shivered at his touch, squeezing my eyes shut.

I finally managed to relax enough to empty my bladder.

After wiping myself, I stood quickly and flushed the toilet. I had to push past him to him to get to the sink.

Damien followed me. "You belong to me now. Let me protect you."

There was no arguing with him. Not when he was in this kind of mood.

Washing my hands under the warm water, I rallied my courage. All I had to do was smile and play nice. Feign innocence. After tonight, when Damien and I were alone, we could talk and I would remind him that I deserved to be treated with respect. After all, I was a Bardot...American royalty.

I dried my hands on a cotton napkin and turned to face him. "We should get back before your father notices."

"He noticed."

I shot him a fearful look.

No one crossed his father more than once.

"Please, explain to the Senator I needed some air."

"You want me to lie to him?" Damien frowned.

"Protect me." I straightened my back. "As a husband should."

"We're not married...yet."

I raised my chin defiantly, trying to hide the fact that he scared me.

His fingertips trailed along my forearm. The gesture seemed too tender for him, and a shudder ran through me as an electric spark seemed to pass between us. This man could ruin something sacred if he wanted to. He could possess a soul for his mere amusement and then destroy it.

He'd destroy *my* soul if I stayed.

"This is the last time you defy me," he said quietly. "Understand?"

"Yes." My eyelashes fluttered rebelliously.

He studied my face. "Usually you're so compliant, Pandora. What's gotten into you?"

I'd remained under his control because he had the power to see my father's ambitions realized. Walking away from an alliance this powerful wasn't what good girls did if they wanted their families to still love them.

"Say something." He tipped up my chin.

He was taller than his brother and a lot stronger—and if at all possible, crueler.

"You've not talked to me all night, Mr. Godman."

"It's Damien, for Christ's sake. Is that what this is…you want more attention?"

"Yes and no."

His expression softened. "You look pretty tonight. Though you always do."

"Thanks for the compliment," I said sarcastically.

"Don't look at me like that. You may come from old money, but your father still needs mine."

"We both know I'm marrying beneath me." I regretted the words as soon as they left my mouth.

"Always a charmer, Ms. Bardot."

It was true his family had climbed the social ladder for decades. They may have amassed an astounding fortune, but their legacy had nothing on the centuries-old noble succession of my family. Which was where I came in, evidently.

"Where does your accent come from?" he asked, scolding me. "At times, you almost sound like Jackie Kennedy."

"Well, I've been molded since birth to accommodate you and your family—to be the perfect trophy wife. I hope to balance your uncouth ways the best I can."

I rushed out of the bathroom but he caught up to me immediately and dragged me against his chest, holding me tight. We were alone in the hallway.

"If you continue with your rebellion, I will have to correct your behavior."

"Did I strike a nerve, Mr. Godman? Being reminded I'm too good for you must sting."

His grip around my waist shot pressure into my spine.

"I'm protecting you from yourself." His mouth loomed close to mine.

I was panting softly, feeling his breath on my lips, his cock pressing into my belly.

"I don't want to announce our engagement tonight," I whispered.

"Want to tell me why?"

"I need more time."

"I'm afraid it can't be stopped."

"Please, Damien."

He let out a long sigh. "You exasperate me."

"Do what you can."

"Let me think on it." Damien leaned in again to brush his lips over mine—teasing me.

My sex throbbed in response to his dark flirting…and he knew it—knew that even if my eyes showed him defiance, my body couldn't help but respond to his charisma and the masterful way he dominated me. Perhaps my infatuation would never be shaken. I'd crushed on the Senator's son at that Debutante Ball because I'd been too innocent to see it was a match-making endeavor. My coming out party presented me as a woman who was ready to be plucked.

"A fruit in need of bruising." He'd teased me with those very words the night we'd met. *"To draw out your sweetness."*

Our first dance together had made my girlfriends jealous. I'd been too naive to realize that the look of excitement on my parents' faces had been because of their successful scheming to have me marry into this family.

To make me his.

Make me a Godman.

Damien gave me a predatory smile—his prey subdued by the strength of his hold and the dominating way he'd captured me. It would be easy to bite his lip, show more rebellion. I was burning up with the heat he radiated from all that hidden passion.

He smirked. "I don't want any evidence of my discipline to appear at the cocktail party. Maybe after everyone's gone."

I flinched as though he'd already hit me. "Don't."

"I don't mean to strike you, Pandora. I'm not a Neanderthal." His glare narrowed. "You're like this because you crave discipline."

I turned my head, refusing to look in his eyes.

His warm breath kissed my cheek. "You're so damn needy. This is why you defy me. You're constantly craving what only I can give you." His thumb rubbed over my bottom lip and dipped into my mouth; as sensual as it was forbidden. "I've arranged for the house at Seascape to be made ready."

That almost made my knees buckle.

He was talking about his private oceanside home that was a helicopter flight from here. The place I'd only heard about. The Godmans had homes all around the world, including New York, Milan, France, and England. I'd never be able to run from Seascape. It was in the middle of nowhere.

Damien's mother had hinted her eldest son might whisk me away tonight after the party, and she'd smiled as she'd delivered the news. Those other things she'd spoken of threatened to haunt my nightmares forever.

I refused to think of them now.

"You and I will spend the weekend at Seascape." He gave a nod. "I believe that once you and I get to know each other better, you'll relax around me."

Did he mean sleep together?

"We have to wait—"

"Go back to the ballroom and pretend you want to be there. Then you and I will have the rest of the evening to ourselves."

He let me go and I headed down the hallway. I was shaking uncontrollably.

"Pandora," he called after me.

I stopped walking, waiting for him to continue without looking back, not wanting to see the victory in his eyes.

"Remember you're a collector's item." Damien quickly closed the gap between us, standing right behind me to speak softly in my ear. "Behave as such."

"There are other women out there you might prefer."

He brushed a fingertip along my bare shoulder. "Be a good girl. Don't make me regret not punishing you for your indiscretion."

I nodded, feeling a shiver run down my spine. "Tell your brother to keep his hands off me."

"I will deal with him. Now off you go."

I hurried along the hallway in the direction of the ballroom, my heart pounding in my ears and Damien's cologne clinging to me, his amber scent scorching my psyche. My continued yearning for him was poisoning me.

As I neared the ballroom where the prestigious guests had gathered for the evening, I raised my chin preparing to face all of these strangers again. I needed to put the fear out of my mind—the fear of being alone with Damien later in some secluded house.

"Miss Bardot!"

I turned to face one of the Godman's staff—a burly man wearing a tuxedo.

"Senator Godman wants to see you in his office."

Fine hairs prickled on the back of my neck. "Damien requested that I go directly to the ballroom."

"This way, please." The man gestured toward a door at the other end of the hallway.

I wanted to listen to my intuition and refuse to be in the same room alone with Gregor Godman.

The tuxedo-clad man was already opening the office door. "Don't keep the Senator waiting."

CHAPTER TWO

Damien

Where was she going?

From the end of the hallway, I watched Pandora walk elegantly into *his* office.

Her deportment was born out of a fierce schooling at the *Institut auf dem Rosenberg* in St. Gallen. Sadly, a place where she'd spent most of her life. Studying in Switzerland had kept her far away from her parents. It made me wonder if all that loneliness was the cause of her flaws; she'd been overindulged in everything. Except love, I suppose.

She displayed a natural grace, but suffered from a terrible naivety. And *goddamn* was she beautiful.

I'd ordered her to proceed directly to the ballroom.

I made my way down the hallway to my father's office.

The guard outside raised his hand to stop me. "Sorry, sir. I've been instructed by the Senator that no one is to interrupt his meeting."

"Seriously?"

He gave a nod. "Miss Bardot's father is in there, too."

That information lessened the tension by a fraction.

"Your father has a meeting with Salvatore Galante in ten minutes," the guard added, hinting they wouldn't be long.

That's right.

Dad had invited over the Chairman and CEO of *Real Nation One TV,* the gnarly television executive who'd built a network from the ground up. Half the population was addicted to his wily news stories that pumped vitriol and well-fluffed lies onto the airwaves. Keeping Galante waiting would be as bad as pissing on a wedding cake in full view of the guests. The repercussions would be endless.

Backing off, I put some distance between me and the door and waited for Pandora to come out.

This could have been prevented. My instructions had been clear. I'd tried to protect her from my family, only so far she'd done a stellar job of leaving herself exposed to all of them.

Her scent lingered in my imagination, fanning the flames of my arousal. My dick chastised me for not banging her against the wall. Agreeably a monstrous act but I'd been in a bad mood for over a decade and couldn't shake my arrogance. This was what my family did…we took what we wanted whether we'd earned it or not.

Pandora was exceptionally pretty, but having a woman forced on you tends to dull your appetite for marriage.

Though I had agreed with my father on one thing—her family's legacy was impressive. The Bardots had a prestigious ancestry that included old money and remarkable connections. Her father, Brenan Bardot, was an oil baron who'd come to Washington with political aspirations. He'd left his eldest son to run his empire in Texas so he could swagger around the city and take aim at the White House.

What pairs well with a billion-dollar oil empire? A dynasty of bankers. Our legacy had been forged from diverse investing and our knack for managing money—making millionaires into billionaires. Unlike the Bardots, we were only three generations away from when we had made our mark on this shitty world.

Before becoming a senator, my father had ruled the financial markets as a brilliant tycoon at the helm of our trillion-dollar company. He'd handed over his philanthropic endeavors for me to manage, which meant my life had a purpose, at least.

Dad had his eye on the ultimate prize for someone desirous of eternal prestige—President of the good ole' US of A.

Both sets of parents, mine and Pandora's, were set on forging a bloodline between our families. If we didn't kill each other first. Our mutual hate went even deeper than Bardot's offshore oilrigs that drilled into the ocean floor, fucking up everything in their wake.

I'd done what I could to prepare Pandora for tonight. I'd gone so far as to give her a list of guests so she could study their individual interests and engage in insightful conversations. I'd needed her to shine. Her usefulness stretched only that far.

Instead, she'd extracted herself from the function—and almost driven off in my car, for God's sake.

She had to regret it now. This was my overriding thought as I gave the guard a stern warning and barged into my father's office.

I chose to stand at the back of the room so I could watch the show continue to unfold. Two more security guards were positioned behind my father's desk. Pandora's father stood before the bookcase with his back ramrod straight and his arms folded. His cold expression could have put out a fire.

This meeting wasn't about making Pandora feel safer—this was about threatening her with what might happen if she didn't comply.

No one walked out on my father. The Senator had a knack for smelling blood in the water a world away, and he went in for the kill without blinking.

Even sharks blinked when they sliced you open.

Pandora sat in a chair in the middle of the room with her back to me. I didn't need to see her face to know she felt intimidated. She seemed to have fixed her stare on my father, ignoring her own dad.

I imagined there was no love lost there. Who gives up their daughter for personal gain? Even Brenan's social-climbing wife, who held her own level of influence in this town as well as in Texas, only wanted more.

Pandora turned and glanced back at me with a hopeful expression. I found it endearing, but now that she was in here there was nothing I could do for her.

My father had strategized and committed a number of questionable deeds to reach the dizzying height of frontrunner. Having a loose cannon like Pandora threaten his progress had left him riled, which was apparent from the way his jaw flexed with quiet rage.

He stood at his oak desk, immune to fear, his shock of white hair revealing his age. Senator Gregor Godman carried the air of a gentleman who knew his fate was to change history.

There was no doubt I was halfway to becoming the same kind of monster. My darkest traits mirrored his...I, too, craved having control over a room full of powerful men.

Only I could alter the course of the trouble heading Pandora's way.

Besides her beauty and grace, Pandora's youth and optimism were valuable assets. Her naivety was annoying, but it would allow her to be molded into the perfect trophy wife.

But right now she was a spoiled princess.

How dare she walk out on an event where she'd been the main attraction? She was the quintessential debutante—the Jackie Kennedy of our times. The woman who would ensure my father would win votes from the youngest generation. Her feminine elegance was the only thing lacking in our brand.

"Pandora," my father's tone sounded polite as he rested his palm on a closed file, "excuse our unusual brand of hospitality."

She drew in a breath. "I was just getting some air—"

He shot me a glance and smiled. "We understand that what is being asked of you could be overwhelming. Trust me, I've been on the campaign trail for months and it's a grueling schedule. You can't even imagine the time and effort, and of course the billions of dollars, it took to get us here."

"I respect that, sir."

He lifted the file. "You're quite accomplished."

"That's on me?" she asked, gesturing at the folder.

"This collection of records is impeccable, Pandora." Dad offered her a kind smile. "Don't make me add a negative addendum."

Pandora turned to look at me, her crystal blue eyes begging for help. I saw her come to the stark realization that she was on her own. Her expression changed to one of resilience as she twisted around to face my father.

Her breathing was ragged, causing her breasts to rise and fall, which was unwittingly bewitching. Here was a damsel who wasn't getting saved.

Pandora was the equivalent of the Hope Diamond—the most expensive jewel in the world, but other than its legendary beauty, quite useless.

But that in itself was a rare gift, really. She was ready to be dominated and then subjugated. She deserved to be treated better, but seeing her vulnerable stirred too much pleasure. My flesh ignited as my mind delivered the images of what I would do to her if given the chance.

I would finally get to have her in every conceivable way.

I would strip her naked and then fuck her into oblivion.

My cock ached at the thought as I stared at Pandora.

"You have a beautiful daughter, Brenan." Dad's attention moved over to Pandora's father. "I'm glad for this match with my son."

"We're sorry for her behavior," said Brenan, his voice void of emotion.

"A small detail that's easily dealt with," I said.

That comment made everyone look my way.

After all, the dark gods had delivered her to us. And now she was mine.

"Give me your phone." Dad held his hand out.

Pandora unclipped her clutch purse and reached inside. She handed the phone over to my father with a puzzled look.

He offered it to me. "Less of this."

Stepping forward, I took the phone from him. My father was right…she seemed to be addicted to the device, using it during the party when she should have been chatting with our distinguished guests. I'd delete her apps later.

She watched me tuck her smartphone into my jacket pocket. "Can I go now?"

"Address my father as sir," I chastised.

Pandora shifted uncomfortably. "Sorry."

"She's very young," Dad said to me, his tone mild. "Considering what's expected."

"Which is why she's perfect," I advised.

"True," Brenan Bardot agreed.

Talk about throwing your daughter to the wolves; that man's ambitions were shameless.

With no ex-lovers to cause a scandal, Pandora would make an ideal bride. If the time ever came for me to follow in my father's footsteps and hold office, she'd make an elegant First Lady.

I strolled over to the liquor cabinet and removed a bottle of Diamond Jubilee. After using tongs to fill three tumblers with ice, I poured some of the amber liquid into each one.

"Whisky?" I offered one to Brenan and gave the other glass to my father, keeping the third for myself.

Dad took a sip and then said, "Pandora, tonight we're going to announce your father as a potential candidate in my Cabinet."

Her expression remained unchanged because she already knew her parents had made the ultimate deal by offering *her*. The price of power for a daughter's future.

"Which is why," I said, my eyes meeting hers, "we should hold off on announcing our engagement tonight." I watched the relief settle over Pandora's face.

I gave her a wink. She'd pleaded with me to delay sharing our news with the world. I needed to get her to trust me and this situation worked just fine.

"Are you sure?" asked my father.

"Let's focus on Mr. Bardot." I turned to Brenan. "Let's create the illusion I got to know Pandora better on the campaign trail. We'll be able to spin it as us sharing the same core values."

Pandora looked back at me with gratitude.

Approaching her, I ran my fingers through her blonde locks

and let them tumble over her shoulders. Looking up, she fixed her grateful gaze on me and I tilted the rim of the tumbler so she could taste my whisky. She was too young to drink, but I thrived on making her break the law in front of everyone as a daring gesture in present company.

"Do you love my son?" asked Dad.

"Yes, sir," she said breathlessly. "Of course."

He offered her a thin smile of approval.

"What was my order earlier, Pandora?" My voice sounded husky from the whisky.

"I was to return to the ballroom," she said.

"And then?" I coaxed.

"I was supposed to host the guests and their wives and make a good impression."

"Correct." I gestured for my father to continue. "She knows her part."

My father gave a nod. "Should you disobey us in any way, Pandora, I'm afraid you'll leave me no choice but to choose a different candidate." He gave Brenan a knowing look.

Pandora drew in a deep breath, trying to hide her panic. She didn't look her father's way…she didn't need to. Brenan's anger radiated toward her like a brewing storm, the air heavy with his disappointment.

My father studied her carefully. "You never leave an event without your fiancé by your side. Appearances are everything. If you have a grievance, you discuss it later with him in private. Understand?"

Beads of sweat spotted her brow. "I won't disappoint you again, sir."

"You are Damien's property, Pandora." He shrugged with the ease of a man who expected as much from his own wife. "You do as he says."

"She understands," I said quietly.

Dad gave a nod of approval. "Let's go spread some rumors, Brenan. Let them know you're my first choice for Foreign Secretary."

Brenan gave a sigh of relief. His political career was still on track...*for now.*

I stepped forward and shook Brenan's hand. "Congratulations, Mr. Bardot. You must be thrilled."

"I'm overjoyed with this opportunity to serve your father," he said. "And the country."

My father approached me. "Damien, correct her behavior whenever necessary. She'll eventually learn the complexities of politics. Make me proud."

His approval meant so much. I'd always admired him for what he'd achieved, but what he stood to accomplish was remarkable. My father was a historical figure in the making.

I felt a fevered rush of anticipation at the thought of flying Pandora off to Seascape later, my body responding to the idea of us finally having the privacy we needed. I was like an addict craving his forbidden fix.

Finally, she'd become more to me.

If I could just learn to tolerate her cultivated snobbery.

Brenan followed my father out of the room without even acknowledging his daughter's discomfort or throwing her a look of reassurance. Her own mother would be harsher, a fact that almost made me feel sorry for the brat.

What had set her family apart from the other contenders for a place in my father's kingdom was *her.*

A female icon in the making.

If she ever realized the power she had over us all, she'd be dangerous.

CHAPTER
THREE

Pandora

The Sikorsky helicopter set down on the helipad.

From the air, I'd admired the impressive house perched on a cliff above the ocean—the place we'd be staying for the entire weekend. We were in the middle of nowhere, and I was glad I no longer had to mingle with a room full of strangers obsessed with politics.

Before opening the aircraft's door, Damien shrugged out of his black jacket and placed it over my shoulders, his heady masculine cologne wafting just enough to remind me why I'd fallen for him. His chivalry gave me hope for the rest of the evening. Maybe here, away from the stresses of Washington, he'd relax.

He helped me climb down from the helicopter and once we'd escaped the heated blast of air from the chopper blades, Damien accepted the two suitcases—one of them I recognized as mine—pulled out of the side panel by the pilot. My mom must have directed a member of our staff to pack mine.

With a nod of thanks, Damien strolled confidently toward the cliff-top home carrying the suitcases, all alpha swagger and boldness. From behind me I heard the sound of blades cutting through the air as the helicopter ascended back over the water.

Into Satan's home it is, then.

He left the suitcases in the foyer. I followed him farther into the home, trying to become acclimated to my new surroundings.

Damien turned as though sensing my gaze on his back. He gave me a devilish grin in response to my wariness. Or maybe he was glad to show me his secret hideaway.

We stepped into the open plan sitting room and I admired the spectacular view of the endless ocean. I wondered if we could walk along the beach in the morning. The expanse offered one the optical illusion of a house floating on water, the sky a blanket of dusky clouds shading the horizon.

I knew what would soon be expected of me, but I still couldn't get there in my head.

I tore my eyes from the mesmerizing view and went off to find Damien, noticing the home's artwork was all modern, and none of it appealing. If the art reflected the owner's personality, Damien had serious issues, though I'd already sensed this.

He was busy in the kitchen. I watched as he pulled a bottle of chilled champagne out of the chrome fridge and then searched the cupboards, finding two flutes. He placed the glasses on the marble central island.

"I'm not allowed," I said.

He uncorked the bottle and it popped and fizzed as he poured the bubbling liquid into the two glasses. "No one will know."

Secretly, I couldn't wait to drink the champagne. I licked my lips with anticipation.

I admired the oak fitted cabinetry and marble island. This was the kind of spacious setting a family would feel comfortable hanging out in. If my infatuation with Damien hadn't faded, I imagine being here would have brought me some contentment.

Damien handed me the glass.

I brought the crystal flute to my lips and took a few sips to garner more confidence, the fizzing bubbles tickling my nose.

A chime went off.

Damien fished around in his pocket and withdrew his Smartphone, his expression turning to one of surprise when he glanced at the screen.

Moving closer, I asked, "What is it?"

He turned the screen of his phone toward me, showing me an article on the *New York Times* website:

WASHINGTON QUAKES WITH THE ANNOUNCMENT
OF
TWO DYNASTIES MELDING

*Presidential candidate Senator Gregor Godman's Son, Damien G.
Godman, to wed Pandora Aria Bardot, daughter of Brenan Bardot
of Bardot Petroleum.*

Damien tucked his phone away.

That was it.

My future was set. Extracting myself from this betrothal now written in stone—or the newsy equivalent—would be impossible.

"Weren't we going to wait?" I shot Damien a look of confusion. "Who sent you that?"

"Welcome to my fucking world." He reached into his pocket and threw a shiny object onto the countertop. I watched as it bounced across the marble toward me, settling near the edge. The ring glinted in the moonlight—a vivid green emerald surrounded by a cluster of diamonds.

It was beautiful, but…

He'd not opened a velvet box to reveal it. Or gotten on one knee to officially propose. There'd been no confession of love… just a gaudy gesture of contempt thrown my way. I counted the cluster of diamonds surrounding the stone to take my mind off its meaning—a stamp of ownership.

Maybe he'd say something soon. Maybe he'd share his feelings for me. With my breath held, I waited for Damien to say that despite all of his questionable prior behavior toward me, he did love me.

But Damien merely pulled open a drawer and pulled out a packet of cigarettes. He peeled back the wrapper and tapped one out, then went on another hunt and fished a lighter out of a small ceramic bowl on the counter. With a flick and a spark, he used it to light up his cigarette.

He took a long drag and blew out a spiral of smoke that snaked toward the ceiling. He flicked an ash into the ceramic bowl.

Acrid smoke reached my nostrils. "Is that ring for me? Or are you leaving it as a tip for the housekeeper?"

"Try it on." He reached for his bowtie and worked it loose until it dangled from his neck.

I set my champagne glass down, my lips quivering with a bitterness that was impossible to hide. I wished it was a sapphire. Petty thought, I admit, but I'd wanted to be there when he chose the ring.

"I'm never going to get down on one knee and propose." He flicked ash from the end of his cigarette into the ceramic bowl. "If that's what you're expecting."

I reached for the emerald and slipped it onto my left ring finger, as though I were perfectly willingly to be bound to him. It fit too well, like it might stay there. It *was* pretty. Striking, really, but this wasn't the way I'd imagined this moment.

He read my reaction. "I'm a victim just as much as you."

"Victim?"

"People like us don't get to decide. We're told who our match will be, that the world will be a better place for it."

"But I thought—"

"You thought I wanted to dance with you at your Debutante Ball?"

Six months ago, he'd made me believe that it was his choice when he took my hand and led me onto the dance floor, slow dancing with me in his arms all night. Gliding me around the floor as though he was a prince who'd come to rescue me from my monotonous existence.

"You're not my type, Pandora."

His words hit me like a bullet to the chest. My heart shattered into a thousand pieces. "Why would you say that?"

"We should at least be honest with each other, right?" He took another long drag.

"What's your type, then?"

"Certainly not a spoiled little brat of a girl."

"I'm a woman."

"You're twenty."

"And I'm not spoiled."

He rolled his eyes. "Maybe we'll grow to like each other."

"I thought you already did—like me, I mean."

He snubbed out his cigarette in the ceramic bowl.

"They're making you marry me?" I asked softly.

He stared at me like I'd just asked a stupid question.

I held my breath for a beat. "Maybe you should forget about me and find a woman that's your type."

"That door's closed."

"I'm still holding out for my one true love." It was cruel, but he'd been crueler.

The air chilled and the weight of his accusatory stare squeezed my heart.

"Maybe my father can help us, Damien. Help us break apart. Release a statement that lands well."

"Your father has an agenda." His expression softened. "This is how it's done."

"They want to see me happy—"

"Yet you're standing in my fucking kitchen."

I let out a long sigh. "What if I refuse to marry you?"

"Have you any idea how many people's lives will be affected if you disobey?"

"My mother—"

"I'm not talking about your family. I'm talking about years of decisions that all led to this moment—" He gestured to me and then himself. "We're standing here with our future set."

I shrugged off his jacket and threw it over a barstool. "How about you call that helicopter back so I can leave?"

"And now you bore me." He slid another cigarette out of the packet.

"You should know I can't stand smoking."

He tilted his head with an arrogance I was accustomed to and then lit the end of his cigarette, blowing out another stream of smoke. "Why did you run out on me at the party, Miss Bardot?" he asked, making my last name sound like a curse.

"Your mother doesn't like me."

"That's not what I asked." He rounded the counter to get closer.

Raising my head high, I stayed silent.

"Okay, then." Damien towered over me. "What did she say? She's entertaining when in full bitch-mode."

"Maybe it was the champagne that made her say those things."

"What things?"

"Your mother hinted you might take a lover. Is it true?"

The tip of his tongue moistened his upper lip. "When did she say that?"

"Tonight."

She, too, could be a spinner of words that cut to the bone.

"You insulted her by walking out on us. I imagine she was waiting for an apology."

"She's had a long wait."

He buried his tongue in his cheek, finding my anger amusing.

"Your mother upset me," I said. "The thought of us not having a proper marriage was too much. I went out to get some air."

"In my BMW?"

"I needed to sit somewhere quiet to think."

He reached around and cupped my ass, dragging my body against his. "I adore your feistiness. You know that, right?"

"The way you treat me..."

"Think you can change me?"

The sensual pressure from his fingers and the bulge in his pants that rubbed against my belly sent an erotic shiver through me.

"The rumors about you are true, then?" I asked, sounding breathless.

"Keep going. I feed off your hate, Pandora."

Actually, the rumors of him had been favorable. He was *the* bachelor to bag, apparently. I wasn't going to tell him that and bolster his already inflated ego.

My lips pressed together, defiantly refusing a kiss.

His eyes lit up. "Seeing you like this arouses me."

I turned my head, refusing to look at him. "I don't like it here."

"Want to go back to my father's place?"

"When hell freezes over, maybe."

He pulled away from me, his cigarette dangling from his mouth as he rolled up his shirt sleeves, revealing muscled forearms that flexed. Moving to the sink, he washed his hands with his back to me.

I let my admiring gaze roam over his form. I could see the hint of a muscled back underneath his pristine white shirt and a tight ass beneath his pants. Closing my eyes, I imagined what it would be like to walk up and press myself against him, pretending we liked each other. Then again, his touch felt like sin; tainting the only good that was left in me.

He brought out several packets of crackers and chips and set them on the counter, then withdrew a cheeseboard from the fridge and set the dish beside them.

"You haven't eaten anything tonight," he said. "This will make you feel better."

"I thought you didn't care about me."

He squeezed his eyes shut. "Let's agree to be polite."

"I am hungry," I admitted.

Damien beckoned me closer as he buttered a few crackers and then placed brie on top of them. A minute later, he slid the plate my way. It was the kindest thing he'd done for me in quite a long while.

I tentatively lifted a cracker and took a bite, tasting the tanginess of the cheese and savoring the crispness of the cracker.

"I'm more of a cheddar man myself."

"I hate cheddar," I lied.

He speared a slice of cheddar off the board and brought the knife to his mouth with the cheese impaled on the end, his tongue tasting it before devouring the delicacy. "That finishing school of yours would throw a fit at half the things I do."

I finished chewing. "More than half, probably."

"You don't ever want to break the rules?"

"Why would I?"

"You'd probably enjoy rebelling."

"I tried to escape tonight. That was rebelling."

"Ah-ha!" He sounded triumphant at my confession.

"I wasn't brought up that way." Nor was I taught to eat off a knife like some kind of caveman.

"You have to feel some sense of rebellion to truly enjoy sex." He set the knife down. "Or you'll never be able to come."

I blushed wildly. "If you've quite finished schooling me, I'm going to have a look around."

He raised his champagne glass. "Enjoy."

Asshole.

I turned back to face him before leaving the kitchen. "Want to know the whole truth?"

"Oh, good, schoolgirl games. As if I'm not being tortured enough."

My jaw clenched. "Your mother told me you already have a lover put up in an expensive high-rise."

"The fuck I do."

Relief washed over me that he'd denied it. "That's why I tried to leave."

"I share a place with Theo Tamer in the city. No one lives there permanently. We had a mutual friend stay there because she was moving into a new place. That was months ago."

"Did you date her?"

He studied me for a long time. "Ten years ago, yes."

"Was her name Madeline Rhodes?"

"You've discovered Google, bravo."

"Were you in love with her?"

"I was twenty-two."

That didn't answer my question. "Are you seeing anyone now?"

"You mean other than you?" He dragged his palms over his face in frustration.

Bastard.

He could have answered *no.*

Pivoting, I hurried out of the kitchen, my heart freezing over because he didn't care about me. Not really.

I could find another lover and cheat—if this was going to be an open marriage. Or I could just give up on finding love altogether. Give up on the chance of happiness.

Climbing the carpeted staircase to the top floor, I began searching for a landline.

I'd call my parents and beg them to extract me from this place. The Godmans weren't the only ones with a fleet of helicopters.

What looked like the master bedroom was lavishly decorated. Gray and white bed linen covered a king-size bed. Window drapes hung from the ceiling and kissed the floor, giving this room a warmer feeling than those downstairs. More modern artwork hung on the walls. It was impossible to make out what the artist was trying to achieve.

Godman's eldest son had a favorite artist or maybe this had been picked out by his designer. She probably hated him, too, and this was the only way she could secretly show it—by framing pretentious art that reflected his personality; dead-hearted imagery.

In the bathroom en suite, there were no prescriptions in the cabinet. No heart tablets hinting of a health issue to give me hope. Unfortunately, he looked like he was in prime shape.

I stepped back into the master bedroom with its oceanfront vista, a moving painting that went on forever. I'd get to wake up to this.

Lucky me.

If this was his weekend home, I'd be living in a house as lonely as his father's back in the city. It made me wonder what that place would be like.

I headed for the bedroom door, my heels clicking on the well-polished floorboards, and paused when I saw a silver picture frame on the mahogany cabinet.

A chill ran up my spine.

I walked over to the photo, my mouth dry as I picked it up. This had been taken the first night I'd danced with Damien at the Debutante Ball in April. His arm was wrapped around my waist possessively. That blissful expression on my face revealing I was overwhelmed with joy to be so close to him. I'd believed my prince had come to rescue me from the tower. How could I have known I was escaping one confining existence to be immediately imprisoned in another?

My lips quivered at the swell of conflicting emotions I was feeling—those crashing waves outside the window reflecting my inner turmoil.

I jolted, realizing that I was no longer alone.

Damien was leaning against the door watching me, his big frame filling the space. I liked him the most when he didn't speak. It was easier to admire his gorgeous face and suave demeanor and pretend he was a different man.

A tremor went through me as I sensed him undressing me with those dark eyes.

"I want my life to mean more," I said.

"Not an uncommon desire." His expression hinted at empathy for our situation.

"How long have you had that?" I pointed to the photo frame.

"Since it was taken."

"Six months ago?"

"I'm hardly ever here."

"Did you frame it?"

"No."

Then who? His mother? Someone wanting to make it look like he cared, perhaps.

"You're very pretty." He shoved off the doorframe and walked into the room. "I should have told you that before. I think you're the most beautiful woman I've ever met."

A neat trick, trying to soften me up before he took me. "You're not bad yourself."

He looked amused and then suppressed a smile. "That look on my face in the photo is what it feels like to pluck out a debutante."

"You're not offended that our meeting was pre-arranged?"

"The illusion of control." He folded his arms across his chest.

"After we're married, I still want to work."

Surprise flashed over his face. "Your job is having the populace fawn over you. Your job is to be my wife."

"I have so much more to offer."

"Can't see it, myself."

"You can't bring yourself to say something decent, can you?"

"Have you considered saying something decent to me?"

I lifted my chin. "You'll never be President."

"That's the kindest thing you've said so far." He looked like he meant it, too.

"Where am I sleeping?"

"Shall I show you?"

"I want to sleep with you."

He hesitated as though not expecting my comment. "If we're in the same bed we won't be sleeping."

"Fucking then."

"Careful, Pandora."

"You should consider yourself lucky to have a woman like me offer you her virginity."

"Your Royal Highness, are you on the pill?"

"No," I said.

He watched my reaction and then turned on his heel and walked away.

My legs went weak and I slumped on the edge of the bed, full of regret for ruining the night even more.

We were never going to work.

I raised my hand to examine the emerald on my ring finger, coming to the painful realization that it would always remind me of our loveless marriage. I went to pull it off, but it was too snug. I'd need soap and water to extract me from Damien's mark of the beast with its many facets of shiny hate.

I smoothed out the duvet, musing that it could have been here on this bed where we first slept together. My first time...

The thought of choosing my wedding dress brought no joy. Deciding on the flavor and look of the cake or even having a say where we went on our honeymoon would not be tasks I could enjoy. All those bridal magazines I'd collected over the years made me look naive.

"Shall we?" Damien stood in the doorway, holding up a condom packet.

I drew in a sharp breath.

He studied me with an intensity that caused a delicious frisson to feather my skin.

I gave a nod, letting him know I wanted this to happen. *God*, how I wanted to feel his body against mine...even if hate was our baseline.

I couldn't wait to be free of this curse. My innocence had been used as leverage to get me here and getting rid of it made me feel a rush of power.

Damien strolled across the room toward a mirror and signaled I was to follow. He gave the mirror a tap and a secret door opened to a staircase.

"Where does that lead?"

Instead of answering, he headed up a spiraling marble staircase. Feeling unsure, I followed behind him anyway, our footfalls echoing around us.

I peered up at the high ceiling, proving the expanse of this place was awe inspiring. Continuing to put distance between me and the rest of the house chipped away at my bravery.

We reached a door at the top and I followed him into another bedroom. An antique four-poster bed was positioned at the opposite end of the room. French-style furniture added a sensual flair, along with the faded soft blue and pink rug in the center.

Strolling toward the window, I looked out at the dramatic ocean view. Up here in what felt like a loft, the vantage point was just as enthralling. My fingers caressed the hairs on my nape—I could feel him staring at me.

I turned to face him.

Then I saw them.

Red silk ties hung down from each of the carved bedposts, the sashes of scarlet suggesting that someone could be tied to that bed.

Someone like me. "You're not…"

"If you remain in this room, yes."

Licking my lips to wet them, I tried to rally my courage. "Will it hurt?"

His shoulders relaxed as he asked, "Do you want it to?"

"I want it to be special."

"I can promise it will be memorable." His eyes narrowed on me. "Would you like that?"

CHAPTER FOUR

Pandora

Damien took my hand and led me toward the bed, his gaze never leaving mine like a hawk watching its prey.

He'd already shown me what kind of man he was, dismissive and punishing. I sensed his brand of love making wouldn't be much different. Everything rested on me surrendering to this moment. Surrendering to him. That's what he wanted to see.

With a gesture he ordered, "Lie down."

After slipping off my shoes, I lay on the bed feeling the firmness of the mattress beneath my body, tulle swimming around my waist. I rested my head on the soft pillow and stared at the ornate ceiling, trying to steady my breathing.

At least he hadn't asked me to remove my dress.

Damien wrapped a silk ribbon around my left wrist and tugged the material to ensure it was inescapable. He moved over to my right wrist and did the same. Then set to work attaching the lower ribbons to my ankles, tying them to the lower two bedposts after easing my legs apart, leaving me sprawled out and vulnerable.

He stepped back. "How does that feel?"

"Nice," I confessed, enjoying the sensation of him stealing all responsibility from me. He'd made it impossible to break free. Guilt for what came next might not even find me in all of this drama. Being tied down meant nothing that happened would be my fault.

I'd secretly yearned for this. For him.

The bed dipped as he reached over to brush a strand of hair

out of my eyes. His gesture could easily be mistaken for someone who had a heart. "Do you trust me?"

When I did not respond, he ran his hand over my dress like I was a plaything—tugging the material and caressing the tulle as though his thoughts carried him far away.

Damien reached out and stroked the ribbon around my left wrist, running a fingertip beneath it. "This is so that you understand what I need."

I exhaled sharply; obviously he was into bondage.

He gave me a slow smile as though sensing I understood. "Follow my rules. Once you abide by them, I will let you come."

"Rules?"

His hand slid down to my neck, his palm resting on my throat. "Please me and coming frequently will be your new reality."

Excitement caused my chest to rise and fall and my breasts to swell, nipples pebbling and showing through the material of my dress.

Having him this close in a sensual way felt like a dream. Damien was too powerful a presence to ignore as he assessed my curves, his pupils dilating at what he saw.

Our eyes locked.

"Are you aroused?" he said, his voice gruff.

"I imagine you'd like that."

He lips curved, showing me he knew the answer to his question was *yes*.

My body tingled simply from hearing his seductive voice. His fingertips grazed my breasts through the material, my nipples beading beneath his circling thumb.

His hand gliding all the way down to my pelvis. "So much to explore."

He hoisted my tulle skirts up and I raised my hips to help him expose my panties.

I jolted when his warm palm cupped me between my legs, causing me to writhe a little at the sensations he aroused there.

Damien was reading every nuance of my expression, sensing my response to the way he commanded my body with his firm caresses and tender stroking, greedily assessing my white thong.

His thumb caressed my clit through the thin material of my panties, causing it to throb and swell.

Feeling frantic from his teasing, I pulled against the silken binds that captured me, but they only grew tighter, making me feel vulnerable. My heart rate skyrocketed, as though I really wanted to be free. Exhilarated, I feigned resistance, as though he'd captured me and was forcing me against my will to feel this pleasure.

I stopped struggling for a moment, aware of the dampness of my arousal.

He pulled my thong aside to reveal the fine strip of pubic hair that was now revealed to him, and with gentle fingers he traced my folds, parting them to expose more of my clit.

I shuddered.

He knew how to touch a woman…how to find the exact spot that would elicit pleasure.

He flicked my clit slowly. "You like this?"

Raising my chin, I gave him a defiant stare. My show of rebellion seemed to please him.

I hadn't begged him to stop…couldn't let those words escape my lips because his thumb was edging me toward orgasm. His fingers eased apart my labia to increase my pleasure.

"You're mine to do with as I want," he said, his voice husky.

My moan betrayed me as I arched my back, giving myself over to him, revealing it was easy to want this intimacy. I needed this release more than anything, even though my mind waged a war against the sensations tearing through me.

It wasn't my fault that it was feeling this good. He'd captured me in this house. Tied me down…made me want him. Each time he entered the room Damien left me spellbound.

No, you hate him.

Then why did I want to know how it would feel when he was

buried deep inside me? On top of me, entering me, riding me into a state of bliss.

Oh, God, please don't let it hurt too much.

"You're so damn wet, Pandora." The raw craving in his voice revealed he was just as turned on by my squirming.

"Faster," I pleaded.

He ignored that and continued the leisurely pace he'd set with a fingertip on my clit. "No one's ever touched you here?"

"No."

"I'm glad I'm your first."

I arched my back with a gasp when he finally relented and set a faster rhythm, his fingers exploring my dampness but not entering me.

I shook my head, whipping my long hair from side to side, wanting more and unable to hide the rising desire that snatched away every last ounce of resistance.

His other hand eased down the bodice of my dress, allowing a nipple to find its freedom. "Do you want me to stop?" His flicking finger slowed on my swollen clit.

"No!" I moaned, not caring about the rules. Or what was expected. This…this was exquisite, and I was free of blame because he'd seduced me.

"Are you mine, Pandora?" He slowed the rhythm again in a tease.

"I am."

"And good girls get to come hard." His fingertip moved slowly but the pressure was more intense.

Close to fainting, I tried to follow what he was saying, his voice luring me into a trance.

"I want you," I said, gasping.

His mouth came crashing down on my nipple and he drew my areola into his mouth, suckling it, sending a luxurious thrill radiating all the way down to my pussy.

My body detonated with the flicking of his tongue on my breast in unison with his finger beating my clit. All coherent thought was gone. All I knew were the sensations bursting through me, surging through my blood vessels like oxygen itself, a life force that couldn't be averted. I reveled in the way he overpowered me, exulting in his control.

If this was suffering, I welcomed it.

Blistering pleasure had me trembling uncontrollably, my own gasps sounding foreign to my ears.

As I came down from my orgasm, he slowed the rhythm of his touch, seemingly respectful of how sensitive my clit felt after his stroking. Shuddering still, I turned my eyes on him as he withdrew his hand and sat up.

My breathing was still ragged.

"Did you like me playing with your pussy?" he asked huskily.

I blushed at the way his mouth so easily formed those filthy words.

He brought his fingers to his mouth and licked the wet tips seductively as though exploring a rare delight. The sticky sensation I felt between my thighs from watching him made me even more flustered.

"You're not quite ready to be fucked hard, Pandora. Not the way I would like. But soon enough."

A long moan of regret tore through me. Should Damien have wanted to fuck me I'd have let him. I missed his touch already.

All logic had left me, and what remained was confusion at this lingering arousal—this man was dangerously erotic.

"Kiss me," I pleaded.

With seeming curiosity, he studied me and then relented and leaned in, his lips close. This was what I had yearned for… his mouth ravishing mine and giving me the affection I'd craved.

I felt his breath on my face and his mouth was almost touching mine when we heard the sound of chopper blades slashing through the quiet of the night. A helicopter was landing, the invasion destroying the special moment between us.

Damien got up off the bed and strolled over to the window.

I raised my head off the pillow. "Who is it?"

He moved back to the bed and freed me from the red silken ties.

"Stay here." He left the bedroom.

Rising from the bed, my thighs sticky, I tugged down my gown and padded barefoot over to the window, making sure my bodice covered my breasts.

Peeking out, I focused on the helicopter that had just landed on the front lawn. Damien hadn't mentioned that anyone would be joining us.

A man leaned low as he ran away from the chopper, but then straightened, standing tall as he approached the house. He was extraordinarily good-looking with aristocratic dark features that made him look like he'd materialized from a different century.

I knew him.

We'd never been formally introduced but I'd seen Theo Tamer at political functions, watching the dashing political strategist from afar. The thirty-something man who worked for Senator Gregor Godman had always been courteous to my father.

My shoulders slumped with the disappointing thought I might have to spend the rest of the evening talking about the campaign.

Theo was dressed in a black tuxedo, having attended the same event as us earlier.

Perhaps an introduction to me would soften the harshness of his expression, cause him to smile.

I traced him in the glass. And then my stomach clenched in panic.

He was looking up, transfixed on me.

His expression was one of intrigue at first, and then it morphed into something that looked an awful lot like contempt. He snapped his attention away and headed into the house.

I left the window and sat back down on the bed, waiting for Damien to return. I was reluctant to be beckoned to join them— for the evening to turn sour. This visitor had ruined what was meant to be our private time.

Half an hour went by, though it could have been longer. I had lain down and curled up into a ball, my body responding to Damien's touch as though it still echoed with rippling pleasure, hips rocking as I yearned for more.

I sat up quickly when I heard footfalls on the stairs.

Damien appeared in the doorway.

I pushed up. "Is he staying?"

"I'm taking you home."

"Back to your place?"

"No, your parents' house."

I climbed off the bed and slipped into my high heels, all the while trying to read his expression. "What happened?"

"I'm needed back in the city." He paused in the doorway and his eyes flashed over the bed.

"I thought we were staying all weekend." Hugging my chest, I willed myself not to glance back at the bed where all of those delectable sensations had flowed. A thrum still rippled through me.

He led me downstairs and through the kitchen, snagging his black jacket off the barstool as we went. I looked around for Theo, but he'd gone to wait for us in the helicopter.

Damien reached into his jacket pocket and handed me my phone back. "No sharing with anyone what happened here, understand? And certainly not on social media."

"I know."

"I'm just making sure you know."

The kitchen had been tidied—the plate of cheese and crackers and the two champagne glasses, and even the makeshift ashtray, were now gone.

All evidence of us being here had been eradicated.

CHAPTER
FIVE

Pandora

I'd wanted to be free of *him*.

But even though I reminded myself of this fact while sitting near the bottom of the staircase in my parents' home, I felt a twinge of disappointment that our weekend away wasn't happening. Damien had dropped me off ten minutes ago, along with my unpacked suitcase—unceremoniously dumping me back to square one.

Back to this palatial home on Chain Bridge Road. Though not as impressive as our estate back in Texas, it had a library, a wine cellar, and a media space. There were more than enough rooms to get lost in and enough life within the walls to keep a staff of five busy.

Not wanting to accept that our weekend had been cut short, I remained sitting in the dark, not wanting to take that walk of shame up the stairs to my bedroom. I should be tired—it was 2:00 A.M.—but the way I'd been hurried out of Seascape had filled me with trepidation and I was too anxious to sleep.

I had never gotten used to these large houses and their strange noises; having spent so many years sleeping in private school dorms.

My parents were undoubtedly in bed. No doubt they'd be surprised to see me at breakfast in the morning.

Just thinking of Theo interrupting our intimate evening made me cringe. When I'd climbed into the back of the helicopter, I'd not been able to look him in the eyes, fearing he'd guessed what we'd been doing. Since he and Damien shared a place in the city, I was certain they knew each other well enough to talk about such things.

I'd fallen asleep in the helicopter with my head resting on Damien's shoulder. The fact he'd let me stay so close to him felt like a small victory.

I expected the month leading up to the election would be strained, but I'd not foreseen this level of chaos, or that it would encroach on my life to this extent.

My fingers trailed along my forearm in a self-soothing gesture, as I tried to mimic how I'd been caressed so seductively in that lofty hideaway.

Damien was devastatingly charismatic. Time with him was never boring, which was probably why I was already missing him. My hands cupped my still sensitive breasts, my body tingling all over as I thought about what Damien had done to me...the memory of that blinding orgasm making me shudder.

Seeing his steely armor relax a little had me liking him all over again.

Damien could easily be invited into the center of my fantasies where I could mold him into doing what I wanted in my imagination.

I sat there wondering what had been so important to drag him away, hoping it didn't have anything to do with his father's campaign. It had been grueling, but the Senator had held up well for a man of sixty-two. He seemed to thrive on the stress.

But having his strategist fly all the way out to the beach house to retrieve his son was a clue that something serious had happened.

"Pandora?" my mom whispered from the top of the stairs.

I turned to see her wearing that familiar Oscar de la Renta satin robe with the feathered cuffs.

I cringed. "Did I wake you?"

"The car lights woke me up."

"Sorry." I stood and ascended the stairs. "Damien had to come back."

"Right." There was no surprise in her tone. "He couldn't leave you at the beach house?"

"Um...no."

Her eyes widened when she saw the engagement ring. "He proposed?"

If throwing a ring across the room could be called a proposal.

She examined my hand and her eyes watered with the emotion of someone who hadn't seen this coming. She'd virtually shoved me at the man at the Debutante Ball.

"They announced it in the *Times*." I studied her reaction. "You didn't see it?"

She reached out to hold me. "I'm happy for you, Pandora."

Relaxing a little, I hoped she wouldn't smell champagne and cigarettes and sex on me. What would Mom think if she knew about those red silken ties? The ones that had made my wrists tingle deliciously.

"You look tired," she said soothingly.

"Do you know why Damien might have been called back?" I asked.

My father appeared down the hallway. "Everything okay?"

"She has a ring," Mom told him.

He approached us, peering over his spectacles at us as he passed by. Heading down the stairs, he said, "I'm going to get a nightcap."

That's strange. I hadn't expected him to gush over the emerald, but actually taking the time to look at my ring would have been nice.

When he'd disappeared from sight, I asked, "Is he even happy for me?"

With a gesture, my mother offered to walk me to my room.

My throat tightened. "What happened?"

"Not here," she whispered, as though hinting a wayward member of staff might overhear.

Just as we had on all those days since Jefferson had left home, we swapped a knowing glance when we reached my brother's room. It was only used when he was in town because he lived in Texas.

My rambunctious older brother had hurtled loudly into manhood. I missed him, but his place was in Dallas running the business as the CEO of Bardot Petroleum. The role filled his days and gave him nightmares.

There were suffocating expectations for everyone living beneath this roof. This was the umbrella of doom we all huddled under.

Mom sat on the edge of the bed and patted the duvet so I would join her. It was a sweet gesture she'd begun using when I'd reached my late teens when she wanted to have a talk.

The gray hairs I saw now had softened her appearance, and so had the lines on her fiercely beautiful face. She had become gentler since entering her fifties, and not so insistent on everything going her way.

Sitting beside her with my head resting on her shoulder, it was easy to pretend we had always been this close.

"How did he seem?" she asked softly.

"Damien?" I swallowed hard at her potential disappointment. "Fine."

She looked wistful. "I hear the views from his beach house are spectacular. Maybe we'll come visit."

"I'd like that."

Thank goodness that bedroom in Damien's house was tucked away—no chance of a wayward visitor wandering up there.

She rested her hand on mine. "Go talk to your father. Reassure him that you'll do what you can, that you'll talk to Damien. Maybe you'll be able to persuade him to make this go away."

"Make what go away?"

She looked worried. "During the party, your father was approached by Salvatore Galante."

"The head of *Real Nation*?"

Flinching, I realized what she was saying. "Did they clash?"

"Galante has a reputation for being…disreputable."

Searching her face, I wasn't sure if I was ready to know what had happened between them. Had Galante insulted the Senator? Thanks to the news stories dished out on his channel, it was well known that he disagreed with the Senator's politics. He released a constant barrage of hate-fueled criticism on how Godman's term in office would ruin the economy.

Had Dad tried to defend Gregor?

"What happened?"

Mom sighed. "Galante told your father he's going to release a story on something that happened in your father's past."

"A story?" A spike of adrenaline had me pushing to my feet.

"We're not sure what he has yet, but there's still a chance we can suppress it. It's all in Gregor Godman's hands now. It's his decision."

Her words echoed in my mind, forming garish images. What had Dad done? Or had this town finally seen the threat my father posed and turned against him, spewing lies and twisting truths?

"Dad might lose his place in the Cabinet?" I asked.

"Perhaps."

"I'm sure Damien will speak with the Senator."

"Go tell your father that. Put his mind at ease."

The thought of asking Damien for such a favor filled me with dread—but there seemed no choice in the matter.

I threw Mom a reassuring smile, feeling a sudden sense of pride that it could be me who influenced my father's position in that historic house on the hill.

I headed back downstairs.

Dad sat in the dark nursing a tumbler of his favorite scotch, seemingly lost in thought, his expression grave. The years he'd spent striving for this very opportunity now hung in the balance. He'd given up running the company to take this chance. He'd sacrificed so much.

Sitting at his feet, I looked up at him. "You don't have to tell me."

He finished off his drink and rested the empty glass on his thigh. "We make the best decisions we can with the information we've got. You can't predict the future."

His confession of wrongdoing made me look away; I didn't want to believe my daddy was capable of anything scandalous.

"Maybe the Senator can make the story go away?" I whispered.

He stared down at me, a melancholy look in his eyes. "Jefferson was always so easy…his future set to follow mine. But you…you were always destined for greatness of another sort."

This was a bad time to bring up the fact I might have wanted to be part of the company myself. Damien had already told me I was selfish, and the fact I was thinking of my own future was proof of that.

I wanted to be a better person. "Another drink, Daddy?"

"Early on, your mother and I thought having a governess to focus on you would tame you."

"I think they call those the terrible twos," I joked, even though there was nothing funny about it.

I'd been placed into the hands of a strict governess when I was a toddler. And there had been several others after her. In my memory, their faces were sewn into a tapestry of discipline, all of those impossible expectations leading up to my tenth birthday.

No further care was needed at home because I was sent to school in Switzerland. Back then, I had no idea there'd be no coming home to live with my parents until I'd turned nineteen. Since I'd returned to live in this house, I had been trying to get to know these strangers again—while my father launched his new career.

Back in Texas, remnants of my childhood lingered in our family home. My old bedroom had helped me recover memories of the years I'd thought gone—dolls and games and toys waiting for me upon my return as though I'd been frozen in time in my mother's mind. All of these frivolities had now been thrown away.

My bedroom décor here was a reflection of what kind of woman my mother had hoped I'd become. It was a space filled with perfect furniture and pristine patterns—fancy wallpaper and plush carpeting. No TV allowed.

At nineteen, I'd begged for my own apartment in the city, wanting to escape this swanky suburb and have some freedom.

My parents had other plans in mind for me.

The independence I craved would never be part of the deal.

Not long before my twentieth birthday, I'd been formally introduced to Damien. And then told to wait for him.

Merely a few months after that, he was ready.

"I'll go see Damien tomorrow," I said softly.

I'd beg him to do whatever he could to make this problem go away, to persuade his father not to turn away from mine. After everything we'd shared, after he'd given me this ring, surely he would be willing to help.

What happened all those years ago?

What kind of scandal were we talking about?

The time I'd spent with Damien at Seascape had brought us closer, his touch lighting me on fire with an unmatched passion. Perhaps he, too, felt the burn of my affection. Perhaps he saw a future for us that would include love.

Maybe he was thinking of me now.

The true testament of what we were to each other would be revealed when I asked him to help us…help my father realize his dream of walking through the hallowed halls of the White House.

Great men had done worse, surely? These aspersions couldn't be proven. Slander could be struck down in a lawsuit. A man like Senator Godman, who wielded more money and potentially more power than anyone else in this country, could make this go away.

"Damien will do anything for me, Daddy."

His hand stroked my hair. "I hope you're right."

My gut twisted in doubt.

I got up and poured my dad another drink. When I handed him the glass, I leaned over and kissed the top of his head, and then left him alone with his scotch.

As soon as I returned to my room, I whipped out my phone and texted Damien. I thanked him for the lovely time I'd had; it was half true. Anyway, Daddy needed me to come through for him.

A moment later I stared at my phone's screen in disbelief. My message couldn't be delivered. Damien had blocked my number.

CHAPTER
SIX

Pandora

Peering through the window of the closed lecture room door, I could see she was attractive...and tall, too. Madeline Rhodes had captured the full attention of the hundred or so students filling the theatre seats all the way to the back. Years ago, she'd captured Damien's full attention as well. According to Google, they'd once been lovers—and it was supposedly true that they'd remained good friends.

From what she'd scribbled on the whiteboard behind her, I had to believe she was smart. This was high-level statistics.

Damien preferred brunettes, apparently. The red blouse and black pencil skirt wearing kind with pointed heels and perfect makeup.

Rhodes would be free in minutes, according to the class schedule, which meant I didn't have much longer to practice what I was going to say to her. I needed to gain her trust and get her to open up and share her insights on how to win Damien's heart.

Or even just to get him to unblock me, for God's sake.

Madeline seemed to sense me staring at her through the glass.

We locked eyes.

Two women with one man in common. We moved in different circles...she in academia and me amongst Washington's elite, never destined to meet. Much to Damien's relief, no doubt.

I wondered if her piercing blue eyes and mature beauty were a possible distraction to her class. She stood by the podium with confidence, commanding the room without compromise.

She ended the lecture with a casual gesture to her audience.

Stepping back, I waited for the Georgetown University students to trail out. They threw curious glances my way as they headed into the hall. Soon, the seats were all empty and the senior lecturer was available.

She held the advantage.

"May I come in?" I asked, approaching the podium.

She picked up a leather satchel. "You're already in."

Rhodes was Damien's type, all right. Or maybe she was his match. Either way she had an intimidating presence.

I paused a few feet away and glanced down at her blood red toenails. "Do you know who I am?"

"Most people know who you are."

Yes, because those long lenses had captured my childhood and they had followed me as I'd grown up—the downside of having an infamous father.

"I was wondering if I could have a few minutes of your time?" I said.

She had the kind of pouty mouth a man would like—enhanced with bright red lipstick. She had tasted Damien's cock with those lips. And he'd tasted her, too.

"Walk with me." She motioned for me to follow. "I'm assuming you're not here to discuss the graduate program?"

We left the lecture hall and I hurried after her, trying to keep up. "I respect that you're busy."

She shoved at a door and held it open for me. "You've got me intrigued."

I slid by and entered her office.

We'd been standing so close that I'd had no choice but to brush against her, feeling her firm body against mine, realizing that Damien knew every inch of her.

Had he tied her down, too?

A million questions circled in my mind. How long had they dated? Why were they no longer together?

"Thirsty?" She gestured to a small fridge.

"Yes, please."

"Coke?"

"Yes, anything. Whatever's easiest."

She studied me. "You're very compliant."

Stacks of exam papers rose high on her desk next to an expensive-looking blue lamp. A glass paperweight pressed down on a few letters waiting to be opened. A laptop had been tossed on a file cabinet, its power cord twisted.

"Thank you for seeing me. I didn't call ahead—"

"No, you didn't." Her sternness stayed with her all the way across the room. She knelt and opened a fridge door, reaching in for a chilled can of Diet Coke.

She strolled over to a cabinet and pulled out a tall glass, then cracked open the can. The brown, sugary liquid fizzed all the way to the top as she poured it into the glass—tipping the can in a way that made her look even more sophisticated.

"Dr. Rhodes, you have the advantage of knowing me." I chose one of the two seats before her desk, thinking of all of the students who had sat here being berated.

"A quick Internet search and you could find out more about me." Her eyes twinkled as she gave me a knowing look. "But you've already done that."

I gave her a sheepish smile. "What exactly do you know about me?"

She handed me the glass of Coke. "Your mother must have a thing for mythology."

"I was teased for it."

"Being named Pandora?"

"The girl who allowed all the evils of the world to escape." I flicked a blonde lock out of my face. "My namesake had a lot more fun."

Madeline smirked as she sank into the chair behind her desk. "Now that's something I'd pay to watch."

I paused for a moment, and then asked, "What's wrong with your laptop?"

She glanced at it with surprise.

"Did it crash?" I took a sip of Coke, and added, "I can have a look if you like."

Her surprised look morphed into one of suspicion. "No, thank you, that won't be necessary. Why did you want to speak to me, Ms. Bardot?"

I swallowed hard and then found my courage. "Why did you and Damien split up? You're beautiful and smart, and clearly accomplished."

"A straight shooter, I like that." She nibbled on her lower lip and it looked seductive. "What happened between the two of you that's caused you to run to my office like a scared little schoolgirl?"

"I'm twenty."

"You look younger."

I lowered my gaze. "I'm hoping for some pointers."

"You make Damien sound like a conundrum."

"That's because he is."

She smiled. "I signed a non-disclosure agreement when we began dating. Didn't you?"

"No."

Her expression told me she hadn't expected that answer. "Well, that'll come about soon enough. Unless…"

"Unless?"

"The rumors are true?"

"What rumors?"

"I still have friends in Washington."

"We're still together if that's what you mean." I hoped the lie sounded convincing.

She glanced at her wristwatch, hinting that I was eating away her time.

"He still loves you, Madeline."

An eyebrow rose as she mulled that over, and then I saw the expression in her eyes soften with affection. It was the kind of reaction seen in those still in love.

"Are you still in contact?" I sensed they were.

"By phone, mostly."

I decided to ask the question I wasn't certain I wanted an answer to. "Why aren't you still together?"

"People grow apart."

"But…you're everything he wants in a woman."

She pushed up from the chair. "I'm flattered you think that."

I'd offended her, and she was kicking me out.

My shoulders slumped in defeat. "I'm trying to understand him. Trying to make this work."

"We don't need a non-disclosure agreement. You and me, we are quite capable of respecting each other's privacy."

I gave a subtle nod of agreement.

"You want me to help fix your relationship with Damien, but your failure was inevitable. If that makes you feel any better."

I set the glass of Coke on her desk and stood, my chair squealing on the hardwood floor as I pushed up. "I'm sorry I wasted your time."

"It's been a delight."

I frowned. "You're making fun of me."

"You're a toy. Power's plaything. Manufactured in a private school abroad and forged for public life."

I wanted to walk away, hating the fact she had the upper hand by knowing all about my background. I wasn't in a position to defend myself.

She stared at me thoughtfully. "Or, Ms. Bardot, you could be more…"

My future was tenuous, but she wouldn't know that.

Soon, like the rest of the world, she would know about my father's scandal—unless I found a way to reach Damien and convince him to make it go away.

Damien blocking my texts felt like the ultimate ghosting. A week had gone by and I'd not heard a word from him, which was why I'd believed visiting Rhodes for advice had been a good idea.

Now, not so much.

Heading for the door, I cursed myself for going to all this trouble. Rhodes didn't care about me. I'd been a brief amusement between lectures.

She leaned forward over the desk, her cleavage showing thanks to her low-cut red blouse. "Are you good with secrets?"

I turned around. "Yes."

"How far are you willing to go?"

"In what respect?"

"Damien has...unusual desires. Surely you've noticed by now?"

I assumed Madeline was talking about the fact he had a thing for bondage.

She reached into her desk drawer and pulled out a velvet box, placing it on top of the desk with reverence. "You must never tell him where you got it. Promise?"

The box was too big for an engagement ring and too small for a bracelet or a choker. My imagination went into overdrive.

I walked over to her desk and picked up the box, holding it gingerly in my palm.

"What is it?"

"A gift. Or a curse, depending on how you look at it. Because it's not meant for girls like you."

I wondered if I should be insulted.

"Or...perhaps you're different." She smiled.

I suddenly had a memory of what the silken ties had felt like—the sensations of pleasure and pain, of writhing to escape and yet never wanting to.

"Pandora, the woman who wears this will get anything she wants."

I smirked. "Are these nuclear codes?"

She glanced at the box in my hand. "What's inside there is a whole lot more explosive."

"Did he give this to you?"

"Not exactly."

"How come you have it?"

"You're wrong. I'm not his type. But you are."

I didn't know how to respond to that assertion, and I still wasn't sure what was in the box.

She looked at me intently. "Has he ever mentioned Vanguard?"

"No." I gave a casual shrug to hide my embarrassment.

She gestured towards the box. "That grants permission. Wear that, and—"

"Permission to do what?" The question carried with it the naivety I was trying to hide.

"For him to do anything to you he wants to do."

My heart rate took off at a thousand beats a second. Finally, I remembered to breathe.

Give it back.

Forget you ever came here.

Her flowery perfume hung heavy around me, stirring memories of that loft...of that secret hour in an oceanside home far from anywhere—my breasts swelling, nipples beading, my entire body thrumming with desire.

Damien's fingertip causing my clit to throb until the pleasure was blinding.

"Pandora?" Madeline pulled me from my daydreaming.

I set the box down on the desk and slid it back toward her. "I appreciate your time, Dr. Rhodes. Really, I do."

I hated Damien...hated him for making me miss him like this—my body needy for his touch.

I wasn't here for me, though.

"I don't want it." I gestured to the box.

"Are you sure?" Her sensual curves were a stark reminder that Damien had enjoyed numerous lovers before me—all of them probably just like her. How could I ever compete against women this sophisticated?

You're his type.

She'd told me that, at least. Trying to read the truth in her eyes, I wondered if there was any honesty in her words.

"I don't think he's really capable of true love," I mused. "I know he felt a great deal for you. What I mean is, he's—"

"A complicated man."

I nodded and then said, "I was never here."

She gave me a smile. "Our conversation will stay between us."

It was best I never knew what lay inside that box.

Seeing me stare at it, she nudged the box closer to me, offering it one final time.

CHAPTER SEVEN

Pandora

"**W**hy hasn't he come over?" Dad muttered beneath his breath.

Mom squirmed uncomfortably in her chair.

"Damien's busy talking with his father's supporters," I said, trying to defend him.

I turned in my seat so I didn't have to watch Damien work the room—while ignoring me.

I feigned indifference, as though his behavior was perfectly acceptable, and focused on the central table display of red roses erupting out of a glass vase, their thorns calling my name.

The St. Regis Hotel's ballroom was the location for this elaborate Saturday night fundraiser. My mom had insisted I dress appropriately for the conservative types and had picked out a Lela Rose floral-embroidered gingham dress for me to wear this evening.

I looked like a pretty doll.

I'd become accustomed to these networking events, mastering the art of the friendly smile to help snag potential supporters for our cause when necessary.

So here I was, thrust into the public eye this evening and ready to be paraded in front of the guests. My orders were to look pretty and charm the hell out of everyone.

Tonight, I secretly represented my father's last hope of being chosen to serve alongside the President—only there was a hitch. Damien hadn't talked to me all night. I refused to let my parents know he'd not called me in over a week. Or that my phone was no longer able to get through to his asshole device either.

A dry mouth made me want to reach for my mother's

champagne flute, but drinking in public before I was twenty-one was taboo. "I'll go over and speak to Damien soon."

Dad gestured for the waiter to top up his champagne glass. "You're engaged. You have a ring."

As though sensing we were talking about him, Damien looked over at our table...then looked away.

Considering our intimacy last Friday night, seeing him throw daggers our way left me chagrined. When he turned his back to us, the rejection hurt my heart.

But even so, I still couldn't drag my eyes away from Damien's suaveness. His tailored suit had been cut to perfection and the black tie made him look edgy. His raven hair had been tamed for tonight's soirée. He stood there casually with his hands tucked into his pockets, yet he still seemed guarded—even stern and unapproachable.

Pivoting back to focus on the table centerpiece again, this time I reached out to touch the stem of a rose and purposefully pressed my finger to a thorn.

"Careful!" My mother slapped my hand away. "Go talk to him."

"I plan to." I clicked open my Bottega Veneta clutch purse and reached in for a tissue. Inside lay that small, black box.

I'd not opened it yet.

Maybe this had been a gift Damien had given to Madeline. Maybe giving it back through me was a message from Rhodes to him, which left me well and truly caught in the middle of her revenge *fuck you* tour.

Because Damien had chosen me over her.

Maybe whatever was inside this box was her attempt to sabotage my relationship.

She needn't have bothered.

Yesterday in her office at Georgetown, Madeline Rhodes had placed such importance on the box's contents, sparking a curiosity inside me that I hadn't been able to resist. But now...I wouldn't be drawn in by her evil scheming.

Snapping the purse closed, I slid the strap over my shoulder and psyched myself up to approach Damien.

Rising from my chair, I gave the guests at our table a polite smile. "Excuse me." I clutched my skirt and raised the hem a little, whooshing elegantly toward him across the ballroom.

Damien was trapped between two senators, Jacob Rommel and Scott Bruno, both good men who fought for causes that mattered.

Mattered to me, anyway.

They were already admirers of Damien's father. I'm sure he did not see the benefit of "wasting precious time" when he could be working the room trying to convert others to Senator Godman's crusade—not with only three weeks left until election night.

Damien gave me a subtle shake of his head in a gesture meaning *not now*.

No, he wasn't going to continue ghosting me in front of all these people. Some of the guests might be watching, and they'd be given clear evidence that those rumors of our estrangement were true.

"Hi, Damien." I forced a smile and turned it up a notch for the senators who flanked him on either side. "Will you both please excuse us while I talk to my fiancé?"

"We're in the middle of something." Damien followed that up with a glare.

Senator Rommel gave me a reassuring nod. "Spend time together. It's what makes these things bearable."

As the two gentlemen walked away, I was rewarded with another unkind stare from the man meant to be my boyfriend. Damien broke his focus away just long enough to read the room, suddenly realizing there were eyes on us.

He leaned forward and kissed my cheek. "Hello, sweetheart."

"Got a second?"

His dashing smile was disarming. "For you, anytime."

"You blocked my number?" I whispered.

"Not here." His tone was harsh.

Walking past him, I made a beeline for one of the many doors that led off the ballroom and found myself in an empty banquet hall. I stood there with my arms folded as I waited patiently for Damien to appear.

Eventually he did, sliding through the door as though trying to be covert. "What do you want?"

"Why are you ignoring me?"

"Maybe this isn't about you."

"I'm your fiancée."

"Can I call you later?"

I narrowed my gaze on him.

He stared back. "You're doubting my word?"

"Yes." I sounded extra snobbish for some reason and I couldn't put the brakes on.

There was just so much riding on Damien being reasonable.

He looked riled. "Quite honestly, Pandora, you're a bad look on me right now."

"Excuse me?"

"That issue with your father years ago just caught up with him. It could ricochet off us."

"That's what I wanted to talk to you about."

"You want to apologize on his behalf?"

"What? No. I want to make it go away."

"You know what he did, right?"

"No, I don't."

Surprise flashed over his face. "Look, I've been told not to talk with you right now." He paused, looking away. "Trust me, this isn't easy on me, either."

My mouth went dry with that revelation. "Are we still together?"

He hesitated to answer.

I raised my hand to remind him of the sparkling engagement ring he had recently given me.

He gave a slight shrug. "Keep it."

A sob caught in my throat. "You used me. You paraded me in public like you'd captured a prize possession. And now I'm not needed anymore."

"Glad you know your worth."

"Actually, I do." *Because there's so much about me you don't know.*

"Look, it wouldn't matter if I'm falling for you. Or if I already have. I don't get to choose."

"Has your father forbidden you to see me?"

"Our families have been rivals for years. You should have seen this coming."

"We're a new generation, Damien. The grandchildren of rivals. What happened between our families was decades ago."

"Hate runs deep between our dynasties, or don't you know your history?"

"Until your family needed mine."

"You should be flattered. You made us look good."

"You did those things to me." I said, my voice trembling. "In your oceanfront home."

"You resent me. Admit it. You always have."

My throat tightened with uncertainty. *Once.*

He looked startled when I failed to deny it, but I knew that any expression of affection for him now could scare him away for good.

Damien raised his hands in frustration. "Your honesty is to be admired."

Tension made the air hard to breathe. "I need a moment."

"Right now, my main focus is getting Pandora Aria Bardot deleted from my Wikipedia page."

"Do you have any idea how you sound?"

He snapped his hand to his chest. "This is what you do to me. Keeping my composure around you is a fucking fulltime job."

"What did I do wrong?"

"Tell me one thing you've done right."

"I've done everything that was asked of me. Even agreeing to marry…"

He sighed. "Your brand of romance is addictive. If you're into self-flagellation."

I tried to read what was really going on, but Damien was so closed off it was impossible to get through to him. "I need you to kill the story on my father."

He looked stunned. "That's why you're here?"

"Well, I wanted to see you regardless."

I saw the doubt in his eyes. "Your father's career in politics is over."

"There must be something you or your dad can do?"

He nudged me back against the wall, placing his hands on either side of my head to cage me in. "It's hopeless. You and your family can sink back into whatever oil spill you all crawled out of."

"Do you have any idea who you're talking to?" God, I was becoming brave.

"You won't let me forget."

"Do you want me to announce our breakup?" I said bitterly.

"Not until after the election." His mouth hovered near mine.

He was going to damn well kiss me—that's what was happening here. His gaze dropped to my lips, which gave me hope. There was still something between us. Maybe I could find a way to get through to him.

"I'm asking for your help," I said softly. "My father's a good man."

His lips dared to brush mine, causing a shudder to run through me.

"You're just doing his bidding." He straightened, moving away from me abruptly as though coming to his senses.

"I admit, Daddy may have asked me to speak with you—"

"Exactly, Pandora. This isn't about you and me. It's about politics. It's about what I can do for you."

"Please don't say that."

"Want the truth?" He stepped closer, leaning over me once again. "You and I have completed our mission."

This time, he really is going to kiss me. Kiss me for the first time…

But he only turned away and said, "Do what you do best."

"What's that?"

"Look pretty."

"There's more to me than just looks."

"Not one thing I've seen or heard from you suggests you care about anyone but yourself."

"I've wanted to do so many things, but my parents—"

"What have you ever done for someone else?"

"I'm here for my family, aren't I? Talking with the most monstrous man in the room."

The smile he gave me didn't reach his eyes. His expression told me he felt he'd made his point.

Tears sprang to my eyes. "I did everything you asked of me."

"You're merely a pawn in the game. Your father's moves have knocked you off the board." He straightened his jacket. "Now, if you'll excuse me, I have a campaign to win for *my* father."

"What about what happened in your loft?" I inhaled sharply. "Did any of our time together mean anything to you?"

I felt lightheaded just remembering how he'd touched me *there*. He was the first man I'd ever been with in that way—and I'd foolishly let myself fall for this playboy.

He hesitated with his hand on the handle, ready to pull the door open, his expression taut as he said, "I remember you saying you wanted your freedom..."

"Please, don't go like this," I pleaded.

Damien looked back at me, his eyes dark with emotion.

And then he left me alone, trembling in the shockwave of his anger.

I fought to get my breathing under control, trying to hold back the tears.

Falling for this man was not the plan, I reminded myself.

No matter what happened next, I needed to escape this life.

CHAPTER
EIGHT

Pandora

I couldn't go back to my table.

Not yet.

I wasn't ready to face my parents and their questions. I didn't want to tell them how terribly wrong it had gone between me and Damien.

I stood there with my hands shaking, trying to figure out what I'd say when the Spanish Inquisition came crashing down on me. I could imagine the angry glances I'd receive from my father and the look of disappointment I'd see on my mother's face. They had relied on me and I'd let them down.

I should never have told Damien those things…even if he'd been just as cruel, just as dismissive and rude. There'd been a glimmer of hope between us and I'd missed my chance. He might have seen past our differences if I'd not blurted out those cruel words.

I'd fucked up.

My father might never speak to me again.

I'd lived without their affection for most of my life, but since returning to the States, I'd found I couldn't exist without it. Their approval was my lifeblood. My brother had stolen the limelight when we were children, but since he was living in Dallas, I'd had my chance to shine.

I sighed. It was time to admit defeat and get the ordeal over with. I had to hold back the tears until I got home and I was alone, locked in my room.

Once back in the ballroom, I looked around for Damien— not that I was ready to face his wrath again. I just wanted to see him one last time.

Would it be the last time?

Damien was leaning against the bar nursing an amber-colored drink, surrounded by sycophants as he held court with members of the Political Action Committee. No doubt those members of PAC were offering to throw money at the campaign to help shoehorn the family into the White House, *if* he promised to return the favor once Daddy was President.

And to think this wasn't even the dirtiest side of Washington.

A woman eased past me even though there was plenty of room around us.

"Excuse me." She touched my arm as she slid past.

Turning, I saw it was Madeline Rhodes.

She strolled away, flaunting her beauty with every step as she headed over to the dessert table. Her exquisite bright red gown had a slit up the side. Madeline wasn't stealing the show, she *was* the show.

And she was back for *him.*

Visiting her classroom a week ago had been a colossal miscalculation.

Pretending to be interested in the sugar feast set before me on silver trays, I perused row upon row of delights—from the selection of delicate chocolate truffles to the classic creamy mousses cupped in individual glasses, from lemon and saffron bites to miniature cupcakes.

"Oh, hello." She sounded surprised.

Seriously?

"Pandora, you look divine." She picked up a set of silver tongs and reached for a tiny cupcake, placing it onto her plate. "Want anything?" She raised the tongs and gave them a click.

"That one." I pointed to a chocolate profiterole.

"Good choice. Very subliminal."

I took a deep breath. "Why are you here?"

She turned to look at me. "Let's talk over there."

Following her into the corner, I tried not to watch her hips sway. My boyfriend's ex, no less, sashaying around like the Queen of England. She pulled a chair out and sat with the same assured style.

"You know whose table this is?" I plopped down beside her.

"Damien won't mind."

"What if he comes back?"

She scooped some icing off the cupcake and brought the spoon to her mouth, eating with a sensuality usually reserved for other pursuits. "How have you been?"

A part of my brain advised me to take notes.

"Dr. Rhodes, friends don't swoop in for the kill when they see a weakness."

She tutted. "I'm going to stop you right there, Pandora. Never reveal a chink in your armor. First rule of war."

"Is that what this is?"

"You know how breathtaking you are. You can't pass a mirror without being reminded." She looked me up and down. "But your parents still have you dressed up like a debutante. Imagine when you're finally allowed to choose your own gowns. "

"I chose this."

She wrinkled her nose at me. "No, you didn't."

Bitch. I hated how her guesses were always right. "I never opened the box," I admitted. "If you're wondering."

She let out a thoughtful sigh.

My fingers tightened around my clutch purse, and I saw her glance at it.

"I'm not here for Damien."

"Then who?"

"You."

Picking up the profiterole, I munched on the round end, making an erotic noise while doing so. The chocolate pastry was delicious.

"Love your style." She gestured to the waiter.

When he arrived at our table, Rhodes ordered four shots of Patrón.

I waited until the server wandered off. "Hope one of those tequila shots isn't for me."

"If you insist on keeping the necklace, you'll need a stiff drink." She licked her spoon, her tongue dancing on metal again. "How shockable are you?"

"In what respect?"

"I'm going to show you something." She set the spoon down on her plate and fished around inside her purse, withdrawing her phone. After swiping to the left a few times, she placed it on her lap and covered it with her palm as the waiter dropped off the four shots.

He looked flustered, which was typical male behavior around Rhodes, I imagined.

After the server left, she leaned in to show me the screen. "Take a peek."

My breath caught as I stared at the image of a naked woman with her hands tied behind her back, red silk ribbon binding her wrists together.

My face felt scorching hot; she knew Damien had done this to me.

I couldn't drag my stare away.

"Ms. Bardot, what is your first thought?"

She knows what happened in that loft.

A sense of betrayal flipped my world and turned an already ruined evening into a nightmare.

"Tell me what you're thinking?" she whispered.

My throat tightened with grief over a breakup there was no coming back from. Damien had told her what we'd done. All trust was lost.

"Why?" My chest heaved with uncertainty.

"This is the tamest thing he likes." She slid the tequila shot glass toward me.

"What?"

She gave me a sympathetic smile.

I gave my head a little shake to clear it, trying to grasp her meaning.

"The moment you walked out of my office with that necklace, I felt guilty. What wearing it brings…"

"What does it bring?"

"Pain, pleasure…everything that traverses the spectrum of bondage. Do you understand what I'm saying? I need you to know what is expected of you if you wear it."

I blinked at her. "He likes it rough?"

She swiped the screen. "Look."

Another photo, only this one was of a woman kneeling before a man in a suit. She was dressed in a bodice with no panties, peering up at him with adoration. Her hands were tied behind her back with black silk.

"How does it make you feel?" asked Madeline.

My nipples beaded, my body shuddering through the realization that I was aroused by what she was showing me. My face flushed with embarrassment as I imagined being that girl.

"Very good, Pandora." She approved of my reaction and slid to another photo. "Now this."

Needing a break from the assault on my mind and senses, I reached for the shot glass and downed the tequila, swallowing the burn. It tasted nasty.

"Want some water?" she asked.

"Just show it to me already."

Oh, God.

Both of us stared down at an image of a naked woman completely bound in rope, hanging from the ceiling. Her breasts were caught in the binds themselves, pink and very pert nipples peeking out between the strands of rope. Her lover's face was buried between her thighs and he was making her come hard, her blonde locks flying wild as he feasted on her pussy, her mouth open as though crying out in agony. Another swipe led to the next image, showing her with a half smile on her face.

Madeline offered me an earbud connected to her phone. I slipped it in, swept away by what came next—actual footage.

On the screen a woman was moaning loudly as two men took her. Both of them had their cocks shoved deep inside her, one in her vagina and the other in her ass.

Rhodes was showing this to me, here—with all these oblivious people around us—in the St. Regis, no less.

Yet I continued to watch…mesmerized by the footage. It was the way the woman looked up at her lovers with wanton gratitude, as though this experience of being taken by two men was a gift meant to be savored. The woman was enraptured by what they were doing to her, her thighs shaking uncontrollably, her moans echoing. I pulled the earbud out to make sure no one else could hear.

"Madeline, why are you showing me this?" I blurted out.

"Because I care about you." She leaned forward to whisper. "I care about Damien, too."

Her expression made her words seem sincere.

She took the earbud out of my fingers and eased it back into my ear so I could continue to secretly watch the video. I allowed myself to awaken to what was possible—that could be me.

The woman's eyelids flickered as she endured a toe-curling orgasm.

"Doesn't it hurt?" I heard myself saying.

Madeline's hand swept up and down my arm to comfort me. "Her master has trained her for double penetration."

"Shush."

"No one can hear us."

My panties were wet; a familiar stickiness I'd come to welcome.

"Do you want that to be you?" she asked, her voice sounding distant.

Yes.

No.

I don't know.

Because right now it felt like my clit was buzzing even though nothing was touching it. All I'd done was imagine myself in the woman's position and my arousal was spiraling toward a pinnacle.

How dare she show me this.

I yanked out the earbud again. "I'm not that kind of girl."

"Your irises are dilated."

I pushed to my feet. "You should be ashamed of yourself, Dr. Rhodes."

She reached out and grasped my hand before I could walk away. "Then you won't want what's in the box."

Madeline had suggested that wearing the necklace would show I belonged to him entirely—like the woman in the video. I knew the term used for those kinds of women.

Submissive.

"Damien will know what it symbolizes?" I whispered.

"Yes." She studied my reaction. "The one who wears it is the chosen one. An elite submissive. This is their emblem."

Reaching into my purse, I pulled out the box. "I don't want it."

"You don't want that level of passion?"

"You got me drunk."

"One tequila shot. What you're feeling isn't the booze, Pandora. It's because your true nature desires this."

"You're a bitch."

"Quite frankly, I'm flattered. And now you know why I'm not the one wearing it." She gave me a sweet smile. "I'm not *that* kind of woman."

"You're more likely to wear a strap-on and fuck them in the ass?" I surprised myself with that one.

"Very much so. I'm a dominatrix." She held out her hand. "Now, Virgin Princess, you have ten seconds to be honest with yourself or I'm taking that back."

"What if I decide to wear it?"

"Your permission is not required for Damien to do whatever he wants to you while the pendant hangs from your throat." She lowered her focus. "Including what I just showed you—and other things."

"What other things?"

"Do you want me to spell it out for you on my whiteboard? I could sketch a level of debauchery that would make those photos look tame."

My breath caught as a rush of adrenaline spiked in me. I was reliving the sensations that had captivated me when I'd been bound with those silken ties.

I glanced around the room self-consciously, as though others might guess what we were discussing.

"He won't care if I'm wearing this or not." I struggled to convey the obvious. "Damien hates me."

"That's because you trigger him."

"In a bad way."

"Not in *that* way," Madeline purred. "He assumes his fantasy of you could never be realized because of your innocence. Which means he's concerned you'd look down on him if you discovered his secret."

"Never."

"Would you like for him to adore you?" She reached for one of the shot glasses of tequila. "How would you feel if you were able to bring him to his knees?"

"He likes that?"

"Figuratively speaking."

Damien adoring me?

Was such a thing possible?

If wearing the necklace meant he would talk with me again, I'd have the time to prove my case. Perhaps he could be persuaded to plead with his father not to pass mine over as a candidate. If I pleased Damien, he'd make that scandal go away.

My body thrummed from the shot of Patrón—or maybe it was from the possibilities of what was to come. Those photos and that footage would likely never fade from my memory, their imagery promising to slide into my dreams and have me soaking wet before I awoke.

I yearned to feel the same level of pleasure as that woman in the video, whose erotic writhing had left me mesmerized. I wanted to be *her*.

"I'd never do anything like that," I fibbed.

I glanced at her phone, wanting to see the footage again.

She gave me a knowing smile.

"What kind of woman does that?" I insisted.

"A woman who respects herself, who is honest about her needs and doesn't let the world dictate her happiness."

"That's impossible for someone like me."

"I disagree."

I yearned to have that kind of life. It was as though Madeline had sensed my deepest and darkest fantasies. She knew what Damien needed...and this was it.

"Are you all right?" she asked softly.

I'd never been envious of anyone until three minutes ago when I'd seen that woman hanging between two men, their cocks buried deep inside her. Such an experience was forbidden to me.

I would never know that level of passion. "Girls like me don't get to have those kinds of fantasies fulfilled."

"You're a woman now. You can make your own decisions." She threw back the rest of the tequila, seemingly not feeling the burn. "Stand before Damien wearing the necklace. Watch his reaction."

"He won't even talk to me."

"Oh, you'll capture his attention."

Doubt lingered in my mind. Could I follow through with what she was suggesting?

Seeing the conflict in my expression, she shrugged. "When in doubt, kneel. Stare at his cock and then look up at him as though he's your only salvation."

I blushed. "The things you say..."

"Pandora." She smiled at me mischievously. "Open the box."

CHAPTER NINE

Pandora

With my head held high, I strolled out of the ballroom, still feeling a buzz from the tequila. I quickly found a private corner and sank into a leather chair behind two large plants with lush, sprawling leaves, feeling grateful for a place to hide.

I clicked open my purse and slowly pulled out the velvet box, glancing up to see if anyone was watching. Then I eased open the lid.

The silver key pendant looked so pretty on its delicate chain. I ran a fingertip over the glinting diamonds that lined the setting. At the top of the key were four round circles and within each of those lay a fleur-de-lis sparkling with secrets.

Still, to me it was just a necklace.

Madeline had called it an emblem.

Curiosity had me lifting out the fine chain and securing the catch behind my neck. Reverently caressing the pendant, I nearly swooned remembering the footage I'd glimpsed.

Surely no one here would know about the necklace's true meaning so there was no shame in wearing it. All I had to do was find Damien and grab his attention. If he responded, I'd lead him away to a more private part of the hotel. We'd get to talk properly this time and hopefully see through our differences.

He's into all that kinky stuff…

Knowing he liked to do all those things that Madeline had shown me would probably make me blush when I saw him again. He wouldn't know why, though—wouldn't know I'd discovered that he liked his sex immoral, filthy and lust ridden and tantalizingly debauched.

Returning to the ballroom, I saw my parents sitting at the same table. They were deep in conversation with another couple. Pride rushed through me that they were entrusting me with such an important diplomatic mission. Letting them down wasn't an option.

My heart skipped a beat when I realized that Damien had left.

Men like him tended to gravitate toward the quieter lounge where they could make their plans to rule the free world. I went looking for him there, and paused when I saw him.

He was speaking to his father. They were huddled close together, proving they were intent on scheming—two intimidating men of power holding tumblers of hard liquor, their private security detail not far away.

All I had to do was say a few words to get Damien's attention and let him see the diamond studded pendant around my neck— if he actually recognized it.

Up until now, I'd believed that strong women didn't bow before their men. They ruled alongside them. I'd been startled by Madeline's confession—she was a dominatrix, a woman who liked to master men.

I could see myself becoming obsessed with all that erotic pleasure…coming hard like all those women in Madeline's collection of evidence she'd pulled out for me. I shuddered while recalling each one…their expressions of lust and a wanton sexuality that I'd only fantasized about.

Damien sensed my presence.

He'd frozen mid-sip as he looked my way, his jaw slack, his eyes ablaze.

I saw a blur of movement to my right and a strong hand grabbed my arm.

"And we're walking. We're walking." Theo led me out of the anteroom.

He gestured to one of the men from my father's security team who was present in the foyer, as though to say, *I have her.*

"Excuse me," I said, annoyed.

"Look over there," he answered, unperturbed by my resistance. "Smile for the camera."

Instinctively, I brightened for the lens pointing our way. "I need to speak with my fiancé."

"He'll call you."

I tried to pull away. "Where are we going?"

Theo manhandled me through the crowd and guided me out through the front door of the hotel. He'd lost his mind. No one had ever dared to touch me like this.

"Where are we going?" I snapped.

With a quick motion to the valet, Theo demanded his car be brought round. He seemed to change his mind as the man bent to search for the keys, seemingly taking too long.

"Fuck it." Theo reached in and grabbed them himself and threw down his valet ticket. "Tell me where my Tesla is."

"I'm staying," I said, feeling bad for the valet who looked panicked at breaking protocol.

A button was pushed on Theo's fob, causing an alarm to ping his car's location nearby. "This way."

"I'm quite capable of getting home myself."

"Not sure I believe you." He cast a glance my way and caught sight of my pendant. "Who have you been talking to?"

My free hand snapped to the necklace. Had it elicited his reaction?

Theo was acting like I'd just revealed a bombshell, so he had to know its meaning, too. He opened the front passenger door of a sporty Tesla and nudged me inside.

"Okay, okay," I said as I settled into the comfortable cream seat.

His eyes focused on something from the direction we'd come.

Following his line of sight through the windshield, blinking into the dusky night, I saw Damien standing not that far away. He had his hands shoved inside his pockets, his glare locked on us, an expression of fury on his face that was pure Godman.

"Shit," muttered Theo, as Damien stalked toward us.

Damien sidled up to Theo and stood chest to chest with him.

"I have no idea," said Theo. "I'm handling it."

Were they talking in code about where I'd gotten this pendant?

"I've got this," said Damien. "Pandora, come with me."

I froze, seeing the stern looks exchanged between the two men.

With a deepening frown, Theo leaned down to look at me and gestured for me to get out of the car. "*He's* taking you home."

I raised my chin in defiance.

"He'll drag you out, Pandora," Theo warned. "And not in a fun way."

"I'm going back inside," I declared.

Damien clenched his jaw. "No, you're not."

My heart did a flip-flop.

What the hell was happening?

Damien nudged Theo out of the way and reached in for me. "Come."

I ignored his hand.

Surprisingly, Damien looked calm. "This is what an order looks like. Obey."

Swallowing my doubt, I relented and let him take my hand to assist me out of the car. He led me towards a limo parked close by.

"I can make my own way," I told him.

"In all honesty, I'm questioning your judgment on any decision right now." Damien glanced back at Theo. "Tell her parents she's with me."

"Will do," said Theo.

Damien opened the rear door of the limo. "In."

He was too quick for the chauffeur, who appeared flustered that he'd failed to open the door for us.

"I've got it, Jacob," Damien reassured him. "Home. Right away, please."

Was he taking me to Foxhall Crescent? It was a place I'd never seen, but I'd heard it was his private home. Climbing into the back passenger seat, I noticed the privacy glass was already up.

"Are you dropping me off first?"

"When we're seen together—" Damien climbed in beside me. "At least try to look happy about it."

"I've been taught to show no reaction to anything either way," I chided. "Hiding my emotions is what I do best."

"You give resting bitch face a run for its money," he muttered. "I know that."

"I would have been very happy to be taken home by Theo."

"Thank goodness it was him who approached you first, you naive brat."

I bristled at his tone. "What are you talking about?"

He turned to face me, glaring, deep chestnut eyes burning an entirely new universe into mine.

A sigh found its way through my trembling lips. I wasn't going to relent, wasn't going to let him bully me.

I realized he was staring at the necklace.

"Explain," he said quietly.

My hand snapped to the diamond key. "This?"

He gave a nod.

"I'm wearing it because I'm worthy."

He looked unconvinced, those muscles along his jaw tensing with suppressed rage. "Have you any idea what that necklace means?"

"Go on, then. Tell me, Damien Godman."

He let out an exasperated sigh. "I'm going around in circles with you. I always do."

"My feelings exactly. You always need to have the last word."

Madeline was right about the necklace. It had sent Damien over the edge. I'd never seen him behave like this toward me.

I felt our passion alighting like a dancing flame, the air crackling with electricity that sparked between us. He had loosened his tie, and his eyelids had become heavy the way they'd done back in his loft when his fingers had grazed my sex.

I tapped the chain. "Clearly you can't handle me wearing this."

He gave me a predatory look. "I'm going to show you what it means."

"I think I'd like that."

"Silence, Pandora. This is where you watch and learn. Think you can do that?" He tugged his tie off. "Turn around."

"Why?"

"I'm going to bind your wrists."

"No, you're not."

"That necklace tells me I can. Now turn the fuck around."

I hesitated, but then turned my back on him to give him better access to my wrists.

It was happening.

He was making me his plaything.

Damien focused, following through on his threat. He yanked my wrists together with force and tugged tight, binding them behind my back.

Leaving me vulnerable.

"That's a clavis around your neck," he said, leaning close to my ear. "Let's see if you know its meaning."

CHAPTER
TEN

Damien

My focus shifted from tying Pandora's wrists to admiring the way she calmly breathed through the process of having her hands bound behind her back.

She was letting it happen.

Her promising reaction caused an erotic charge to surge through my veins—awakening a need in the darkest part of my psyche. I felt a spark of affection flare inside me, lowering my guard, allowing me to see her in a new way.

This wasn't the girl I thought I knew.

She glanced back over her shoulder at me, her plump lips pouting.

"Are you even still a virgin?" I chided.

The look on her face led me to believe she might be. Still, what kind of virgin wears the clavis, the mark of a submissive? Either way, the symbol riled my diabolical side, which she was about to become acquainted with. I'd hidden that part of myself from her, assuming she'd never see me like this—now I felt hope rising for a relationship between us I'd believed impossible.

How the hell had she ended up wearing this key?

I could be over thinking the situation, but Theo had been wondering the same thing—who the hell had given it to her?

With her hands tied at her lower spine, Pandora was forced to push her chest forward and keep her back straight—the glint of diamonds at her throat assuring me of her willingness to comply with utter submission.

What she'd done was the equivalent of setting a match to

gasoline and watching the flames fan around her. She gave her consent the moment the catch closed at her nape.

Her vulnerability was stirring my debauchery; it flared white hot and blinding.

It would be easy to do whatever I wanted to her in the back of this car as retribution for daring to wear what she had no right to.

Vanguardians...owning a submissive was our veritable right.

"I want this," she whispered.

Really?

You dare to tease me? After I've bound your fucking wrists.

What was meant to follow was me diving deep into my proclivity, forgetting what day or even month it was within minutes. A surge of arousal heated my flesh and caused my dick to ache for this. I wanted Pandora to need this just as much, for her offering to be real.

That pendant could unlock her hidden desires.

I'd devour them as my own.

Be the fucking adult here and shut this down.

Or, something altogether different—strike with retaliation for her haughtiness to think she could pull this off and I'd fall for it.

Because she had dared to tease me, I placed my palm at her throat, squeezing her neck tight for the delicious entertainment of it. Fear flooded her eyes—a gift from a submissive to her master.

Could this be us?

Could we make this work?

No.

Right now, it was imperative I see through her scheming and scare her off. There'd be no compromise. In reality, she'd never agree to my demands. Lesser submissives had crumbled under my sway.

She was no different.

Finding a woman I loved who would succumb to my needs

was an ambition I had yet to realize. She'd need to publicly shine like a goddess and in the bedroom shimmer under my complete dominance.

My hand slipped from her throat and she sucked in oxygen, gulping hungrily.

Cue her screaming...

I watched her face closely, waiting for the hysteria, bracing myself for a torrent of curses being flung my way. Maybe she'd realize she was close to drowning in the deep, dark ocean of my lust.

Her breathing slowed as she assessed me with her crystal blue eyes, her gaze roaming over me and settling on my erection.

"You have my attention," I said gruffly. "Do I have yours?"

"Yes, sir."

I taunted her with a sneer. *Nice try, but not convinced.*

"Show me what happens now," she whispered.

"You mean if that necklace stays on?" I reached for the catch at her nape. "Which it won't."

She shifted away a little. "No."

"If you keep it on, I will punish you for wearing it."

A shade of doubt clouded her eyes, but then she lifted her chin. "I deserve it."

Very well...

I eased the straps of her gown off her shoulders and pulled the bodice down, along with her bra, until her breasts were bared. "I'll start here."

I pinched her nipples to punish her, taking my adrenaline-soaked arousal out on those beaded buds until they responded to my twisting.

"Oh, please," she said, gasping.

So many ideas flashed through my filthy mind about how I could abuse her, get off on having her subjugated before me.

Pandora let out a long groan inviting more punishment, her wrists twisting to escape as she writhed before me, her hips rocking on the leather seat as though imagining how it would feel to ride me.

I massaged her breasts with the authority of a man who knew how to wield bliss, and was rewarded with her throaty, needy cry in response. The erotic sound caused my cock to harden even more.

My hands moved beneath her hem and past her panties, my thumb rubbing her clit to prepare her for finger-fucking.

Think.

And not with your balls.

If she was a virgin and this was a ruse, fucking her in the back of a car could traumatize her.

I wasn't *that* kind of monster.

But she thought I was…

I pulled my fingers away from her and brought them up to her mouth, letting her lick her own juices.

"Show me what you like," she whispered.

Having a sub wear this emblem was a rare and beautiful accomplishment. It was possible, but only the highly trained and well-prepared lovers endured what their masters demanded. It didn't make sense that she was wearing the necklace.

I tried to flood doubt out of my thoughts, leaning in and drawing a pert nipple into my mouth and suckling, letting the way my tongue formed sensual circles around her areola serve as a precursor to more.

Six months of not having this, of dating Pandora and remaining loyal, because that was the only way my heart had navigated around what we were. Here, now, my soul was rejoicing that my sexual starvation was over.

If only she knew what I was capable of. The gifts I yearned to give her if I kept her as a toy. If I allowed myself the privilege of believing she wanted this, wrecking Pandora was going to be the grandest gift I gave myself.

Because she was Pandora Aria Bardot—the most exquisite sub a man could own.

"It's not enough," she begged.

I freed her hands from my necktie. "Patience."

Pandora's natural beauty felt like a trick of nature. She seduced with her presence, her exquisite blue eyes promising mystery. The way her tongue darted to wet her lips was a thing of beauty and dangerously arousing—she'd be exquisite to watch when coming with my dick inside her. Her awe of being subjugated would be equivalent to modern art.

Lifting her gown, I pulled her thong down her legs and off her feet, shoving it in my jacket pocket. She knew my next command was imminent. All the power she had left would soon be gone.

She was my plaything.

Her thighs opened wider as she welcomed me exploring her wet folds with a delicate touch, her tender clit throbbing as my index finger brushed along the nub.

"Hold yourself like this." Taking her hands, I had her ease back her labia. "That way I can do this."

Smack! I tapped her clit.

She flinched and gave me a look of shock.

"Do I have your attention?"

She gave a frantic nod.

"Again," I demanded.

Her breaths were panicked and her eyelids heavy, but she obeyed, reaching low and pulling back her labia.

This time, I slid down onto my knees on the floor of the car and leaned in between her thighs. "Make no mistake," I said fiercely. "This is not me bowing before you. This is me giving you what you deserve. Am I making myself clear?"

A subtle nod.

I planted kisses up and along her left thigh and when I almost reached her pussy, I moved my attention to her other knee, causing her entrance to pucker in a rhythm of want.

"Play with your nipples."

She placed her fingertips at her breasts and tweaked the buds just like I had, mimicking the way I'd teased her.

"Harder," I demanded.

She obeyed my command like a well-trained bottom, twiddling her areola with verve.

"Continue like that," I demanded.

Her clit swelled at its tip at the first touch of my tongue. I thrummed it delicately at first, and then more insistently before dipping into her entrance just enough to make her gasp.

God, she'd be tight when I entered her, sheathing my erection like a vice, hungry and needy, with her selfish cunt clinging to my full length. I'd be balls deep soon and thrusting if I didn't slow this down.

I lavished her pussy until her breath hitched and she neared the edge over my feasting. I tasted her sweet juices, devouring and plundering every crevice; savoring what was mine.

I peered up at her. "Tweak your nipples to the same rhythm as my tongue, understand?"

She gave a nod and her eyelids became heavy; dark lashes flickering, her jaw slack as she followed my command and played with her nipples to the same beat as my flicking tongue. Swirling in a circle as wide as it was slow, I could feel her clit swell and harden, its response pleasing.

This was my privilege, to perform cunnilingus as many times a day as I desired, wherever we were, in any setting.

Beneath my touch she came alive, rocking her pelvis. My hand reached down and felt her toes, delighted to find they were curling—proving she was close to coming.

I continued to lick her clit as my hands reached up and nudged hers away from her breasts, taking over playing with her tits. I wanted her to relax so she could savor her climax as the luxurious gift it was.

I devoured her sex as only an obsessed master can.

Her body stiffened as an intense trembling stretched all the way through her body. She climaxed long and hard, her deep-throated groaning revealing her pussy was truly possessed by me.

Her cries became panicked at the intensity of her never-ending orgasm.

My mouth let her down slowly, lapping at her until she was seemingly boneless and breathless. She slid down the seat a little, dazed and gasping for air.

She looked over at me, unable to hide the pleasure she'd enjoyed, her blue eyes bright and her smile dreamlike.

I pushed myself up.

Subs deserved after-care no matter the treatment, but Pandora hadn't earned the right to wear the necklace.

I sensed that much was true.

It had been the way she'd followed my every move as though seeing it for the first time. She'd been mesmerized by each shift in movement, each lap or kiss, and each suckle.

Grabbing my necktie from where it lay on the seat, I weaved it around my shirt collar until it hung from my neck and then twisted it into neatness.

With that done, I eased her breasts back into the cups of her bra and pulled down her gown, ensuring her hem was over her legs to hide what I'd done to her.

All in silence.

All done with the precision of a master who was merely warming up.

With a push of a button on the console, I lowered the glass divider exposing us to the driver once more. He glanced in the rearview mirror to check on us and then turned his focus back to the road.

Fucking her before we reached the house was still a possibility. *If* she opened her big mouth again. If she made one complaint.

We were ten minutes away.

Enough time to get my heart rate below sixty. I fished around in my pocket for my smartphone.

My cock was rock hard.

"You may wear these again." I handed the thong to her.

Pandora discreetly slipped her underwear on with the endearing shakiness of a novice.

Popping in my earbuds, I tapped the music app on my phone

and selected Puccini's *Madam Butterfly*, letting the agony of the soprano flow through my soul. I stared dead ahead, getting myself in the mood for when we reached home and I could torture the truth out of her.

The pleasure to come would be sublime.

CHAPTER
ELEVEN

Pandora

T his was the kind of progress I'd given up on.

Finally, I was standing inside Damien's Foxhall home, despite our argument at the St. Regis an hour ago. We'd been tentatively dating for six months and in one brave move, I'd leaped all the way here to his private sanctuary.

His kitchen, to be exact.

This... the transformative effect of a simple pendant.

I'd also dragged him away from the event. There'd probably be repercussions for that later. The polls would be closing in just over three weeks, so every event mattered. Time was too valuable to waste.

I studied him now, in case that exact fact might have pissed him off, but I couldn't read his expression.

I set my purse down on a barstool, my gaze shifting to the wide windows that would welcome the light in during the day. The dark wood paneling of the room complemented the open floor plan. Every time Damien took me to one of his homes, I dived deeper into his world and got to see another side to this mysterious man.

God, I still felt tingles down *there*.

Still reeling from what he'd done to me in the car, I reminded myself why I was here—not to have him overpower me, but for me to keep the upper hand.

Wandering over to his kitchen table, I looked down at what appeared to be architectural designs. "What's this?"

"The Fairfield Project." He walked over and folded them, his body language changing as he gathered them up protectively.

Watching him carefully, I asked. "Can you tell me more about it?"

He turned to face me. "Want a drink?"

"No, thank you." I slipped off my high heels seductively, grateful for the feeling of relief.

He leaned back against the wall and watched me take in the décor of the home he'd never before brought me to—because I'd always been a token and nothing more.

"Well?" he said, interrupting my musing.

"It's beautiful." I looked at him. "Do you have any staff?"

"No." He shrugged. "A housekeeper. Once a week."

"You cook?"

"Yes, Pandora, I am not helpless like some people we know."

"Funny." I looked around the kitchen, impressed with its simplicity. "I like it a lot."

"I've been told I should sell it. The Secret Service hates all this glass. I have a wall around the property, but drones, you know. They can fly over."

Once, when I was sunbathing in our back garden, a drone had flown over and taken a snapshot of me in my bikini by the pool. The photo had appeared soon after in *The Inquirer*. Privacy was a rare privilege for people like us.

Damien strolled over to a wall panel and pushed a button. The windows went dark. "Now we have privacy."

"No one can see in?"

"No." He shrugged out of his jacket and threw it over a corner chair.

"I'm glad we've called a truce."

He folded his arms in a *no we haven't* pose.

"Then what are we now, Damien?"

"You tell me."

"More than friends?"

"These are the rules while we're here together," he said, ignoring my question. "You never discuss your family. We don't ask any favors of each other...ever. We forget the outside world. Most importantly, we're honest."

"I can do that."

He glanced at the necklace. "Want me to begin?"

"Begin?"

"Where did you get it? And don't lie to me."

I crossed my arms. "I have my own rules."

He raised his hand to stop me from saying anything else. "Don't bother. With *that* around your neck you have no say."

My hand snapped to the key at my throat. "This is who I want to be."

"You have no idea—"

"I have some idea."

"I ought to take you home right now."

I pulled the straps of my gown down and let the material fall in a pool around my feet, then stepped out of it, reaching back to undo my bra. When I'd removed it I threw it down on top of the dress, standing before him in only my panties.

His harsh attention raked over me as he straightened to his full height, as though he was preparing to intimidate me.

I waited for him to say something.

When no words came, I slipped my fingers beneath my thong and eased it off my hips, slowly wiggling the panties down my legs and then stepping out of them.

I stood before him naked now.

Damien's eyes locked with mine as he walked closer.

A shudder ran through my body when he loomed over me. Leaning in, he dipped his head to my throat, capturing the key pendant between his lips and sucking it. His daring sensual act stirred lust-fueled memories of our journey here in his chauffeur-driven car.

He wasn't touching me, but he was close enough for me to feel the power dripping off him. Still suckling on my necklace, his soft cologne teased me, hinting of things to come.

Finally, he let the pendant drop from his mouth. Stepping back, he tilted his head, his eyes narrowed on me, assessing my reaction. "What happens now, Pandora?"

I have no fucking clue.

Dropping to my knees, I recalled the advice I'd been given back at the St. Regis, to peer up at him with adoration, which was easy because his looks were so striking—even now, after a long evening, with his hair sensually disheveled and that smoldering burn in his eyes boring through me knowingly.

With me on my knees, lips parted and eyes wide and pleading for his approval, I saw an internal switch seemed to flip within him. His stance became aggressive and dominant as he glared down at me with a fiery certainty. He knew what he was looking at—a woman who was willing to do anything to accomplish the impossible...make him fall in love with her.

But, oh, God, this was going to hurt. I might even stain his high-thread count with the blood of my innocence.

"Get up," he snapped.

I obeyed, pushing to my feet.

"This is what will happen, Pandora. You are going to get dressed and walk back the way we came, down the hallway to the front door. My driver will take you home."

I don't want to leave.

Not after the suffering I'd endured all these months. Not when his touch felt like it turned a key within me—awakening my sexuality.

"I'm making this easy on you," he said with a rare kindness in his tone. "I'll call you, okay?"

That flash of decency he was displaying might be a once in a lifetime event, a compassionate effort to help me avoid a shameful mistake.

Don't fall for his charm.

I turned my face away to hide my flushed cheeks.

"Ms. Bardot, if you choose to stay you will suffer the consequences of that decision."

"I know," I said, my voice trembling. "I...I want to."

Just breathe, that's all that's required.

"Do you want to risk it all? Turn right instead of left. Head through the red door and down the set of stairs. Walk to the end of the corridor..." He raised an eyebrow.

Swallowing my nervousness, I ran through my options. Leave and he may never speak to me again—although his promise to call made that decision easier. But the reason I came here would be lost. Stay and I would have to face the dire threat of what he would do to me becoming my reality. Madeline had revealed that much at least.

"This is what concerns me," he said darkly. "You're wearing a clavis but have no idea of its origin." He tucked his tongue into his cheek as though finding this fact amusing. "Are you really this brave?"

I tried to answer but no words would come.

He smirked. "Are you willing to obey the directive of the clavis?"

I gathered my dress off the floor, along with my underwear, unable to look him in the eye. Grabbing my purse off the barstool, I scooped up my high heels as I went, clutching everything to my chest as I hurried naked into the hallway, heading fast for the exit.

I pulled my gown on at the end of the hallway, but I paused before opening the front door.

There was a different kind of suffering my body craved, a deep yearning buried within me.

It made me turn around to stare in the opposite direction—at the long shadows falling over a dark red door.

CHAPTER
TWELVE

Damien

She'd turned left instead of right, and then she'd changed her mind.

Glancing at my Rolex, I timed how long it would take before Pandora reached my dungeon. She'd be looking around at the instruments of pain positioned strategically around the room, ready to be used on the willing.

That should be enough to have her running for the car. If this glimpse into my psyche would accomplish that, then so be it.

I should be down there now, watching her reaction so my diabolical side could snag a few minutes of entertainment before she made her escape.

The thought of Pandora in that room was a revenge play for all the crap I'd taken from her these last few months. Hating her had become my favorite sport. Our arguments were so damn arousing it was enough to make me believe that, subconsciously at least, I liked being around her.

I had to admit that the scent of a woman within these walls lifted the loneliness, but it was only temporary. She'd be gone soon. Pushing that aside, I reasoned I was used to the quiet.

I headed over to the liquor cabinet and uncorked the Cognac, pouring some of the dark amber liquid into a tumbler. I took a sip, waiting for Pandora to fly by the door leading to the kitchen and out the exit. It made me chuckle…the thought of scandalizing my pretty debutante.

This was a decent brandy—sweeter than a whisky, tasting of fruit and citrus. The bottle's contents had been aged in an oak barrel that had been switched out each year to ensure its quality. Not bad for a four-year-old liquor. I swirled my nightcap around in the glass to let the liquid breathe, savoring the scent.

Hmmm. She isn't coming out.

My move.

I headed out into the hallway to find her.

Wait.

You need answers before you dive in and potentially fuck up your life…or hers.

Doing a one-eighty, I went back into the kitchen and grabbed my phone off the central marble island. If my suspicion was right, calling this number would confirm the clues I'd deciphered. There were a handful of intimate friends who knew about Vanguard—most of them men. And only one woman.

Madeline answered her phone on the third ring. "What a lovely surprise."

I listened for any hint of where she might be at this late hour. "Thought I'd say hi."

"I'm flattered," she said. "I know how busy you are."

"How's teaching?"

"Fulfilling. You?"

"Honestly, I'm exhausted."

"You need to take some time for you, Damien. A day off once in a while."

"I wish."

"I've been following the polls. It's looking good for the Senator. How does it feel?

Your dad's going to be President! Oh, my God, you have to invite me over to the White House."

She made me smile. "Consider yourself invited. But let's not pick out new curtains yet."

"Are you freaking out?"

"No."

"How are you this calm?"

"It is what it is." I paused. "It's good to hear your voice."

"The feeling is mutual. To what do I owe the honor?"

"You're a great distraction from the work I have waiting on my laptop."

"I'm so glad," she purred.

Her husky voice always did things to me—it was like melting butter. My balls

remembered the feel of her mouth…the way she'd suckle my sac like that was all she cared about. Like it was her goddamn job.

I adjusted my pants to accommodate my reaction, cursing the day ten years ago that Madeline had told me she wanted to top. I'd been twenty-two and balls deep into the lifestyle. Balls deep in her, too.

Weeks later, she'd officially become a dominatrix, a waste of a good submissive.

Still, she was happy and therein lay the wisdom of that decision. She'd found what I'd been searching for—fulfillment. I was glad for her. If not a little jealous.

"Still there, Champ?" she said with affection.

"There's a submissive inside my dungeon. Waiting for me to fuck her into

oblivion while I burn off some stress."

Silence lingered on the other end.

"I have an excellent selection of toys to use on her," I continued. "A few new pieces shipped in from Italy." I smirked. "Some antique torture devices from medieval times. She'll be destroyed by the morning."

"I thought you had work to do?"

"I consider this a gift to myself. Some night play. This need has been building for quite some time. I'm going in strong."

"Damien," she scolded.

Yeah, you better break, bitch. "I'm listening."

"Okay, okay, I gave her the clavis."

I felt a rush of relief at knowing this ruse had been orchestrated by Madeline and not some deviant with a political objective.

"Keep talking," I coaxed.

"I thought Pandora would be good for you as a submissive." She breathed out a sigh.

"Since when do you decide what I need?"

"Since I decided I love you. And I know you, too. I know what you need to keep you sane. You're starving, Damien. I can see it in your eyes at the pressers."

"You watch my interviews?" I downed the rest of my drink in one go. "I'm flattered." Citrus and spice danced on my tongue and heated my throat.

"Be gentle with her. Ease her into it."

"She's using me."

"I showed her Amelia."

"What?"

"I showed Pandora the video of Amelia being taken by Theo and Landon at the same time—you couldn't see their faces in the footage."

I raked my fingers through my hair.

"You should have seen her reaction, Damien. Pandora was mesmerized. It was like a light being turned on full beam. Her response was pure sub. I tested her with some other photos and—"

"Where?"

"At the St. Regis."

"You were there tonight?"

"I was."

"Where?"

"Ballroom. You were off wheeling and dealing in the anteroom."

And we both knew we couldn't be seen together. This job was stifling.

My back stiffened. "You showed her those things with all of those people around?"

"Yes, of course."

"What were you thinking?" I scolded.

"That she was being forced on you. Might as well make it a

good relationship. For both of you." The rustle of sheets revealed Madeline was in bed. "I watched her reaction. You know I have a knack for spotting subs. Pandora watched the footage and pressed her hands to her breasts. She wasn't even aware she was doing it. She only watched five minutes and was hungry for more. There's your new sub."

"I'm quite capable of finding my own."

"Really? If your father makes it all the way to that house on the hill, you'll be locked out of Vanguard. Those are the rules. No further access."

"What the fuck do you know?"

"Everything. I still visit."

"Vanguard? I thought you hated that place."

"Not since certain changes were made." She chuckled. "A dominatrix runs it now. So, it's well suited for the female gaze. It's now more respectful and emotionally fulfilling for female members."

If I wasn't hard from knowing Pandora was waiting for me in my dungeon, I certainly was now. Rhodes was a scholar in and out of the classroom. I'd always wanted the women in Vanguard to get as much out of it as the men.

"I respect your opinion." A session with Madeline was probably mind-bending. She thrived on the play as much as I did. "And if I'm ever in the mood to be topped..."

"Like that would ever happen."

"True. I fucking hate it."

"Enjoy her. That's all I want out of this."

"She's not here to be dominated, Madeline. She's here to use me."

"I don't necessarily believe that. It's probably what she's telling herself. Either way, use her right back."

"This could blow up in my face."

"Or..."

"She's probably in shock at what she's seeing right now."

"You'll find her kneeling. Her mouth ready for your cock."

"You always were eloquent." I drew in a breath. "Did you tell her to do that? To kneel?"

"Your balls are tight. I can hear it in your voice. Usually, I'd say don't think with your cock, but you know…"

"I'm hanging up now."

"I need you to remember that this is her first time."

"You know the Italians really were cruel fuckers in medieval times. You should see the variety of devices I've got lined up in my dungeon for tonight's game of 'Let me see how long it takes to make you cry.'"

"I'm serious, Godman. Slow but sure with this one."

"I'm serious, too. The taste of a virgin's tears and all that."

She laughed. "You love your gift."

I hung up on her.

CHAPTER
THIRTEEN

Pandora

The lighting was dimmed in a soft red haze. Unfamiliar shadows danced over furniture and certain devices I recognized from the porn I'd managed to sneak a peek at while hidden away in my bedroom.

I stripped down naked again and placed my dress, underwear and shoes on a corner chair.

An impressively carved four-poster-bed was positioned in the center of the room. But instead of red silk ribbons, there were chains attached to each bedpost with metal cuffs on the end.

This sense of fight or flight or fuck was cranked up enough to have my nipples beading and my clit throbbing; my pussy was already soaking wet.

I'd felt just as intimated back when Damien had tied me to the bed in his oceanside home. There'd been no regrets over that evening. He'd warned me it would be memorable, and it was. Though he'd done hardly anything to me there.

Which was why I hadn't left this room yet. A replay on that night was as alluring as it was terrifying. I recalled my disappointment when I'd been escorted out of Seascape in the early hours and whisked away in a helicopter with the unspoken threat that I would never return there.

I ran my palm over my right arm, feeling it tingle at the memory of Damien's touch, trying to comprehend why I had this craving.

For him.

For this.

For more.

The excitement inside me elicited a heady sense of arousal that had me craving his affection, yearning for more of his roughness.

And admittedly his love—or at the very least, his approval.

What he'd done to me in the back of that chauffeur-driven car on the way here had given me the merest taste of the way he liked to dominate. God, I wanted it.

Wanted it all, only...

I looked around at the walls and shelves that offered up strange contraptions promising an alternative to pleasure. It made me recall the images Madeline had shown me—a glimpse into Damien's depravity, a whole spectrum of perversion, apparently.

To be taken like that...shared, even. Owned like that woman in the video.

Footfalls were heading in this direction.

I gasped and hurried over to the end of the bed, kneeling before it and assuming the same pose that had seemed to please him upstairs.

I only had to wait a few more moments before he walked into the room.

He moved toward me with a stern demeanor that sent shivers up my spine. He'd already removed his necktie. I watched as he peeled off his watch strap, placing it on a high table.

He rolled up his shirt sleeves and casually moved about the room, opening drawers and pulling out contraptions, laying them all in a line on top of the mahogany table.

Daring to raise my head a little more, I peeked at the nipple clamps he'd chosen. The magic wand that lay beside them looked familiar, and I saw a mysterious metal device that was unappealing. I tried not to betray my thoughts, but was unable to hide my concern.

He leaned back against the table and returned his focus to me, crossing his ankles casually as though gauging my reaction to the objects he'd put on display.

I went to speak, wanting to ask what came next.

He raised his finger to stop me. "Eyes diverted. That was your first mistake. Second, your palms should be turned upward. Ready to receive. Any of this sound familiar?"

"Don't send me away," I blurted out.

"Give me a good reason not to."

"If I don't experience this now, I never will."

"That's not necessarily true."

I shot him a glare. "You know this is not the world I come from."

"Second mistake, you're still speaking. Which offends me."

I slapped my hand to mouth to stop myself from interrupting.

He pushed off and strolled toward me. "This chamber has rules. You broke all of them."

I averted my eyes, aware of him kneeling before me, sensing his dangerous demeanor. He even seemed to dominate the air I had to breathe.

His hand reached between my thighs and he touched me. I jolted when his fingertip brought an instant of bliss as he stroked my sex. Then he pulled away to examine the sticky wetness on the tip of his fingers with curiosity, rubbing the thickness between his thumb and forefinger like a teacher grading a task.

Reaching for me again, he cupped my pussy, his firm hand pressing against my softness. "I shouldn't have had to wait for this. You've been mine for months."

"Let's make it special between us," I said breathlessly.

"It's my understanding that you're here for a different kind of special, true?" His thumb grazed my clit.

I shuddered as his fingers slid along my wetness. *Oh,* it felt so good. My feelings were gliding between affection and wanting him to be the man I'd imagined he was.

"So wet." His finger flicked my clit.

I flinched forward.

"Good girl." A nod, hinting I'd passed a test.

He pushed to his feet and stared down at me, looking intrigued.

I reached for his zipper.

"Another rule broken."

I let my hands fall to my thighs with my palms facing up. "I thought you might like it."

"What do you want?"

"My wish is to be taken by you."

"Are you hoping that will work in your favor?"

I looked away, considering how to answer his question. Damien was Yale-smart, and street-smart, too. He'd know I was lying if I denied it.

"This room," I whispered. "It's like a womb."

His sternness softened for a beat. "Scared?"

I leaped to my feet and hurried over to the bed, reaching for one of the chains lying there and slipping my wrist through the metal cuff. "This is what I want."

"That's not what I asked."

"I thought wearing this—" My free hand reached for the pendant— "might get your attention. Persuade you to help me and my family. But now I find myself not caring about any of it."

"Tell me who the necklace came from."

"I promised not to say."

"Madeline Rhodes?" He studied me carefully.

If I said yes, I'd be breaking a confidence.

"There's a serial number on it." He arched a brow. "Each necklace is worth thousands of dollars because of the diamonds. All I have to do is look at it under a magnifier."

This felt like a mind game.

"I gave my word."

"I'll give you exactly what you're asking for," he said quietly. "Break that promise to whomever gave the necklace to you, and I will do everything in my power to have your father's position realized."

I'd always been the good girl. The one sent across an ocean to be forged into a valuable asset to be used later. For the first time, I wanted to do something for me. Have my own experience that felt sacred and not waste another second pleasing others. I felt no animosity toward my family. This was about me needing to breathe and have my own life.

"Answer," he said.

Climbing onto the bed, I reached for the other chain and slid my wrist through it, lying flat on the duvet and spreading my legs, showing off my soaking wet pussy and not caring—giving in to whatever happened next as my head sunk into the satin pillow.

"Full transparency," he said, his tone turning kind. "I just spoke with Madeline."

My head snapped up.

"I know she gave you the pendant."

"I want to earn the right to wear it."

"I'm impressed you didn't give her name to me, Pandora—especially considering the stakes. This pleases me."

"You can trust me."

"I believe you."

I felt a rush of relief.

He gripped the left bedpost and leaned in. "I'm going to film what I do to you. How do you feel about that?"

"To show someone?"

"Perhaps, but more for my own enjoyment."

"Like a sex tape?"

"I'm going to be taking a virgin. I want to document it for my collection."

I threw a nod toward the high table and the objects that rested on top. "Will you use those?"

"First, a conundrum."

"A puzzle?"

"You're not going to like it."

"I'm listening."

"Stay, and you will *never* get what you want for your father from me. Leave now, and I will do everything in my power to see his ambition realized."

These were mind games.

"I don't understand."

"Be here because you want to be. I don't need a martyr in my life. I want a submissive to dominate. Someone to fuck wherever and whenever I like. A woman who will give herself completely to me. A woman I can cherish."

If I stay...

Upon the wall hung paddles, whips and chains—and more instruments that looked like they could inflict a lot of pain...

He clicked his fingers to get my attention. "You will obey me in all things. You're a spoiled brat, Pandora. It's going to be a tall order."

"I'm here, aren't I? Tied to your bed."

"You're not tied to it yet. But once I clamp those handcuffs, you're staying. You're going to be gagged. Am I making myself clear?"

"I can stay?"

"Are you sure you want to? Staying means that potentially your family's aspirations are over. It's a lot to consider. I can give you some time to think about it." He gestured his willingness to leave.

With my chest heaving, I tried to decide if I was willing to throw away everything I'd been trained for—a life dedicated to being my family's commodity. Now, instead of saving a dynasty, I was considering his offer.

If I stayed, I'd be *his.*

CHAPTER
FOURTEEN

Pandora

With all this pendant had achieved, it felt sacred to me now, resting delicately against my throat as I lay back on the bed. Damien snapped each of the metal cuffs closed—after he'd stretched my limbs wide and positioned me spread-eagled on the satin bed cover.

I tried to control my breathing, tried to keep my mind from spinning. Tension rose in me as I watched him take his time preparing the room.

Candles were lit and placed here and there, their shadows dancing over my naked form. A camera pod was stationed to our left, the lens pointed directly toward the four-poster bed to capture the scene, a blinking red light confirming that filming had begun. I looked over at the mahogany table where the instruments glinted threateningly.

Finally, Damien appeared ready.

He kicked off his shoes and then stripped off his shirt, revealing a toned body with sculpted abs and a lean waist. He watched me as I stared, pulling his pants and briefs off and tossing his clothes on top of mine.

My eyes settled on his enormous cock, curling up his abdomen, the head round and smooth. That would be inside me soon. The thought of it caused me to feel a wave of panic as I watched him stroke it from base to tip, causing it to grow in size.

He ripped open the small square packet in his hand and eased out a condom, pinching the end and rolling the shiny sheath over his impressive length. His cock continued to grow larger as he secured the condom with nimble fingers.

My head crashed back onto the pillow.

At last, it was happening.

The sound of my rapid breathing filled the chamber. He came at me slowly, crawling from the end of the bed and soon closing in on his prey, causing the mattress to dip slightly as he leaned on his elbows.

His thumb brushed over my lips. "Ready?"

I gave him a hesitant nod and glanced over at the camera.

"Keep your eyes on me." He brushed a wisp of hair out of my eyes. "It's going to be uncomfortable. Bite down on my shoulder if it helps. Don't worry about me. I like it."

My mouth went dry and I licked my lips as I fathomed his words.

"Want something to drink?"

Just do it...get it over with.

"If you want me to stop at any time, just say." His thumb slipped into my mouth.

I suckled on it, surrendering to the sensuality.

His hand moved, cupping my cheek. "Slow your breathing."

I wanted to tell him to be gentle, but the contents of this room screamed that it wasn't his way. This man appeared to search out pain and probably drenched himself in it. The same level of endurance would be expected of me, no doubt. All I had to do was survive seconds and minutes and possibly hours of discomfort.

Yet despite my trepidation, my body craved that same agony, like a numbness needing to be clawed at—a fragile body needing to be proven strong.

His honesty soothed a part of me, as though his promise of torture might cancel out a past of privilege—that side of me that had been coddled and protected and kept safe, lifting me out of the dullness of my existence.

"I'm ready for the pain," I whispered.

Dark eyes seemed to see through me. "Silence."

After dipping a fingertip in his mouth, he placed it upon my nipple and circled the areola, moving slowly until it pebbled; an erotic torment that brought a surge of arousal. His attention moved to my other breast, and he used the same hypnotic method to make me moan.

I saw approval in his eyes.

His mouth crashed down on mine, his tongue darting in and exploring, fiercely searching, warring with my tongue.

This was our first kiss and it felt divine, as though we really were lovers who were obsessed with each other. Wanton and needy, he hungrily savaged my mouth and I gave into his demands willingly, groaning with pleasure, eliciting a deeper kiss.

When he pulled away, he studied me carefully, as though seeing me in a whole new light.

My arms ached to reach out and pull him to me. I wanted to hold him against me and let the hour slip away with us in an embrace. But I was bound and prevented from moving. I was his to do with as he pleased.

Exulting in my capture, he rose and positioned himself between my spread thighs, dipping his head, his tongue beginning to explore my pussy, causing my back to arch.

Pouting, I tried to endure the way he thrummed my clit, causing it to throb and swell. He devoured that most private part of me with an aggression I would never cease to want, my hips rising to press my pelvis into his face.

"Want to taste yourself?" he asked huskily.

I want it all...

I nodded frantically and he answered my need by moving up over my body to kiss me fiercely, sharing my sweet taste as his tongue lavishly spread what was forbidden.

He pulled back, resting on his elbows above me so that his engorged cock was visible, looming close to my entrance.

"Do you want me to stop?" he whispered, his eyes blazing with desire.

"I thought you were going to gag me."

He leaned in and planted kisses along the crook of my neck,

sending tingles along my skin, distracting me with the gentle affection.

He followed the soaking wet line of my cleft, inserting the tip of his erection into my entrance and pushing in a little.

A pinch.

He watched my reaction.

My thighs were sticky from how wet he'd gotten me. I sucked in a lung-full of air as he shoved in a little more, stretching me wide, causing a shock of pain in my pussy.

I snapped my gaze over to the lens that captured every move, every whisper, every sigh—my sacred moment his to enjoy later.

I'd demand to watch it, too.

Remembering what he'd told me to do and feeling like it might help, I lifted my head a little and suckled on his shoulder, my teeth biting into his flesh.

"Harder," he coaxed.

Reluctantly, yet needing the relief, I dug my teeth into firm muscle.

My reward for this action was his hand sliding down between my thighs and his fingertip settling on my clit. He beat a perfect rhythm, causing my pussy to clamp down on the head of his cock.

He shoved all the way in—breaking through, breaking me in two...a glorious agony that made me let out a deep-throated groan. I squeezed my eyes shut to endure the pressure as he moved deeper inside me.

"God, you're tight." He gritted his teeth as though in pain, his expression taut and focused, perspiration spotting his brow. "I'm going to fuck you now."

I arched my back, trying to endure his first full hard thrust, gasping with the discomfort, a terrible ache forging its way into pleasure. It was too much, yet it wasn't enough, his filling me entirely with a threat of tearing. His finger flicked my clit, trying to edge me on as he pulled out a little and then eased back in, the sound of my slickness and stickiness no doubt caught on film.

My trembling certainly was, too, as were my moans as I squirmed beneath him. Unable to reach for his back, I strained against the cuffs, my wrists and ankles sore from the metal; but the sensation of restraint was pure ecstasy. I welcomed the sense of helplessness…being conquered by this man.

He rested his head on my chest. "I want to pound you but it's too soon."

"I want it."

He shook his head. "Not yet. How does it feel?"

My jaw slackened as he rolled his hips in a circle. "Oh, it feels good, my pussy feels so…"

He nestled his face into my hair and whispered, "Say how your cunt feels out loud."

This was him asking for the sake of the camera, I just knew it. Instead of hating him for it, I adored the idea of this being recorded to be savored at another hour. I didn't care if he showed it to anyone. The idea of others watching him fuck me caused my arousal to spike—proving my desires were similar to his. I shuddered as my imagination overflowed with all the possibilities of what else he might do.

That video I'd seen of the ménage-a-trois rushed back into my thoughts, and I realized how nearly impossible it would be for me to endure being taken by two men at the same time. One man was more than enough.

"Your cock is so deep," I cried out.

"And?"

"I'm so wet!"

"Good girl."

"It feels so good." I squirmed furiously beneath him, my breasts rubbing against his hard chest.

"Fight me, baby," he growled. "Resist me."

My hips lifted with each thrust, welcoming more of him.

His cock burrowed even deeper, causing me to arch and writhe and yell for more. I wanted to touch him.

"Play with my clit," I begged.

Damien withdrew his length and I cried out at the loss of fullness, struck by the cruelty of him denying me what I'd grown accustomed to…what I deserved.

He reached for the metal cuffs around my ankles and unhooked them. Damien sat up and then lifted my legs to pull me closer so that I was half laying on the bed and half on him, my thighs wrapped around his waist with my ankles together behind his back.

His throbbing cock found my entrance again, shoving all the way inside and giving me what I begged for.

His left hand eased apart my wet folds and his right finger vigorously flicked my clit, slowing down to move in a circular motion as my body welcomed his hard thrusts.

It felt like my soul was being obliterated, the intense, blinding pleasure becoming unbearable, stealing the breath from my body.

I finally caught air into my lungs and let out a scream, intoxicated by him and his masterful dominance. My thighs spread farther apart, my hips bouncing to demand a deeper fucking from him. Taking over, I pummeled him right back with my own frenzied thrusts, submerged in this wild place of insatiable need that drove me to pound myself against his cock as though only this would save me.

I stared at his face as my frenzied movements began to slow, glimpsing in his eyes the pure lust he was feeling for this new me. For what I could become.

My thighs trembled violently and I took in rasping breaths, rising from what felt like a dream, aware of Damien pulling out but too weak to demand he stay joined with me.

I watched as he sat back and ripped off the condom, my thighs still splayed wide, soaking wet pussy throbbing and sore.

His right hand tugged on his bulging cock, working himself with swift hard strokes, his expression contorted as though possessed by agony at the moment he shot a stream of cum over my pelvis in arches of white.

A mask of dominance on his face, his gaze roamed over me with pride—the gift of his orgasm shimmering over me. His semen had anointed my skin.

Am I yours now?

Intoxicated by him, reeling from the delirium, I reveled in the beauty of this silent moment...the first true song of my heart.

Bowing his head between my thighs, he planted a soft kiss upon my pussy.

CHAPTER
FIFTEEN

Damien

I drew a bath for her, letting the water flow over my hand as I allowed myself this respite from reality. The world and its constant demands could wait. That external forces ruled over internal needs was a lie I excelled at perpetuating.

I needed this. I needed…*her*.

Her taste lingered. Like the memory of peering down at her tight pussy clenching my cock. She'd given me her virginity. And I'd taught her the meaning of the clavis.

It felt like oxygen was finally moving through this house again, through me. I'd been starved for the type of action that had just happened between us. I could feel the strain in my shoulders finally releasing, making my muscles less tense. My balls were no longer tight with need.

From the wicker chair in the corner, Pandora sat waiting for the tub to fill, watching me as I added bath salts to the water. She was quiet—probably because of the profoundness of what this meant to her. This was more than aftercare. It was me making sure she had no regrets for giving me the gift of her innocence. Even if she was meant to be mine—a lie we'd lived with for too long.

It was my job to help her work through any doubts so that when she left she was in a good headspace. What I'd revealed about myself was a lot to take in.

Pandora had been methodically cultivated and refined, created for the sole purpose of being used as an asset. Highly educated abroad. Molded into social perfection. Released into the world on a pre-determined trajectory. Both of us were set to rise together to the highest office. Happiness had never been part of the equation; a happy marriage was a throw of the dice.

Ten minutes ago, I'd freed her from the dungeon where I'd taken her for the first time. Beneath my handling she'd blossomed brilliantly. If anything, she'd shown an instant addiction to rough sex. Never had I seen such a profound response to pleasure before. A dark craving that had lain dormant waiting to be unleashed.

Of course, tears could possibly follow such an experience, and I was ready for them.

"Climb in," I told her, helping her slip out of her bathrobe and guiding her into the large tub—all the while admiring her nakedness and the way she moved with grace as she sank into the water.

She relaxed low in the tub, with her head peeking out above the water and her hair pinned up high, which somehow made her look even younger. The frown lines around her eyes were now gone.

No doubt the endless orgasm she'd experienced with my cock buried deep inside her for the first time had left her body relaxed—her rapture captured on tape for posterity. My cock hardened with the memory of taking her for the first time, but she deserved to rest now.

I'd be fucking Pandora into oblivion again soon enough.

Disrobing, I climbed into the tub and settled down in the opposite end, the warmth soaking into my flesh and warming my bones. Breathing in the scent of sandalwood, I settled back with a sigh, admiring the beauty who could be mine permanently. A blonde pouty submissive, with a rousing interest in the lifestyle, proving she'd been hungry for more as she'd licked her lips while I'd jerked myself over her porcelain flesh to consecrate her.

"Moving forward," I said, "we should be open about our feelings. Think you're up for that?"

She looked at me coyly.

"Shall I begin?" I coaxed.

"Sure."

"What we do in this house has nothing to do with anyone but us." I cupped a handful of bubbles and crushed them in my palm. "Tell no one."

"I promise."

"Let's talk about what happened downstairs."

She looked relieved. "Does your family know you have that room?"

"I meant what happened between you and me. And no, that room is private."

"I've had fantasies."

"Go on…"

"Of doing those kinds of things."

"Any concerns?"

She looked surprised. "Never. It was everything I thought it would be and more."

"I imagine you're sore. Want some Tylenol?"

She took a deep breath and I glimpsed a hint of pink nipple above the bubbles.

"What's the worst thing you do to your submissive?"

Glancing away, I thought about how much I should reveal. "Tie you up. Hang you from the ceiling—" Fixing my glare back on her. "Engage my imagination."

"You use those devices?"

I stared at her. "I have a fetish that involves seeing you…"

"Scared?"

"Vulnerable."

"In peril?"

"Yes. And obedient to me."

"Will you take me to Vanguard?"

"Where did you hear that name?"

She dragged her teeth over her lips suggestively. "You have your demands. I have mine."

I rolled my eyes. "Madeline?"

She rested her head back and slid into a knowing smile, a few stray locks swirled like sea creatures around her shoulders. She looked ethereal, with her cheeks flushed and her eyes bright with yearning.

I'd been the one to awaken her.

Sliding my leg between her thighs, I pressed my big toe against her clit.

Her eyelids fluttered and her jaw went slack. Soft thighs widening as far as possible.

"You like that?"

She gave a nod.

"Talk," I coaxed her. "Tell me what you want."

That spark in her eyes revealed she had secret desires. "I want you to take me to Vanguard."

"What do you know?"

"You go there. You do things." She seemed lulled by the pressure of my toe against her sex. "I want to see."

"Madeline showed you some photos, I hear?"

"I liked them."

"One condition."

She opened her eyes as though ready to hear it.

"You go as my submissive."

"I want that."

"You must agree to do all I ask of you."

"What kinds of things?"

"I'm talking of ways to protect you."

"What if we're recognized?"

"We'll be wearing masks. The lights are dim at Vanguard. The events are different for each room."

"How do we choose which one to enter?"

"I choose."

She reached down and held my foot between her thighs which was her way to keep my toe playing with her pussy. "I've been kept in a glass cage. Never allowed to do what my friends did. No sleep overs. No getting drunk. I literally had to beg for a library card."

I chuckled. "Did you get one?"

"Eventually, but I'd trail in there with my father's security detail and it got old."

"What kind of books were you searching out?"

A blush rising on her cheeks.

"Maybe it's time to lock you back up in that glass cage, young lady," I said sternly. "I can see you becoming trouble."

Her thighs splayed even more. "I want you to show me everything."

"Where would you like me to start?"

She bit her lip suggestively. "Just take me over the edge."

The thought of taking her to Vanguard caused a torrent of euphoria to rush through me—the real me didn't need to be hidden from her anymore.

My toe rewarded Pandora's clit, indulging her need for my brand of debauchery.

Seemingly dazed, she was already gone, riding through a heady climax, her body shuddering and her breasts trembling, her pink nipples pert. Her soft sighs filled the room and then she screamed my name.

"Take me to Vanguard as yours," she begged a moment later, gasping. "Promise me you will."

"Not yet, but soon."

CHAPTER
SIXTEEN

Pandora

I'd never had the chance to look around Damien's home. With nothing on me but one of his white shirts, I went exploring— my mind dragging me back to last night. To that room below.

God, that room and all that went on within its walls. Those endless orgasms. Him taking me for the first time, making it as memorable as he'd promised. And that leisurely bath we'd shared during the wee hours.

Afterwards, feeling shaky and overwhelmed with so many emotions, I'd let him take my hand and lead me to his bedroom. He'd climbed into bed beside me and pulled me close. Spooning, we had slept together all night.

I'd woken up just after 7:00 A.M. to the sound of him showering, and decided to take a tour of the house.

A rush of excitement hit me when I walked into his impressive study. I'd stepped inside the reflection of a man, noting the simple modern desk surrounded by tall shelves of books covering a wide range of subjects. Reading some of the titles, I recalled that Damien had studied history at Yale.

He also had what looked like a full collection of Chuck Palahniuk novels on the far shelf, along with some Tom Clancy books, too. That was a nice surprise.

"See anything you like?" Damien was leaning against the doorjamb, his hands around a large mug.

He was already dressed in a white shirt and black slacks, looking so damn suave and fresh.

The memory of what he did to me caused me to shiver.

"I'm making myself at home."

"I can see that." He softened it with a smile.

"This is where it all happens for your dad's campaign?"

He shrugged. "Actually, I'm hardly ever here."

I gestured toward the books. "What is it they say?" I pivoted to look back at him. "If you don't learn from the past, you're destined to repeat it."

"We always fucking repeat it. Same story. Different decade."

"That sounds…"

"The truth sucks, as they also say." He winked.

I smiled. "You went to Yale, right? I guess it was great."

"Well, you needed a bike to get around."

"I wanted to go to Brown University."

"You'd have fit in."

"What? No condescending retort, Damien?"

"That was one. You're privileged. Lots of your spoiled friends would have joined you there." His smile faded. "I'm sorry you didn't get to go."

"Were you raised by a strict governess? Because most of my friends were."

"Point taken."

"All my nightmares are set in my childhood home in Texas." I'd never told anyone that before.

He hesitated and then gave me a look of sympathy. "We'll make up for it."

"How?"

He came over and placed his arm around me, pulling me into a hug. His lips pressed down on my head with affection, his body firm and warm against mine. I breathed in his soft cologne, feeling protected.

My escape plan was getting derailed by this man because he was becoming easier to be around. And I was craving more moments like this.

Figuring out how to extract myself from this arrangement had always been a mystery. I'd never factored in the possibility that I might want to stay.

It made me wonder if he sensed my scheming.

"Come on." He turned to go. "Let's have breakfast."

We ate waffles and fruit at his round kitchen table while he read three newspapers at the same time, searching out stories printed on his dad.

I sat opposite him, sipping orange juice and reading news articles on his iPad.

He looked up knowingly. "It's quicker for me this way."

"You discuss what you've read later with your dad?"

"That's right."

"Can I help?"

"Sure." He slid a newspaper toward me. "Let me know the tone of what you read."

"Want to go see a play this week?" I asked.

He dragged his eyes off an article. "Um...yes, when all of this is over."

"Are you going to keep me hidden?" I pressed my lips together in embarrassment for asking the question.

"That was the plan." He took a sip of coffee.

This was like being punished for something I'd not done.

Changing the subject, I said. "It's like turning a tanker during a storm."

Damien raised his head and gave me his full attention. "You mean the campaign?"

"Yes, you read these—" I rested a finger on an article. "You adjust your reaction by a fraction. Too much and you're admitting truth in the situation. Not enough of a response—"

"Could leave fractures that become fissures later."

"This article," I said. "In *The Atlantic*. The Senator is being accused of being out of touch. We're too close to the election for articles like this to be ignored. The Senator needs to press home he cares about the small things."

He gave a smile. "Valid observation."

"I didn't mean to offend you."

"Well, coming from you it's...insightful."

"How do you mean?"

"When was the last time you went shopping for anything other than designer bags?"

"That's unfair."

"Go on, then, tell me the price of a gallon of milk."

"I've been advised it's a security risk."

His brows narrowed. "To be amongst people?"

"When was the last time you went food shopping?"

"Yesterday." He conceded with a nod. "I might have shaken a few hands while in Trader Joe's."

"Made it a thing," I jested.

"I wore jeans and a baseball cap. Still…"

I'd undone the last few minutes of conversation—reminding Damien I was more out of touch than anyone.

"It's not your fault, Pandora," he said kindly. "You're enlightened now. Once you wake up from the illusion of privilege you can choose to make a difference."

"I've always wanted to make a difference."

"I believe Salvatore Galante is bluffing."

"About my father?" I hesitated, remembering the rule.

"Let's continue to be seen in public." He went back to reading a paper. "It's perfectly reasonable for now."

Reaching for my juice, I brought it to my lips, my heart soaring. Despite facing the impossible we were still an item, which meant there was a chance for my dad. Pushing that thought aside, studying the way Damien's intelligent eyes scanned over the papers, I couldn't help but be mesmerized by his staggering beauty.

A ping went off on his phone and he dragged it toward him, his expression becoming pained. "I have to go."

"Where?"

"Downtown." He pushed to his feet. "Let's get you home. Don't discuss what happened here last night, okay?"

"You mean with my parents?" I smirked. "I thought that's what our sex tape was for."

"Fuck off." He grinned as he grabbed his jacket off the back of a chair.

"You fuck off," I said just as playfully.

He rounded the table and dipped his head to kiss me, his hand cupping my cheek, his mouth firm against mine. "Take your time getting dressed. Make yourself at home."

"You don't mind?"

"I like having you here." He grabbed his wallet, phone and car keys and headed for the door, stopping for a beat before reaching the hall. "Pandora."

"Yes?"

"I'll have a car pick you up in a couple of hours from your parents' place. Be ready. I'll meet you at my dad's."

"Is that wise?"

"You need to acclimate to the intensity of what we're up against." He looked down his nose at me. "A change of scenery from spending your days in the lap of luxury."

"My gilded cage. Lucky me." I pushed to my feet. "I want to go to Vanguard."

"No."

"Why not?"

He looked thoughtful. "If you perform to a satisfactory level this evening, I will consider taking you with me to Vanguard. Now sit and finish your breakfast."

I sat back down immediately, tingling with expectancy as his dominance vibrated through me, my nipples beading at the way he'd barked that order. Why did his voice have such a primal effect on me?

Damien watched my reaction. "When you get home, pack a suitcase full of clothes. Something for every occasion."

"Am I staying here again?"

"We need you ready for anything." He pivoted and headed out.

CHAPTER
SEVENTEEN

Damien

A riot of morning sunlight surrounded me where there would one day be walls. Right now the structure was merely a husk and I felt a gut-wrenching panic that work had stopped abruptly on the Fairfield project.

How quickly life goes tits-up.

I'd been on a high since I'd awoken this morning, knowing Pandora was in my bed. Watching her sleep had been sublime.

We'd taken an important step forward with an authentic evening getting to know each other on an entirely new level—an evening spent in a dungeon that clung to my psyche as only a taste of perfection can. Truly, those were the best hours we'd spent together.

Here, now, was as low as it could get—some fucker had shut down construction.

A voice boomed from across the vastness. "Thank you for coming."

Blinking through the dust, I turned to see the construction supervisor Al Shaffer, who approached me wearing a hard hat.

He gave a friendly wave. "Mr. Godman, a minute."

Walking carefully along what would one day be a foyer, I joined him out on the street.

"Guess you heard we received a notice to close down all construction this morning," he said.

I nodded. "Just glad no one's been injured."

"Nothing like that."

"Who told you to shut down?"

"It came from your father's office."

Had I misheard him?

Hiding my reaction, I gave his hand a shake with the reassurance we'd be back on track by this afternoon. Getting this affordable housing off the ground—along with the adjacent after-school program—would be one of my proudest accomplishments. This place would inspire the youth who lived here. My ego told me we'd be making the sports champions of the future, giving kids the chance for a better life. Or at least produce a lifetime of friendships out of this forward-thinking setting.

Back in the car, I shot off an urgent text to Theo to schedule time with my dad. It was imperative I delivered the news before the press got word.

I drove to my father's place in a blur.

Making it into the offices in record time, I braced for his reaction when he heard someone was interfering with my project. No doubt I'd have to face a barrage of questions that I wouldn't have the answer to. Who the hell had shut it down?

Theo cut me off in the hallway. "Damien, he has a meeting. Can't be interrupted. Walk with me."

I followed him away from my father's office, more out of politeness than anything. Theo worked around the clock to ensure Dad's schedule went smoothly. Making his job easier was a courtesy.

I respected Tamer. Usually his judgment was as solid as it got.

He was also a member of Vanguard and we'd experienced some stellar times together at the society. Late nights spent at that place had seen us bonded like brothers. The secrets we kept were enough to destroy empires.

But apparently even Theo couldn't rush me in to see Senator Godman on a day like this—even though he was my fucking dad, for God's sake.

When we made it to a private office space, he asked, "Any updates?"

"That's what I'm here for."

He cringed. "Consider how you're going to broach the subject."

"Why?"

"The Senator is conflicted with the situation."

"What does that mean?" With rising annoyance, I took in the round table and chairs in the room, remembering all the crisis meetings that had taken place here. I'd attended many of them as our team had strategized, putting out fires and lighting some, too.

It was me being *handled* in here now.

"We need to control the optics," he said.

I stared at him, finally realizing the truth. "Did my dad shut us down?"

"Damien, let's talk this through."

"Years." I clenched my fists. "I've been working on this for *years.*"

"I get it," he said, lowering his voice. "Providing houses for lower income families was important to you."

"You do realize you're using the past tense, right, Theo?"

"There are many charitable projects that are important to your dad. You can get on board with those."

"This was mine! The project had the public's approval. *This* is what I brought to the table." I rubbed my hand over my face, barely suppressing my fury. "Why shut it down?"

"Maybe this is a wise choice? We throw money at it...make it go away."

"Why? What happened?"

"There was some other interest in the land."

I took a deep breath. "I'm still in this fight."

"I'll do everything I can to turn his decision around."

"He listens to you. Get me in that room."

Theo shook his head. "Your father has meetings all morning."

"Why do I feel like he's avoiding me?" I headed for the door. "I'm going to see him."

"Not yet."

I was suddenly curious as to why Theo didn't want me to see my dad. It was more than annoying—it was suspicious.

"Who's in there with him?" I studied his reaction.

"Twelve years we've been friends. I've dedicated myself to your family," he said softly.

"What are you insinuating? Your hands are tied? That whoever intercepted my project is unscrupulous."

"You're the only man I trust in this town, Damien."

What the hell was his point here?

"We're as close as two men can get," he added.

"Why, because you've seen my dick?"

"And a very nice dick it is."

I ignored his retort. "You know how important this is to me."

"I will always be in your corner. You know that." Theo always had a way of calming me. "I'll put this on your dad's desk as a top priority. See what I can do to get this decision reversed."

"How could someone persuade him to do this to me?"

"No comment."

"I get it," I said, raking my fingers through my hair. "You can't serve two masters."

"Right."

"Do you have a cigarette?"

"You gave up smoking, didn't you?"

"No comment."

"I gave it up because you gave it up." He slapped his arm, where I assumed a nicotine patch was stuck to his bicep. "That's why I'm wearing this shit. This was your fucking idea."

"The patch made me antsy." I shuddered to make my point. "Do you have a cig in your office for emergency purposes?"

"You're going to have to learn to not smoke during tough times, too."

"Thank you, Captain Obvious."

"You don't want to set off the fire alarms."

"Fuck it."

I stormed off to find someone who was more agreeable,

stopping in my tracks when I saw people walking out of my father's office. Amongst them, strolling confidently in four inch high heels and a pencil skirt was Helen King. I didn't need to see her face to recognize the fifty-something brunette who'd made my life hell.

Three weeks ago, her lawyers had called mine and made me an offer for the land where my affordable housing was going to be built.

Interesting timing.

Peering through the open doorway into my father's office, I saw him sitting behind his desk surrounded by staff, no doubt discussing the meeting he had just had with her.

"Godman, no!" Theo warned.

Heading on in, I said, "Dad, got a minute?"

He looked hassled. "Not a good time."

I forced a polite smile. "Everyone out, please." All it took was a wave of my hand and the men left the room.

The last man closed the door on his way out.

"Why do I feel like you're avoiding me?" I didn't care to sit.

"You know what it's like being out on the trail. I'm here for a few days to regroup before heading out again."

"Did you hear what happened?"

"Fairfield?" He leaned back in his chair and clasped his hands behind his head. "I know it meant a lot to you."

Shouldn't he be more pissed off? More reactive instead of sitting back and looking like I was wasting his time?

"Did you shut it down?" I stepped forward and leaned on his desk, knuckles white as my fingers curled.

"After this election we'll explore the possibility of proceeding with your efforts again."

"I'm not stepping away. Not after all this work."

He pushed to his feet and rounded the desk. "We've worked too hard for too long to let a small detail like this trip us up."

"People are depending on that housing."

"You can't fight every battle. We have to choose carefully—"

"What is more important than this? We're talking about kids, here."

"You need to take a couple of days off."

I threw my hands up in frustration. "The work on the foundations has begun."

"This is hard on you. I get that."

I fought the old urge to let Dad convince me defeat was the only way.

"Sorry, son. Look, I have another meeting. You know how grueling my schedule is."

I headed to the door, turning back to look at him before opening it. "Was it Helen King who shut me down? I just saw her leaving your office."

"She's one of our biggest donors."

"No! Dad…"

He wouldn't do this to me. Not to his son. I'd dedicated my life to his ambitions.

A knock at the door distracted him. "Come in," he shouted.

Theo peered in. "Sir, your 11:00 A.M. is here."

Dad looked vaguely apologetic. "We're out of time, son. Let's pick this up next week."

My back stiffened. "Next week will be too late."

I was being unceremoniously ushered out. With my pride decimated I gave a respectful nod and walked through the door Theo was holding open.

Once the door had closed behind us, I glared at my friend. "How can this not be a priority for him? How could he not fight for me?"

"He's got a lot to deal with, Damien." He clutched my shoulder. "I'm assuming he told you to take a few days off. I think that's a good idea."

"What will I say to the construction crew? What will it make me look like?"

"Cathy's on this," he said. "Your dad's executive director has everything covered."

"No. This is my mess. I'll clean it up. I'll reach out to everyone."

Theo gave a shrug. "Your dad needs you at one hundred percent. No distractions."

This wasn't about money. It was about political leverage. My father had sold me out for influence. If Helen King was involved, a deal had been brokered in private. She was a brilliant strategist, but her price was always way too high.

Adrenaline surged through my blood. This betrayal would never go away.

Theo was watching me carefully. "Need a minute?"

I straightened, making a mental vow to put this right. "Stall for me. That place is getting built or there'll be blood spilt."

Theo went to speak but thought better of it. Instead, he motioned for us to head toward a quiet corner. "How are things with Pandora?"

"If you're going to change the subject at least be less obvious."

He smirked.

I zeroed in on what he was insinuating. "Things are fine. Why?"

"Did you talk to her about the key pendant?"

That's right. Theo had seemingly tried to protect my innocent fiancée back at the St. Regis last night.

I gave a casual shrug. "The pendant was a gift. She had no idea."

"Damien, I know what I saw."

"What was that?"

"A Vanguard clavis."

"Now's not the time."

He moved closer. "She knows you're a member."

"When did you talk with her?"

"Half an hour ago. You invited her here. You had a car bring her over from her parents' place."

"Where is she?" I asked.

"The kitchen. She wanted to know more about Vanguard."

"What did you tell her?"

"To discuss it with you."

"What's she doing in the kitchen?"

"She knows the chef. This isn't her first time here."

Cringing, I recalled all those times we'd sat together here during our family functions over the last few months, while I mostly ignored her. Having treated her that way felt abhorrent to me now.

My annoyance softened. "If and when I decide she's ready for Vanguard, you'll be the first to hear about it."

"Not all the fun's at Vanguard."

"True."

And I had been thinking of exploring more of her erotic side. I'd told her that this morning.

"Tell me what you need," he said, seeming to read my mind.

No wonder he had women lining up to be his subs. A slew of wannabees never to be sated by the bad boy of Vanguard. He was just too selective.

I walked backwards offering him a grin of mischief to rile him up.

"Seriously?" he asked, grinning back at me, his interest piqued.

Damn it, I was stressed out and Pandora was desperate to begin her erotic awakening. If not now, when? My life had derailed. I needed to play dirty like I needed oxygen.

"Think you can deliver?"

He gave me a quick nod of conviction. "The Ritz-Carlton. 7:00 P.M. Black-tie. Private suite."

My brows arched in interest. "Text me the room number."

With that confirmed, I walked away.

And reality returned to punch me in the gut.

Helen King was offering my father more than money for his campaign. She was probably promising him access to influence, too. That wily bitch wanted to build a shopping mall or high-end apartments on the site that was mine. She had set her sights on a billion-dollar profit.

God, this town was ruthless.

Turning this around seemed impossible—but I had to do it.

It was an interesting state to be in—I was filled with wrath for Helen King and lust for tonight's willing victim.

I headed off to find the lovely Pandora.

CHAPTER
EIGHTEEN

Pandora

P lacing the thinly sliced Swiss chocolate rolls around the edge of the mousse, I showed the Godman's chef, Thomas Davenport, how this dessert was finished off—a mouthwatering chocolate torte I'd learned to create back when I'd attended those intense cooking classes at school for ladies who intended to entertain.

The Godmans' master chef had sat on a barstool at the kitchen counter watching me with his chin resting on his hands. He could see I was whipping up something super special for him.

Thomas' dreadlocks were the mark of his proud heritage, the gray at his temples adding wisdom to his joyful eyes. This wasn't the first time I'd snuck down here during a visit to see him. I was always guaranteed to be welcomed with kindness—and enjoy a good laugh because he was as funny as hell.

Having once worked at the White House for the President, Thomas had a bunch of riveting stories to share. He'd grown up in New Orleans and taught himself to cook before talking his way into a job at The Ponchartrain Hotel, an historic gem in the Garden District.

Being with him was a welcome break from all of the stuffiness upstairs—an escape from the staffers coming and going and the tension that went along with the daily running of a senator's office.

Damien strolled in with a serious expression on his handsome face.

An hour ago, Theo had told me Damien was on his way in from downtown and was hoping to get a meeting with his dad. I wondered how it had gone.

Memories flooded in again of what we'd done together in his dungeon last night, and I had to tear my gaze away from his.

"Hey." I pointed proudly. "Look what I made."

Thomas straightened up from the countertop. "Ms. Bardot's teaching me some mean tricks with Swiss chocolate, Mr. Godman."

"You can call him Damien," I said.

"Sure can," Damien said as he reached for the dessert knife. "You do realize that Mr. Davenport is a Michelin chef?"

"Of course I know."

Damien threw him an apologetic smile. "I'm sure Thomas can top this any day."

"Pandora's a great cook," Thomas said warmly.

"Allow me, sir," said Damien as he cut off two slices, sliding the plate over to him. "Good luck."

"Hey." I punched Damien's arm playfully.

As Thomas tasted the creamy mousse his face lit up. "I better watch out for my job."

Damien tasted the confection. "You're hired, Ms. Bardot. Let's start you off with washing dishes."

"No way," Thomas defended me. "She's my new pastry chef."

I gave him a bright smile, excited that such a renowned chef had enjoyed my dessert.

Damien offered his thanks to Thomas for being my company. With a nod of his head, he indicated I was to follow him out.

"Bring a slice," he demanded. "I'll finish mine later."

Thomas hurried to throw a big slice of the dessert into a glass dish. I gave him a hug before leaving.

Carrying the chocolate mousse, I tried to keep up with Damien's long strides. "I'm not allowed to bake at home."

"Don't take this the wrong way, but Thomas doesn't have the time to entertain you."

My feet stuck on the tile as I watched him walk off. He'd gone from cordial this morning back to moody.

"Hurry up." He held the door open for me.

I scurried through. "I was showing him a new recipe."

"Right, a Michelin chef. I'm sure he appreciated that." He cast a disapproving glance my way.

We exited the building and he gave a courtesy wave to the two security officers as we passed by them. Damien quickly reached the passenger door of the SUV and ushered me in.

We both settled into the back seat of the car—the same one that had brought me here. My suitcase had been stashed in the back. With Damien's change of mood, I wondered if he regretted inviting me over to stay tonight.

"How was your meeting with your dad?" I asked.

"Seatbelt on," he snapped.

Pulling mine on, I asked, "What about yours?"

He was too busy texting. "Do as I say, and all that."

"Damien, what's wrong?"

He glanced at the chauffeur. "Not now."

Turning to face him, I felt a rant building inside me. "This is how it always goes. Don't do that. Do this. Be like this—"

"Bad time for a tantrum."

"I'm expressing how I feel."

"Feelings are irrelevant in our business. Or didn't they teach you that at your finishing school?"

"If you're asking if I studied politics, yes, I did," I replied. "I'm fluent in several languages—including computer programming. I can play the piano well enough to get by at a dinner party—"

"I saw your resume," he said dryly. "Very impressive. Want a standing ovation?"

I poked a finger into his ribs. "I could have gotten into Yale."

"Your point?"

"If there's a problem, maybe I can help."

"If I need someone to hack into a computer, I'll call you."

"You know I can actually do that, right?"

He shot a warning glare at the driver. "She's joking."

I reached over and gave his arm a squeeze. "Tell me about it when we get home."

"Very well." He didn't sound convincing.

I touched my pendant, making sure he saw my revenge play.

He pretended to ignore me and focused on his iPhone instead, tapping away on the screen, no doubt sending off emails and reading texts that made him cringe now and again.

Something had him extremely upset, going by his deepening frown lines and the occasional expression of defeat I saw on his face. Seeing him like this was difficult.

We drove the rest of the way in silence.

Once out of the car, Damien pulled me closer. "There's a lot going on."

"I'm here if you want to talk." I watched him walk over and lift my suitcase out of the back of the SUV.

He rolled my suitcase up the driveway as I followed, which seemed to make the driver uncomfortable. Damien turned back to face him. "Take the rest of the day off."

The chauffeur brightened and gave him a grateful nod.

Damien might be a class-A asshole, but at least he was a gentleman to the staff.

We headed into Foxhall.

Being back here so soon after this morning felt like a small victory. We entered the kitchen, where we'd had breakfast this morning and made an intimate memory of our first morning together.

"I was going to take you out to lunch," he said, his tone apologetic. "But I've lost my appetite."

"What happened?"

He shook his head, refusing to go there, rubbing his tired eyes.

Setting the glass dish on the countertop, I opened his fridge. "I'll make us something to drink." I poured sparkling water into two glasses, adding ice cubes and a slice of lemon in each.

Damien moved around the kitchen looking for something. He caught me watching him. "Secret stash."

I shook my head. "Those things are bad for you."

He yanked open a kitchen drawer. "I do this thing where I hide a cigarette hoping to forget about it. Then I forget I found it."

Lifting my skirt, I flashed him a look at my panties. "This is me saving your life."

"Jesus." He raced over to the wall console and punched a button to close the blinds. "The windows."

"We have nothing to hide."

He stepped closer. "If only that were true."

After slipping out of my panties and dropping them on the floor, I lifted myself up onto the central island and sat on the edge, leaning back and spreading my thighs. I took a deep breath in anticipation, turned on at the thought of being so exposed. "Let me make you feel better."

He didn't move. "Actually, I wanted to talk with you about this evening."

"Oh?"

"No fucking around until tonight." He started to say something else and then paused, staring at me. "Maybe we can."

Biting my lip suggestively, I leaned over and took the lid off the glass dish.

In a flash, he was standing in front of me. "Let's taste that dessert of yours."

"You've never tasted anything like this," I said, as he pushed my skirt up around my waist.

"Hmm, I might have." He smirked as he dipped his finger in and scooped up some of the chocolate mousse, smearing it over my sex.

Oh, yes.

His finger caressed the delightful softness between my folds, causing a rush of sensations to spread through my body.

Damien leaned down and ran his tongue along my clit. "Best dessert I've ever tasted."

"Train me to be your submissive."

He straightened, his dark eyes studying me. "First, you must agree to no more outbursts like you had in the car."

"No speaking my mind?"

"Yes, no more of that."

"I'm not sure that's something I can do."

"Allow me to demonstrate how you'll be rewarded for your obedience." His head dipped once again, his mouth lavishing affection on my sex like a starved man, his tongue darting and exploring, no doubt tasting the creamy richness of the chocolate.

My breath caught at the searing passion coming off of him.

My head fell back and I stared up at the ceiling without really seeing it. I was lost in oblivion as he kissed my thighs, teasing me with the pleasure he was denying me before returning to that sensitive place where he bestowed endless pleasure.

I reached over to dip my finger into the dessert to give him more.

He gripped my wrist to stop me. "You're all I want," he whispered, his words resonating like a poem...

Easing my folds back, I offered myself willingly and he ravished me there, his tongue swirling and conquering and owning that part of me.

My thighs trembled, my body shaking and my back arching, as I came in waves, my hips rocking as my climax possessed me.

He possessed me.

Damien planted kisses up my thighs and then rested his cheek against my stomach, taking a moment for himself, as though he wasn't ready to part from me. I selfishly craved more times like this, never wanting this closeness to cease, not now, not ever.

His lips pressed to my public bone. "I needed that more than I realized."

Trailing my fingers through his hair, I whispered. "I want to take your mind off it a little longer."

"Off what?"

"What's upset you."

He shook his head.

I nudged him back so I could slide off the central island. "Let me do this for you."

I sank to my knees, reaching for his pants and undoing his zipper, peering up at him with a seductive little smile. I gently eased his cock out, feeling it begin to harden in my grip as my hand slid from base to tip.

I dipped my head and took my first taste of him, my tongue exploring the rounded head, licking and lapping. Damien's left hand reached out to grip the countertop.

I took a deep breath and then drew his girth all the way to the back of my throat, lips stretching wide to accommodate his size.

"Suckle my balls," he demanded.

Using my right hand to stroke him, I dipped my head lower to draw his right sac between my lips, feeling the firmness surrounded by softness, then worshiping the left one as I suckled harder.

"Pandora, let me know where you want my cum…"

I leaned my head back to look up at him. "I want to swallow."

He gave a nod as I took his length into my mouth again. Rocking his hips, he reached for either side of my head, fisting locks of my hair to thrust deeper into my throat. Breathing in through my nose, I followed his pace, excited for his taste, thrilled to be the one to send him over the edge.

His deep-throated groans revealed the nearing of his climax.

"That's it," he said huskily. "Don't stop."

My moan vibrated against his steely silkiness.

"I'm coming," he grunted.

His heat shot into my mouth, and I tasted the salty warmth of his cum, thick and creamy and seemingly endless as I swallowed and swallowed and tried to keep air in my lungs—my fist stroking him from base to tip as he went ridged.

I'd stolen his breath, too.

Looking up at him, his height intimidating, I read the torturous bliss in his face as he climaxed, panting heavily. I lapped his shaft to thank him for letting me have him like this—it was everything I imagined it would be.

It was a gift I'd need again soon, seeing him come undone before me. For the first time, the power had been mine.

He eased out of my grip and tucked himself away.

I blinked up at him. "Did I do it right?"

He stepped forward and brought my face to rest against his belly, his taste still on my tongue.

I settled against him, still on my knees, feeling calm and sated, giving him time to recover. I closed my eyes, savoring this rare moment of quiet affection between us.

CHAPTER
NINETEEN

Pandora

L ater that evening, I readied for the uncertainty of what
Damien had planned for us.

I'd wanted to dabble in an erotic playground, but it felt
altogether different in reality. The unknown closing in made me
apprehensive—even if my body yearned to explore. Even if I felt
like I was breaking out of the confines of my life and doing something unique. My body ached for what was to come.

Fingering my silver pendant, I understood its symbolism
now. It felt like a key had been turned and my desire had been
unlocked at last.

Wanting to look uber sexy for my new adventure, I chose my
Saks Fifth Avenue short black halter-neck dress that I'd packed
earlier today.

Damien was in a black tuxedo, his mood lifting as I got ready
around him, passing him now and again and reaching out to
touch his hand or lean in for a hug. He responded with affection
and seemed to draw comfort from my small gestures.

I styled my hair so that loose waves tumbled over my shoulders with sensual elegance. Then I applied some light foundation,
dabbing on mascara and eye shadow and choosing my bright red
lipstick to fit my vixen mood.

"No underwear," he called over to me.

"At all?"

"For tonight, you should respond with 'Yes, sir.'"

"Before we begin role playing?"

He shrugged.

"Why won't you tell me what's wrong?"

He raked his fingers through his hair. "It's complicated."

"Maybe I can offer a different perspective."

"You may bring your phone, but it must be turned off the entire time." Damien strolled over to the window and looked out. "Our car's here."

With masterful strides, he moved across the room and pulled a shoebox off the dresser. Kneeling before me, he eased my feet into the exquisite heels he had bought for me. They were higher than any I had ever worn before, the black straps weaving around my ankle with precision.

"They're beautiful."

He gave a ghost of a smile. "Thought I'd introduce you into the scene gradually."

"I'm excited." I reached down and cupped his cheek.

His eyes closed for a beat before he pushed himself up. "Come."

Grabbing my clutch purse, I followed him downstairs.

We entered a chic-looking dining room that contained a long table surrounded by eight high-backed chairs. A crystal chandelier hanging above the center cast a prism around us, reflected in the impressively large mirror on the far wall.

It made me wonder if he liked to entertain in here.

Moving closer, I watched him place a series of playing cards on the dining room table, facedown.

"Sir," I said, leaning forward to get a closer look. "What's this?"

He rested a fingertip on one. "This will enable us to express a desire without having to speak one word."

A shudder of anticipation ran through me.

He tapped one of them. "You choose one. I choose one."

"Turn them over."

"They're explicit."

Oh, my God, these were sex cards—the implication obvious.

"Do we choose one randomly?" I asked meekly.

He shook his head. "Choose the one you want to happen to you tonight."

I took a deep breath, feeling a bit lightheaded. "I can do that."

"For this to continue, you must abide by the rules. Ready?"

I nodded.

"Face forward over the table."

"Why?"

His hand crashed against my ass leaving a mark, no doubt. Quickly, I leaned over the table, an electrifying zing buzzing through my body as his fingers hoisted my dress over my hips to expose me. The breeze on my butt caused me to shiver.

"Thank you, sir."

"Better."

To my left, he unraveled a velvet cloth, revealing a collection of five bejeweled butt plugs, all in various sizes. He reached for the lube beside them and squirted some onto his fingertip.

"You're putting one of those in me?"

"Keep this in all evening." His sticky finger worked the lube around my hole, dipping in a little. "Smallest first."

His hands eased my cheeks open and I felt the taut pressure at my entrance. My face flushed wildly as the small anal plug went all the way in. An erotic moan escaped my throat as my pussy spasmed in response to this dreamy sensation. No one had ever seen that part of me before.

"How does it feel?"

"I feel turned on," I admitted.

He gave my ass another slap. "Up."

I straightened, trying to ignore that gentle, arousing force inside me causing a shiver up my spine—and trying to hide my embarrassment.

He returned to the cards and flipped one over. It was a drawing of a woman on her knees giving oral sex. Damien and I swapped a knowing look. We'd done this one a few hours ago in his kitchen. I suppose that meant it didn't count.

With a twist of his wrist, he flipped over another card and

then another, one after the other until all of them were laying face-up. How many submissives had played this game with him? I didn't care. The danger of the unknown and the lust-filled promise of endless pleasures with him were too alluring. I peered down at all the sexual acts on display, my heart racing.

I peered up at Damien. "I choose now?"

"Give me any of these cards and your fantasy will be granted."

So many choices. So many devilish positions and variations to experience. "Any of them?"

He leaned in and trailed gentle kisses up my neck and along my jaw, his cologne a teasing reminder of the night ahead that would mean our fantasies being fulfilled.

"Do you want me to choose first?" His finger hovered over one card and then another and then landed on the one in the center.

"Oh, you went with that one." My pussy clenched tight and a pang came from the plug in my ass.

"I take it you approve?" he said, his voice husky.

That card—what he wanted of me—would have me bending over a high table and showing myself to two men while they touched me at the same time…fingering me *there*. But who would be the other man?

"Do you trust me?" He sensed my question about who might be joining us.

I suddenly wanted to raise the bar to see if I could shock him. I pressed my finger to another card and then picked it up, handing it to him. "This one, please."

Damien's brows rose and he gave me a nod of approval.

He gestured toward the front door. "Shall we begin?"

CHAPTER
TWENTY

Damien

There was only one man I trusted to pull off this fantasy for Pandora alongside me. Theo was a guy with integrity, a gentleman who cared for his submissives and wanted his lovers to thrive—not just in an erotic setting, but in life, too.

He was a man capable of not only ensuring the five-star hotel suite was pleasing, prepared with all the luxuries, but also free of recording devices.

The Ritz offered up one of the best private suites available—it was spacious and had a decadent spirit, regally designed in the Louis XVI neoclassical style with gold trim and a generous display of blue wallpaper. The lighting was minimal to enhance the forbidden mood.

Should Pandora explore further, she'd find two full bathrooms with generous tubs that we might try later. A generously stocked bar in the living room invited guests to partake in the leisurely atmosphere of decadence.

There would be no sleeping here.

The play was real—the emotions always true to form.

So far, I saw no regret in Pandora. She was taking in the luxury suite with a look of approval. Complimentary champagne and chocolate-covered strawberries had been placed on the central table and would appeal to her taste. A vase of fresh roses set the romantic scene—a feminine touch to represent her as the center of attention.

"If at any time you want it to cease," I told her, "express that."

She gave a nod, but instead of trepidation, the expression on her face was one of exhilaration. "The other person?"

"He'll be here soon." I cupped her elbow and guided her toward the bar.

She didn't need to know that Theo had come earlier to prepare the room so that she didn't see him. He would wait in the foyer until 9:00 P.M. and would soon take the elevator up to join us.

"Drink?" Rounding the bar, I set about pouring two shots of tequila—a warm-up to the rule breaking she was about to explore.

After sliding the drink her way, I returned to her side again. We clinked our glasses and threw our shots back. She gaped at the burn of liquor down her throat.

"Tell me what your expectation is?"

"I'll lean over the bar." She waited for my nod of approval. "You and another man will…touch me?"

"You're forbidden to move."

"You'll be gentle?"

"Show me where you expect to be touched."

She pressed her palm to her sex.

"We'll both play with your pussy. Understand?"

Her irises dilated and she licked her lips, proving she was ready, needy even—her arousal crystal clear.

"Should that go well, we'll move on to what you requested from the card you chose."

"You'll make sure…"

"You're soaking wet down there? Trust me, you will be. I will guide your every step. If at any time you're unsure you must communicate that to me. If it's too much…"

"What if it's not enough?"

"Your eagerness is to be applauded." I reached into my pocket. "Tonight, you'll wear this. At no time take it off."

"A blindfold?"

"If you do well here at the bar, we'll advance."

This was the start of something wonderful for her. A woman caged all her life and finally able to break free and follow her own needs and desires. Watching her flourish under my control felt divine.

Her face looked flushed from the tequila.

It was enough to help her relax and give her the courage to see her reverie come to life. She looked beautiful tonight, but she always did. Her short black dress hugged her curves and the new heels gave her more height. Her blonde locks cascaded down her shoulders. Soon, when I pulled her dress down, her nipples would peak between those golden strands to tease.

The twinkling of her necklace represented the possibilities of what lay ahead, moment by moment, playing out like a prism of erotic colors. She was giving herself over to be controlled.

"Turn around," I ordered.

I wrapped the blindfold around her eyes and fastened it behind her head with the black silk. "*I* own you. Remember that."

"Yes, sir." She shivered against me as I pressed up against her.

"I'll position you." I took her hand and guided her over to the bar.

She leaned over it, her head resting on the wood paneling, her hair cascading around her like golden waves.

"Grip the other side." I eased her hands forward to show her where to place them and watched her delicate fingers curl over the wood.

After getting her comfortable, I lifted up her hem and hoisted it over her hips. Seeing her pussy glistening beneath the soft lighting made me want to savor this offering alone. My hand caressed her rounded cheeks, exploring her delicate porcelain skin.

A familiar frisson went through me—the thrill of anticipation for what was to unfold.

Someone knocked on the suite's door.

"He's arrived." My voice sounded gruff from my arousal.

She nodded eagerly, letting me know she was ready.

"He will see your cunt the moment he walks in. How does that make you feel?"

"Oh," she said softly, her voice dripping with lust, "I want this so much."

CHAPTER
TWENTY-ONE

Pandora

*C*alm *your breathing.*

Damien's last words before the room went silent—the only sound was his footfalls walking away.

Until I heard the door to the suite open.

I could see nothing, but wearing the blindfold brought me a sense of protection. Damien had to have known it would. This pose had been the gentlest of all the cards he'd shown me. He was easing me into the scene, maybe even building my trust.

Damien could be harsh, though when we dived into play he was totally engaged with me and charming. As though this was where he flourished within each sensual moment…promising so much more that the ordinary.

My body was sparking with energy, each cell craving attention. I was bent over, exposed, with them standing behind me. My flesh felt heated from the anticipation.

Please…

I'm so ready.

I tried to imagine what the stranger might look like, if he was as gorgeous as my lover. If his touch would be gentle or firm.

My fingers clenched the end of the bar—following orders was a blissful way of surrendering…giving over all my power and relinquishing all guilt.

Good girls didn't do this kind of thing. That had been my mantra all my life and it had imprisoned me. Now, in these unfolding seconds, I felt the bars opening on my confinement. My face burned when I felt a trickle of wetness from my arousal slide down my inner thigh. That sight would serve as an invitation to them, surely.

Oh, God, the stranger would see that jeweled plug in my ass. I felt a flash of humiliation that my butt was on display.

But right now I was merely a plaything.

"You will obey," commanded Damien. "I'm pleased to give you what you asked for."

I'd begged for it. This felt raw and real and the vibrancy caused my body to shimmer with desire. Listening, I heard what sounded like the removal of jackets and them being thrown on a couch or a chair—perhaps the rolling up of their sleeves as they prepared.

I suddenly panicked at the thought I might be alone with the stranger. "Damien?"

"Spread your legs," he ordered.

Relieved he was still here, a rush of need zinged through me as fingers trailed over my butt and squeezed. A hand pressed the arch of my spine to get me to raise my hips even more as firm fingers pinched my flesh—followed by a spank.

"A butt plug," said the stranger, his voice deep. "I approve."

My body thrummed as someone twisted that bejeweled toy around, causing me to gasp.

My reaction seemed to incite one of them to hold my hips in place. My breaths came fast as I tried to hold still, unsure how to maintain this pose as another hand slid up my thigh, feeling the dampness there. My cheeks flamed knowing this stranger was caressing the evidence of my slutty imaginings. I clenched and relaxed my pussy, knowing they'd see.

It was easier not having to look at them—Damien had known this, too. Making eye contact with them and then watching their reaction was something I wasn't ready for...not yet.

A shudder went through me when hands pressed against my ass cheeks, pulling them apart, as though offering me to those gentle fingers that now traced my folds and explored my pussy. I felt a sudden push, a shock as fingers penetrated me.

"Nice and slow," advised Damien.

Because just yesterday, he'd been the first to ever enter

me—the first man to ever take me there. My channel tightened fiercely around what felt like two fingers probing, then pushing farther in and slowly forging a rhythm of entry before withdrawing and reentering me. Soon the finger fucking was a constant stream of force—in and out as though the stranger was getting familiar with my form, penetrating in a rhythm until my thighs trembled and I felt a rush of vertigo.

I was the centrifuge, suspended in time and place…separating into different particles. My asshole clenched my bejeweled toy to bear the unceasing fingering.

"Play with her clit," said Damien.

Gritting my teeth, I dealt with the shock of the sudden withdrawal of those firm fingers, a desperate moan escaping my lips. Those same fingers were now wholly focused on my clit, forging ahead with a frenzied flicking that delivered pure pleasure.

The stranger caressed my clit while my vagina was being explored, the feeling delicious as two fingers pushed deep, probing, like they were sharing their exploration of my sex.

I heard the sound of my stickiness, aware of how filthy all of this was for me. How I was being subjugated.

What sort of girl does this?

Let me be this unchaste, have this memory to cherish and recall later…my own personal secret, knowing two men had finger-fucked me.

Were finger-fucking me.

Firm hands eased my thighs wider apart—what I assumed was Damien's grip holding me in place so there was no escape. Captured by his strength, I squeezed my eyes shut in surprise as a mouth met my sex, the shock of a firm and inquisitive tongue traversing along my folds.

The stranger devoured me, fiercely lapping and licking, forcing pure delight into me, and through me, expelling doubt and fear as I gave myself over to them both, exulting in these heady sensations while pushing back into his face.

"That's enough for now."

No, it wasn't.

I needed more. Needed to be brought all the way—that orgasm snatched cruelly away, leaving me frantic with my hips rocking in wanton need.

"You moved your legs," came the chastisement from Damien. "When I place you, you stay in that exact position. Understand?"

"Yes, sir," I answered breathlessly.

A harsh hand came crashing down on my ass, bringing agony ricocheting through my flesh, causing me to cry out. But then that same hand smoothed over the sting with a gentle caress.

"This is your punishment," the stranger warned.

That voice...so familiar.

Knuckles white, I gripped the edge of the bar as a torrent of strikes came crashing down on my buttocks, stinging my flesh and bringing heat, followed by a flood of arousal.

My moans filled the room.

"Want to move on to the next card?" asked Damien.

Was I ready?

How could I not be? Damien knew more than I trusted myself to know. He helped me straighten up and led me across the room, my feet moving cautiously from the blindness he'd imposed upon me, heading toward the couch and chairs, if I remembered correctly.

A belt was being unbuckled; trousers being shed.

"I'm putting a condom on," Damien reassured me.

With firm hands around my waist, I was turned and then pulled down to sit on top of Damien, right onto his lap facing forward. We were in one of the armchairs—I could feel the velvet beneath my fingertips as I gripped the armrests on either side. I felt the press of Damien's erection against my back.

This was what the card had displayed—a woman riding her lover as another man knelt before her and leaned in between both their thighs to get to her pussy.

A tremble of exhilaration ran through me.

I felt no trepidation at the thought of being seen this close up, ready to be impaled on a cock. Damien's strong hands lifted me up and positioned his erection so that he slid in easily with my slickness, spearing me completely, my thighs wide and quivering.

The unbearable fullness morphed into flashes of white in my imagination that lit up the darkness caused by my blindfold, like fireworks exploding in my solar plexus.

We were together.

Him and me and our secret lover.

I was locked with Damien, my thighs pulled wider apart by unseen hands; my sex exposed for that dark stranger to admire. My wet pussy stretched taut by that cock, dangerously close to coming because the plug was stretching me beyond what I'd imagined possible as I felt the strain of double penetration.

"Arms behind your back." Damien ordered.

Responding quickly, I brought my hands behind my back and held my wrists together, feeling even more vulnerable and unguarded from that second man who had to be close by now.

Damien's hands undid the halter-neck where it was tied at my nape and dragged down my dress until my tits were exposed and pebbling from the sudden cold. Fingers circling each areola tenderly, thumbs sweeping over beaded nipples. My breasts rose and fell rapidly beneath firm massaging and pinching. I felt a thrill from not knowing whose fingers were now stroking and touching and tweaking, as both men explored and probed each part of me.

Feeling the heat of breath on my sex let me know the stranger was now leaning in fully between my thighs.

I twisted my head, demanding a kiss from Damien.

First, he bit my lower lip and then his mouth covered mine, forcing my lips wider so that his tongue could conquer me there, too.

What that card hadn't shown, what it couldn't have shown, was the blinding pleasure I felt as their mouths crashed on my lips... and on my lips...

The stranger was relishing each crevice and fold between my thighs, delighting in my taste with erotically charged noises of gratification as he indulged his mouth.

I wished I could watch as he lavished attention on my sex, his tongue exploring, sweeping over where that mighty erection stretched my entrance. His frenzied worshiping of my clit in fast flicks and meaningful circles brought a heavy pang that morphed into an impossible nirvana.

My mind splintered into nothingness.

My body was being ravaged from every angle, breasts pinched and twisted, Damien's cock filling me completely, my channel tight and grasping. My sphincter clutching that bejeweled plug with needy spasms. Damien was surely feeling the pressure against his erection as my muscles milked him—every part of me utterly seduced and tamed by them.

"Come together," demanded Damien, his voice gruff.

Head back, shuddering violently, I climaxed into the center of this blinding pleasure, wrecked and ruined, eyes rolling back as freedom found me and I surrendered completely, shuddering and writhing; disappearing into the center of euphoria.

Damien's body stiffened behind me and his breath caught with the upward push of his hips, causing me to quake as he released his heat with a jerk.

Stilling, our breaths slowed, limbs softening.

Feeling cherished by them both, I slumped back against Damien.

I had been adored and loved, all with nothing expected in return. *This*…this had been everything and more that I'd asked of him.

He pulled me back into a hug, wrapping his arms around me. "That was perfect," he said huskily. "Well done, Pandora."

Again…

I wanted all of it again.

CHAPTER
TWENTY-TWO

Damien

C urled up like a kitten in the same chair I'd fucked her in, Pandora appeared spent and close to falling asleep. She was still wearing the blindfold to protect Theo's identity.

Quietly, I escorted him out of the suite into the hallway, keeping my foot stuck at the base of the door so I wouldn't lock myself out.

I tapped his arm with gratitude. "Thank you."

"My pleasure." He shrugged into his jacket.

"You'll be able to make it home?" I was referring to the boner that had gone unsated because his role had been merely to lavish devotion on Pandora.

He gave a smirk. "I can handle myself. She seemed to like it, right?"

"She responded well."

"That was very generous of you, Damien, considering this arrangement could be temporary."

I shushed him. "Keeping her happy is my priority."

"So you like her now?" He looked unconvinced. "I thought she was just a PR move."

"Lower your voice."

He gave me sympathetic look. "I love you, bro. You always get the rough end."

"That's not strictly true."

He moved closer. "It looks like her father's scandal can't be disappeared."

Which meant the death knell on our relationship had been rung.

No, I wasn't giving up so easily—not when I'd begun to find her so desirable. Not when I couldn't push her from my thoughts when she wasn't around. And certainly not when I'd had her come so deliciously on my lap five minutes ago.

"Maybe it's time to negotiate with Salvatore Galante? See if we can get him to drop the story."

Theo arched a brow. "Your dad wouldn't approve. No negotiating with the enemy and all that."

"I'll think of something."

"You've no choice but to break it off with Pandora." He glared at me. "You're capable of doing that, right?"

My mouth tried to form the proper words, and failed.

"Damien?"

"As soon as the optics look favorable." Saying it caused my chest to tighten.

I wasn't done with her. There were more scenarios to play out with Pandora, more time needed to explore her secret fetishes—and mine. I had to admit that just being with her at times was enough.

"Her parents threatened to send her back to Switzerland if her dad is locked out of the Cabinet."

"What the fuck?" I glanced up and down the hallway to make sure no one could overhear.

Theo rested his palm on my shoulder. "Give a woman that experience—" He pointed back into the room— "and she's going to be hard to get rid of."

"She asked me to expose her to more intensive play."

"Maybe it's time to do the deed."

I gave him a pointed look. *No, I don't think I will, Theo.*

He fished his phone out of his pocket and stared at the screen. "Shit. You've been summoned."

"By who?"

"Apparently you're not answering your phone."

I rolled my eyes in annoyance. "Let me take Pandora home first."

"Make it her parents' place." He tapped his phone's screen. "I'm getting a car for her right now. It'll be here in fifteen."

"Stop trying to manage me. I'm not a campaign."

"Did you tell the construction crew on the Fairfield project to keep going?"

"Might have."

He squeezed his eyes closed in frustration. "I'll handle it, okay? Go home. I'll take the call and face your dad's wrath."

"I'll call him in the morning."

Tonight, I'd been able to forget all that chaos.

I trusted Theo. He was more of a brother to me than Carter. He'd never held it against me that I was a Godman and carried the weight of privilege. Instead of breaking him, life had carved out a gentleman—though it had bestowed upon him a need to indulge in the forbidden. Tonight he'd proven again he was equal to me in all things debauched.

Theo headed off down the hallway, adjusting his pants to disguise that enduring erection. I pushed the door open and headed back into the suite.

Damn it.

Pandora stood a few feet away in the center of the room. Her dress had been rearranged back to decent—and the blindfold dangled from her right hand.

How much had she heard?'

"He's gone," I told her. "Let's enjoy the room."

"It was Theo?"

I shouldn't have left the door ajar. "Yes." I watched her expression. "How do you feel about the fact it was him?"

"He's certainly good at certain things."

"Theo's a brilliant man. I'm lucky to call him a friend."

"You're taking me back to my parents' home?"

I studied her face to gauge her mood. "Yes, I believe that's best."

"Salvatore Galante can't be persuaded?"

"You heard everything?"

"You can't make my father's scandal go away, can you?"

"What was our agreement, Ms. Bardot?"

"I'm not to bring it up."

"If you ever eavesdrop on me again, I will…"

"You will what, Damien?" She looked fierce. "You're breaking it off with me because of my father's scandal?"

"We can remain a convincing couple to the public."

"This relationship is still a fake one to you?" She threw the blindfold at me.

It hit my chest and dropped to the floor.

She wore the same pleading expression that had persuaded me to bring her here an hour ago. Only this time she was asking to be loved. That same look had inspired me to honor the mark of the clavis; the wearing of that pendant she had yet to earn.

"Pour me a brandy." I pointed at the bar. "And while you're at it, think of all the ways you're going to apologize for your behavior."

She headed over to the other side of the room, and then paused to look back at me. "I'll never love you, Damien. If that's what you're afraid of."

My jaw flexed, and I suddenly felt a dull ache where my heart used to be before emptiness filled up that void. "Well, good," I said. "We agree on something."

Her lips quivered as she glared at me.

"Hennessy Timeless Cognac," I said. "No ice."

Pandora rounded the bar and set about pouring me a drink.

Seething at how badly this had gone, I watched her throw ice cubes into the tumbler. She uncorked the Cognac and filled the glass.

She headed back across the room with the drink, moving with the kind of elegance I'd become addicted to, with her petite frame gliding as she approached me.

I eyed her suspiciously when she stopped a few feet away, refusing to hand the drink over.

"I will continue to act like I'm happy to be around you at

social gatherings." She sipped the Cognac—my drink—and then added, "And you will continue to keep your end of the bargain."

"Continue to fuck you?" I pointed to the velvet chair. "Like the pet you are."

Her cheeks flushed bright red as she took another sip of Cognac.

My cock hardened at the memory of her on my lap, her pussy being devoured by Theo at the same time…the way she'd responded to us both—and how hard she had come.

She sipped some more of the drink. "The sex was fantastic. Only it's a shame it's you on the other end of that dick." Pandora finished off the Hennessey in one gulp, delivering a burning punishment to her throat—the same throat I should be fucking.

I forced a smile. "Let's take you back to Mummy."

"That's generous of you, considering you don't actually like me!" She bit out the words that Theo had spoken in the hallway.

"All power returns to me."

"You gave me the illusion of power. But you never gave it up."

"That's the first insightful comment you've ever made. Get your purse. We're leaving."

"Why are you like this?"

"Like what?"

"I don't understand. I thought you and I…"

"Tonight, you were awarded a gift while leaning over that bar, and then again in that very chair. You should be thanking me."

Her lips trembled and she looked like she was biting back tears.

"It's true, your father's ambitions probably won't be realized."

"Some part of me believed you might…"

Love her? Was that what she'd been about to say?

My look of astonishment caused her confidence to shrink. She wilted like a flower scorched by the sun—once thriving below dazzling rays only to be utterly destroyed, savagely burned by my words.

"These are precarious weeks. I need you to be obedient."

"I was coming around to the idea of you," she admitted.

Push her away.

It will be easier on her in the end.

"You were never anything more than my plaything."

She looked unsteady on the heels I'd bought her. The same ones I'd taken my time to pick out for her. Placing them on her feet had felt like a sacred ritual.

Destroying Pandora Bardot should be something I savored, a gift to myself and to my family. In order for that to work, I was going to have to get my head back in the right space. Back to the same position I'd held before Pandora had walked through that red door last night and given herself to me—her innocence enduring even after all I'd done to her.

I struggled to drag my gaze away from her beauty, trying to remember a time when I'd once felt nothing for her.

I headed for the door. "I'll wait for you outside."

I stood in front of the hotel. Pandora took her time before joining me.

In silence, I escorted her all the way to the chauffeur-driven car parked outside the Ritz. The hotel valet opened the rear door and I assisted her into the backseat. She refused to make eye contact or speak to me.

Seeing her like this shouldn't have hit me quite so hard, but it did. I felt like I'd ruined a good thing—a goddamned brilliant arrangement.

Not an arrangement, a relationship.

Seeing her in pain made me feel like acid was burning my soul.

"Ms. Bardot's home, please," I instructed the chauffeur.

I returned to the hotel, striding fast for the elevator that would take me back to our private suite. I couldn't go home just yet, for no other reason than it was hard to focus. I was being assailed by too many conflicting thoughts and emotions, and there were no easy solutions.

Clearly, I had been letting my heart do the thinking for me. It was a colossal mistake I wouldn't repeat.

CHAPTER
TWENTY-THREE

Pandora

O n my way downstairs the next morning, I tried to come up with the words I'd need to describe the current situation. When I stepped into the dining room and sat down to have brunch, saying *"I fucked it up,"* probably wouldn't land very well.

Back at The Ritz, I'd blown up any chance of continuing a relationship with Damien. Before our argument the evening had been magical. I'd reveled in their erotic games, being their plaything, and finding freedom in my sexual desires—fucked hard in that velvet chair while having my pussy devoured at the same time by some secret stranger, who'd turned out to be Theo Tamer, a man just as devastatingly handsome as Damien.

Last night…

I relived an endless array of powerful sensations—the lingering soreness I felt below proving it wasn't a dream. Leaning my head against the dining room door, I tried to recover from the arousing memories that still made me breathless.

Maybe I'd also thrown away any chance of having that type of experience again. I crash landed with the unforgiving truth that Damien had admitted to Theo in the hall that he would be extracting himself from this marriage of inconvenience.

All that was left to do was share the news of our breakup with my parents and tell them my future as a Godman wasn't looking so good.

I should be happy. I should be glad that my escape was imminent, but all I felt was heartache. I didn't want us to end just yet.

Nudging the dining room door open, I strolled over to the

long table where my parents sat, their conversation ceasing when they saw me.

Mom looked bright and full of hope. "Damien is such a gentleman."

"How do you figure that?" I asked, as images flooded in of last night's escapades.

If they only knew.

"He brought you back home last night." She reached for Dad's hand. "You can only imagine the peace this brings."

Yes, but two nights ago, Mom, he tied me to his bed in his own private dungeon. Facts are important, after all.

"He has his moments," I said, keeping my amusement to myself.

Mom reached across the table and covered my hand with hers. "We know you're doing everything you can to appease his family."

"Is there any truth to what Galante is threatening to reveal?" I watched her expression carefully, as well as Dad's.

"I was a businessman long before I went into politics, Pandora," he replied flatly.

Mentioning his scandal as a career-ending event before lunch was not allowed, I knew that much.

"This is nothing for you to worry about," he added.

Well…another banal comment from a man unwilling to share the all-important details with his daughter—the same daughter who was meant to save his place in the Cabinet.

"Just keep at him," said Dad. "Keep Damien on our side."

Right.

The way our evening had ended at The Ritz, I was fairly certain that would be a tall order.

I noticed there were only two settings for brunch, and asked why. "I was going to join you."

"I thought you had a thing?" Mom rose and walked over to the sideboard to fetch a gift box with a bow. "Damien had his driver drop this off. His chauffeur is outside ready to take you to Number One Observatory Circle."

"Today?"

"Yes, it's the Vice President's garden party."

"Are we going to that?"

Dad looked frustrated. "I'm not. But you are. Reaching across the aisle is essential. You know that."

Mom looked exasperated as she handed me the gift. "You forgot?"

No, that asshole forgot to mention it—that's what had happened here. I'm sure he got some sordid pleasure from imagining me scrambling to get ready in a rush. This was his way of punishing me for our argument last night.

Still, considering I never expected to see him again, this news actually stopped my heart from aching.

Oh, Damien.

You're such a loveable bastard.

Lifting the box, I gave it a rattle and tried to guess what was inside. "Suppose I should get ready."

I headed out of the dining room, thinking I didn't want to go to a garden party, or a press mixer. Especially when half the staff there would know who I was and what my father represented, which was an extreme version of all their backward policies. No doubt the other guests would give me crap for it.

Part of me wanted to forget Damien Godman existed because the thought of having to face him and his intimidating wrath…not too keen on that, to be honest.

Halfway up the staircase, I unraveled the ribbon on the box. Maybe this was a peace offering and his way of apologizing. Maybe he'd chosen this gift himself and inside was a beautiful snow globe or some other pretty ornament.

I entered my bedroom and removed the box's lid.

Oh, my God.

Thank goodness I'd not opened this in front of my parents! Damien was the devil incarnate.

Easing back the tissue paper, I peered in at the sapphire-beaded butt plug. One size up from the other bejeweled item I'd removed last night. His plan to prepare me for butt sex was still underway, apparently. Last night, I'd removed the other one and had hidden it in a Louis Vuitton pouch that was currently shoved into a corner of my underwear drawer.

Also in the box was a handwritten note from Damien:

Don't be late, Ms. Bardot.

Well, he was going to be disappointed.

Insert your gift. Wear it during the event. You'll also find a complimentary object d'art. Make sure you are wearing this, too. There will be consequences if you fail to follow these simple instructions.

See you soon, my love.

—DG

I rummaged around and found a velvet pouch inside.

Hmmm…

The pouch weighed less than the plug. Clearly, he still needed me to uphold the illusion that all was well within the kingdom of the Godmans.

Tipping the velvet pouch, I blinked in confusion at the two ornate blue spheres that fell into my palm, both connected by a fine strand of silk. They were beautiful. Then it dawned on me where he wanted me to place them.

I was already half an hour late. My palm closed around his gift and I tried not to imagine how this would feel inside my pussy.

I wanted to hate this man.

I wanted to hate the way he made my body ache for more of his dark fantasies, his dirty, erotic schemes that were so addictive. I rubbed my thumb over the sapphire plug, craving its insertion.

I hated myself for craving his games.

CHAPTER
TWENTY-FOUR

Pandora

A ll I had to do was stay out of everyone's way.

It was a skill I'd cultivated when having to make an appearance at prestigious events like this, smart enough not to become the center of attention—simply playing the role of a pretty wallflower.

If this was war then I was ready for it. I'd worn my bright red Giambattista Valli long-sleeved midi-dress with accented lace—the one my mother insisted was too mature for me. My scarlet lipstick complemented the radical color.

Music from a string quartet rose above the chatter inside the Vice President's historic residence. Many of the excitable visitors had thrown down a handsome sum to schmooze with the movers and shakers of Capitol Hill.

I was fulfilling my end of the bargain by attending. It didn't mean I had to talk with any of the senators, or their partners, who were cutting through the crowd looking for their next victim to intimidate and persuade.

Besides, I was all hot and bothered from the sensitized tissue of my sphincter, caused by the sapphire gift that kept on giving, enhancing the heady stimulation I felt from the two spheres inside my vagina.

Avoiding Damien was also in my well thought out plan.

I was here to be seen, but I would simply refuse to talk with him.

Counting down the minutes until I could go home, I lingered at the long table covered with delicacies from around the world. Everything looked appetizing to my eyes, considering I'd missed brunch. I nibbled on the lobster truffles from France, and then noticed the Polish pastries, which were similar to crepes. I used the tongs to reach for one.

"Have you tried the Parisian soufflé?" said a familiar voice.

Turning, I dropped the tongs back on the table. "Mr. Vice President."

VP Aiden Palmer cut an intimidating figure at over six feet tall. His African-American heritage graced him with a sophisticated authority that was easy to trust.

"Ms. Bardot, how are you?" he asked.

"I'm fine, sir, thank you. How are you?"

"As bored as you are by the looks of it." He winked. "Is your father here?"

"No, he couldn't make it. Daddy sends his apologies."

"Right." Palmer smiled. "Has a date been set?"

I wiped my hands on my napkin, and gave him a puzzled look. "I'm sorry?"

"Your wedding day?"

"Oh, no, we decided not to set a date until the election is over with. Not that we're trying to push you out or anything. That would be rude. I mean, this is your home…and it's beautiful. You must love it here. And um…I'm rambling, aren't I?"

He laughed. "I'm used to it."

"Thank you for inviting me."

"Well, you are Damien Godman's plus one." He gave me a mischievous grin. "His father is here to ruin everyone's appetite."

"Oh, how wonderful," I said with sarcasm, grinning back at him.

He pointed at me. "And you're here to be beaten down by my staff so we can get intel on Godman's campaign."

"Love your honesty, Mr. Vice President." I leaned in. "Put me to work. I might be able to help you out."

He laughed raucously. "I was impressed by the guest piece you wrote for the *Washington Post*."

"The one about social media?" I felt a rush of pride. "You read that?"

"Yes, in fact, if you ever want to come and work for us, we'd love to have you."

"That would be awkward. My father's policies—and Senator Godman's—kind of clash with yours."

"You believe everything Godman stands for?"

"I'm respectful of what he's hoping to achieve. Some real change in a new and positive direction. I'm passionate about many of the forward-thinking policies he's running on. Their hope is to inject a new vitality onto the Hill. And as you know, Damien is dedicated to modernizing public housing."

"As are we."

"Kind of slow to make things happen, sir."

"Everything hits a wall at some point. No matter how well intended. Surely the Godman campaign know you're their secret weapon? Or maybe they're holding back until they can unleash you days before the election."

I held my arms out with a palms-up gesture. "Unleash the sorceress!"

"I can only imagine." He scrunched his nose. "They don't know how lucky they are."

"Thank you for the offer of work. I'm flattered. I mean, if it was up to me—"

My body erupted with sudden pleasure—the space between my thighs wired with a potent pulsing, a deep-rooted vibration within my pussy. "Oh, God!"

Palmer looked concerned. "Sorry?"

"What?"

"Are you okay?"

With my face burning up, I tried to catch a breath. "I just re-membered I have to talk to...somebody. It's amazing. I mean, it's been lovely to see you again."

"Likewise." He gave a bow.

With a look of apology, I hurried through the crowd searching for Damien.

No one walked *away* from the Vice President. It wasn't what you did, ever. It was always the other way around. You followed protocol and respected his rank as first in succession to the President.

My sex was alight with sensations coaxing me toward an orgasm—right here in the middle of a fucking garden party.

I'm going to kill him…

My fake fiancé was using a remote to pulse those spheres inside me to what felt like maximum oscillation.

I glared at him as I approached.

Damien raised a finger to indicate he was deep in conversation within a circle of journalists, and then waved to impress upon me he couldn't be interrupted.

Ignoring him, I eased through the gathering and whispered, "Turn it off."

He offered a polite smile to the men and women around him. "Excuse me for one second."

Damien's strong grip led me a few feet away. "I'm in the middle of an interview."

"How dare you? Of all places. Turn it off."

"I don't have the control," he said flatly.

"What?"

He smiled, seeing the blissful torment on my face.

"Listen to me," I seethed. "If you don't want me screaming—"

"You're not a screamer." He gave a shrug. "That's what I've learned so far. There's more of a slow, quiet build up and then your expression is one of pure joy. You moan softly when you finally climax." He played with a strand of my golden hair. "No one will notice. Except me, of course. Come at will."

"I'm serious."

"So am I." His thumb caressed my bottom lip. "You're my break from the tediousness."

"People are looking, Damien."

"I love your dress. The color is—"

"Mr. Godman!"

He hesitated and then admitted, "I seriously don't have the control."

"Who does?"

"Theo's in charge of that side of the operation."

I rushed away from him, searching for Theo in the crowd, my face blanching and my heart racing—feeling mortified that it was Godman's senior campaign manager controlling the device. I'd never be able to face him again.

Damien had gone too far.

Theo Tamer stood across the lawn, looking dashing in a slate gray suit. He, too, was engrossed in conversation with Damien's father, no less—a Presidential candidate who was surrounded by secret service officers.

One of them gestured that I wasn't to approach.

Pivoting away, I hurried through the crowd with my heels clicking on stone, entering the house and pushing past the other guests who were between me and the restroom. I'd be just as enamored as them with the historic elements of the place if my labia wasn't about to explode.

I made it to the restroom and shoved the door open.

But as I turned to lock it, the door swung forward and Damien stepped inside with me.

"No." I shoved at his chest. "Get out."

He turned, locking the door, and then pushed me backwards until my back hit the chintzy wallpaper. Reaching for my wrists, he dragged them above my head and held them there as he boxed me in, watching me intensely.

"I have to take them out," I pleaded.

"They are to stay in for the duration of this event. Those were my orders."

"You don't understand."

I felt myself rising into the stratosphere as his erection pressed against my belly through his pants, causing raw, exquisite sensations to surge through me.

I gasped, my body squirming as his firmness rubbed against my lower stomach making the torture worse. It was impossible to remain still.

My wrists twisted in his grip as I writhed against his firm chest, his all-seeing stare locked on me. The butt plug and balls inside me worked in unison, setting off each other, rendering me a throbbing mess of need as I rode out this euphoria against Damien's firm body.

"Good girl," he soothed.

I licked my lips to ease the dryness. "It's too much."

"You're doing well."

Breathless and boneless, I shimmered through an orgasm, small sobs escaping at the unfairness of this delectable thrumming. My legs went weak, my body feeling limp. He was the only reason I was still standing.

"Fuck you," I said softly.

He dragged me in for a kiss.

"Theo?" I asked, turning my head away. "He controls this?"

"He has a right, now that he knows what you taste like."

The dark truth that they were both playing with me snatched the remaining air from my lungs. My deep-throated groaning broke through the quiet, my breasts swelling and clit panging for contact against something. That something had to be Damien's groin as I ground against him, out of control, chasing after these dangerous compulsions…these multiple orgasms savaging my ability to speak. All the while he held me tight, his focus never leaving, watching me intently as these sensations continued to wreck me.

Finally, the frenetic buzzing ceased and I was able to breathe again, able to get my bearings and come down from the exhilaration.

"Why?" I managed one word.

Damien pushed off from me and stepped back. "When you defy me, like you did last night—" His hand reached out to cup my face. "I punish you."

Too exhausted to fight back, I rested my face in his hand as my breathing returned to normal.

"How does your pussy feel?" he asked huskily.

I fell against him, reaching around to hug him tight to thank him for this luxurious buzz that endured even now…thanking him for this reckless game.

His arms failed to embrace me back.

I pulled away, trying to regain my composure. I gave a nod to confirm I'd almost recovered.

He led me over to where a roll of toilet paper sat on an ornate holder, pulling off a few reems. Then he lifted my hem and eased my panties down. With my thighs spread a little, he wiped me there, tenderly, easing away evidence of my arousal, and then disposed of the paper, flushing it away.

As I tugged my dress down, he said, "Pull yourself together. I need you pretty and obedient. I need you by my side."

He left me standing there, stunned at his coldness.

Leaning on the vanity, I caught my reflection in the mirror, seeing my frazzled expression and disheveled hair. I was caught up in the depravity of one of Washington's most powerful men.

Nothing could be done.

Being used like this was never going to end.

You don't want it to end.

I scraped my fingers through my locks and reapplied my lipstick. Then I raised my head to practice how a woman might stroll through a crowd and not reveal her post-Damien high.

I stepped out onto the lawn, recognizing Brahms' String Quartet No. 1 in C Minor. The piece heightened my dramatic march over to where Damien was standing.

True to form, he'd nabbed himself a glass of champagne and an orange juice for me.

"Thank you." Taking it, I sipped thirstily, and then threw the other guests around us a warm smile.

"Good girl," he teased. "That's right, act like you're head over heels in love with me."

"Asking for the impossible?"

"You admitted it last night."

"I didn't finish the sentence."

"You implied it."

"It was the tequila."

"You can't get enough of me."

"What makes you say that?"

"Your pussy is still throbbing. And your ass is spasming as you imagine my cock buried deep inside you instead of the jewel. We'll get there. Just keep that plug in as instructed. We'll increase the size incrementally so you can accommodate me."

"You're crass." I looked around for Theo to see if he was watching me.

"You're lucky I don't get you to kneel before me in front of everyone."

"You're lucky you're not wearing orange juice on your shirt."

Damien reached for my wrist and gripped it with an ironclad hold. "One more word of contempt and those balls are buzzing again. Fancy another multiple? This time I won't let you retreat to the house."

"Let me go or I'll scream."

We stood there together, him glaring and me with my chin raised in defiance.

He let go and sipped his drink. "Just two more weeks of this, Bardot. Then you're free."

"I imagine you're counting down the days. I know I am."

"I'm proud of so many of my achievements. But I'm especially proud of the fact that I've captured the famed debutante Pandora Bardot's cunt."

I slapped him hard across the face.

He didn't even blink.

"Are people looking?"

I meant the press…and the senators, and the Vice President and his wife. I wondered if the world might soon be seeing a photograph of me striking Gregor Godman's son.

Damien reached around my waist and yanked me toward him, pressing his lips to mine, forcing my mouth open to accommodate his lashing tongue exploring and pillaging and warring with mine. He stirred up all the same feelings that had surged through me in the restroom.

I was hyper-aware of each sensation, including the feel of those spheres in my pussy. His ferocious kiss sparked arousal as he battled with my tongue; soaking my trepidation in confusion. Yet I surrendered to him anyway, desirous of the affection I'd been deprived of, wanting to love him again like I'd once believed I had.

His hostile takeover of my mouth continued vigorous and full of vitriol, a merciless attack that made my body quake and relent to his—both of us still holding our glasses and not spilling a drop—like consummate professionals who knew how to endure a disaster with grace.

Damien pulled away. "And now you smile, like your god-damned life depends on it."

Because it did.

CHAPTER
TWENTY-FIVE

Pandora

Anyone would be thrilled to be in the back of a chauffeur-driven car that was parked beside an enormous Dreamliner at Reagan National Airport, ready to fly first class to a private resort on a sunny Saturday morning. Unless of course that person was me, because my travel companion was none other than Damien G. Godman.

I'd once read the G stood for George, because Damien's mom had a thing for British royalty, and their empire building ways. That entire family was fucked-up.

If he thought I was stubborn before, my refusing to leave the car and board that plane would really piss him off. My suitcase had already been carried on to the flight and I was mulling over ways I could reclaim it.

Despite me telling Damien I didn't want to go, he'd picked me up from home. My parents had literally shoved me out of the house and into the back of his waiting car. I'd been greeted by a surly Damien in the backseat. He'd ignored me for the entire journey here.

Apparently, I'd brought this unexpected out of state jaunt on myself. There was the embarrassing matter of Washington D. C.'s journalists printing snapshots of yesterday's garden party. Note to self: Don't fuck up when the entire press core have their cameras trained on you and your beau.

"Here comes the persuader," I mumbled to myself.

Theo Tamer had just climbed out of the car ahead of us, the same one that had escorted us to the airport. Proving Damien's father wanted us out of the city and wasn't willing to risk one of us bailing, since this trip had probably been arranged to correct yesterday's "optics."

The car door flew open and Theo gestured. "Don't keep Mr. Godman waiting."

"I'm not going."

"Then why did you get in the car?"

"Why do you think?"

Because Damien knew full well my parents wouldn't have accepted me missing out on this opportunity for us to spend more time together.

I stared at Theo. "Did you enjoy the other night?"

"I have no idea what you're talking about."

I flashed a wary glance at the chauffeur then focused back on Theo. "Our private time at The Ritz."

He shrugged. "What happens at Fight Club stays at Fight Club."

Great, he'd used a Chuck Palahniuk reference, one of Damien's favorite authors.

His eyes narrowed on me. "I need you out of the car."

"Why?"

"I'm more than happy to say it here, if you want."

"What happened to 'what stays at Fight Club'?"

"What can I tell you…I'm light on my feet when it comes to threats. Now get the fuck out."

I let him take my hand and escort me across the tarmac. We stood at the base of the metal staircase where we could talk freely.

Theo lowered his voice to a whisper. "What happened at The Ritz should be considered a present from your lover. He's possessive, but still let you have that experience—"

"I'm so embarrassed it was you."

"Why? You were beautiful. Damien controlled every aspect. You asked for that fantasy and he gave it to you." He pressed his palm to his chest. "He knows I'll put you first in any scenario."

I closed my eyes. "What we did in that room…"

"Your secrets are my secrets."

My face blanched at the thought that this man had been intimate with me, yet he stood here as though nothing had happened, acting all business-as-usual, like it was no big deal that he'd gone down on me.

What the three of us had done at The Ritz would be a secret I'd carry with me forever, never to be shared with anyone.

"Go on, up you go."

My heart couldn't take much more of this angst. "Tell me how to make him love me."

Theo gave me a sympathetic look. "Earn his trust. Pure and simple."

"He thinks I'm with him for all the wrong reasons."

"Convince him otherwise."

"I want to visit Vanguard." *I want more.*

He hesitated. "Tell him."

"I will." And I had, only so far there'd been no favorable response.

Theo pointed to the stairs. "Be the woman he needs. You're a rare gem. He knows that but he needs to see you're capable of falling in love with every side of him."

How could I not trust his words? Theo's touch during our shared intimacy had been gentle and respectful, and he continued to be loyal to Damien.

I stood on tiptoe and planted a kiss on his left cheek. "Thank you."

"I'm here for both of you."

"It's so hard to be around a man who hates me this much."

"There comes a time when hate can flip over to love. You're already on the way to making that happen."

"I hope you're right."

With a nod of gratitude, I made my way up the stairs and into the cabin—stopping short when I saw the plane was empty of passengers.

CHAPTER
TWENTY-SIX

Damien

I'm not quite sure why my father thought I could have a relaxing trip to Sanibel Island when I had to bring along the most contentious woman in the city.

"Go have fun," he'd said, "create some photo ops."

Meaning: Fix this fucking mess.

He'd ordered us to leave Washington D. C. for the weekend—after also delivering the devastating news that the construction on Fairfield was indefinitely stalled…again.

I leaned back against the headrest, reassuring myself that once I returned on Monday, I'd be back at it, right in the center of the fight. Nothing would derail my endeavor. I'd make my social outreach program my life's work and not just because of how it looked to voters. The fact it was my dad stifling my efforts was heartbreaking.

Escaping this city, even if it was only for a little while, wasn't such a bad idea.

We were traveling in style on Dad's Boeing Dreamliner, usually reserved for the campaign trail. It was a commercial jet big enough to accommodate his entire team and anyone else wanting to hitch a ride to those designated states where he needed to nab more votes.

I glanced at my Rolex, my impatience rising.

Where the hell was Pandora?

We'd driven here together, though admittedly in silence. She was meant to be right behind me. I'd gone on ahead so I could chat with Andrew Holt, the co-pilot. We'd even managed a pre-flight check while waiting for Her Highness to board.

Bardot finally appeared in the cabin looking as irritatingly gorgeous as ever as she brushed blonde locks out of her face. Her cream pantsuit and jacket had been designed for an older woman, but she wore it well. A pair of shades rested on top of her head—she was ready for the sun.

She looked around. "Just us?"

"Obviously."

"Where would you like me to sit?"

"On the floor. Where you belong."

"Let's keep it to ourselves that we're the only passengers. Carbon footprints and all that."

My jaw flexed. "When the plane lands in Florida, it will pick up a hundred Gulf War veterans and bring them to D.C. They will then be provided with a tour of the White House."

"Oh, that's nice."

"Why do you suddenly care about the environment, Bardot?" I said tersely. "Usually you only care about yourself."

She plopped down beside me. "My chat with Theo was enlightening."

I glared at her, and then softened my expression as Becca our flight attendant brought us both tall-stemmed glasses of white wine.

"Drinking so soon?" Pandora chastised me.

"Got to drown my sorrows somehow," I mumbled, reaching for the glasses on the tray, and handing one to Pandora. "Thank you, Becca." I gave her a grateful smile.

She headed back up the aisle.

I set my wine on the tray table next to me and pushed to my feet. "Excuse me."

Pandora looked panicked. "You better be staying on this plane."

"Where else would I be going?"

"I don't know. You seem extra pissed off today, that's all."

"This is what you get when you slap a man in front of the world. At the Vice President's residence, no less."

"Speaking of Vice President Palmer," she continued brightly, "we were having a lovely conversation before it was interrupted. He was telling me how much he'd enjoyed reading my opinion piece in the *Washington Post*—"

"You wrote an opinion piece?"

"Yes, please follow along."

"It's hard when I'm trying to avoid boredom."

"The VP invited me to go work for him."

My expression reflected my disbelief. I mean, that man was more cautious than the President. Pandora was far more progressive. Not to mention, he was on the wrong fucking team.

She continued with flushed cheeks. "Just as we were discussing the details of my new role in the White House—"

"You wouldn't have taken the job."

"Maybe I would have. Maybe I'm ready to do the opposite of what everyone expects. But that's not the point."

"What is?"

She raised her index finger with indignance. "While we were discussing the details, you set off a firestorm inside my pussy. You timed it for that exact moment when I was talking with him."

"I didn't have the controller."

"You asked me why I slapped you." She glared up at me. "It's because you used that despicable word."

I blinked as though confused.

"You know which one," she snapped.

"Cunt?" I grabbed her pointing finger and gave it a waggle. "I recall elegantly describing it as a famous debutante's cu—"

"No!" She pulled her hand away. "No more of that in front of me."

Her response sparked my amusement; I kind of liked this version of her. "What did you and Theo talk about?"

"Vanguard." She threw me a triumphant look.

"That's not something he would discuss."

She tapped her necklace. "This gets me in."

Glancing at my wristwatch, I feigned disinterest.

"From your reaction, Mr. Godman, you've considered taking me."

I smiled. "You're not ready. I doubt you'll ever be. For starters, you have to be able to lean into the word cunt."

"I want separate rooms when we get to the hotel."

My jaw tightened. "We have to pretend that we more than just like each other. After the *New York Times* printed a front-page photo of you slapping my face this morning we've had to fine-tune our public persona." I threw up my hands in frustration. "The headline was *Trouble in Camelot?*"

"I thought my father's scandal was about to hit the press." She casually took a sip of her wine. "Which meant you and I would never see each other again."

I studied her face. "Is that what you want?"

Becca appeared and got my attention. "Sir, Andrew's ready."

I gave a nod of thanks.

"I doubt the staff at the resort will care how we act together," said Pandora. "Anyway, this is my first vacation and I want it to be special."

"What are you talking about?"

Her father was a billionaire, for God's sake. That didn't make any sense.

"This is my first trip without an escort. *You* don't count."

"I'll do everything I can to make it memorable."

I started to turn away, but she grabbed my hand and held it. "When my brother gets defensive it's because he's hurting," she said. "Tell me what's hurt you. Tell me what made you angry last night. And don't say it was just me."

"This is beyond your scope of comprehension."

"If the Vice President, who should hate me because I'm his opponent's daughter, can see my value, then so can you."

"I want to protect you from all that."

"That should be my decision."

I sighed. "They shut down the Fairfield Project."

She looked horrified. "Damien...oh, my God—you should have told me. I'm so sorry."

All that good had been suspended indefinitely. I stared straight ahead, feeling a sense of powerlessness that savaged my ego. No, it was more than that. It was about social justice and equality and about tackling corporate greed.

Her frown deepened. "Why would they shut it down?"

"Politics."

"Is there anything I can do?"

"Just be you, okay? Let's see if we can spend the weekend together and not kill each other in the process." I gave a smirk. "Stick to your brand."

"I'm not sure what that is."

"Well, you have two and a half hours to think about it before we land."

Pulling away from her, I headed up to the front of the plane, not wanting to admit to myself that I missed the touch of her hand.

CHAPTER
TWENTY-SEVEN

Pandora

My emotions were all over the place.

Perhaps all the times I'd endured loneliness had been worth it; a bleak prelude to me finding a life that had purpose, one that was filled with devotion. If only we could get there. If only we could get to a place where our relationship was authentic.

It was hard to deal with all these heart-wrenching ups and downs, trying to understand Damien's complexity, to understand the man who'd been preordained as mine.

Or maybe never would be.

I sat there musing on what my "brand" actually was, and I realized I'd always gone for understated—always trying to go un-noticed. Maybe it was time to start reinventing myself, having fun with a future I finally saw opening up.

There came a jolt and then the scenery moved outside my oval window. Within a minute, we were jettisoning down the run-way at full speed. I felt a sudden panic at the thought I was sit-ting alone, my fingers clutching the hand rests. A shudder went through me as the wheels lifted off, that familiar weightlessness of going airborne, then seeing the shrinking views of the city off in the distance.

In pure Damien fashion, he'd left me to endure my nervous-ness alone.

Pulling the console down in front of me, I selected the menu for the onscreen entertainment and scanned what TV shows or movies might be fun to watch, looking out for something I could recommend to Damien—perhaps a nice documentary about animals eating their prey while their victim was still alive…causing no end of suffering.

Something I could relate to.

It seemed like it was just me in the middle of this big plane, with Damien sitting up front somewhere, probably flirting with the flight attendant.

I sipped my wine, trying not gulp it down when the thought of him giving her his phone number sprang into my mind…or even her giving him a blowie.

A ping announced we'd reached cruising altitude. Unclipping my seatbelt, I pushed up and moved into the aisle.

If you're going to dump your travel buddy, at least be courteous enough to excuse yourself first.

I gazed over the rows of seats ahead, looking for Damien, my concern rising when I didn't see him. I approached the restroom door and knocked.

Becca poked her head out of the galley. "There's no one in there."

"I'm looking for Damien."

"He's up front." She gestured to the cockpit.

"Talking with the pilot?"

"Usually we don't allow that, but as it's you." She smiled at me.

"They won't mind?"

"Of course not. This is his family's jet. What time would you both like lunch?"

"I'll ask him."

"Great. I'll put a menu where you're sitting."

"Thank you." I reached out to shake her hand. "Pandora."

"Becca." She smiled brightly as she shook my hand, and then turned to tap on the cockpit door. "You have a visitor, sir. Ms. Bardot."

There came a muffled voice through the door.

She pulled it open and gestured for me to step forward.

Peering inside the flight deck, my jaw dropped open. Damien was sitting in the pilot's seat.

Wait.

What.

Another pilot sat to his right and both men were wearing headsets, looking supremely confident before the high-tech panel that was lit up before them. Lights were flashing and indicators blinking. The vast window stretched all the way around to reveal a flurry of clouds whipping by.

Damien looked over his shoulder at me. "How was take off?"

"Smooth?" I'd made it sound like a question. In shock, I watched him flick a switch on the panel. "You're flying the plane!"

The pilot to his right gestured at Damien. "You didn't know your man can fly?"

Yes, he'd probably mentioned *something* about it.

But this was surreal. "We're in a passenger jet! I mean, it's big."

Damien laughed. "No complaints so far."

"But this is a Dreamliner!" I burst out.

"Wait," said Damien. "This isn't a Cessna?"

The men both chuckled.

Feeling shocked, I realized that he'd been the one in charge of our take off.

The first time I'd met him I'd admittedly swooned, and that had been the last time he'd elicited that kind of response in me… until now.

It was sexy the way Damien had removed his jacket and rolled up his sleeves to reveal firm muscled forearms as he handled the controls, chatting with air traffic control, using the lingo and showing no fear.

"Do you want anything?" I asked, trying to act like this was no big deal. "Becca was going to make some lunch."

"We'll have lunch when we get to Sanibel," he said. "Go relax."

With a nod, I turned around and made my way back down the aisle, my hands using the seatbacks on either side of me for balance.

There was so much more to this man I didn't know.

CHAPTER
TWENTY-EIGHT

Damien

When it came to a weekend getaway that would suit our purposes, Sanibel Island in southwest Florida was the perfect place, with its pristine beaches, crystal waters and beautiful landscaping. It had just the right amount of exposure to the public while still allowing us some privacy.

The luxurious beach resort promised hours of relaxation.

If only that was on the agenda.

I guided Pandora around our holiday cottage, showing her where she could hang out and chill.

"Your room." I gestured to the king-sized bed and continued on over to the window that overlooked the pool. "Will this do?"

She studied me, as though realizing this meant we didn't have to sleep together. I saw confusion reflected in her eyes.

She followed me out, continuing down the hallway to the double glass frontage of the cottage.

"Your father owns an island," she said.

"Your point?"

"Why did you choose this place?" She peered out the window. "I do love it. Only, people might be able to see us."

"Do you want the romantic version or the truth?"

She spun round to look at me. "This isn't just about getting us out of Washington?"

"When we're in here we can spend as much time apart as we want. Out there—" I pointed to the beach. "We act like we care about each other."

"Why not just call off our engagement, Damien?" She

gestured her frustration. "No one need know."

"Everyone must play their part."

"I'm feeling very used."

"Your father has many supporters. They adore you. We can't risk losing one vote."

"I'm aware of my currency."

"Look, I know you and I haven't always seen eye to eye. But as a form of punishment, spending a weekend in paradise isn't too bad in the scheme of things."

She studied me carefully. "Why didn't you tell me you'd be flying the plane?"

"Thought it would be a fun surprise."

"A jet liner, though."

"I once wanted to be a commercial pilot. Obviously, it didn't happen."

"I thought you studied history?"

"It's possible to do both."

She looked sad for me. "Were you expected to join your dad's business?"

"Of course."

"How often do you fly?"

"Enough to keep my license valid. I get the hours in whenever I can."

"It was impressive, seeing you in the pilot's seat."

"Wait. Was that a compliment?"

"Yes, I'm teaching you how they're delivered." Her tongue rested on her upper lip and then she pivoted away toward her room.

I headed in the opposite direction and entered the kitchen. We could make this work. I'd take the main bedroom and den. Pandora could have the rest of the place. I'd set her up so she could stream TV shows in the entertainment lounge.

The kitchen was fully stocked with enough meals to feed a family of four for a week. I may come from privilege, but I wasn't as spoiled as her Royal Highness.

Reaching into the fridge, I lifted out a chilled bottle of beer and popped off the cap. I stood sipping my beer and admiring the view from the kitchen window. Tall palm trees lined the way to the pool. A bird hopped between them as though he, too, was used to all this decadence. It was one of those birds tourists mistook for flamingos because of its distinctive pink feathers.

"Damien, will you do my back?"

I turned to look at Pandora and felt a spark of arousal at seeing her in a red bikini—and a skimpy one at that. She might as well be naked. I admired her toned curves and the pert nipples visible through her skimpy bikini top. She was holding up a tube of sunblock.

With my thumb, I pointed toward the window. "Roseate Spoonbill."

"What?"

"It's a bird. Outside. You should take a look."

She came closer and peeked out the window. "Oh, yes."

"They can be confused for flamingoes."

"They go bald when they get old."

I shot her a look.

She raised her sunblock. "You don't mind?"

I took several gulps of beer. "We should do that outside."

"I'm meant to apply it before I'm exposed to the sun."

"I know, but…"

She looked horrified. "Are the press out there already?"

My lips twisted into a rueful smile.

"I have to change." She set the sunscreen on the nearby counter. "I have a swimsuit that doesn't show off so much skin."

I moved over and picked up the bottle of sunscreen. "You look fine. Come on, I'll bring my Kindle and you can sunbathe beside me. Our pool is private."

"Not from a long angle lens."

"Which is why you and I are going to work hard at being nice. All that's expected of you during this trip is for you to not show how much you hate me."

"Ha." She turned and padded on bare feet to the door.

After making a quick change into my swimming trunks and grabbing my sunglasses, I joined her in the midday sun by the pool. This might even be fun if I didn't over think it.

Pandora knelt to dip her hand in the sparkling pool water. She looked ethereal from here, golden wisps of her hair caught on the breeze, her big blue eyes taking in her surroundings.

I felt a stab of guilt that she'd been dragged into this family like a bright star being sucked into a black hole.

I walked over and placed my palms on her shoulders. "You'll burn."

"Are you serious?" She hissed under her breath.

"Give me the lotion." I snatched it from her and gestured to the lounger. "On there."

She rose gracefully and then laid face down on the lounger, that thong of a bikini bottom covering nothing of her firm, round butt. I slapped her ass.

Pandora winced. "Ouch."

"Pretend you like it." I opened the lotion bottle.

She looked at me over her shoulder. "Can't get over how lucky I am. *The* Damien Godman, Cosmo's number one bachelor, is currently applying cream to my bum."

"Shut the fuck up." With a dollop of cream in my palm, I moved down to her feet and began there, lathering it on her toes and arches, working my way up her calves and thighs, and then her hips and back. Her muscles relaxed beneath my touch.

My fingers caressed her nape, my cock already half erect. "Turn."

She rolled over onto her back with her face turned away, those sunglasses on so I couldn't see her eyes.

Beginning at her feet again, I worked my way up her body until my fingers danced over her thong. I slipped a thumb beneath the material and caressing her clit.

She jolted with surprise. "Someone might see."

"This is how it's done, Pandora. We act like we believe no one is watching. That way our affection appears real."

She relaxed again, giving a nod so that I would continue. With her consent, my palms trailed upward over her belly. When I reached her breasts, I slid a palm beneath her top and caressed her nipples.

"Unless we're making another sex tape," she said tersely. "You better watch where you put your hands."

Grabbing a beach towel, I threw it over her bottom half. "No one can see when I do this." Exploring her hips, I eased apart the ties of her thong to free it, sweeping my hands over her pubic bone.

Her body responded favorably as I secretly explored her pussy beneath the towel, finding her soaking wet.

She inserted her fingertip into her mouth and suckled it in an erotic display.

Very fuckable lips.

Her thighs went slack in invitation.

I eased a fingertip into her pussy and then another, setting a sensual pace of finger fucking her. Her hands clenched the top of the towel and her mouth parted, her breath hitching when my thumb rested upon her clit and swirled.

"They'll know," she breathed.

"Know what?"

"If they see a photo of your hand under the towel."

"And what would it look like?" My thumb increased its pace, beating that throbbing nub.

She peered over her sunglasses. "I mean, it looks like we're…"

"That's the point."

"It looks like we're crazy for each other."

"I agree, it does."

She pulled off her glasses and looked at me. "Why can't this be us for real?"

"You like this?" I inserted my little finger into her ass, just a bit, and penetrated her pussy with my thumb at the same time.

"Oh, you're putting your…"

"You've been wearing your ass jewel?"

"Didn't bring it because of…s…s…security." She was breathless.

"My finger will have to do for now, then."

She nodded frantically. "Why can't you always treat me like this?"

My touch stilled.

"Don't stop," she pleaded.

I resumed my probing of both her orifices with my right hand and flicked her clit with my left. "We can't be more, Pandora. You hate me."

Her neck tilted back as she neared orgasm. My firm fingers pounded her faster as I strummed her clit furiously. She was soaking my hands, causing my dick to harden.

She arched her back, her thighs shuddering, toes curling, her body going rigid—her climax was a thing of beauty.

She found her breath again. "I'm in love with…the way you touch me."

"Not with me?"

"You wouldn't want that." Her eyes softened with confusion. "Would you?"

Looking away and then finding her eyes again, I tried to convey that I could never love her. My throat constricted at the lie. She was infuriating, and totally spoiled, but she was the first woman I had ever agreed to marry when my father had broached the idea to elevate our status.

I wiped my hands on the towel and tossed it on the ground.

"What are you thinking?" she asked softly.

Pandora was pretty and sweet, and pliable, and should she prove as kinky as me and be willing to explore the depravity I craved, I could see us becoming more. Not just as a token to please society but with a relationship that went deeper—maybe even leading to love.

She was reading me and for the first time since I'd known her, I sensed she could see through me like glass, my soul bared for her.

"Did you enjoy me fingering you?" I asked huskily.

She sat up on the lounger. "Can we continue this conversation in private?"

"We can discuss it here."

Her eyes widened with insistence. "Inside."

Here it comes, the first argument of our trip.

Pushing to my feet I said, "Tell me what you want."

She glanced at my cock. "I'm ready."

"For what?"

"To be taught how to be your submissive." She licked her lower lip sensually. "I'm done with foreplay. Prepare me for Vanguard."

She wrapped a towel around herself and stood up and padded toward the villa.

When she reached the door, she glanced back at me with a sultry look, her hair blowing in the wind, her face flushed and lips pouty.

And here I was, captured completely in the snare of Pandora Bardot's aura—my life interwoven with hers as though we'd always been destined to be together.

She'd left a trail of her flowery perfume in the air. My soul yearned for the endless ocean between us to disappear, wanting nothing more than to plunder the treasure that was her.

The fact she wanted this, too, felt surreal—like all my expectations for her as a sub might come true.

I headed inside after Pandora, finding her in the luxurious sitting room.

She sat on the edge of an armchair. "Where do you want me?"

"Talking is good," I began.

Her brow knitted together.

"Look, when I introduced you to my dungeon, we were in a different place."

She shot to her feet. "You're talking about optics?"

I sighed. "I only want a submissive in the bedroom. Other than that, I want my partner to be equal in all things."

"So only submissive in the dungeon?"

"Correct."

"Okay, I like that."

"Yes, but the fact is, should you become *my* submissive, you'd fall deeply in love with me."

"Maybe not."

"You will, Pandora. It's inevitable."

"Are you saying what I think you're saying?"

My silence was her answer. Our future was never destined to happen.

She stormed past me.

I grabbed her arm to stop her from leaving. She pulled away, then came at me and shoved my chest.

My hand snapped to her throat and I walked her backwards towards the wall and pressed her against it, my lips close to hers, but not kissing her.

"Go to your room," I said sternly.

She looked devastated.

"When you are willing to obey me you may come out," I said. "And perhaps we'll discuss this further."

I released her and walked away.

CHAPTER
TWENTY-NINE

Pandora

S tirring from sleep, it took me a few seconds to orientate. *That's right. I'm in a cottage, miles from home…with* him.

And I'd just woken up from an afternoon nap, after being scolded by Damien as if I were a schoolgirl. I wiped my mouth, hoping he hadn't seen me like this—my makeup smudged and my hair a tangled mess.

I wanted Damien, but staying with him meant I'd be willingly closing the cage on my life. He'd all but admitted he didn't love me, that we were over in every sense other than a pretend show for the public.

Earlier, I'd almost blurted out my love for him.

Almost.

Caressing my chest, I tried to decipher these swirling emotions around my heart.

This wasn't a bad place to hide out from the world—even with the threat of the paparazzi looming. There seemed to be areas in the garden I could hide.

I climbed out of bed and spent a few minutes in the bathroom to freshen up and deal with my smudged mascara and messy hair. I looked like I was strung out from a sexcapade.

I put on my yellow Fendi floral mini sundress and gold sandals and went looking for Damien. He wasn't anywhere in the cottage.

Popping on my sunglasses, I left the cozy setting and strolled down the pathway toward a garden surrounded by lush foliage and tall palm trees. An opening revealed another sparkling pool with lounge chairs and a table set for a late lunch beneath a sunshade.

Damien was swimming laps in the pool, cutting through the water with his back muscles bulging and his toned arms propelling him along. This man had endless endurance. It was easy to stand here and enjoy the impressive display.

Eventually, he swam to the tile steps and rose up out of the water, his muscular form covered with shimmering droplets across his sun-kissed flesh. His dark hair turned sable when wet, highlighting his deep brown eyes. His blue swimming trunks did nothing to hide his major asset.

"You look nice." It was all I could think of to say.

Looking amused, he whipped a towel off the back of a lounger. "Yellow looks pretty on you." He studied me for a beat and then dried his face off. "We'll shop later. You need shorts and T-shirts."

I shrugged. "That's fine."

"You dress like a princess."

I smirked back. "An American princess."

His expression softened. "How are you feeling?"

It was hard to know what he was referring to—the finger fucking earlier by the pool or our argument. He continued assessing how I felt about everything we'd done *he'd done.*

I shrugged. "Okay."

He tossed the damp towel on a chair and pointed to the table. "Hungry?"

Ambling up to him, I whispered, "I suppose us eating a late lunch together is expected—another photo-op."

He loomed over me. "They'll possibly have a body language expert break down each photo. Be mindful of the way you behave around me. No more slapping allowed. Unless it's my hand on *your* ass." His lips hovered close to mine.

"Then conduct yourself appropriately, Mr. Godman."

He smiled. "You do realize I'm your 'get out of jail free card.'"

"How?"

"With me there are no rules. Anything you want is yours."

"Except my independence."

"You're living in the free, privileged world. You'll never go hungry. You'll never know what it feels like to be homeless, or sick with no access to medicine. And you can walk around here naked if you want with no fear of having your human rights removed."

My throat tightened with shame.

"Too much?" His lip twitched in amusement.

I couldn't think of a response.

"It's not your fault. You've been protected from what goes on out there."

"There can't be that many people out there like you described, though, right?"

"Are you fucking kidding me, Pandora?" He reached out and grabbed my head and shook it. "Earth calling Planet Privilege."

"Well, I've been kept away from the real world."

"You don't watch the news?"

"We were discouraged. I mean, I was."

He pressed a fingertip between my breasts. "You've been protected so as not to ruin your sensibilities."

"Is that why you hate me?" My mouth went dry with the realization.

He sighed. "I'm a moody bastard. I get that. But my blinders are off and I see the world for what it is. That way, I know what I need to do to make it a better place."

"I'll work on myself." I breathed through my humiliation.

His shoulders dropped. "Once you see the truth it can't be unseen."

The thought of anyone lacking the basic necessities of life made my heart sink. I was the living definition of spoiled.

"Come on, Marie Antoinette." He reached for a strand of my hair and ran it through his fingers. "We should kiss now."

"If you think it will help."

"For the photogs."

"Right."

He reached behind my head and dragged me in, our mouths locking in bondage as our tongues fought with one another, my moans escaping as urgent wanton desires sparked inside my core. The memory of what he'd done to me by the pool filled me with delicious sensations.

He bit down on my lip and made me wince, leaving me breathless and panting when he pulled away.

"I imagine that looked…convincing." Damien followed that up with a dashing smile.

I felt giddy and ashamed at how easily his suaveness had bypassed my defenses. His kisses were like arrows of unrequited love right into my heart.

Breaking away, I feigned the kiss had not affected me at all. "Oh, a shrimp salad. My favorite." I moved over to the table, glancing back to see him still focused on me. "Thank you for this."

"Allow me." Damien pulled out my seat.

After sitting down, I felt the brush of his lips on my neck, firm and affectionate, trailing along my shoulder and causing me to shudder.

Please, let this be real…

His warm hand pressed against my nape. "Thank you for playing along."

I swallowed the lump in my throat. "Of course."

He put his sunglasses on and sat opposite me. His laptop rested on another chair to his right.

Pointing to it, I said, "You were doing some work?"

"While you slept." He reached for a napkin. "I find it hard not to keep busy."

"What are you working on?"

"Research on why someone might want the land meant for the Fairfield Project."

"Can I see?"

"Maybe later."

This man was never going to let me get close. All that could be done was surrender to the inevitable.

I was still up for playing nice. "This place is lovely."

"We needed a location that was understated. Not too flashy.

That never looks good. A hotel that would accommodate a long angle lens but prevent the reach of listening devices."

"They're going to an awful lot of trouble."

"The Oval Office rules the world. Trust me, you're worth it."

"I'm flattered."

"Settle in. It's going to be a bumpy ride."

"Speaking of bumpy rides, you need to work on landing planes."

"It was a flawless landing."

"If you're fine with your passengers feeling like they're on a roller coaster."

He looked amused. "You've regained your feistiness after your nap. Maybe we should make that a regular occurrence."

"When I'm asleep I'm not thinking of my situation."

He lifted his fork and skewered a shrimp. "Your father is still part of the same political party as ours. He stands to gain a tremendous amount from us winning the election. You and me, we're playing our part."

"I know."

"I'm doing my best to make this situation easier on you."

Having him show his true feelings was what my heart yearned for. Still, to be reminded I was merely an asset stung. I reached for my knife and fork and cut through the leafy greens.

He pulled up his laptop and typed away as he ate dinner. It made me wish I'd brought my Smartphone or a book to read.

Usually, when my glass was empty, a hovering staff member would quickly fill it. Here, it was Damien who reached for the water to refill our glasses, preferring a more relaxed dining experience.

I pushed to my feet, rounding the table to stand before him.

"Yes?" he said, curious.

"At first, I thought you were wrong in so many ways. To break with tradition all the time. Ignoring etiquette. But I like it. Your ways are different."

He sat back and studied me. "I'm waiting."

"For?"

"Your caustic criticism."

"For as long as I can remember, I was told 'this is the only way,' but it was from centuries of regulated rules. A legacy as one of America's most celebrated families. And yet all along, I was destined to be sold off to the highest bidder."

He pulled me onto his lap. "Tell me what I can do to make you happy."

I wrapped my arms around his neck and whispered, "You have to ask?" Surely, he knew.

"You're a very complicated young lady."

"Have a guess, Damien Godman."

"You used my full name." His lips curled at the edges. "Now I'm in trouble."

"I've told you about me…"

He gave a nod and drew in a breath. "Unlike you, who comes from old money and old traditions, my family are considered *nouveau riche*. We're bankers, as you know. My great-great grandfather, Charles Godman, lived in India. He opened a bank in Mumbai." Damien's smile widened. "He met my great-great grandmother, Adhira, there and married her. She came from Indian royalty. Charles brought his young bride back to London. In that thriving city he set up a financial establishment that set my family on a path to become the dynasty it is today."

"And your family moved to Tennessee?"

"Yes. Where we continue to grow the empire."

"You reject your privilege."

"I learned early on that it wasn't the things that were handed to me that made me happy."

"I don't care for money either."

"That's because you've always had it."

"Earlier, you accused me of hating you."

He leaned in, his lips hovering close to mine. "If this is hate, I'm all in."

CHAPTER
THIRTY

Damien

Frantic, I searched the garden for Pandora.

This wasn't how I wanted to spend my Sunday morning—heart pounding, phone in hand and ready to make *that call*—searching for the woman I wasn't meant to care about. The fear of losing her ripped at my heart. My mind kept seeing the horrifying highlights of what might have happened.

Last night, we'd slept in separate rooms. That was the last time we would ever do that—from now on, we'd be sleeping together.

When I'd gone to check on her this morning, she wasn't in her bed or anywhere else in the cottage. We were supposed to be having breakfast together, lounging by the pool, swimming and spending time together.

If anything happened to her, I'd have to explain to the world how I'd let their beloved princess out of my sight just long enough for her to succumb to harm. I'd have her blood on my hands...two weeks before the damn election.

The thought of her suffering threatened to break me.

Yes, we had security, but we'd been dodging them the last seventy-two hours and they were probably used to our bullshit.

Pandora had breached my defenses and lately I'd seen her in a new light, peeled back the layers she hid behind to see the sweet girl beneath that high-class shell. Fucking her had felt like a spiritual practice I couldn't be without.

I'd been selfishly pursuing the one goal my family had chased after for decades, unwittingly forgetting what had been important to me all along: people. I'd gone through the motions of serving the public but deep down I'd felt like I was fighting a losing battle.

I'd lost my way.

Through Pandora I'd found it again.

Pressing my phone to my ear, I resigned myself to suffering the consequences of alerting our security team. It would, of course, trigger an alert that would be sent back, the fallout monumental. Not ready to call that number yet and bring hell down upon us, I put the phone back in my pocket and kept going, willing Pandora to be okay.

Hurrying out of our private garden, I made it to the pathway that led along the ocean front, hoping to see her walking along the beach.

Farther down, a gardener was shoving some exotic plant into the dirt, his tan-weathered face a testament to the sun.

"Did you see a young lady come this way?" I tried to keep the panic out of my voice. "Probably wearing a sundress."

"Is she blonde?" he asked.

My heart rate took off. "Yes."

"A young lady, a blonde, headed off in that direction about ten minutes ago." He pointed. "There's boutiques down there." He gave me a knowing smile.

"Thank you!"

Sprinting, I rounded another cottage and saw a luxury line of stores. Starting at an ice-cream shop, I kept peering through the windows, moving rapidly from one store to another until I'd gotten all the way down the boulevard to a jewelry shop.

Pandora was in there, standing before a glass counter and talking with a woman on the other side. The shop keeper appeared bright and engaging.

Adrenaline continued to surge through my veins.

Taking a calm breath and at the same time finding true religion, I opened the shop door.

The doorbell drew attention as I entered.

I was greeted by a wide smile from Pandora. "Hey, you found me."

My nod probably appeared out of place, half casual, half subdued panic, as though my mind hadn't gotten the memo she was okay.

My fiancée stood before me looking devastatingly beautiful and unaware of the dread she'd caused. Her value had always come from her status, the fact she was a Bardot. Now, here, I saw beyond all of that.

She was a sweet-natured girl, kind and worthy of a man so much better than me.

"Find anything you like?" I tried to sound nonchalant to hide how unhinged she'd made me.

She looked sheepish.

The glass cabinet was filled with blue stones, a collection of sapphires and all of them engagement rings. I gave her an inquisitive glance and then flashed a smile at the emerald on her ring finger.

I was suddenly reminded of how I'd thrown that ring at her in the kitchen back in my oceanside home and I squeezed my eyes shut for a beat.

What an ass.

The piece she wore was not even chosen by me. I'd merely had my assistant reach out to her family and inquire as to what kind of stone she favored. They'd told me emeralds. Clearly, they were wrong.

Maybe no one really knew her.

"Sapphires?" I said with a smile.

She touched the emerald self-consciously.

Stepping forward, I peered through the glass. "They're all impressive."

"She likes that one," the shopkeeper said.

The sapphire was small and delicate and not at all what I'd have guessed Pandora would have liked. It was understated.

"Not that one?" I pointed to a larger gemstone mounted upon a platinum band.

"Too flashy," she said.

"Which one is your favorite?"

"There's an ice cream store a few doors down." She wrapped her fingers around my arm. "Shall we treat ourselves?"

"It's nine in the morning."

She gave the shop assistant a sheepish glance.

Guilt flooded through me with the realization that I, too, had been cruel to her—treating her the same way everyone else did with a disregard for her feelings. All this time I'd misread her shyness for snobbery.

"I think it's a fun idea." I pulled her in and kissed the top of her head, closing my eyes and letting the relief saturate my soul. "Having ice cream for breakfast."

"Really?" She brightened. "Because it feels like we're being super rebellious."

Right...of all the things that made me a rebel this wasn't even in the same realm.

Feeling like my life was back on track after having found Pandora safe, I led her out of the store and along the pathway, looking for any sign of the security team tasked with protecting us. If they were here, they were discreet. They should have read my panic and approached me. Though I had given them strict orders to *stay the fuck away*, so, there was that.

Being a bastard was hazardous, apparently.

Inside the ice cream store we picked up two chocolate cones and enjoyed them as we made our way back to the cottage. I found the sweetness of the creamy treat soothing.

Beyond, the twinkling beach reflected the rising sun; the clear blue ocean spreading out and sparkling.

Pausing, I took in the view. "We should go for a walk along the sand."

"We're allowed?"

"Of course." I paused, taking a few more seconds to watch her lap her chocolate cone. It was purely erotic and she was so devastatingly unaware of it.

She seemed more herself, her usual stuck-up demeanor replaced with a naturalness as though her defenses had come down. I felt like she was finally letting me in.

I was letting her in, too.

She shrugged. "I've never been in the ocean."

"What?"

She reached up and wiped cream from the corner of my mouth, and the small gesture moved me beyond ordinary feelings. I dabbed my face with the napkin before throwing it into the trash.

She crunched on the last of her cone. "We can dip our feet in."

The beach was deserted except for us; we'd have all the privacy we needed.

"We can do better than that." I reached over and slipped a finger beneath an extra strap on her shoulder. "You have your bikini on?"

"Yes."

Sweeping her up in my arms, I carried her along the pathway and over the white sand, feeling it squish between my toes. She squealed with delight in my arms and kicked her legs playfully. We would seem like two lovers with no cares or troubles.

Once near the lapping shore, I set Pandora down and grabbed her dress by the hem and eased it up over her head, dropping it on the sand. Kicking off my shoes, I pulled off my shorts and T-shirt until I was only wearing my swimming trunks.

I picked her up again and carried her toward the shoreline, wading all the way in until I was chest deep with her still in my arms, enjoying her laughter.

I let her down slowly.

She sank into the water and her face lit up. "It's so warm."

"Let's swim out a bit." I waited for her to catch her stride.

She swam easily beside me, the ocean buffering us with small waves and the sun shining down on the clearness of the ocean.

"We found it," she said, her voice full of awe. "Damien, we found paradise."

I threw my head back in a laugh. "I suppose we did."

Or maybe paradise was wherever Pandora was.

My throat grew tight again as I thought about what I'd put her through, having to be seen as mine, for having to endure my world and all its flaws. It was like my heart had cracked open, leaving me vulnerable.

A tremor ran through me as I suddenly realized I had let myself fall in love with her.

CHAPTER
THIRTY-ONE

Pandora

"**A**ll I'm saying is, let me know if you want to leave. I'd
like to go with you."

I sat back on the couch, sipping my coffee. "I should
have left a note."

He'd wrapped his hands around his coffee mug, too. His expression was softer than I was used to—gone were the frown lines and all traces of concern.

Half an hour ago, we'd returned from our swim in the ocean and had even showered together. It was a nice romantic touch after our virtual standoff.

"Just be more self-aware," he said.

"Security are still out there." I looked in the direction of the team I never actually saw, toward the invisible men who gave us the illusion of freedom.

"I'm responsible for you." His brows shot up. "Is that my laptop?"

I'd placed it next to me. "Yes."

"You want to check your email?"

"I have my phone for that." When he wasn't going around confiscating it, that is. "Let's find out who sabotaged your project." I lifted his Mac onto my lap.

"How do you intend to do that?"

"You told me the project has been shut down. Come on, we're losing precious time." I patted the seat beside me.

Damien gave me a suspicious look as he sat on the couch next to me. "Something tells me you're about to surprise me."

"I'm polite enough to ask for your permission to access this information."

He leaned over and tapped in his password. "Please tell me you're joking."

"Yeah, maybe not."

With a few taps of his fingers, we were in. "There you go."

"What's this?" I pointed to the screen. "Is this the Fairfield Project?"

He leaned over and pressed his fingertip on the mouse pad, bringing up a series of architectural designs. "These are the schematics for my youth center with an after-school program." He pointed to the adjoining building. "An indoor and outdoor area where we'll hold sporting events." He pointed. "See, the housing is over here. This is where they can safely walk from here to there, back home."

"This is incredible."

"Right up until they ordered us to stop."

I gestured, indicating I needed control of the keypad.

Damien's hand rested on mine. "You don't need to do that."

"You know who hijacked your land?"

"Have my suspicions, yes."

"Who?"

"Helen King." Damien sat back, his expression pained.

My chest constricted. King refused to hide her contempt for political forward thinking. She was power hungry. If she had shut the project down, it would surprise no one.

"Were you going to try to figure it out?" said Damien.

"I was going to hack into the Title Office. See whose name was on record as taking over the land."

"Follow the money, and all that."

"This town is all about favors. Some cost more than others."

His brow arched. "Maybe I should be more wary of you."

I broke into a smile.

CHAPTER
THIRTY-TWO

Pandora

I t would have been polite to swim toward Damien and take that glass of freshly squeezed orange juice from his hand. He stood at the edge of the pool in his swimming trunks holding up two drinks, offering me one.

The view was regally spectacular. He looked tall and devastatingly handsome, his toned muscles kissed by the sun's golden rays as he presided over paradise.

He noticed I was staring at his assets, and waggled his eyebrows playfully.

Nibbling on my lower lip self-consciously, I continued to admire his striking, majestically sculpted form—perfectly proportioned as though plucked out of the Galleria dell'Accademia in Florence.

Our school trip to Italy had seen the entire class staring up at an exact replica of this man carved in marble. We'd gawked at the statue's perfectly chiseled features.

My gaze traveled up Damien's muscled calves to his firm thighs, that classic V a prelude to a taut belly and six pack abs.

"I see what you're doing there," he said, finally wading in toward me.

"I was looking over your shoulder at an exotic bird."

"Is that right?" He looked amused.

I waded forward to meet him halfway and accepted the drink from him.

"If you kiss me," I said, "I imagine it would make a great photo."

"Not sure that's necessary." But that sidelong glance told me he liked the idea.

"I think it's important we play our part," I added.

"You mean something like this?" He leaned forward and nuz-
zled my neck, his lips tracing my jawline and gliding to my ear-
lobe, causing a shiver of need to run through me.

He reached for my drink and moved over to set our glasses
on the edge of the pool. "Or are you thinking of something more
like this?"

He cupped my face and leaned in, pressing his mouth against
mine, sparking a passionate response from me. Our kiss erupted
into a frenzied attack. We explored each other's mouths with
firm lips and sensual tongues, deep and needy, wanton and full of
truth. Our secret affection spilled out, exposing our hearts.

I wanted this to be real. An authentic *us*, but I knew a love
like this wasn't possible. We were too entrenched on the path that
was expected of us and there'd been too much hate between our
families for this relationship to ever work.

He would always keep holding back.

For some reason, it hurt to believe this…and it shouldn't. I'd
been working for so long on not caring, but I couldn't get enough
of his touch. I found myself missing him even when he was close,
as though our love existed in an alternate universe and was bright
and vibrant but totally inaccessible.

He cupped my face and kissed my forehead. "You're not the
girl I thought you were."

"Is that good or bad?" I asked breathlessly.

His smile widened against my lips, feeding my anticipation,
causing hope to flare inside me.

"Damien…"

"What do you need? Tell me."

"Help me escape," I said quietly.

He pulled back abruptly and stared at me.

"Help me get out of this life."

Surprise filled his eyes. "You want me to…"

I tried to let my true feelings show in my eyes. "After the election, obviously."

"I can't do that."

My lips quivered. "But I can't live like this—as another person's symbol. No ability to choose my own way."

Because if I couldn't have him, it would be no one.

He pressed a fingertip to my lips. "I'll make it bearable."

So many times, I had secretly plotted a way out of this existence, planning to extract myself from a loveless family.

And later, *this* man.

Damien may have shown me his true colors and they were bright and vivid and so addictive—but it was an illusion.

Maybe it was all this pristine water that was having a healing effect, or the fresh air and the bright sunlight and the wildlife that showed little fear for humans. My thoughts were clearer because the clutter of chaos was gone.

Damien lifted me into his arms and waded over to the tile steps, carrying me out of the pool and over to the Jacuzzi. We descended the steps into the hot water and he nudged me up against the tile.

The shock of the steamy heat was welcoming. Bubbles caressed my skin and my thoughts wanted to wander free. My soul had been tricked into believing I'd found freedom here with Damien.

From his kisses trailing along my sensitive neck, to the way his lips found mine again and savaged me with a scorching passion that stole my breath, he halted time. Our frantic hands were searching and grabbing—his for my bikini and mine for his swimming trunks—until we'd set our bodies free to enjoy skin on skin contact with nothing between us but our lies.

His flesh felt hot against mine as we deliriously fought to remain close. Desperate to be closer still, I lifted my legs and wrapped them around his waist, drawing his cock toward me, tipping my hips in a way that begged for him to enter. That first thrust of his erection stretched me open.

Fully immersed, with only our heads above water, we moved against each other rhythmically, up and down, secretly fucking. We were one now. Every caress, every glance, and every touch tender and loving. His gestures first gentle and then savage, taking everything from me. Our feelings rose and clashed and fought for new ground, our passion rising to heights we couldn't deny—our awed expressions showing we were both aware of the bridge we'd crossed where there could be no more pretense.

Coming hard, my orgasm stole my breath and I tried and failed to catch it, feeling as though I were submerged beneath the water, drenched in him.

Time seemed to dissolve…

Damien pulled out and threw me a rueful smile. "We needed a condom."

His lips quickly found mine again, ravishing me, as though he wanted me to know we were something greater than before.

Both of us naked and hidden by trees, he carried me out of the Jacuzzi and along the pathway and into the cottage. Damien threw me down on the couch and knelt before me, easing my thighs apart. That same hungry mouth captured my other lips, the ones between shaky thighs, my clit tingling with bliss as his tongue traced along it lovingly.

My body went rigid, completely owned by him as he gave me over to euphoria, my body quivering as he effortlessly stole my soul. Love fluttered out of me like a blossoming flower as Damien unlocked my heart.

A blast of air-conditioning hit the droplets of water on my flesh, causing me to shiver, but all I cared about was being devoured by this man. His firm hands spread my thighs wider, until he'd seemingly had his fill.

Pulling me back up, he carried me down the hallway and kicked open the bathroom door.

Grabbing a condom from a discarded box on the countertop, he then pulled me toward the open shower.

In a daze, leaning against his bare chest, I felt the rush of heat from the water pouring over us. Here is where I wanted to stay… snuggled within these glass walls within the arms of my lover whose touch short-circuited my brain.

I watched as he pulled on the condom, his cock hard and ready.

He dipped his head to suckle on my nipple, his fingers generously remembering the other, sending shockwaves of deliciousness into me. Lifting me, he directed my thighs to wrap around his waist and then he plunged deep inside me with one thrust, sliding in and out like a steady piston.

"I'm going to fuck you hard, baby," he said, his voice full of sex and need.

I managed a nod before holding on, digging my fingernails into his back to endure the luscious sensations that soon morphed into a blinding intensity. Damien pounded me with fury against the tile, taking me higher again only this time I felt it was his turn to slip away.

His lips at my throat, I heard his moans mix with my cries, captured in the bondage of his masterful fucking.

Damien searched my face as he rode out the rest of his climax. His eyes locked on mine, his expression a mixture of lust and love. Withdrawing from me, he eased me down onto my shaky legs.

I studied his face.

"Don't do that," he said.

I looked at him inquisitively through the shower of droplets.

"Don't over think this," he added.

My hand moved swiftly to his nape and I pulled him in for a deep kiss, fearing my words might betray me. If spoken, they would bind me to him.

He pulled away as though needing to examine my reaction.

My lips quivered with emotion. "I thought all of this meant we might change the way we are with each other."

"The way we are?"

"That we'd be kinder."

He pulled me into a hug, squeezing me against his firm chest. "I might frighten you if I admit…"

My eyes shot up to meet his.

"I'm on the precipice." His eyes were filled with an emotion I'd never seen in him, the expression on his face held an aura of compassion as he gently stroked my arm.

But he hadn't fallen yet. Or maybe he had, and he was refusing to admit it. Though showing it seemed inevitable. The way he was with me felt more intense, more connected. His affection flowing freely.

Away from the shower, he dried me off and wrapped a towel around me, then dried himself off.

Reluctantly, I headed off in the opposite direction, wrung out from sex, glancing behind me to see his long, confident stride carry him away from me.

In the bedroom, I blow-dried my hair into waves and applied some light make-up. I decided to put on my flowery sundress and pumps.

Sounds from the kitchen drew me in that direction.

Damien stood at the central island preparing a large salad in a wooden bowl, filling it with lettuce, tomatoes, cucumbers and olives. Other vegetables waited on the counter to be chopped and added. The faint scent of garlic and roasting chicken filled the kitchen.

"You're cooking?"

"Don't sound so surprised."

"I want to help."

Glancing over to the main table that we'd not sat at once since we'd been here, I spied eight place settings.

"You invited people over?" I thought we didn't know anyone.

Damien uncorked a second bottle of wine and placed it on the dinner table. "I know it's our last evening, but we've had two days alone together." He came over and planted a kiss on the top of my head. "You've had fun, right?"

"You know I have."

He smiled. "I'll see that you have everything you need when we return to Washington."

"I want you to be happy, too, Damien."

"Then no more talk of escaping." He gave a nod of conviction. "We must show a united front."

I swallowed hard and pointed to the dinner settings. "Who's coming?"

"You and I weren't alone, even if we wanted to pretend we

were. There were secret service agents working around the clock protecting us."

"You invited them to dinner?"

"Yes, this is how we thank them—preparing a home-cooked dinner to show our gratitude."

"Have you done this before?"

"It's what my family's always done. Yours don't?"

"We give bonuses." It came out wrong. "Unless they're paid by the government."

"Never forget what we do." He pressed a fingertip to my chest. "We're here to serve."

Hugging him, I tried to fathom how I'd gotten this man so wrong. That time I'd been in his oceanside home, I'd seen a vicious man who was hell-bent on ruining my life, and now he was acting like some kind of gentleman.

A knock sounded at the door.

"Ask them what they want to drink. Two of them are still on duty so they'll decline alcohol. Help me make them feel welcome." He pointed a finger at me. "You can't drink in front of them. It's illegal in Florida."

"Sneak in a sip?"

"No." He grinned. "Not until they've gone."

"What will we talk about?"

He looked surprised. "Them. We make this about them. Because it is."

This was spontaneity; the ability to mingle with whomever I wanted. The normalcy I'd chased after.

With a wide grin, I headed for the door, opening it to be greeted by the warm smiles of the men, and one woman, who had protected us all this time.

I welcomed them in.

CHAPTER
THIRTY-THREE

Damien

The only person I wanted to see was *her*.

I searched the faces of the guests at this prestigious cocktail party, the burning sensation in my throat from this glass of Macallan doing nothing to distract me from thinking of the woman I wanted in my sights.

I'd missed her.

I'd gone four days without seeing her. How was it Friday already?

She'd be here soon. I wouldn't have to endure this black-tie event alone. Having all these people in my dad's home was stifling, even though the place was vast. I'd never been one for all this luxury; the lavish furnishings and parquet floors, the staff with endless drinks being offered to loosen tongues.

My fingers dug beneath my bowtie. It was hard to tolerate this stifling tuxedo after the casual T-shirts and shorts I wore during our brief escape to Florida.

We'd returned to Washington on Monday to the bleakness of the city…to the intensity of all that waited. With tensions flying high and tempers frayed from the chaos of the campaign, men had been broken by less. A billion dollars had been pumped into this endeavor and human lives were at stake from the policies we hoped to implement.

Losing wasn't an option.

I'd dived right in to join Dad's staff, spending my days and nights here. Giving over my soul to help see his vision realized as he ran for office.

Pandora had remained at her parents' place all week. The decision had been mine so she'd not feel lonely at my Foxhall house, since I'd not be able to visit.

I'd been working twenty-four hours a day—or so it felt.

We'd not seen each other since our return, only sharing a few cordial texts here and there. That was it.

Within the confines of that Sanibel cottage, my desires had taken over all reason. I'd been shaken, well enough to see what I wanted my life to look like.

My family hoped to carry America through a profound political awakening and there was no bandwidth for fragility.

Many of the guests had brought along their agendas that only my father could see realized. This was a playground of sharks. Scanning the crowd for the worst of them all, I looked around for Salvatore Galante. I'd grab some time with him later and try to extract what he had on Pandora's family. If anyone could persuade that fucker to drop the story on her dad, it was me. I'd go for diplomacy.

I'd do anything for her.

I downed the rest my Macallan to get rid of the taste of bitterness. Avoiding the more nefarious guests, I resigned to at least mingle and seek out the policy changers. The men with integrity. The game changers who genuinely cared about social issues. Equality, fairness, and a respect for humanity.

Hushed whispers hinted that someone important had arrived. It was her.

Like a breath of fresh air.

Dazzling.

My heart stuttered at the beauty of Pandora as she gracefully entered the ballroom.

She held her head high until she saw me, then she broke into an iridescent smile, looking stunning in a shimmering silver gown that matched her delicate clutch purse. Her hair was styled in a chignon, making her look both youthful and sophisticated, her classic style complemented by twinkling Van Cleef jewels.

Pandora behaved like a queen about to greet her people—regal and haughty, with that same closed-off demeanor I knew her for.

Both of us were starkly aware of the stares locked on us.

"Hi," I greeted her, reaching out and taking her hand.

"Damien." If her chilliness was meant to intrigue, it did.

I felt a rising desire to fuck her red pouty mouth with the burn of passion I'd suppressed for days. Somehow, I'd find the time for us to be together tonight.

My hand slid from the middle of her back to her lower spine…a physical prelude to what I was going to do to this woman later. I would start slow and then ravage her. Taste and devour her. Make her come again and again. Have her forget there'd been any lost time between us.

Her cautious eyes threw me a warning.

I followed the direction of her gaze and saw her parents standing amongst an elite crowd of billionaires. They were sipping champagne and making small talk. Many of the guests were hoping to find time alone with my father to offer their demands in exchange for helping pave his way into the White House. That door was closing fast.

For her parents, I was willing to accommodate a meeting with my father. After all, it was something she would want. Even now when my dad was being dragged in every direction, I would make it a priority.

I pulled her aside. "How are you?"

"Fine, thank you."

"Everything okay?"

"Yes, of course."

"You seem a little…chilly."

"It's cold." She turned from me and perused the room.

The ice maiden was back.

"Want my jacket?" I went to shrug it off.

She put a hand on my arm to stop me. "You can't be seen without it." Her expression softened. "But thank you."

"Let your father know I've secured time with the Senator tonight."

"The Senator?" She narrowed her glare. "You're so formal at these things."

I pointed to my chest. "*I'm* formal? If you were any more formal, we'd be calling you Your Majesty."

She threw me a sideways glance. "You must be pleased. Our trip to Sanibel was a success. How did the *New York Times* put it? '*The haughty daughter of Brenan Bardot finally knows her place.*'"

I cringed. "Thought you didn't read the news."

"You encouraged me to."

"The photos of us by the pool were quite something."

"I noticed."

"At least they had the decency to print the ones of us with our clothes on." I flashed a carefree smile.

"You used me at Sanibel. For your father's campaign."

I nudged Pandora into an alcove. "Not true."

"The press insinuated it."

"Fuck them. The public saw another side to you."

She read my face carefully.

"I had fun," I said with a playful smirk. "You didn't?"

"I respect the fact that things are busy for you—"

"Really? Because you seem to have no idea what really goes on in the world."

She went to walk away, but I grabbed her arm, smiling at a few guests who might have caught it. "Don't walk away from me."

She turned and faced me. "The polls are rising. You must be pleased, Mr. Godman. I'm no longer needed, apparently."

"We still have a week to go."

Her expression filled with pain as she eased out of my grip. "Darling, I'm off to powder my nose."

Her stride was as elegant as it was swift and full of pride.

Immediately, I regretted not sharing the truth—I'd fucking missed her. That every night I'd woken in a cold sweat because it was too late for me. Our weekend away had driven a passionate stake through my heart and somehow gotten it to beat again.

I'd been thwapping my cock in the darkness at night as I'd

tried to ease the strain of obsessing over her. Whatever spell she'd cast had burrowed deep.

I should go after her, demand she listened to the truth of what she'd done to me and how I really felt about her.

I'd fallen.

Like a million men before me with everything to lose.

Go tell her that.

Damn it.

Dad was signaling me from across the room—there was someone he wanted me to meet.

Telling Pandora my feelings would have to wait.

If she didn't leave before I got to her.

CHAPTER
THIRTY-FOUR

Pandora

Confusion now clouded my mind and my heart had been pulverized by Damien's coldness. I walked away from him, keeping my expression stony-faced to hide the pain I was feeling from all the people who watched me pass by. The agony of rejection wedged itself deep in my chest.

I'd been counting down the days and minutes and seconds until I could see Damien again. But the man who'd swept me off to a romantic getaway on Sanibel Island was now gone. Maybe my perception of him had only been an illusion.

More agonizing still, I'd fallen for his ruse to get me to appear carefree in that lush vacation setting, giving the press all they needed to present the Godmans as kings of Washington.

They had needed me to perform and Damien's charm had been a sure bet to get the ice maiden to crack so they could use me for his family's gain. He'd snagged a living, breathing Bardot.

Tears stung my eyes as I pushed onward toward the restroom. Ironically, it was the same one Damien had brought me into during their last event three weeks ago. He'd stood over me as I'd peed with the same quiet contempt he had shown tonight.

Staring at my reflection in the mirror, I realized how much of my heart I'd given to him.

All of me.

Every facet of myself had been given to Damien and delivered with my own hands, no less. Those dark circles beneath my eyes, hidden by makeup, were evidence of all the sleepless nights I'd suffered.

Leaving the event wasn't an option. Last time I'd left a Godman party, I'd been summoned into the Senator's study.

I looked into bright eyes that were good at faking happiness—I'd had many years of practice to master the art of suppressing emotions. All I had to do was return to the ballroom and search out a glass of water to swallow this lump in my throat. Then I would continue to perform my duty, offer a willing smile at anyone who looked my way and engage in pleasant conversation.

Damien doesn't love you.

I struggled to hide my grief for a relationship that could never be, dealing with regret because I'd promised myself I'd escape. Being away from him hurt. But what hurt more was knowing we could never have a truly loving relationship.

I left the restroom and saw Theo Tamer halfway down the hallway. He was leaning against the wall staring at his phone with his earbuds in, seemingly lost in thought.

I kept my eyes down as I walked past him.

"Hey," he called to me.

Pausing, I turned and gave him a wary look. "Hi."

Tamer was no doubt part of this conspiracy to manipulate me for the Godmans' benefit. We'd had an "interesting time" at the Ritz Hotel but he'd proven he was on Damien's side.

He removed his earbuds. "Heard you had fun on Sanibel."

"You shouldn't believe everything you read."

"That came from Damien."

"He set up some great on-camera moments."

"You okay?"

"Don't I look it?"

He stared at me. "Who upset you? I will hunt them down and make them pay."

My response was a slight shrug and a *nothing can be done* expression.

"Give me a whirl. I'm the go-to guy for the Powers That Be when shit needs fixing."

"Something tells me I'm one of the problems."

He closed the gap between us. "Haven't I proven my loyalty?"

I stepped away. "To everyone else, yes."

"Did someone say something?"

I headed down the hall. "Sorry to have interrupted your phone call."

He caught up and walked alongside me. "I'm listening to Duran Duran while I wait for someone."

"Who?"

"You've never heard of Duran Duran?"

I shook my head. "Who are you waiting for?"

"A new staffer needs briefing." Theo raised his phone. "Duran Duran's an 80s band." He looked amused. "You make me feel old."

"You're the same age as Damien."

"I'm older by three years. You make him feel old, too."

The tears I'd been trying to suppress stung my eyes. "I believed him. I believed he was enjoying himself on the island. That it wasn't just me who felt this way."

"You love him?"

I let out a sob. *That's why it hurts.*

"This is a good thing, right?" he soothed.

"He doesn't feel the same way."

"You guys had fun. Once this is over you'll have your entire life ahead of you. You'll meet someone super cool."

I took off down the hallway, not wanting to cry in front of him.

Theo shouted. "Pandora!"

Needing to compose myself, I quickly put distance between us, heading in the opposite direction of the event. I needed time to figure things out.

There was no other way—I was going to have to find another solution to my dad's looming scandal and stop that news story from going live. There had to be some kind of leverage I could use. I had the means, too. Access to contacts. The ability to dig deeper using tech.

I'd do it myself.

Oh, no.

Damien's brother was talking with someone at the end of the hallway.

Pivoting fast, I turned right, lifting my hem and scurrying off. A security guard stood at a doorway gesturing I couldn't go that way. I tried to retrace my steps but I couldn't remember which way I'd come.

I picked up speed as I rounded a corner—and bumped right into Carter's chest.

"Steady," he said, grabbing my arm and leading me away. "You can't be here. My dad's having a drink with the Ambassador of Germany. Security's a bitch."

"Let go." I was dragged behind his tall frame.

He glanced left and right as though checking to make sure no one was looking, and then he opened a door and pulled me inside an empty room, shoving me up against the wall.

Trapping me.

My breaths came short and sharp against the pressure of his firm chest as my arms pushed against him, my heart rate thundering in my ears. I tried to break free but he was too strong, too tall and too threatening.

"I heard about Sanibel." He whistled.

"Get off."

"No, I don't think so. My family paid for you fair and square."

"What are you talking about?"

"You for a seat at the table. I'm just taking what's ours."

"The last I heard my father wasn't in the running anymore."

"I know Damien is doing what he can to deal with that dumpster fire."

"He is?" It came out wistful.

He clutched my jaw. "Anything to get you to open your legs."

My face twisted in disgust, his touch causing sickness to roil in my stomach.

His lips snarled in a rebuke. "Those photos of you were something else." He dug his fingernails into my jaw.

"What?"

"You didn't see yourself in *The Inquirer*?"

My breath caught in my throat as the door flew open.

Damien barreled toward us and grabbed his brother by the scruff of the neck, yanking him back and thrusting him up against the door.

He pointed a finger in his face. "If you ever touch my fiancée again, I'll end you."

Carter smirked. "You don't even like her."

"That's not true."

"Really? I was there when you stormed into Dad's office and demanded a way out of your engagement."

"Asshole. That was before I'd met her."

"I'm the asshole?" He scoffed. "You're the one who was sent away to fix the mess you made. *Two* weeks before the election."

Damien glanced my way. "The issue's resolved."

"She's an issue?"

"That's not what I meant."

Carter shoved him back. "What I'm hearing is there's no sharing your bitch?"

The strike of Damien's fist into his stomach made Carter double over.

"If you come within one mile of my girlfriend—"

"Which one?" Carter gasped, his hand on his stomach. "So hard to keep up with them all."

"What the fuck is wrong with you!" Damien stepped back. "You're a sociopath."

"They always did say I take after Dad."

"That's not a compliment."

"Well, the last time I checked he's about to become President."

"He's just waiting for you to fuck it up, Carter."

"I'm not the one with a stalled multi-million dollar construction site. Fairfield was destined to fail."

Damien spun around to look at me, trying to appear calm.

"Did he hurt you?"

Trembling, I managed to shake my head to show I was okay.

"It's like arguing with a fucking wall." Damien straightened and tugged his jacket down, his demeanor becoming more composed.

"It's unlike you to lose it," said Carter.

Damien seemed to realize this, his brows knitting together as his gaze scanned over me. "I apologize on behalf of my brother."

My heart swelled with hope knowing that Damien had found and saved me.

Clutching my hand tightly, he led me out of the room.

We made our way through the mansion, reaching a sitting room that had a door that led out to a patio. We walked across the sprawling lawn and took a path over to a private terrace with a fountain in the center.

The tall sculpture at the top poured out a torrent of crystal clear water that cascaded down onto several levels. The sound was a welcome change from the chattering and raucous laughter of the guests.

"I won't leave your side again," said Damien. "Not when you're in the vicinity of anyone in my family."

"I walked away from you," I admitted.

I'd forgotten how many monsters were lurking nearby.

"I should have come with you." He looked me up and down. "Tell me you're okay."

"I am now."

We sat on the stone ledge of the fountain, me resting my head on Damien's shoulder and him hugging me into his side.

"Let me guess," I said. "Carter was bullied?"

Damien shook his head. "No, he's just an asshole."

"You can be just as arrogant, Damien."

He looked at me with mock surprise. "Me?"

I nodded slowly.

"How?"

"Remember how you were at Seascape?"

"Sure that was me?" He smirked.

I suppressed the emotion in my tone. "Things right now are chaotic. I get that."

He sighed. "We've come so far. We just need to stay the course. Everyone's exhausted and wound tight. Including me. I'm sorry."

I rubbed my hand up and down his back to soothe him. "You're giving it everything. I know that."

He kissed the top of my head. "I've been thinking."

"About?"

He straightened. "On Sanibel, you told me you wanted out. You never wanted this—" He pointed to our surroundings. "All of this had been thrust on you."

"I shouldn't have told you that."

"You asked me to help you escape. Now it's all I can think of."

"I didn't think you and I would work out."

"That's not what you want anymore, though, right? To be free of this commitment? Of me?" He looked conflicted.

"Could you ever love me?"

He stared at me. "You don't know?"

"Know what?"

He clenched his palms in frustration. "I promise to do everything in my power to make you happy."

"Phone me, that makes me happy." I loved hearing his voice. When he didn't call it felt like a strike to my heart.

He let out a frustrated sigh. "What if the way I feel traps you."

"I admit to saying those things."

"You're still young—"

"No, don't do that."

"You talked about wanting a career. I ignored what you were saying because I couldn't see any other way forward."

At least we were talking. Sitting here in the quiet garden finding time to just be together.

He pulled away, turning to look at me intently. "Tell me what you want."

I want you to love me.

"Other than your ridiculous name, you are too fucking perfect—from your blinding beauty to your ability to endure a man like me."

"You think my name's ridiculous?" I grinned at him. "Yeah, and wow—do I ever endure a lot."

His expression softened. "I want us to work."

"Because we have no choice?" I asked softly.

He broke into a sweet smile. "I'm quiet in the morning. Is that something you think you can cope with? I mean, until my first mug of coffee reaches my brain."

"Are you asking me…?"

"Move in."

"Aren't we meant to wait?"

"I'm done with appeasing others."

"I'm not sleeping in your spare room."

He pulled me onto his lap, his face nuzzling my neck.

Wide-eyed, I tried to comprehend the words he'd spoken, the invitation to live with him before we were married, my heart stuttering with the realization he was sincere.

Damien was going to say it…

He was going to confess his love. I held his stare, disappearing into chestnut eyes that reflected a multitude of complexities that now shone with tenderness.

My heart was beating faster than it ever had. I craved this man, craved his intoxicating touch.

"I have something for you." He slipped a hand into his pocket.

"Oh?"

Damien frowned in frustration as he looked up the pathway.

Someone was approaching.

It was Theo. "Sorry, bad time?"

"No, it's fine," I said, refusing to budge from Damien's lap.

Because we had the rest of our lives to tell each other how we felt. My love burned brightly for this man who held me in his arms.

My heart is telling me to stay.

Theo looked down at the bottle of tequila he was holding. He held three shot glasses in his other hand. "We have a problem, Damien."

"We do?" he replied.

"Pandora confessed to something shocking," said Theo.

Damien and I swapped a wary glance. My thoughts circled back to my discussion with Theo, and I tried to figure out what he was about to say.

Theo nodded slowly, frowning. "She's never heard of Duran Duran."

Damien threw his head back and let out a bark of laughter. "We have to rectify this."

"I know, right?" Theo stepped forward and raised the bottle.

"In all honesty, Duran Duran was before our time, too. Tamer's an 80s music geek." Damien lifted me off his lap and stood alongside me.

I leaned in and wrapped my arms around him, not wanting to return to the party just yet. His right arm tightened around me.

"Come on," said Theo. "She needs to experience one of the most successful bands of the golden era in music."

"You forgot to mention the hairstyles." Damien laughed and it made him look adorably young and carefree.

"I want to hear this music," I said.

"The lady has spoken." Theo uncorked the tequila bottle with his teeth. "A shot each to make the rest of the evening bearable." He set his phone on the edge of the fountain and pressed play.

"You realize she's too young to drink," said Damien, winking at me.

Theo ignored him. "This is from the Rio album."

A moody synth style sounded around us, a man's smooth lyrics mimicked an almost erotic groan.

"This one was written by lead singer Simon Le Bon."

Damien reached out and took the bottle of tequila from Theo, tipping it back to take a gulp. His mouth made an O as though the liquor burned his throat. "Pure genius."

"I like it," I said, amused as Damien sang along.

I gestured my insistence for a drink.

Damien grabbed a shot glass from Theo and poured some tequila into it, then offered it to me, the spark from his touch sending electricity into my hand.

"Tamer, what did you really want?" asked Damien.

Theo looked at him. "Salvatore Galante isn't coming."

Damien flinched.

Watching his reaction, I wondered if Damien had intended on speaking with Galante tonight. Theo and Damien swapped a look of frustration.

I raised my shot glass in a toast. "To new adventures at Vanguard!"

"No." Damien gave a forced smile.

That sounded like him taking back control.

"Godman has only one more week left to visit Vanguard," said Theo. "Then he's cut off."

Damien smirked. "Those days are over."

Theo seemed to be studying his reaction. "One week, buddy."

"I need you to piss off now." Damien gestured for Theo to leave. "Take your 80s band with you."

"Fuck off." Theo threw him a big grin as he reached for his phone.

He walked back up the pathway with the enticing bottle of tequila; probably a good thing as I was going to have to rejoin my parents at some point.

I studied Damien's face. "You're not going back to Vanguard?"

He ignored that and stared into the fountain's pool of water. "What I was going to say before we were interrupted..."

"What?"

"Make a wish." He pointed to the fountain.

I closed my eyes and sent out a secret prayer *for us.*

I heard him approach me, felt his presence.

"Keep your eyes closed." He took my hand and placed an object on my palm. "Have a look."

I opened my eyes to see a blue sapphire ring—the same one from the store on Sanibel Island…the one I'd fallen in love with.

"That was your favorite?" He looked hopeful.

"Yes! It's beautiful."

The one I'd dreamed of.

He eased the emerald engagement ring off my finger and tucked it into his pocket, replacing it with the sapphire ring, the blue stone shimmering.

I pressed my body to his chest. "You remembered."

"Of course I remembered." Damien looked at me, his expression pleased. "This is how I prefer you. Smiling."

"I'll move in with you."

His face lit up. "Now it's my turn to smile. Not that you had any choice in the matter." He nudged my arm playfully.

CHAPTER
THIRTY-FIVE

Pandora

Whenever I'd imagined what kind of man I'd end up with, I'd never considered the possibility he'd be into this: a dark dungeon filled with unusual devices.

Having only moved in yesterday—the same day Damien had asked me to—I suspected this would all become familiar. Damien would frequently lead me down here and choose one of these pieces to use on me.

Opening a drawer, I peeked inside and removed a leather strap with a chain on the end, realizing I was holding a leash. My smile flittered when I imagined him using it on me.

"You need a collar," Damien's voice boomed from the doorway.

Pivoting, I clutched the leash to my chest. "Do I get one?"

He looked devastatingly handsome in his white shirt and ripped jeans, his dark hair ruffled casually.

He stepped in and walked across the room. "See anything you like?"

"Am I allowed in here?"

"As long as you don't use anything to pleasure yourself, yes."

"Because only you're allowed to touch me like that?"

"Masturbation is forbidden."

"Unless I can't help myself," I teased.

He didn't laugh. "Want your collar?"

"Yes, please."

"Then earn it."

How would this work if I was always compelled to rebuke him. I suppose that was the point, we'd find our way in all of this—him bossing me around and me reveling in the way he mastered me.

Falling to my knees, I assumed the position and gazed down at the floor, remembering the pose he'd once told me to hold.

"Permission to speak, sir."

"Granted."

"I want to see our sex tape."

"You mean my sex tape?"

"Yes, sir."

"Why don't we familiarize you with everything in here first."

Damien closed the space between us and assisted me to my feet. He escorted me around the room giving me the grand tour, showing me his collection of nipple clamps, sex tongs that widen a woman's labia, whips and chains and toys and restraints, paddles and blindfolds and feathers, a suede flogger, and a collection of vibrators.

More alarming still was the antique collection of torture devices he had hung on the walls, which he pointed out were merely for décor.

Though with him anything was possible.

Already my panties felt damp from the expectation of how a scene with him would play out.

"Am I ready?" I asked softly.

"Are you?"

"Yes."

He brushed a few strands of hair out of my face. "Get undressed."

Damien was no longer touching me, but my skin felt like he was as I slid off my pumps and stripped out of my jeans and blouse. I pulled off my underwear slowly, the blue sapphire twinkling on my left ring finger…a reminder that whatever we did in this room we did as lovers.

Naked, I was led across the room by my master, who directed me to stand between two tall posts. He slipped my wrists into cuffs, pulling the straps wide so that my arms were stretched out on either side of me. There was no getting out of this. My legs were free, but even those he controlled by showing me how to stand with my feet apart.

I wanted to ask him not to hurt me too much, to keep the pain at a minimum, but I felt exhilarated, too.

Standing before me, he held up an iPad and showed footage that had been recorded in this room…in the bed where he took me for the first time. Mesmerized, I watched the moment when he had thrust deep inside me, taking my virginity. My body couldn't help responding as though it was happening all over again. I recalled having him above me, that pinch of pain, the deep ache and then what followed, a sense of euphoria.

He must have been reading my expression because his eyes softened, as though asking an unspoken question.

"Whatever happens, I'll always be yours," I said, my voice a mere whisper.

"Let's begin."

He set the iPad down on a long table and brought back two metal clips that he worked to fit each nipple. Damien tightened them until the pinch became a throbbing sensation; the same one I'd craved. The same one that seemed connected to my pussy.

Lifting a leather whip off the table, he tapped it in his palm as he approached me slowly, threateningly, then let it glide along my limbs until my flesh tingled with need. He strolled behind me and I felt a flash of pain and heat as he struck my butt. My breaths came short and sharp as he continued to strike my buttocks.

Damien moved on to a small spiked roller that he weaved around my chest, right over my over-sensitized nipples that were still captured in clamps, causing me to jolt and gasp.

I felt dizzy by the time he stopped, and then I watched him remove his wristwatch and throw that on the table, too. He stripped out of his shirt revealing his toned, tanned muscles and six pack abs.

In a haze, I was lulled by the toys he brought over, one after the other. The vibrators that he seemed to carefully choose, the same ones he placed on my clit to thrum it into another universe.

"Today, it's all about Pandora's pleasure," he whispered.

Unable to answer, I merely nodded, peering down as he pried open my labia with his fingers to reveal how wet he'd made me. He placed a rounded wand on my clit and it cherished that small nub with a violent tremor. I forgot to breathe.

Then he pulled it away just as quickly.

"I need more," I managed.

"You need what?" he teased.

"To come."

He moved over to a corner of the room and fetched what appeared to be a curved red seat on a sturdy base. He eased open my thighs and slid it between my legs so that I was sitting on it—straddling the saddle. With my hands outstretched and secured in cuffs, I couldn't refuse him anything.

He flicked a switch on its side and the seat vibrated with a dangerous ferocity, causing my entire bottom half to shudder vigorously. It shocked my pussy into an instant orgasm. My cheeks flushed as I realized I was copiously soaking the seat with my arousal.

Another climax snatched away my self-consciousness and thundered through me like a runaway freight train. I gripped the seat with my thighs, jaw slack, exulting in this full body explosion of sensations with my tits bouncing, their clamps tugging, feeling another detonation of pleasure.

I was only vaguely aware of Damien as he stood back watching my violent ride, his expression serious, as though gauging my reaction to the intensity of the undulating seat.

My moans and screams echoed around us.

Head back, I rode out yet another orgasm. Owned by this moment, by him, I could do nothing but endure another forced cresting.

Having almost passed out, I felt him undo the cuffs and set

me free. He carried me across the room and laid me on the bed, his hand brushing over my face to bring me back to reality.

I tried to smile, tried to find a way to express how profound this experience had been for me.

"Fuck me," I said at last.

Damien's zipper was already undone and his tip quickly nestled against my slick entrance, then his cock was thrusting deep, thrusting hard, pounding me as though he was aware it was him I really needed most.

Small tremors shook my body like little earthquakes.

My legs wrapped around his waist as I was snatched up into another climax, oblivion finding me as I felt him lose control.

Finally, I drifted off to sleep in Damien's arms.

CHAPTER
THIRTY-SIX

Pandora

When you find the perfect life, you naturally want it to last forever. I found that I was willing to do anything to keep Damien.

Even this...

It was the biggest risk I'd ever taken in my life, turning up unannounced at Salvatore Galante's Granger Street office.

It had been a gamble thinking I could gain access to the Chairman and CEO's top floor suite. His security was high because of the number of death threats he probably received. The AFN served as an extended arm of the party that couldn't be trusted—or so my father insisted. "A propaganda machine", he'd called it.

I imagine the fact I was here to see him wasn't even passed on to Salvatore. Either that or he'd guessed I was going to beg him not to run that story on my father, and no doubt wanted to avoid the drama that would ensue from meeting with me.

I'd failed to get any farther than the receptionist's desk in the ground floor lobby, ending up back in the car that had brought me here. Randolph, one of my parents' drivers, threw wary glances my way from the front seat.

"I needed to speak with someone, but I was turned away," I explained. "Thank you for being patient."

"Of course, Ms. Bardot." He gave a nod. "Can I help?"

It was risky, but I couldn't see any other way. "I need to speak with Salvatore Galante."

He looked surprise. "Did you make an appointment?"

"Not exactly. But as it's me, I thought he'd be intrigued."

"Does your father know you're here?"

"I plead the Fifth."

Randolph paused, studying my face. "Here's a thought. We could drive to the 118 News Club on Third Street and wait for him to go in." Randolph glanced at his watch. "We'll arrive before him if we leave now."

"How often does he eat there?"

"Every day, I believe. Your father eats there on occasion. I've driven Mr. Bardot to the club and seen Galante go in there, which means he's also a member. I imagine that's where he picks up a lot of political tips."

"Okay, let's try that," I said. "Thank you, Randolph."

Traffic was slow, but we made it to the club in less than thirty minutes. I knew what Galante looked like. Everyone in this town did—he and his three sons ruled the airwaves with their hateful rhetoric and twisted stories. They'd ruined reputations and left a trail of devastation. That kind of thing tends to make you stand out.

We parked next to the curb outside and waited for him to appear.

Popping in my earbuds, I tried to listen to music to make the time go faster…songs from Hozier to Adele to Billie Eilish.

My heart skipped a beat…

Galante's car had parked behind ours and he was climbing out. The crowned head of news appeared just as tall and intimidating as he was on TV, looking ruggedly handsome in a white fox kind of way—if you were into evil, that is.

He was immediately flanked by two bodyguards.

Once out of the car, I headed in his direction, managing to catch up with him at the stone steps leading up to the 118 News Club.

"Mr. Galante!"

He looked my way, his glare taking me in. "Do I know you?"

"Kind of." I stepped forward, wary of his guards who were poised to shove me back. "May we speak in private?"

"Make an appointment," he snapped.

"Your secretary failed to pass on my message?"

It was as though a veil lifted and he recalled where he'd seen me before. "You're Brenan Bardot's daughter?"

"Yes, sir."

He looked me up and down, making my skin crawl with the arrogant way he surveyed me. "Is this about your father's scandal?"

"I'm asking you not to discuss those lies on your network," I said.

He looked intrigued. "Did your father send you?"

"No, and I would be grateful if you would show respect by not mentioning it. Either in public or on your news station."

"Have any updates you want to share?" He looked triumphant. "Like any contradictory information to what we might have?"

What did they have on my father?

"I think you'll find your information false, Mr. Galante. We'll file a libel lawsuit."

"We'll countersue." He went to step up and then paused to look back. "You're Damien Godman's fiancée?"

"I am, yes."

He gave a nod, his tongue running along his lower lip. "Quid pro quo."

"Are you asking me to betray my boyfriend by giving you something on him?"

He shoved his hands into his pockets. "I am."

I folded my arms, my heart aching.

"Well?" he pushed. "I'm waiting. What have you got?"

"Can I think about it?"

"Sure."

"I've thought about it. When hell freezes over." I'd just spoken those words to the most powerful man in television.

Galante smirked. "I hear you once wanted to be a journalist, Ms. Bardot?"

"I wrote a piece for the *Washington Post*."

"That's right." He reached into his pocket and handed me his business card. "My number. Let me know when you're ready for the exchange of information on the Godman family. You have until Saturday. The news story about your father goes live at 5:00 P.M."

That was just days before the election.

"Never going to happen," I said.

"Well, then, get some marshmallows to roast on the fire. It's going to be a scorcher."

Bastard.

He didn't care about people. Just his stupid ratings and his ability to ruin lives with his news show spewing lies.

Holding his business card in my fingers, I peered down at his name embossed above the *Real Nation One's* logo, the station designed to manipulate viewers into thinking this man cared about this country. All he cared about was his ego and wielding his influence in exchange for power.

Galante reacted to something he spotted down the street and then turned and quickly ascended the steps to the club.

Following his line of sight, I couldn't see exactly what had drawn his attention. A few people were heading this way. Tucking the business card into my purse, I walked back to the car.

A pretty brunette strolled by me. She looked out of place in her ripped jeans and baseball cap, like she didn't want to be seen. She was looking up in the direction of the club. I caught a glimpse of a mole on her right upper lip. Except for the dark hair, she reminded me of Marilyn Monroe. She wore a ruby pinky ring. An interesting choice; I wondered if she knew wearing it on that finger represented self-love and an aversion to commitment. Monroe's doppelganger elegantly ascended the stone steps to the entrance.

Her lack of confidence was glaring. I'd grown up with the type of women who thought nothing of strolling into elite clubs filled with alphas with their heads held high. She didn't fit the profile. I wondered what she was doing here.

On a hunch, I followed her up the steps.

The interior was pleasantly designed with marble flooring and classic wood molding to enhance the swanky style.

Peering through the front window, I watched her stroll across the foyer to greet Galante. He put an arm around her shoulders and they walked through a doorway.

Were they having lunch together?

It was none of my business, but it certainly looked like an affair. Or maybe she was his daughter and I was over thinking it.

Defeated, I returned to the car.

"Thank you for making that happen," I told Randolph.

"You're welcome, but please don't tell anyone," he said nervously.

"Never." Pulling on my seatbelt, I said, "The Foxhall residence, please."

"How did it go, Miss?" he asked.

I sighed. "As expected."

CHAPTER
THIRTY-SEVEN

Damien

What the fuck were you thinking?

I didn't say it though. I merely leaned on the kitchen counter and offered Pandora a kind smile to reassure her that I was glad to see her home. She'd walked into the house a minute ago and stopped short when she reached the kitchen.

I wasn't alone and it seemed to startle her.

Bardot had only moved in with me three days ago, and already, she'd almost destroyed an empire in less than twenty-four fucking hours.

From her expression of guilt, she knew that we knew what she'd done. Her uneasy gaze bounced from me over to Madeline. She was also probably wondering if she'd walked in on something between me and my ex.

I rounded the central island and pulled Pandora in for a hug, kissing her tenderly on the lips to show her all was well—or at least as well as it could be when your girlfriend had just met with the most dangerous media mogul in the world.

She had put herself on his radar, which meant I was now, too.

I rested my hands on her shoulders.

She forced a smile at Madeline. "Hey."

"Hey." Madeline gave her a warm smile back.

"Coffee?" I moved away, not waiting for an answer, needing to keep my hands busy while my brain ran through the best way to deal with the situation.

"Damien invited me over," Madeline began.

"I'm glad." Pandora looked fine with it, but then again that was her. Always accommodating and effortlessly presenting her best self.

I slid the fresh mug of coffee over the countertop toward her. "I know about your meeting with Galante."

Pandora approached the barstool and sat down, her brows knitting together. "I thought so. But how?"

Madeline cast a glance my way. "Galante is dangerous. We think it's best—"

"We?" Pandora's frown deepened.

I let out an exasperated sigh. "Just come out and fucking say it."

Madeline's fingers traced the handle of her mug. "Not sure if you Googled me some more or not, but if you dug deep enough, you'd have seen that ten years ago I was a media strategist with a brilliant career ahead of me. That's how I met Damien."

"Stick to the point," I said firmly.

Madeline shook her head at me. "Damien, don't interrupt."

I gave a nod of apology.

Madeline continued, "Galante threatened to run a story on me and my lover at the time. The threat of it being published chased me out of politics."

"What did he have on you?" asked Pandora.

Madeline pursed her lips. "Photos of me as a dominatrix."

Pandora studied her face. "That's why you're a lecturer now?"

"Galante's threat fast-tracked me into a new career. This is also why Damien and I are never seen in public. In case those photos ever emerge."

Pandora genuinely looked sad for her. "Why did he threaten you?"

"Galante was intent on dismantling the entire campaign staff, of which I was a senior member. It was his way of influencing the election. I was caught in the middle...collateral damage."

Pandora flashed me a confused look.

Madeline sighed. "The man who was also in the photos with

me was my male submissive. He had everything to lose. Had I let Galante show the photos, his career would have been over. He deserved my protection."

A man whose name she wouldn't say...

"Did you date Damien before or after the photos were taken?" asked Pandora.

"Before...him," I told her.

Pandora frowned. "Salvatore gathers something on everyone, doesn't he?"

I nudged my mug aside. "Except on my family, as far as we know."

"Senator Godman is always careful," said Madeline.

"What did you discuss with Galante today?" I asked.

Pandora stared at me. "Who told you?"

"Answer the question," I insisted.

"I asked him not to run that news piece on my dad."

"And?"

"He wouldn't listen."

"You brought the spotlight down on us," I scolded.

Madeline moved around the island and grabbed her Hermes bag on the way. "I should go."

"Thank you for stopping by." With a gesture, I offered to show Madeline to the door.

We made it to the hallway without looking at each other, both of us aware that Pandora would be keeping us in her sights.

Madeline pulled a scarf up and over her head, putting on sunglasses to round out her disguise. "I like her," she whispered.

"She's *the one*." I shrugged at how easy that felt to say.

"I think you're right."

"Thank you for encouraging it."

Her lips softened in a knowing smile.

On the front porch, I tried to find the words to say what I had always failed to express to her. "I'm sorry I couldn't save you back then."

She shook her head. "I would have brought you down, too."

I would always cherish our friendship and I would always admire the sacrifice she'd made. She'd put herself last and protected everyone around her.

"Galante's unstoppable," she said.

"Maybe he'll drop dead from a heart attack. Everyone's wishing it."

"Thoughts and prayers." She lowered her sunglasses and winked.

I watched her head up the driveway toward her car and then I turned and went back inside.

Pandora wasn't in the kitchen.

In the hallway, I noticed that the red door was open…she'd gone down to the dungeon. Following her, I braced myself for a possible argument about my ex being here. Maybe I should have texted her to let her know.

When I found Pandora, she was sitting in the dark on the edge of the bed, seemingly lost in thought.

She looked up. "What can be done?"

"In what respect?"

"How are we to stop him from releasing the story?"

I loomed over her. "If you ever decide to go rogue again, I will lock you in here and never let you out."

She started to stand up but I nudged her back down. "Are you listening?"

"You told me I can't talk about it in this room."

"Then why are we in here?"

"I needed somewhere quiet to think."

"I get that."

She nibbled on her lip. "Where do we keep the sex tape?"

"In a safe place." I threw her a reassuring smile.

"If he runs that story, you and I will be like you and Madeline. We won't be able to be seen together in public. Ever again."

She was right. We'd be torn apart. Her father's scandal could cause my father's people to panic. What would follow would be them asking the impossible of us.

A ripple of dread caused me to freeze—I'd known it could happen, but I'd been in denial. I'd fought hard to do the right thing for everyone.

Pandora fell back onto the bed. "I've only just moved in."

I lay down beside her, staring up at the ceiling, futility finding me in the darkness. Part of me felt like I'd already lost her.

CHAPTER
THIRTY-EIGHT

Damien

Being given permission to walk into a room to speak with my dad wasn't a new experience. Though now, with the security cranked to the max and the hustle and bustle of staffers and the campaign crew filling the hallways of my family home, it felt like pandemonium had been unleashed.

I finally entered Dad's office, gladly closing the door behind me to cut out the noise.

"You wanted to see me?" I threw a contemptuous glance at my brother as I walked across the room.

Carter stood beside Dad. He'd been leaning over his shoulder and pointing at something on his desk, a smarmy expression on his face.

My father sat behind his desk with a dangerous glint in his eyes. Paperwork was stacked so high on his desk it would be a miracle if he ever got to all of it.

"I'll see you later, son," said Dad.

My brother shoved past me, his shoulder deliberately pushing mine. His shot of aggression didn't go unnoticed.

"What's that all about?" Dad pointed to the chair opposite his desk.

"A misunderstanding." I left it at that.

I took a seat, casually crossing my legs.

Telling him how badly behaved Carter was around Pandora wasn't what he needed to hear. Dad had international issues to worry about and this was the way it had always been—us protecting the head of the family from trivial matters.

"How are you?" He leaned over the desk and weaved his fingers together.

"Fine. More importantly, how are you?"

"I'm proud of the man you've become, Damien."

"Thanks, Dad." I hid my surprise.

"I want to bring you in."

"Are you offering me a position in your Cabinet?"

"Nepotism is just working with the people you trust most."

"I'll always be here for you, you know that."

"Then your answer is yes?"

It was a *no*, but he didn't need to hear that right now.

When I hesitated, he shook his head at my reticence and slid a file across the desk towards me. "Take a look."

Okay then, business as usual.

Lifting the file and skimming through it, I was surprised to see a collection of photographs, all of beautiful women. "Do these come with resumes?" I looked up at him, confused.

"We'll get more info on them."

"What am I looking at? Your top picks for a press secretary?"

"Keep the file. Let me know your choice."

"Well, it would be helpful to know the context."

"We got an advanced copy of the story *Real Nation One's* going to run on Brenan Bardot." He slid another folder over to me. "It's worse than we thought."

"In what respect?"

"It's all in there."

"Make a deal with Galante." I threw the folder of potential staff back on the desk. "Once you're in the White House give him some extra access for his channel."

He tapped the folder I'd just handed back. "Break it off with Pandora."

"What are you talking about?" *But I knew.*

"That folder contains prospective girlfriends."

"What the fuck, Dad? No, you're not doing that to me again." I flicked the file his way. "Fuck off."

"A scandal like this…"

I pushed to my feet. "I'm not calling it off."

"We've discussed this with her parents. They're going to explain it to Pandora."

"You don't get to make that decision for us."

His fist thumped the desk. "We've come too far to have our chances ruined now."

"I'll find another way."

"Your Fairfield Project. How much do you want it?"

The air crackled with tension; his threat weaving around a punishing promise. The truth of what he'd done—and what could be undone—reflected in those dark irises.

"What are you saying?" I asked softly.

"Family comes first."

How could it be worth it? To gain the highest office but lose your soul.

"We can't be seen as weak, son."

"I know that."

"Maybe construction will resume on Fairfield." he said with the calmness of a sociopath. "If you do the right thing."

The right thing…

What was this? Blackmail? Yes, that's exactly what this man was doing…to his eldest son…to the boy who'd grown into a man feeling nothing but admiration for his father.

Until now.

My mouth went dry and I couldn't form the words to respond to his abhorrent offer.

"You have until the end of the day." He shooed me away. "Send in Theo."

Fetch Theo yourself.

You're not the President yet.

I walked out of his office, my gut twisted and wrenched, fearing they had already gotten to Pandora.

CHAPTER
THIRTY-NINE

Pandora

H ad he forgotten his key? Or maybe because of the down-
pour Damien didn't have time to dig for it, I thought,
listening to the insistent rapping. I rushed to the front
door to let him in.

Theo was hunched beneath an umbrella and getting soaked,
his voice almost drowned out by the driving rain.

"Hurry, come in," I said, opening the door wider. "Put your
umbrella there."

He shook it outside first and then rested it in the corner.

"Let me take your coat."

"I'm fine." He followed me toward the kitchen. "I have a key,"
he admitted. "Didn't want to scare you."

"It would have been fine." I watched to see if he glanced toward the red door. At least he was polite enough to feign no interest at what went on downstairs.

"Damien's not here." I headed over to the coffeemaker.

"Figured."

"Let me get you a hot cup of java. Unless you'd prefer tea?"

I reached for my phone on the countertop.

"Don't look at that right now." He raked his fingers through
his hair. "I need you to trust me. Do you think you can do
that?"

"What's wrong?"

"Can you pack a bag? I can help if you like."

"Where are we going?"

"We have a place in the city. Damien will meet us there."

"You still share a place with him?'

"It's where we host meetings when we don't want to bring people to our homes, and for times when the office is too formal and hotel lobbies are too public."

He'd mentioned the place once. Told me something about Madeline staying there while she was buying a home. "Did he say why we have to go there?"

Theo's frown deepened. "I don't need coffee. Best if you turn it off, actually."

After unplugging the coffeemaker, I tried to figure out what he wasn't saying. "I'll call him." I reached for my phone again.

"We need to go, actually. Right now."

Theo hurried me upstairs to the bedroom and watched me pack. I gathered my toiletries from the bathroom and stuffed my clothes into my bag, all the while going over a thousand different scenarios as to why we had to leave so suddenly. I longed to question Theo, but he was insistent we talk on the way there.

My heart was thundering and my hands were trembling. I'd been ushered out of places with little notice before but usually I knew why—a security threat or a last-minute meeting that meant we all had to cut our day short and hop on a plane somewhere. Once your father enters politics your day becomes fluid.

After locking up the house, Theo drove us across the city.

To my frustration, our conversation did not cover why this was happening.

By late afternoon, we arrived at Ten Ten Mass, a tall building in the heart of Washington D.C. We walked through the lobby and Theo thanked the bell boy for helping wheel my suitcase into the elevator. He told him we would continue on alone, both of us ascending rapidly to the top floor.

"How long will we be here?" I asked. "I'm cooking for us tonight. It's a surprise." I'd searched out a recipe and ordered the ingredients. I was excited since it would be the first time I'd done anything like this for Damien.

"Sounds nice." Theo reached for his keys.

Pulling my suitcase along, he ushered me out of the elevator and along a swanky private hallway. We reached the front door and with a turn of his key, Theo let us in.

Once inside, I stood in the sparse living room feeling confused.

He didn't miss a beat, just went on ahead and insisted he provide a tour of the place. "The kitchen's nice, fully stocked. But you can order anything you want from the menus on the counter over there," he said, pointing. "There'll always be a security officer outside. Order food for them, too. Best way to win them over."

"Has there been a threat?"

"No." He continued to show me around. "Down there is another bedroom. That one has a bathroom en suite. I think the main bedroom will be yours."

"And Damien's."

"Right. In here's an office. Feel free to use it. Oh, let me show you the TV controls in the sitting room—" He ushered me back that way. "We've set up all the channels: HBO, Netflix, and Hulu."

"I can work it out." Panic rose inside me as we entered the sitting room. "How long am I staying?"

"It'll be best if Damien explains."

"When will he be here?"

Theo glanced at his watch. "Soon."

This isn't right.

Everything felt wrong as I tried to peer through the rain-drenched windows, seeing only murky grayness. "Theo, tell me what's going on."

Theo fished his phone out of his pocket. A relieved expression crossed his face as he read a text. "Okay, good. Damien's in the elevator."

Oh, thank God.

"I'll leave you two to talk." Theo stepped forward and started to hug me, but then seemed to think better of it. "You have my number. Call me if you need anything."

"I have to call my parents." I reached for my phone.

"Don't. Not yet. Not until you've spoken with Damien."

"Is something wrong with my family?"

"No, trust me on this. Damien's got it." He gestured. "I should go."

With the slam of the front door, I was left alone. I looked around at the masculine décor with its silver and brown tones and its minimalistic furniture.

Scurrying into the bathroom, I peed and then washed my hands, listening for Damien's arrival. Clean towels were hung over the bathroom door and I used one to dry my hands. Two plush bathrobes hung on an ornate hook.

I already missed his house.

Near the sink, I saw a selection of bottles and creams of *Rare,* Damien's favorite product line for men, proving he used this place. Opening a cabinet, I peered in at the row of toiletries…and packets of condoms.

This was a fuck pad.

Damien's voice echoed down the hall, beckoning me.

Retracing my steps, I met him in the sitting room. Damien stood there, tall and handsome in a droplet-covered raincoat. His eyes looked haunted and his face wore a conflicted expression.

The hairs on my nape prickled.

"I don't like this place." I took a deep breath. "Can we go home?"

He turned his attention to the blurred landscape through the murky windows.

Answers had been within my reach, if I had chosen to use the phone in my handbag. This was why I'd failed so many times—trusting others to know what was best for me. Not listening to my gut when it told me to take action. I'd always let others decide what was right for me.

"Damien, what's going on?"

A little shrug as he failed to meet my gaze. "Nothing's changed between us."

Stepping back, I put some distance between us as though it would stop the pain from reaching me.

There'd been no rushing forward to embrace me. No big smile to greet me. Just a guilt-ridden expression he couldn't hide.

My fingers scrunched my sweater as I worried over his anguish.

"I want you to stay here." He gave a nod. "You and I will privately continue to see each other."

"What's happening?"

He shook his head. "I couldn't persuade him."

Who? His father?

It was actually happening.

The ground beneath my feet felt unsteady. Through a haze, I heard the rain striking the window as the torturous seconds seemed to drag on for an eternity.

"I'm sorry." He looked at me, his dark eyes full of pain. "Your father's scandal—"

"Do you know what he did?"

"I can't stop the story from running."

I shook my head. "What is this place?"

Damien seemed to realize my insinuation. "Theo uses it more than me."

"When was the last time you were here?"

"Can't remember."

"Tell me!"

"A month, something like that."

I pointed to the bathroom. "Are those your condoms?"

He stepped closer. "Don't accuse me of being that man."

"What kind of man are you? A man who always does what his father asks?"

He pinched the bridge of his nose. "I'll visit you."

"And what? You and I will never be seen in public together again?" My chest tightened as I struggled to control my emotions. "You're breaking off our engagement?"

"You and I are still very much together."

"You're denying me in front of the world because of something my father did twenty years ago?"

"We have to keep our heads down until this is over."

"It will never be over."

"In four years—"

"Your dad will run for another term!"

"This place is temporary. They won't look for you here."

"You're keeping me in your fuck pad?"

His eyes widened as though realizing what he'd done.

I'd never be anything more than a lover he couldn't acknowledge.

He was destined to marry someone else, someone good for *their* image.

In the meantime, my father's reputation would be decimated, his career in politics sabotaged by misconduct committed ages ago—a stain permanently on our name and a dynasty sacrificed so that the Godmans could rule.

What had Madeline called herself? Collateral damage.

"You expect me to stand by and let you do this to my family?" I whispered.

He sighed. "What else can you do?"

"You underestimate me." I swallowed hard. "Did you ever love me?"

"Yes, of course."

"Do you love me now?" My hand shot up when he moved closer. "Stay there."

"I'll always love you."

"This is the first time you've ever said it."

"You told me you wanted out. I was waiting to see if you changed your mind."

"Tell me when you last fucked a woman here."

"Don't."

"I want to know." *Needed to know.*

He ran a hand through his hair. "We're not having this discussion."

"Last week?"

"I haven't slept with anyone since you and I were thrown into a fake relationship." He shook his head. "It wouldn't have looked good."

I reached for my handbag, my fingers fumbling for my phone. "I need to know what they're saying about me."

"The news isn't out yet. Just speculation. My father is working on damage control."

"I'm a liability?"

All of this was being done in backroom negotiations. This was why Theo didn't want me looking at my phone. My parents would demand my return home.

"Have you talked with my dad?" I asked.

"It will happen tonight."

"With me?"

"No, just your parents and me. A meeting at their place."

"A meeting? I should be there."

"Let me handle this."

"What about what I want?"

"I have to prove to them I'm worthy of you. Give me the chance to show them I'm willing to fight for you."

Shaking my head, I tried to fathom how our paradise had turned into a personal hell. "It's decided then."

"This is a machine, Pandora. It's bigger than both of us. The stakes are incredibly high. We're talking human rights. The environment. Health care for all. Freeing those wrongly imprisoned. We're talking about millions of lives affected for the better if my father gets elected."

"My father has so much to offer, too."

"I don't disagree."

"I have to think of who else might benefit…" My eyes widened at a sudden realization. "He promised you the Fairfield Project would resume if you ended us."

"Yes, but—"

"You get what you wanted. You all get what you want."

Except me.

"Lay low. That's all I am asking of you. Until I figure this out."

"I will not stand by while my family is destroyed."

"This is why our families have never agreed in the past. Only one can rule."

I grabbed my bag and ran for the door.

He caught me by my wrist and walked me backwards until I hit the wall, my bag dropping to the floor. He towered over me, his lips hovering dangerously close to mine.

I peered up at him. "Are we really over?"

"I will find a way. I need you to believe me."

"After the media has thrown us to the wolves, my life will be over."

He pulled me into a hug. "Listen to me, I will not give up on us. Not now, not ever. Stay here. Don't go home. They'll send you to Switzerland. Or somewhere I'll never find you." He pressed his lips to my forehead, his kiss firm and unrelenting.

Our powerful families had thrust us together for one purpose only. They'd succeeded in bringing us together because that is what they did—they always got their way.

Those same dark forces were now trying to rip us apart.

"No one will know you're here." He lifted my chin. "Unless you tell someone."

"They can't make me leave the country."

"Who knows what they're capable of doing. I need you to promise me you'll stay here."

The chasm of love between us kept widening.

"I don't need protecting."

"We do what they want for now. After the election, we'll find a way to be together."

I was now simply a Plaything of Power.

My future was set; marrying Damien was never going to happen. I could only be his lover.

Our chance at a real relationship had been an illusion all along. A battle that could never be won.

Rallying my courage, I felt my steely nature returning. I, too, could throw in a chip to bargain with. "I'll stay here on one condition."

"Say it and it's yours."

CHAPTER
FORTY

Pandora

Theo drove us across town in his Tesla.

We couldn't travel in one of the official cars or have security escort us as this evening had to be kept a secret. Damien wanted it to be Theo who took us to Vanguard since he was a trusted friend. With Theo being a member, too, there'd be no questions about our time at the club.

This had been my one condition to stay at Ten.

I'd have stayed anyway, but it was fun to negotiate with the master negotiator himself, my former fiancé. I was still wearing his ring, so there was that, at least.

Though wearing panties, I'd been stripped of my bra before we left, the kinkiness having begun before we'd even departed. Damien had purchased me an expensive black bobbed wig to wear. I looked super cute, like a Charleston flapper girl. It was fun to be someone else for the night. I peered out at the passing view, my fingers nervously trailing over my key pendant.

This necklace had brought me so far.

Theo wore a hoodie pulled over his face, his casual clothes a contrast to ours. We'd dressed according to the code—cocktail dresses for women and tuxedos for the men.

"You Say" by Lauren Daigle piped out of the speakers, providing an emotional backdrop to us spending precious time together. The world might be trying to rip us apart, but they couldn't steal our memories. We would always have those.

Damien and I sat close together holding hands, his fingers interwoven with mine as though claiming me. It was a protective gesture that I appreciated—the anticipation swirling inside me was almost unbearable.

But I wanted this, wanted tonight to happen more than anything. Being this daring, this reckless, made me feel like I was spreading my wings to the fullest.

We stared out of our respective windows, Damien dressed in black-tie and looking incredibly suave and me feeling feminine in my silver Stella McCartney halter-neck mini dress and these Jimmy Choo glitter sandals. With the small key pendant marking my right to be here.

We were already wearing masks. I'd been gifted a bright red sparkling masquerade disguise that covered most of my face. Damien's black-beaked mask covered his face completely. I understood why, but getting used to not seeing his face all night would take a while. I'd been warned never to remove it. I couldn't imagine why I'd want to. Especially with the way this town gossiped. I loved the secrecy…the sense of doing something so forbidden at a party where all the guests were anonymous.

Digging my fingernails into my palms, I tried to distract myself from this feeling of uncertainty and coming to terms with the idea that this was my new status: Damien's lover. I'd always been destined to be a trophy, but with him I'd believed I could be more.

There would be no marriage, but at least we would have each other.

And maybe he would have to marry at some point; I just wished it could have been me. I was to be only a concubine—one who adored him enough to give up being with any other man. My future had quickly begun to unravel.

Damien looked over at me and I tried to read the expression in his eyes, hoping to see how he felt about finally bringing me to Vanguard. The exhilaration I saw in him proved to me that he needed this more than he was willing to admit. It was the way his hand tightened around mine, that long look of desire we shared containing a multitude of emotions.

The town car continued along dark roads leading away from his city apartment. We passed a sign for Woodland Drive.

Damien stared at me. "Don't you dare remember that."

"Remember what?"

He could have been smiling behind his mask. "This is where your amnesia begins."

I drew in a sharp breath, realizing that all my dirtiest fantasies could come true. I wasn't even sure what I wanted from tonight. Other than to experience what had been out of reach before.

"Happy now?" asked Damien. I sensed his smirk. "Seems to me you always get your way, Bardot."

"I thought we were forbidden from saying our last names?"

"Good point. It won't happen again."

"Maybe I'll spank you later for it."

"Yeah, not going to happen."

The tone of his voice sent a shiver down my spine.

Damien reached over and his fingertips grazed my throat in a leisurely tease, causing tingles beneath his touch as he paused at the dip of my dress. "Obey me in all things."

I rested my head back. "Always."

He turned my head so our gazes met. "What do you want to happen?"

"I want to watch."

"Do you want an experience?"

"I'll let you decide."

"It's a simple yes or no."

I licked my lips. "Yes."

Theo was decent enough to keep his eyes on the road; if he had an opinion on anything we'd discussed he was keeping it to himself.

"Ready to play?" asked Damien.

A rush of feathers fluttered within, causing my core to tingle. "I feel it."

"A frisson?"

That's exactly was this was, a sudden sense of excitement that made the hairs on my forearms prickle. My skin felt flushed with awareness.

Lush, imposing trees lined the roadway as though guiding us toward a private estate. The view of land opened up around us and a grand gothic house came into view.

"Do as I say," Damien ordered.

My heart was racing. "I will." A thrill of anticipation caused my chest to tighten.

"Disobey and we leave," he said sternly.

His dominance was making me wet. Didn't he know that's what his sternness did to me? It caused my sex to quicken for his touch, made me long to have his cock buried deep inside me, his forceful thrusts dominating me.

I want it all.

My trembling fingers checked my mask yet again, finding it secure.

We pulled up to the front lawn of the property. A fountain statue of a seductively posed nude woman spurted an arc of water from her mouth.

"Stay close," he said.

I hoped we'd slowly be introduced to what was happening within those brick walls and not thrown into the fray too soon.

A butler exited the mansion wearing a black tuxedo and waited for us near the front entrance. Damien climbed out of the car and assisted me, my high heels landing on gravel, his grip on my forearm forceful as he led me toward the manor.

He didn't even throw a glance at Theo, perhaps not wanting to draw attention to him. I heard the sound of wheels crunching small stones as Tamer drove back down the driveway.

Trepidation rushed through me, but it was too late to back out—we were at the front door.

Damien nodded at the doorman. "Any new art I might like?"

"Yes, sir," replied the butler. "A Monet."

"Hopefully it's Waterloo Bridge?"

"It is, sir."

I suppressed a smile. Damien had given the password to get us in. I assumed it had to change from time to time.

After that intriguing exchange, I was escorted inside the manor. Waiting for us was a waitress who offered up a tray of champagne-filled glasses. Beside them lay a selection of red bracelets. Damien accepted only one drink and handed the flute to me.

I lifted my mask a little and sipped the golden bubbles as we walked, grateful for something to quench my sudden thirst.

With Damien's fingers interwoven through mine, we strolled through the foyer and beyond, working our way toward the center of the mansion.

"I need to talk with you," he whispered.

I glanced at him questioningly. "Okay."

"Let's find a quiet place."

I admired the lavish décor around us—the high ceilings and stone brick walls. Enormous fireplaces and curvy wrought-iron sconces illuminated the place with dusky lighting. Large gilded mirrors reflected the low hung chandeliers—all of it lending to the theme of glamour and decadence.

"No one will touch you unless you're wearing a red bracelet."

"That's good."

"If you want to touch someone, make sure they're wearing one."

I downed the rest of my champagne. "Can I have another?"

"You've had enough." He took my empty glass and set it down on a table. "Nervous?"

"Curious."

"Did I tell you that you look pretty?" His hand reached down and squeezed my ass.

"Yes, you did."

"I thought we'd start off with your fantasy."

"Oh?"

"I believe we'll find what we're looking for up here."

We ascended a staircase that had been hidden from view around a corner. It felt secretive.

A masked couple hurried by, laughing.

"How do you know what's happening in each room?" I asked.

"The rooms up here have themes."

"If you enter, you're consenting?"

"If you take a seat on the bed, you are showing consent. So, no sitting down unless you want to be part of the scene."

That was easy to remember. The doors were painted in different colors and I guessed that's what Damien was following as he guided me along.

He paused suddenly.

Bumping into his back, I saw what he saw, a masked woman sitting back on a generously sized travel trunk with her legs spread wide while a man between her thighs suckled her pussy. They didn't seem to see us; they were too caught up in each other.

It was deliciously obscene, her throaty groans echoed around us. She turned her head and noticed us watching, her expression revealing she was pleased to share this moment with strangers. Her head fell back as she focused once more on her frenzied lover devouring her sex.

We strolled by them, and I looked straight ahead, unsure whether staring was taboo. I felt my cheeks burning as Damien's curious eyes studied me.

It made me wonder what kind of things he liked to do when he visited. Maybe he, too, had taken a stranger like that in the middle of a hallway for all to see.

We paused before a purple door.

Inside the room my eyes adjusted to the dim light and I blinked at the large bed covered in a purple silk sheet. Two men wearing tuxedos and a woman in a long green gown sat on the edge, talking softly. All three of them wore masks. A few other couples had gathered around apparently to watch them.

We huddled in the farthest corner, close enough to see but far enough away to not draw attention.

This is what Damien meant—my thoughts flashed back to

the footage Madeline had shown me on her phone at the hotel. The same evening she'd told me that Damien loved this adult playground. Inspiring me to learn more. *Be more.*

"Madeline told you," I whispered.

"We can leave if you want."

"No."

His palm traced my spine. "It's going to get explicit."

We were about to watch the scene play out before us. A thrill in my solar plexus felt like sparking electricity had fused with my soul.

All three of them stood and began removing their clothes, the men helping each other remove their tuxedos and then helping the woman strip out of her gown. One of them eased off her heels as the other leaned in for a kiss, their sensuality deeply touching.

She sat between them on the edge of the bed as they explored her body, their hands tracing over her pert nipples and tweaking them. Their cocks erect now as they took their time surveying her nakedness.

Both of them eased apart her labia as though wanting to expose more of her to the crowd. Complying, she parted her thighs to show her glistening sex, her legs trembling as they ran their hands over her and played with her pussy, dipping fingers and teasing her labia. One held her folds open while the other played with that small swollen nub, gentle fingers flicking as knowing looks were exchanged between them.

Hidden in the shadows, I hoped no one looked our way, because for a second my hand had slapped to my chest in shock. It was erotic and brazen and daring…and arousing. Already the dampness between my legs revealed how turned on I was.

"You okay?" Damien's voice was almost imperceptible.

I managed a nod, my attention riveted on the ménage à trois.

The masked beauty was on her knees now with the men before her, dipping her head to take in one cock and then the other with her wide-open mouth—her hands working where her mouth had left off in a hypnotic rhythm set in motion as she deep-throated them in turn.

In an explosion of passion, the men grabbed her up and ravaged her body, their mouths exploring every inch of her. Writhing together, the three bodies merged as they moved in sync upon the bed, all hands and mouths, stroking and tasting.

One of the men reached down for his jacket, removing a small object. Then he smeared something on his finger…lube. His fingertip reached between her ass crack to smear the clear gel there and then he took her from behind, thrusting deeply until he'd buried himself inside her. Their lover moved swiftly to lay next to her, his erection disappearing as he thrust into her pussy, joining them.

Just as I'd been spellbound by the footage, I was mesmerized here, seeing it in real time and being part of this erotic display. My heart soared when I saw that familiar look she offered to her lovers—a wanton gratitude for being taken so well by these masked men—her eyes darting to one and then the other. It was as though no one else was here. All three were too lost in each other to care about their audience.

The woman seemed enraptured as she neared orgasm, groaning loudly, her thighs shaking as she writhed between them.

My sigh matched hers as she came hard.

Damien took my hand and pulled me from the room.

"Well?" he whispered.

Leaning into him, I said quietly, "No words."

"Want to take it up a notch?"

"Yes!"

I wondered exactly what he meant, but was too aroused to care. Both of us hurried down the hallway until we made it to another door.

What happens in the Blue Room?

The answer was soon revealed as we entered a dark dungeon, the furniture and contraptions unmistakably for BDSM. Only one other couple was present—a masked, naked submissive was secured to the Saint Andrew's Cross with the back padded for comfort. She was being whipped by a male bare-chested master. Red welts covered her flesh. Proof of her arousal glistened between her damp thighs.

Damien pulled me over to a long chain that hung from the ceiling. Raising my hands up in a gesture of consent, I watched as he took my wrists and clipped them into two metal cuffs, securing me with my arms above my head and my heels barely touching the floor.

Exhilaration mingled with the addictive thrill of exploitation. In Damien's eyes flashed dominance and desire, his need to see me vulnerable obvious from the way he mastered me.

"No," I said, playing along with his fetish.

He paused, assessing my reaction.

"How dare you!" I scolded him. "Do you know who I am?"

His breathing became rapid and his pupils dilated, that familiar supremacy ruling our scene.

"Fuck me hard," I bit out. "Because you'll never have me again after this."

"Jesus." He went for my jaw, clenching it tight.

A spark of arousal lit up like fireworks between us, our chemistry bubbling like a delicious poison both of us craved. His fingers reached behind my neck and unfastened my dress, dragging the top down to expose my breasts, causing my nipples to bead. Firm fingers worked around the pebbles of arousal as my eyes flittered across the room to the submissive.

Her master's left hand had parted her labia and he was tapping her clit with a whip. Gentle and seductive, as his sub's half-lidded gaze hinted she'd tranced out.

"You like that?" asked Damien.

My focus returned to him. "Oh, yes."

He tugged at my dress until it shimmied over my hips and I stepped out of it. Then he knelt before me to slide my thong off until I, too, was as naked as that submissive, other than my high heels, which brought me a little closer to Damien's height.

The risk that someone could walk in at any second felt divine—the sense I was someone else…someone afraid of nothing.

The scene on the opposite side of the room continued as though we weren't here, other than an occasional glance I swapped with my counterpart, staring through our masks at each other—both of us being controlled and cajoled by our masters, teased and flicked, and licked and suckled, with our sighs intermingling and whispers resonating.

Her master was holding a vibrator to her clit, causing her to shudder through her first orgasm, her deep-throated moans sounding primal as they rose higher as she climaxed.

"Look how wet you are." Damien's fingers rose to my eyeline and he eased a fingertip into my mouth.

I tasted my own musky sweetness, eyes flitting back to our mirror image of master and submissive. They were fucking now.

"You just can't look away, can you?" Damien's voice sounded stern.

"No, sir."

She'd wrapped her legs around his waist, her hands still tied to that device so all she could do was hold on with her thighs and let him have his way.

My wrists were smarting from their metal bindings above and deliciously sore. I felt totally enraptured by this game, this flawless aura that had me obsessed with this spectacle.

I'm here.

Part of the play.

From behind me, Damien's strong hands positioned me to bend a little so that my ass came up. I heard the sound of his zipper coming undone, and felt eager for what came next. I rose onto my tiptoes, balancing in high heels. There came the glide of his cock along my crack, moving lower until it grazed my wetness, the tip nudging my pussy. I tipped my hips eager for that first thrust, and gasped as he buried deep. His hands controlled the thrusts that came hard and fast—a furious pounding.

Two couples fucking in front of each other…our echoes

mingling, the scent of sandalwood and raw carnal pleasures as we romanced each other with our dark fetishes. Our perfect coupling made me high.

My orgasm was expertly held off as, on and on, euphoria stole my breath and held me suspended. The pleasure became blinding when Damien's fingers reached around and flicked my clit to enhance his fucking.

I was only able to stand due to the metal binds that held me secure. I felt him withdraw, leaving me feeling bereft, my cry of need drawing attention our way. But then his slick cock slid back to rest against my puckered hole.

"Ready?" he said huskily.

He'd be slick from my soaking wet pussy, I knew that, but this was new and though he'd prepared me with his bejeweled toys my heart still skipped a beat at how it might feel.

My master was already there...he pushed the tip of his cock in, invading that space, bringing the sensation of fullness with his invasion, causing my thighs to tremble as he impaled me.

Muscles within gripped him tight as a detonation of pleasure burst inside me, my pussy jealous of his cock and the intense sensations that kept unfurling.

I slowly rocked my hips with him behind me, wedged deep, as his erection glided in and out until all I knew were us and them...and the space between.

His warmth entered me suddenly, his body going stiff against me as he came, his arm around my waist holding me still so he could ride out his climax.

I want to stay like this forever...

Leaning forward, dangling from cuffs, my thighs spread wider for balance as he let go. My breathing was ragged and I was feeling awestruck by what we'd done, a stark beatitude rising as though this was our church and we were the worshiped ones... our sex as primal as it was sacred.

My soft sighs filled the room.

He untied me and I fell against him, needing a few minutes

to just be, to breathe. No words were needed because all we'd wanted was this moment of no barriers between us—a dark evening to cherish.

Damien gathered my dress and panties and led me into an adjoining bathroom. Both of us nurtured each other as we made ourselves ready. He tenderly washed away the remnants of our adventurous lovemaking.

As he helped me dress, our eyes locked, and still no words were necessary.

We walked back out into the hallway and descended the stairs, swapping knowing glances with each other. Sated, we searched out refreshments to quench our thirst.

Damien hunted down some champagne and we toasted to my first time here.

"I want more," I admitted.

"What do you want to see?"

"Another submissive," I said softly. "I want to see my future."

Raising his mask a little—and mine too—he brought me in for a leisurely kiss, his tongue tangling with mine, his lips forceful and unforgiving—as though punishing me for my insatiable need for more erotica.

With our masks pulled back down, we were ready to proceed.

"This way," said Damien, leading me on.

Soon, we would leave this place never to return and for the first time I knew the sacrifice Damien had made. His true nature was being twisted this way and that until nothing was going to be left of his private life.

"Back home," I said, walking beside him, "wherever we go, we'll create a place where we can be us."

His eyes showed understanding. "This is why I adore you."

"Teach me everything."

Damien gestured down a long corridor. "This is a good place to start."

CHAPTER
FORTY-ONE

Pandora

Beneath the dim lighting and between the tight walls we made our way down into what felt like the heart of the manor.

I saw recognition on Damien's face as he greeted another butler. "Giles."

Giles gave a low bow. "Do you want access to the Burgundy Chamber, sir?"

Damien gave a nod of thanks.

"You may proceed." Giles motioned toward another corridor that had a sharp turn.

When we made it to the end, Damien opened the door and we went inside the room.

The décor followed the theme of "heavy on the male DNA" we'd seen in other areas of the mansion. A leather couch and several chairs sat on a blue and red Persian rug in the center of the room, with lots of space left around this staged furniture.

On the walls were portraits of historical men, sharply dressed famous figures, who'd somehow influenced American history. Was this a hint that the secret club went back centuries?

The room was already filled with men and a few women; some with submissives kneeling at their feet. The air crackled with electricity. They stood around the outside of the room leaving a space in the center. At one end was an empty armchair and at the other end a naked woman provocatively knelt, delicate silver chains dangling over her body but covering nothing of her pert nipples and closely shaven sex. Her head was bowed as though waiting, the half-mask over her eyes only revealing a stark prettiness framed with long brunette curls.

She sat calmly, waiting—the key pendant twinkling against her skin.

My hand snapped to mine as though I'd found my soul sister, a woman with whom I shared a commonality. We were both submissive—both of us daring to explore our sexuality, but clearly, she was far braver.

Giles returned to us carrying a silver tray and offered us drinks. We took the two glasses with gratitude. Sipping mine, I confirmed he'd given us sherry.

Giles bowed and backed out of the room, leaving us.

Damien took the drink from me and placed it behind us on a bookcase.

My hand reached up to massage the back of my neck, trying to relieve the tension—anticipation making me anxious. I still felt the pang of where he'd fucked me in my ass. I was sore but sated and reveling in the way my skin remained flushed. The memories of that room would always be cherished.

Damien's hand replaced mine at my nape and his fingers dug into tense muscle.

"Can you see?" he whispered.

"Yes." The sweet taste of sherry had soothed me a little.

With his hands on my shoulders now, Damien moved us so that we stood at the back of the room, right behind a leather chair.

He directed me. "Here."

We were hidden a little by the high-backed chair.

At the opposite side of the room a door opened. A man entered through it, also wearing a tux, and like everyone else he, too, was wearing a mask. He strolled across the space and sat down in the armchair opposite the kneeling woman.

The room hushed.

The naked submissive crawled the distance to where he sat.

My face blanched for her—she was willingly performing for this crowd of fifty or more guests, unabashed at her own nakedness. She knelt upright between the man's thighs.

Damien pulled me into a hug against his chest. "She likes being watched."

He knew her, or he'd seen her before, of that I was certain.

Responding obediently, the submissive placed her hands on the man's knees. With a nod from him the brunette unbuckled and then unzipped his pants, exposing him. She licked her lips expectantly as she eased out his cock. She wiped a bead of pre-cum off the purple head and licked her finger sensuously.

Dazed, I watched her stroke his erection as though no one watched, brazenly working her palms up and down the length of him, examining his cock adoringly.

She drew him all the way into her mouth and suckled, then pulled back a little, leaving him shiny with wetness as she lavished her tongue along the top of his shaft. She dipped her head to suckle his sac.

"See that," said the man, his voice husky, "how she likes to focus on my balls?"

She gave a half-distracted nod to confirm this, running the tip of her tongue around his head and causing him to lift his hips.

A deep, low throb in my pussy caused me to keen a little, and I put a hand on the back of the chair to steady myself. Damien's arm tightened around my waist.

My clit throbbed deliciously at the sight before me of a woman's head bobbing between a man's thighs. I tried to behave as though this scene had little effect on me, but all the while my thighs were becoming sticky with arousal. Licking my lips, I imagined what it must feel like to have his fullness stretch my lips wide as I sucked on the length of him, feeling my jaw stretch from his girth.

Jolting me out of my trance, Damien's hand slid up my dress, gliding up my thigh, his fingers trailing closer to my panties.

My thoughts cycled around the idea that the woman on her knees may have done this to the man before. I searched his masked face and then hers for any clue they knew each other.

Damien's warm hand cupped my sex, sending a shiver of

delight through me. I swayed in a daze, more than a little aware of the dampness at the triangle of my panties. I widened my thighs a bit to give him more access to my pussy.

"Good girl," he whispered at my compliance.

I continued to watch the couple, the way the man's lips parted as his breathing became ragged, his long lashes fluttering, body tense.

I made a note of what the woman did to send him into a silent frenzy, the way her tongue ran around the head of his cock, flickering at his frenulum, the way she took him deep into her mouth and at the same time held his stare.

His thighs opened wider and his head fell back against the chair as he sunk into the seat, resigning himself to her actions.

I wondered how she'd found this place and come to be here. Her heavy-lidded eyes were aflame with desire as she swapped erotic glances with her master. She looked up at him with awe… and how could she not with his dazzling control?

Damien's fingers dipped beneath my panties and found my clit. My face flushed wildly beneath my mask at this hidden act— yet I wouldn't have wanted to experience this any other way. He flicked and teased my sex, easing its desperate ache for attention. Though all these people couldn't see his actions, knowing he was doing this with them so close was exhilarating.

"Taking notes?" he whispered.

"Yes," I managed.

Between my thighs came that familiar rising of sensations that were close to stealing my breath away, lulling me, revving me into a state of wonder. Damien's fingers continued relentlessly, unceasing.

The man in the tuxedo at the center of this erotic play flicked his fingers in an order.

The woman sat up and raised her chin, preparing for what came next. He rose to his feet with his right hand stroking his shaft as he positioned himself over her.

Entranced by their wanton glances and moans of lust, soft

sighs escaped my lips as the scene played out. My sex was soaked with arousal, my pussy tingling more with each passing moment.

The mysterious man became rigid, letting out a groan that caught in his throat, his hips rocking as he stroked his cock from base to tip with a steady rhythm. He came hard, glistening streams arching and then showering upon her breasts.

With her head up, her hands massaged the creaminess over her tits, seemingly swooning as his warmth bathed her in spurting jerks. She tweaked her nipples as she raised her focus obediently to meet his.

Wanting it all.

Grateful.

A perfect submissive, her brazen sexuality a remarkable gift to treasure.

Would I ever act so wantonly in front of so many? I wasn't sure, but I knew that being here was the greatest privilege.

Damien's fingers continued to adore me during these drawn-out minutes in the only way a Godman could—with a scorching passion that left my sex throbbing.

Even when he pulled his hand away leaving me sated, I couldn't stop wanting his touch.

Finally, he'd given me *this*.

My focus returned to the center of the room as the man sat back down as though waiting for something else to occur.

"Out," he ordered.

The pretty brunette hurried from the room like a scorned child, turning to glance back at me through that half-mask with a smirk before exiting. It was then I noticed a familiar birthmark on her upper lip. *A brunette Marilyn Monroe.*

Damien pulled me into a hug, and I sank against his body, his warmth enveloping me. His strong arms wrapped around me possessively as though he felt proud that we'd shared another first together.

I didn't want to leave this place. There was so much more to see and to experience. He'd given me permission to explore my sexuality and I adored him for it. My body was still wracked with arousal, shuddering through the images branded into my mind of that beautiful woman who'd rushed out of the room all too quickly.

"Did you like that?" Damien asked huskily.

I gave a nod, cursed by this need to be fucked again and soon.

"I thought that might be something you'd like." Damien reached for the sherry glass and offered it to me.

"You don't think I've had too much to drink?"

He turned his back on the crowd. "Clearly you haven't had enough."

He lifted his mask a little and raised the sherry glass, drinking the liquor.

I smirked at his retort. "Where did the submissive go?"

"To freshen up, I imagine." Damien chuckled as he lowered his mask. "She'll be back. This is her fantasy, after all."

"Hers?"

"This room was orchestrated to fit her reverie. This is her fantasy come to life."

I felt relieved to know she was the mistress of this setting.

Oh, my God.

There had been a pinky ring on her left hand—a ruby.

I suddenly remembered where I'd seen the woman before. The shock of this realization stunned me into silence.

CHAPTER
FORTY-TWO

Pandora

T he only place in Vanguard I was allowed to visit alone was a female spa. It was empty, except for *her*...the girl with the ruby ring. Curious, I'd followed the mystery submissive to see what I could discover.

When she'd removed her mask, I was sure she was the woman I'd seen at the 118 News Club with Salvatore Galante.

There was no way I could remove my mask—even if she asked me to.

She stepped out of the communal showers having washed off all the evidence of what she'd done in that room. Grabbing a towel, she dried herself off in front of a locker.

I approached her. "Hey."

She looked at me intently, as though trying to work out my identity. "Hi."

"Are we alone?"

Her brows drew together. "I think so."

"That was amazing...what you just did."

"It felt amazing."

"You're so brave."

She glanced at my diamond key necklace and her expression turned inquisitive. Clearly someone who wore this pendant should be used to that kind of erotic play.

"Do you have a second?" I whispered.

She glanced at me suspiciously. "I've not met you before, right?"

I felt a wave of relief that she didn't recognize me.

She gestured to a small alcove. "In here."

Still naked, she wrapped the delicate chains back around her body. "I'm Phoebe," she said. "I have to go soon."

"I'm…"

"That's okay. I'll call you O."

That made me smile.

She fixed the chain around her breasts and looked up. "Want me to orchestrate a fantasy?"

"Um, no. How long have you been a member?"

"Why?"

"I'm curious."

"You want a threesome with your boyfriend?" She smirked. "I can do that."

"No. But thank you." I stared at her sparkling pinky ring.

"Why are you looking at me like that?"

"Have you any idea what they'll do to you?"

"What?"

I took a deep breath. "How long have you worked for Galante?"

She froze; her expression panic-stricken.

Shit.

She really did work for Galante.

"You're in so much trouble," I said.

She swallowed hard.

"I can help you, Phoebe."

"I have no idea what you're talking about."

"So it's fine for me to go tell one of the butlers here?"

She shook her head. "You're wrong."

"See you later, Phoebe." I went to leave. "Have fun."

"Please don't say anything," she said breathlessly.

I looked back at her. "How much does he pay you?"

"Hardly anything. Galante fucking owns me."

"Why?"

"I was turning tricks at a private club. He threatened to give the evidence to the police."

"Wouldn't that be safer for you than this?"

She was a spy at Vanguard, reporting back to Galante. The risk she was taking was unthinkable. Some of Washington's most powerful men undoubtedly frequented the club. I dreaded to think of what would happen to anyone who betrayed their secrets.

"I'll pay you," she stuttered. "I don't have a lot but—"

"I don't want money. I want to help you."

"Why?"

"I have my reasons."

She looked distraught.

"What can you tell me about him?"

"Nothing."

"If I leave this room, I'm going straight to the top."

"We can't talk here," she whispered.

"I don't have much time, so spill."

Damien was outside, probably wondering where I was by now.

"You need to trust me," I said. "I came straight to you. I didn't tell anyone."

"How did you know I'm connected with Salvatore?"

"You go first."

Phoebe gave a resigned nod. "He's the most powerful man in Washington. He likes to call himself the King Maker."

"Wow." He was full of himself.

"I once overheard Galante say he owns everyone in this town because he has the body."

"What?" I sputtered. "He killed someone?"

She shook her head. "Not that kind of body. BODI. It's an anagram."

"What does it stand for?"

Phoebe stepped forward and whispered, "Box of Damaging Indiscretions."

"Scandals?"

"Promise me I can trust you."

Placing my hand on my heart, I gave her a nod.

"He owns them…everyone he's ever collected a scandal on.

Some people don't even know they're in his collection. He waits for the right time to release evidence of their misconduct. He blackmails men with what he knows."

"Where does he get his information?" And then I realized— from women like Phoebe.

"He has many sources. He pays for stories. Like TMZ, but they go nuclear."

"Where does he keep the BODI?"

"I can't talk here. I'm meant to be back."

I wondered what else she'd be doing in that room. This time watching her was out of the question.

"You can come in if you like," she offered.

"I'm fine. You like being here?"

"I fought hard to become a member." Her fingers traced her key pendant.

"You're a trained submissive?"

"Of course." She glanced at my necklace. "You too, right?"

"Meet me tomorrow at the Emissary Café at four. Do you know it?"

"On 21st Street?"

"That's it. We'll talk more there."

"I didn't want to do it. This place is everything to me. But Galante told me he'd ruin my life. I've seen him do it to so many people."

"We'll get you away from him. Hang in there, okay?"

"He's dangerous," she whispered. "I think he's going to sabotage the election."

A chill slithered up my spine. "How?"

"Later. I have to go."

She ran from the room.

My chest tightened. The voting booths would open in five days. What did Galante have on Senator Godman? Had Phoebe overheard a threat?

I hurried out of the spa, and found Damien waiting for me at the end of the hallway.

"Everything all right?" he asked. "I was close to coming in there."

"Just freshening up," I said calmly. "Can we go home?"

"We can do anything you like, sweetheart. Did you enjoy yourself?"

"Every moment," I said wistfully, taking his arm.

He glanced at his watch. "Tamer's coming back at midnight. We can sit by the pool until he's here."

"I know it's your last time here." Cutting it short felt unfair, but still.

"I have you now. You're as good as it gets."

I nudged his shoulder playfully. "We don't need this place to get kinky."

"We certainly don't."

With a brave face, I walked beside him out to a garden with a sparkling pool. Guests were scattered about enjoying the evening air, as well as the steady flow of free drinks being served by the masked staff—a few of which were scantily-clad.

It was too soon to tell Damien what I knew. His involvement would put him and his family at greater risk.

Handling this myself was the only way.

CHAPTER
FORTY-THREE

Pandora

I sat in Damien's BMW watching the café door.

It was overwhelming to think the election might hinge on the actions of the two of us. Senator Gregor Godman was an arrogant man, but he was also capable of doing so much good. He had the ability to help so many people in so many ways. People are complicated and Damien's father was a testament to that fact.

If Phoebe realized I was a Bardot, she'd be able to bribe me. I'd kept my mask on the entire time at Vanguard and I felt certain she hadn't guessed my true identity. Meeting with her now was reckless—even though I was wearing my Charleston flapper, bobbed wig disguise.

Damien had once accused me of being self-centered and having no influence on the world. Here, now, I had my chance to prove him wrong.

My phone buzzed with a text. I cringed at his timing.

Damien: *Where are you?*

I hoped he wasn't at the apartment. I started to type a reply, but paused for a moment when I saw Phoebe scurry inside the café with big sunglasses on and a baseball cap pulled low.

I quickly replied to Damien's text: *I'll call soon.*

Outside the car, I put on my sunglasses and approached the café, my bobbed wig camouflaging my blonde hair. The sports clothes I had on gave me a dressed-down look—not the kind of outfit I usually chose to wear when going out.

Inside, I purchased two coffees and joined a nervous-looking Phoebe in the corner booth. She had every reason to be scared. Should she return to Vanguard after her secret was revealed, they would rip her to shreds. If she didn't turn up at Galante's home as scheduled, he'd probably destroy her life. She was caught between two powerful entities—essentially trapped.

"Glad you made it," I said.

Her eyes went wide as she studied my face. "I knew I'd seen you somewhere before."

"Our little secret, right?"

"Of course." She set her sunglasses on the table.

I gestured to her purse. "Turn off your phone."

While waiting for her to comply, I looked around at the other few customers in the café, making sure no one would overhear our conversation.

She shoved her phone back into her purse. "Aren't you meant to be marrying the President's son?"

"He's not President yet."

She eyed me suspiciously. "Did they send you?"

"No. And they'll never find out. Right?"

"I won't tell them." She blinked nervously. "Who were you with at Vanguard?"

"I wasn't there," I said boldly.

She nodded. "Me neither."

"Right."

And after all, we both knew I hadn't handed her over to the men at Vanguard who would have done God knows what to punish her for being in Galante's pocket.

Her eyes watered. "You think you can help me. You can't."

"What if I told you that all the evidence Galante has on you is accessible, which means it can be destroyed."

"You don't think people have tried that?"

"Maybe they tackled it from the wrong angle."

Perspiration spotted Phoebe's upper lip. "What are you going to do to me?"

"That's up to you." I rested back against the plastic seat.

She reached for her coffee and pulled off the lid, blowing on the drink to cool it.

"I can't go back to Vanguard," she said.

"You're done there," I agreed.

"I loved that place. I could just be me, you know?"

"I'm sorry."

I understood her regret, since I'd probably never go back either. Even though I'd only visited Vanguard once, I already felt the pull of addiction caused by those mysterious rooms; the atmosphere of the place gave everyone permission to explore.

"What will I tell Galante?"

"Nothing."

Her trepidation seemed to morph into hope. "What do I have to do?"

"How often do you meet him?"

"Usually every Friday."

"Tonight?" I felt a surge of apprehension. We'd have to move fast, but as the story on my father was being released tomorrow, the timing was perfect. Could I really be the one to save him— and save a Presidential election?

As long as my plan didn't go off the rails, that is.

"His wife arranges for him to get a massage," she said, her voice low. "I'm one of the masseuses."

"And you do more than that, I imagine?"

Phoebe's lip curled in discomfort.

"Does his wife know?" I asked.

"She pretends she doesn't. But she's over having to suck his dick herself."

"That could be your way out, Phoebe," I told her. "We can use his manipulation. Maybe get him to admit to it."

She shook her head. "We can't prove it."

"What else can you tell me about him?"

She shifted uncomfortably in her seat. "Like I told you already, he's rumored to keep records on some of the most powerful men and women in Washington. He uses that to bribe them."

"How did Galante find you?"

"I was an exotic dancer. He waited for me to come out of Archibald's."

"Is that a gentleman's club?"

"I stripped there sometimes. Anyway, he was waiting for me outside. I was told to get in the back of his car. I assumed he wanted a blowie."

"Then he blackmailed you to work at Vanguard?"

"Yes."

"How much does he pay you?" I asked.

She hesitated.

"You have to be transparent." I reached for her hand to reassure her. "If we're going to set you free from all of this."

She let out a sigh. "It depends on what I bring him. What kind of gossip I overhear. The members talk at Vanguard. They assume we aren't listening."

There could be a record of payment between them, at least.

I was scared to think of what she may have already relayed back to Galante—and the damage it may have caused. She'd been blackmailed into taking part in his terrible scheming.

Phoebe's lips trembled. "Can you still help me?"

"After all the evidence on you is destroyed," I said, "I'll give you enough money to set up a life anywhere you like."

"How do I know you're telling the truth?"

Reaching into my handbag, I pulled out an envelope and slid it toward her. "Ten thousand dollars." I rested a fingertip on it. "Get me into Galante's house tonight and I'll give you a lot more."

"You're insane."

"That's all I'm asking of you."

Phoebe went for the cash.

"Does he keep the dirt on everyone in a vault or a safe?"

"I think he did once. Someone tried to destroy it. He had a fire at his office about a year ago."

"I need his home address, and a sketch of the layout. Everything you can remember."

Phoebe looked at me with doubt.

"Have you seen how he accesses his computer?"

"I saw him on his iPad in the car." Phoebe chewed her lip

thoughtfully. "He just swiped the side of his wrist across the screen instead of typing in a code. It was kind of weird."

Did Galante use a biometric encryption key?

"You don't want to be on Salvatore's shit list," she said. "One feature on his political talk show can wreck a reputation."

"I'm well aware."

"Does he have something on your fiancé?"

"Not that I know of."

"You're here for his dad, then?"

"Actually, it's someone else that's motivated me to be here. He has something on someone I care about."

"Do they know you're here speaking with me?"

"No, and they never will."

"I want to help."

"From what you're telling me, the key to the BODI is not in his watch. It's embedded in his wrist." Raising a finger, I added. "Probably."

Phoebe realized what I was suggesting. "What the fuck..."

"I believe what you saw was him using a biometric encryption key."

"Like a microchip implant?"

"That transmits a signal. Exactly."

"I've heard of employees getting bonuses by having an implant that clocks them in, tracks their workday, follows their movements."

"They can store medical records on them, too."

"There's no way in hell I'd let them put one of those in me."

I laughed. "I feel the same way."

"Why would he do that?"

"He's using it as a security measure. No one else can access the intelligence he's gathered."

"How the fuck do you know all this shit?"

"What's the first thing that comes to mind when you think of Swiss private schooling?"

"I don't know...tennis."

"You were thinking short skirts and gossiping girls, weren't you?"

She looked apologetic.

"Truth is, they're turning out potential world leaders from my old school. Switzerland is one of the most innovative countries in the world. Our education reflects that. I wasn't just taught how to bake a nice soufflé."

"That's where you learnt about…"

"Bio tech, yes. Amongst other things." I rummaged around for my phone to check my messages. "You can only imagine my surprise when I returned to the U.S. and was told 'your job is to look pretty.'"

"And I thought I had it bad."

"I'm privileged, I get that. But it's like being bred as a racehorse and not being allowed to run."

That made her laugh.

I looked down at the slew of texts from Damien.

"Is your phone on?" she asked, panicked.

"Yes, it's totally fine." I threw her a smile. "I'm the one that needs to trust you, remember?"

"*Jesus,* are we doing this? Are you really going to try to get inside his house?"

I pushed to my feet. "What time is your appointment?"

"Seven."

"Meet me a few houses down at six-thirty. I want to see you before you go in."

"I can do that." She picked up her coffee and handbag and pushed to her feet.

"Go home. Pack a suitcase. Once we're done tonight, you need to go straight to a hotel. Can you do that?"

"Leave my shitty studio apartment?" she asked in mock horror. "I can try."

"I have a friend we can trust. He'll set you up somewhere really nice."

She cast a suspicious glance around the café. "What if after I help you, I'm of no more use to you?"

"I'm interested in stopping Galante," I reassured her. "Protecting his victims. And you're one of them."

And if we were caught, it would be the end of the Godman campaign. I'd be sent abroad never to return. Hell, they'd probably try to send me to Siberia.

My temples began to throb just thinking about it.

"We need each other, Phoebe." I stepped closer and embraced her. She smelled of lilies…like a wild, untouched garden. "We have no choice but to trust each other." I pulled away to meet her worried expression. "I know what it's like to be controlled by powerful men. This is how we take our power back."

I waited for Phoebe to leave the café before I made my way back to the car.

A sense of dread came over me as I climbed into the BMW. Phoebe was scared and alone and it was up to me to help her. I'd taken a huge risk involving her in all of this, but she was my only viable option to get into Galante's home.

I called up my Google map and searched out a shopping mall that was close. I needed an alibi for when I returned home and faced Damien's wrath.

CHAPTER
FORTY-FOUR

Damien

"**A**m I being insensitive?" I asked Theo. "We are days away from E Day."

"Maybe she went home?"

"She knows that's risky." I was struggling with my bowtie in front of the bathroom mirror. "Where do we keep the cigarettes?"

Theo leaned against the doorframe, watching me. "You told me to throw them out."

I glared at him. "I noticed how you forgot to throw out the condoms!"

He cringed. "She found them?"

"She thought they were mine."

"You haven't had a woman here in a year."

"Try telling her that." I raised my hands. "How do I look?"

"Fine."

"Just fine?"

"Like a stud."

I slapped his back. "Not so bad yourself."

My frustration with Pandora was rising. She had merely sent a couple of texts in answer to my half dozen—the last one saying she'd be back soon. I understood that my girlfriend probably wanted to be with her family, what with *Real Nation One TV* about to drop her father's scandal onto the airwaves tomorrow.

But not answering her phone?

I'd move Pandora to a better place. This apartment wasn't good enough for her.

Maybe that's why she wasn't here. She was used to luxury, not this minimalist style. She was used to staff and having company. Maybe she was lonely. I should have thought about that.

Damn it, this is as far from a home as you can get.

Like me, Theo was wearing a black-tie suit and looking suave. But unlike me, he was behaving as though everything was business as usual. I felt like my life was deteriorating with each passing second.

"Ready to call off your engagement?" he asked. "Your dad mentioned leaking it to the press tonight."

"Don't let them send it out. I'm going to talk with Dad. I'm fucking done letting him dictate who I can have in my life." I realized the truth in that statement. "Pandora's annoying at times, but I love her."

"She gets you. I can see that."

"We've both been used and we're over it."

Until I told my father I'd ended it with Pandora, the Fairfield Project would remain stalled. The damage between us now felt irreparable. What was that saying? To win in Washington you have to be able to kill your darlings? Well, bravo, Dad. I'm dead inside if that's what you were going for.

I'd chosen to get ready here so I could at least see Pandora before heading out for the cocktail party at the Fairmont in Georgetown. Going without her was hell. I wanted to be able to walk into the hotel with my arm around her. I was proud to be seen with her, and not just because she was a Bardot.

I wanted her by my side permanently.

I'd turned up the air-conditioning thinking that was the reason my chest felt tight. But no, it was her not being here that made me feel like I couldn't get enough oxygen.

Pandora had eventually texted to say she was on her way, but until I saw her I would be filled with trepidation.

That little minx had ditched her security and gone off on a jaunt in my BMW. I knew driving around town without an escort was her way of rebelling against the system that had held her captive all her life. Still, even as my lover she'd have to stay within the confines of my security detail.

I will marry her one day. I'll find a way.

I followed Theo back into the sitting room. "Did you fire everyone yet?"

"Can we wait, please? Hear what Pandora has to say?"

Unable to draw in a deep breath, I loosened the bowtie I'd been wrestling with in the bathroom. "I'll fire everyone myself then."

I heard the sound of a key turning in the lock.

We both turned to watch Pandora walk through front door, both of us letting out a collective sigh of relief.

She strolled in as though her being out in the world alone was normal, carrying high-end shopping bags and looking unfazed from breaking the rules.

What the fuck were you thinking?

Days ago, she'd gone to see Salvatore Galante. Anything was possible with this girl. Keeping an eye on her was essential. I may love her, but Pandora going rogue again wasn't an option.

I made sure my expression did not show the anxiety she'd caused me. Of course, I was glad to see her, but I had the urge to smother her in a revenge hug.

She looked different in an unexplainable way. I saw an internal conflict reflected in her eyes, as though she'd been touched by an inexplicable experience.

Or maybe it was just me.

Maybe I was seeing her as just a girl who'd been wronged all her life; being privileged but having gone unloved for all these years—a kind of hell camouflaged in luxury.

She needed someone to show her the purity of love. And I wanted to be that someone.

She threw the shopping bags onto the couch. "You both look nice."

My back straightened. "Where have you been?"

"Just in case you changed your mind about tonight, I needed something to wear."

I stepped closer, a look of apology on my face.

"I'll wait in the car," said Theo, moving by her. "Please don't evade our security detail."

"You mean Damien's security detail," she said abruptly.

"Damien's, then." He forced a smile. "If they fail to protect you, they'll lose their jobs. Let's not forget that."

"As of right now," she replied, "I'm a free agent. Let's not forget that."

Theo looked affronted.

"Theo, I've been stashed away in a fuck pad across town while the adults decide my future—advised not to return home because my parents want to ship me off to God only knows where…again." She looked defiant. "And so, I wait to see what's decided on my behalf. What will it be? Will I be a whore stashed away in a nice chateau as a plaything? Or will I disappear in the quiet of the night to a place where even you can't find me." She brightened. "Or I can take my power back."

"By going shopping without an escort?" said Theo.

"Why, yes," she faked a southern belle accent. "For starters."

Theo let out a huff and headed for the door with his head bowed.

With him gone, Pandora stood before me with her arms folded and her expression taut.

"Your parents called me," I admitted. "They've expressed their concern. It looks like I've kidnapped you."

"You have."

My throat tightened with that accusation. "Want me to take you home?"

"No, thank you."

"What's going on with you? You're worried about something. I can see it. Is it your dad? I know tomorrow's not going to be easy on any of you."

"Galante might change his mind."

My heart squeezed at her need to deny the inevitable. I closed the gap between us, but she raised her hand to stop me.

"No."

"I can't hug you?"

"If you hold me, I'll tell you everything…and then you'll stop me."

"What are you saying? What's going on?"

"This is the most important time of my life. I don't want to fuck it up."

"You're talking about us?" I stepped back. "We'll be together. There's no compromise. You know that, right?"

"You've asked me to trust you. I need you to do the same for me."

"Pandora, you ditched your security. Want to tell me where you went?" I glanced at the shopping bags, which I now believed she had used as a ruse.

"I went to a coffee shop."

This was good…Pandora was opening up. My only concern was why she went there alone.

"You wanted to experience normality?" I reasoned.

"You're going to be late."

"If you need me to stay—"

"You can't, though, can you?" She arched a brow. "Optics."

"We're mere days away." I read her reaction and cringed. "What I mean is, they'll focus on more important issues other than—"

"Our suitability."

"We're almost there, sweetheart."

"Damien, I need you to remember I fought for you, too."

I went to embrace her again, but she sidestepped me.

She walked across the room to the window. "I'll call my parents."

"What will you tell them?"

"The truth. That I'm never going home."

"You must do what's right for you," I told her. "I've decided this place isn't good enough for you. I'm going to find somewhere better."

"But not your home in Foxhall?" Her beautiful eyes reflected a terrible sadness as she read the truth in my face.

"I'm in love with you, Pandora."

Her eyes closed as though the words were too much to endure.

I moved closer. "I'm a selfish bastard for not helping you escape all of this and me along with it. But I want you...for keeps. I want us to make a life together. For the first time I can remember, my life is bearable."

"Oh, Damien."

I walked over and bent down on one knee before her. "Pandora Aria Bardot—"

"You told me you'd never get on your knees."

I let out an exasperated sigh.

"Oh, you're..."

"Yes. I'm asking you to marry me. Officially. This is me letting you know I'm not going to stop fighting them until you're my wife."

"They won't win," she said softly.

"They won't win," I repeated, gazing up at her, letting my love show.

She tumbled forward into my arms and I buried my face against her belly. I felt the serenity my heart had yearned for, quietly worshiping this woman as mine. Her fingertips trailed through my hair to soothe me. This was how surrender should feel—no longer as a sense of loss but of gained freedom. There was no other place I'd rather be than here in her arms.

But I had to tear myself away. She needed to see a show of strength, needed to see I had what it took to fight for us.

Pushing to my feet, I grabbed my wallet and phone. "I'll be home as soon as possible. Don't wait up in case it's late."

She gave me a wistful smile as I headed for the door.

Leaving her alone after baring my soul felt like the hardest thing I'd ever done.

CHAPTER
FORTY-FIVE

Pandora

P hoebe and I sat in the car holding hands until it was time. I'd only just gotten to know her, but already we'd bonded over these strange set of events. Both of us had so much to lose, but if it worked, we'd be truly free.

Damien would have made it to the Fairmont Hotel by now. He'd be schmoozing with all those high-brow types. If he found out what I was doing, I feared it would mean the end of us.

With that thought eating my brain, I repositioned my short-bobbed wig. A few days had passed since I'd met with Galante, but should he see me I needed to look different. *If* he saw me, it would mean everything had gone wrong.

I could change my mind. Let those who'd found themselves on Galante's list fight their own battles. But my dad was on that list, as was Phoebe and Madeline and her lover from all those years ago. Even a potential President was on that list, his first term hanging in the balance.

It made me wonder about all the women in history who'd played their part in American politics, but had gone unrecognized.

My mind went around and around assessing if this risk would be worth it. If I succeeded, careers would survive, lives might even be saved. If I failed, the damage would be irreparable. I, too, would end up as a name on Galante's list.

"Are you second guessing yourself?" Phoebe threw me a wary glance.

"The consequences…"

"I'll get my life back." She turned to face me. "Your friend will be protected."

She meant my dad, but she'd never know his identity. She probably suspected I was doing this for the Godmans, too.

"Could we could end up in prison?" She squeezed my hand.

"What?" I hadn't thought of that…

The alarm on my phone signaled it was time.

Phoebe saw it and reached over to pull me into a hug. "Let's do this."

We embraced like two sisters, full of hope and fear, clinging to one another as though waiting for the other to see reason and call it off.

I wondered if we'd remain friends after it was all over.

Phoebe got out of the BMW and walked toward Galante's home.

If I could just calm my racing heart a little, slow my breathing, this would all be bearable. My hands wouldn't stop trembling. I hadn't made my way into his impressive home yet and I already felt guilty.

In the duskiness of evening, I regretted getting Phoebe involved and encouraging her to be a part of this crazy scheme. But deep down I knew this was the only way for her to ever be free of Galante.

There was no choice, not really.

On foot now, I made my way toward the house knowing security cameras would capture a person of interest in sweatpants and a hoodie making her way around the back of his property. I hoped this disguise would help me buy some time at least.

I huddled on the back step of Galante's home, waiting. Galante was important enough to have a high-tech security set up but I knew he didn't have security guards patrolling his property.

By now, Phoebe would be set up in the massage room.

Chewing on a fingernail, I thought through the different scenarios. Phoebe being too scared to break away from the room to sneak to the back door to let me in. Or worse, her telling Galante about my plan to garner favor with him.

What would Damien say if he found out what I'd done? He'd blame me personally if his father lost the election because of one girl's mistake—mine.

Minutes felt like hours.

Finally, the back door clicked open.

My heart hammered painfully against my chest as Phoebe ushered me in. Pausing briefly, I stepped inside and looked around to make sure this wasn't a trap. Maybe I wouldn't know until it was too late.

I followed her down a hallway.

She grabbed my arm. "Make sure the iPad has no sound. No beep, or anything."

"I know, I've got it."

She pointed. "His office is the last door on the right."

So far, Phoebe had come through for me. She really was brave, proving how much she wanted to get out of her dilemma. I needed to come through for her.

She hurried back toward the massage room. I went in the opposite direction, walking softly until I reached the room Phoebe had indicated.

Once inside, I rounded Galante's enormous desk and searched for his iPad. Within a minute, I'd located his briefcase. Amongst a stack of envelopes in there, I found the sleek device. With no way of knowing the battery life, I plugged it in to make sure it had enough juice for when we needed it.

Footsteps trailed past the office door and I ducked behind the desk and waited. Phoebe was going to provide Galante with a sixty-minute massage. At the thirty-minute point, when he was most relaxed, she would open the door to the massage room as a signal.

With time being relative, it felt like I'd been in the office for hours, but only twenty minutes had passed. I unplugged the iPad and made sure the sound was off.

My timing had to be precise.

There was also the risk of bumping into other members of his staff on my way to the private massage room. Or even his wife.

Peering around a corner to make sure the way was clear, I went for it. Forgetting to breathe, I scurried down the hallway, almost biting through my lip with dread.

Finding the door ajar, I sucked in a deep breath and peered inside the room...

Galante lay face up and was naked except for a towel covering his waist and a cloth over his eyes. His tall frame filled the length of the leather table. Phoebe's hands were digging into his right arm as though working out a knot.

I stepped lightly into the room.

Phoebe glanced up at me and gave a nod to indicate she was ready. Then she continued massaging Galante's right arm, looking as nervous as I felt.

The scent of sandalwood hung heavy in the air. I'd be triggered by that smell for the rest of my life. It was a fear-inducing scent that would always remind me of the scariest moment of my entire existence.

My hands were trembling so bad I was scared I'd drop the iPad on the hardwood floor. Phoebe seemed too terrified to make eye contact with me again. If this went wrong, she'd be destroyed by him.

Kneeling at the center point of the massage table, I lifted the iPad and waited for Phoebe to bring Galante's right arm toward it. She adjusted his wrist so it didn't come in contact with the iPad. Then swept his wrist left.

He raised his head. "Is that a draft?"

The hair on my forearms prickled.

"I don't feel anything." Phoebe's eyes were wide with fear.

Gently, she swept his wrist across the panel again. "I'll check in a second, sir."

The iPad's screen remained dark.

Shit.

"Again," I mouthed to Phoebe.

She shifted her attention to his hand, massaging his fingers. "You've got a lot of tension here, sir," she said. "Let's work it out."

He let out a sigh of frustration. "Yeah, well, if only people did their goddamned jobs."

"I know how that feels," she said, cringing at her ridiculous retort.

Again, I raised the iPad and Phoebe slid his wrist across the panel. The screen flashed on.

We were in…

Both of us stared at the blue colored screen as though still not expecting this to work. I had a minute, maybe, to search for the link to the BODI. I slid my finger across the glass, blood surging in my ears as I scoured the device for what we needed: the link to a file that was evading us.

There it was.

With another sweep of his wrist across the base of the iPad, the file opened. We had access to the BODI.

Clutching the iPad, I tiptoed toward the door.

Leaving Phoebe inside the room alone with that man felt wrong. But we were so close now to pulling this off. If we were lucky, this would be the last time she would ever have to be in that room with him.

Heading back toward his office, I tried not to pass out from sheer terror.

Breathing normally again back inside Galante's private office, I returned to my secret hideout beneath his desk. Hands trembling, I checked the battery life and then cracked open the BODI.

Names. Hundreds of them. Incidents attached to each one. A collection of scandals…of lives hanging in the balance waiting to be destroyed.

Then I saw it—Phoebe's profile.

As promised, I wiped out everything that Galante had on her.

I had fifteen minutes left to get out of here…

Mouth dry, heart racing, I opened up Google and logged into my personal drive, tapping in my code to access the cloud.

I checked the transfer time…sixteen minutes.

I didn't have that long, but I went for it anyway.

I implemented a mirror scan in case Galante had a back-up file of the BODI stored anywhere. Finding none, I opened up a brand-new document in the cloud.

And hit TRANSFER.

CHAPTER
FORTY-SIX

Damien

I should have brought Pandora with me to the Fairmont.

Her absence felt like a strike against me. All my life I'd done exactly what was expected, but I was over that now.

In my alcohol-infused state, I studied the guests. They drank the booze my father had provided for them—champagne and hard liquor, while the hotel staff offered up a variety of canapés and confections.

There were at least five hundred guests mingling in the ballroom, everyone networking their hearts out to forge the way for their own personal gains. Phones came out and heads went down between calculating conversations, the lights from their devices shimmering amidst the mass of bodies.

I'd mastered the art of escaping to a quiet corner where I would hang out with those few sincere friends I'd made over the years. Though right now, I stood alone nursing a drink. Solitude didn't reflect my ambition, I had plenty of that still left in the tank. This was about me wanting to fight for my own causes—the ones that lifted poverty off the shoulders of the needy.

I would not be derailed.

Sipping my Macallan, I reluctantly offered friendly nods to those who looked my way. With Pandora not being here, the event felt even more stifling than usual.

"Hey." Theo rested a hand on my shoulder. "How's it going?"

"Hey." I gave a shrug.

"It's going well so far, right?" He looked around as though genuinely interested in the crowd.

I arched a brow to reveal he'd triggered my senses. He knew I was on to him.

"They asked me to do the deed." He cringed. "Not sure why."

"Because I trust you?"

That blow hit him hard enough to make him flinch. "Need a cigarette?"

"I don't smoke. I gave it up, remember?"

"I know, but for some reason you're always asking me if I have one anyway. And I have one."

"You told me I had to be strong during times of stress." I looked over at him, noticing his frown. "What's wrong?"

He let out a frustrated sigh. "I have the piece they're going to run in a few hours. It'll explain why you and Pandora haven't been seen together for a while—the fact that lately you've had to put some distance between the two of you. But it's vague."

I glared at him. "Right before *Real Nation* runs its story on her dad tomorrow."

"I'm sorry, Damien." He raised his phone. "Want to see?"

"No."

"It needs your approval." He looked apologetic.

"They're gonna have a long wait."

"There's some movement on the Fairfield Project, I hear."

Raking my fingers through my hair, I tried to keep my expression serene for any of the political influencers who might be watching. "Sure does sound like blackmail."

"Want to go outside for some fresh air?"

My back stiffened. "The Fairfield Project will go ahead as planned, regardless."

"That's what we all want, right?"

"With a caveat," I ground out.

He gave me a reluctant nod; this was as shitty as it got. The fact they'd sent him was cruel to both of us.

I threw my drink back. "Should I decide my relationship is over, my father's team will be the first to know."

"That's your answer?" He looked uncomfortable, no doubt

dreading having to deliver such bad news.

"*And* let them know I won't be blackmailed with my own project."

"I'll tell your dad you need more time."

"Tell him the truth, Theo." I gestured to the barman for another Macallan.

"Right." He tucked his phone into his pocket. "Now I feel like crap."

"Why? Because you and I are best friends?"

"I've always been your wingman."

"And I yours." I slapped his back affectionately. "It's because of you we've come this far, Theo. Just in case no one ever tells you, thank you for all you've done. You're a good man."

"I don't feel like it." Theo walked away, navigating the crowd to find wherever the team had hunkered down in this big hotel, scheming and making plans that seemed to always benefit everyone else.

In four days, my father could very well be announced as the next President of the United States. The polls were looking too favorable to deny the possibility of him sitting in the Oval Office by early next year. The Godmans were about to step into history and leave a mark so indelible I'd have a book to add to my history collection about *us*.

The Godmans' speeding train had left the station and there was no getting off. On Tuesday, the polls would open, and our family would gather to watch the number of votes coming in, right alongside the American people. Soon after, the calls would pour in from leaders around the globe congratulating my dad and welcoming him to the world stage.

I'd worked tirelessly right alongside everyone else on my father's staff. I knew the privilege of this position—excitement should be the resounding emotion rushing through my veins. Yet all I could think of was *her*.

Another sip of Macallan did nothing to soothe my emotions. *Oh, hell no.*

Helen King was making a beeline for the bar.

I spun around and gestured to the barman for a glass of water. I wasn't in the mood to talk with the bitch. She'd already ruined my year. Though when the hairs on the back of my neck prickled, I knew she was behind me.

"Damien," Helen said, determined to grab my attention.

With my back to her, I tried to erase the grimace on my face. It took a few seconds to school my features into a mask of friendliness.

I pivoted to face her. "Hello, Helen."

"How are you?"

"Fucking fabulous." I tried to smile but it crashed and burned on landing. "You?"

Her fingers seemed to be gripping her glass a little too tightly. "I'm totally fine."

That statement made me wonder what other devastation she was about to unleash. Or maybe she was just here to flaunt her betrayal.

She smiled weakly. "Damien, I want to apologize for slowing down the construction on your building."

Wait…she's admitting it?

"You can be reassured it will resume first thing tomorrow."

I studied her face. "But I suppose it will have your name on it?"

"No, it will have yours."

"My father managed to persuade you, then?"

"We haven't spoken."

That was confusing. "What were you going to build there?"

"Doesn't matter now. Damien, I'm asking for your forgiveness."

What the fuck.

I'd stepped inside the Twilight Zone. I was speaking with the most ruthless woman in Washington. She'd slashed budgets that could have saved lives, cut salaries, wiped out pensions, and had always proudly taken the sickeningly large bonuses offered after the fallout. Body snatchers had grabbed up Helen King's soul. This couldn't be her.

"Do you have a twin?" I asked, sarcasm dripping from my tone.

"Excuse me?"

"I don't know what to say, Helen."

"I'm glad it all worked out in the end," she said.

Perhaps my father's people had worked their magic behind the scenes, keeping my father out of it to protect him. Though that didn't quite add up. I'd not broken things off with Pandora yet, and that was the deal, after all.

Her breath stuttered when she saw someone across the room. Following her gaze, I tried to see who'd rattled her. The evening was getting stranger by the second—Helen was staring at Pandora.

My lover approached us, looking dazzling in strappy heels and the shortest dress I'd ever seen her wear, showing off her beautiful bare legs. She was oozing sensuality, her golden locks curling over her shoulders.

She clutched a silver purse, and upon her elegant throat rested her silver key pendant.

At first I thought my inebriated state may have produced a mirage—was I really seeing this vision of loveliness? I was like a man in the desert who was desperate for sustenance. All I wanted was to taste her lips and hold her in my arms.

Wait.

She was meant to be back in the apartment where I'd hidden her away.

Pandora walked toward us with an easy grace, drawing the attention of everyone in the vicinity. She always looked striking but tonight there was something different in the way she carried herself. It was more than confidence…self-assurance, that's what she exuded tonight. I'd seen a glimpse of it back at the apartment but for some reason beneath these glittering lights it was exaggerated.

Pandora stopped a few feet away from us.

"Hello, Helen," she said with a nod.

"Ms. Bardot," said Helen respectfully.

"You two know each other?" My eyes darted from one to the other.

"We've only just met, actually." Pandora gave her a smug little smile. "We had a lovely chat a few minutes ago, didn't we, Helen?"

Helen snapped her attention back to me. "It was lovely to see you again, Damien. I wish you all the best with your project." She glanced at Pandora. "It was...nice meeting you, Ms. Bardot."

I blinked in disbelief at the impossible statistical occurrence of Helen King looking shaken. She walked away from us as though her confidence had been obliterated. The woman who had taken down kings had been intimidated, and only a source of ultimate power could have had such an effect. The possibility of my father becoming President had unnerved her, clearly.

"That was strange." I watched Helen disappear from view and then focused my attention on Pandora. "The project's back on."

"Oh, that is good news." She flashed me a brilliant smile. "I had a good feeling about it."

My heart surged with the knowledge that the Fairfield Project was happening. All those families would be given a chance to live a better life. I felt a rush of warmth and it wasn't from the whisky.

My smile widened. "You couldn't stay away from me, could you?"

She batted her eyelashes at me and snagged a glass of orange juice off a passing tray.

"I think that might have alcohol in it," I warned.

She pressed the rim of the glass to her bottom lip. "Oh."

"I thought we agreed that I'd see you later?"

"You made a decision. I vetoed it."

My lips quirked. "We're not supposed to be seen together."

"We're just having a friendly chat. People can make of it what they will. As long as there's no physical contact."

"Right...if we stand too close it would contradict the party line."

"How close is too close, I wonder?"

"If I was to step forward—" I closed the gap between us. "And, for example, put my arm around your waist…like this." I pulled her against my chest.

"That's forbidden," she said softly, her lips hovering near mine.

"Exactly." My grin widened. "It might even look as though I'm about to kiss you."

"We'd be breaking the rules."

"I hate rules."

"But they're so fun to break," she said huskily.

"Come with me." With my arm firmly around Pandora's waist I led her through the crowd, aware we were being watched as we left the ballroom.

We made it to the elevator. "Want to tell me what happened between you and Helen?"

"Not right now, no." She leaned against me.

"I insist, Ms. Bardot."

"I might have shared how important Fairfield is to you."

"I think my dad got to her."

"Ahh."

"We have a suite here. It's my dad's. They're fully booked so we can't get our own room."

"Hope it's empty."

"You're not suggesting?" I stared down at her.

"Goodness, no. That would be totally against the rules."

We ascended with lightning speed.

Once out of the elevator, I took long strides to make it to the suite, pulling her behind me.

I nodded respectfully at the security guard standing as a sentry at the door.

"Anyone in there?" I asked him.

"I don't believe so, sir."

With a slide of a keycard I opened the door for us, ushering Pandora inside.

I let go of her hand. "Let me check to make sure we're really alone."

The luxury suite had three bedrooms—all of them empty. This was a place my father or his staff could visit should they need privacy. Most of the time it went unused—it was merely a courtesy added on by hotel management.

After scouring the place, I came back into the sitting room.

Pandora stood there dressed only in her bra and panties, having removed her short dress. She still wore high-top stockings and had not slipped out of her strappy heels. I admired the sight of this erotic goddess waiting to be devoured, an exquisite beauty teasing me with her sensual decadence.

Approaching her, I tried to fathom how I was meant to live without this woman. It would be like expecting me to live without breathing—because that's how it felt when I wasn't with her.

My hand reached around her neck and I dragged her in fast, our lips close but not quite touching in a fierce showdown, as though seeing who would break first.

Me. I leaned in, trailing kisses along her neck slowly, my body thrumming with need as I breathed in her soft perfume.

She looked up at me, her eyes wide and pleading.

My hand slid up her thigh and I snagged her thong, easing her panties down so she could step out of them.

I shoved them into my pants pocket.

She looked around as though guessing where I might fuck her.

I gave her a devilish grin, unzipping my pants and pulling out my cock, and then reaching for her again. My fingers trailed along her sex to make sure she was ready.

And, oh, God, she's so wet for me.

I lifted her easily and heard her inhale sharply in surprise, instinctively wrapping her legs around my waist.

"Here?" she asked warily.

"Right here. Right now." I guided the tip of my cock between her swollen folds.

Pandora opened for me like a budding flower, gifting my cock entry into her slick warmth. I thrust deep inside her tight channel.

Pandora squirmed around me as her arousal spiked and her breaths came short and sharp. She buried her face in the crook of my neck as she moaned, her pussy milking me.

Gently rocking her to obtain deeper thrusts, I fucked her where I stood and felt a shuddering rush at the thought of being caught by anyone walking into the room. She was petite in my arms, my devastatingly beautiful lover.

The woman I was forbidden to see…

Didn't they know they'd made her more desirable? Made the taste of her even sweeter so that fucking her felt like a victory? Making her mine and letting the world know it felt like a strike against our enemies.

Having her tremble against me as she came hard felt like my birthright. She'd been bred and molded to be perfect.

She'd been created for me and that was our curse to bear.

And that was why she had to be mine.

Pandora felt like my true calling—this woman was my compass and without her I was lost.

We climaxed together, giving ourselves completely and leaving nothing unsaid.

CHAPTER
FORTY-SEVEN

Pandora

B eing careful not to wake Damien, I sat up and tried to orient myself to our latest surroundings. We'd ended up in one of the hotel's suites and had fallen asleep in each other's arms.

I felt a headache forming as I recalled the happenings of the previous evening. That's right…last night I'd broken into a news mogul's home—all in a day's work for a debutante who'd been wound too tight all her life.

After Phoebe and I had snuck out of Galante's mansion, hugged and parted, I'd driven straight back to the apartment to change. Then I'd turned up here at the Fairmont in Georgetown, dressed to the nines in the new dress I'd bought yesterday.

What the fuck had I done?

With my grogginess lifting, I replayed how I'd risked everything to carry out my scheme. But doing nothing under the circumstances would have been equally as dangerous. We would soon know if we'd fucked up. If *I* had fucked up. No one else deserved to take responsibility for my actions. This entire escapade had been my idea.

I pressed my fingers to my temples, trying to relieve the throbbing ache. All this uncertainty was making me lightheaded.

Would this be the day I lost Damien?

Don't be silly…you've gotten away with it.

I felt a tightness around my heart where there should be happiness, butterflies tickling my belly.

I pulled my panties out of Damien's jacket pocket and put them on, smiling as I remembered last night and what we'd done to each other in this suite. We'd fucked in every single room. I slid into my Versace mini dress and glanced at his sleeping form. He lay on his chest with his arms stretched languidly above his head.

I found it hard to believe that I'd been able to get so close to this mysterious bachelor. He had already been cautious when it came to love. It was hard to think I might end up hurting him if my scheme backfired.

I glanced at my watch...1:00 A.M.

We'd slept into the wee hours.

Padding toward the sitting room, I searched out something to quench my thirst and found a bottle of water. I unscrewed the cap and took a big swig, then noticed my reflection in the mirror on the far wall.

Jesus!

I almost jumped out of my skin.

Carter stood behind me, staring daggers my way.

This was his father's suite, meant to be used during functions, so his being here wasn't really a surprise. It was the way he looked at me with such arrogance and distain that sent shivers of uncertainty down my spine.

"You scared me," I whispered.

"Where's Damien?"

Raising a finger to my lips, I gestured for him to be quiet because Damien was still asleep—then immediately regretted it. Damien would shoo this asshole away, if necessary.

Carter rolled his eyes. It was obvious that we'd used this suite to have sex.

"Your father wants to talk with you."

I frowned at him. "Dad's here?"

"Downstairs."

"I have to check my hair." I hurried over to the round wall mirror and tried to brush out my disheveled locks with my fingers.

The advantage of sleeping in makeup: I actually looked well-rested with just a smudge of mascara beneath my eyes. I wiped it away to look decent again as Carter stepped forward and reached into his jacket pocket, offering me his comb.

"Thank you." I took it, wary of him.

I dragged the prongs through my golden locks and handed the comb back to him.

"My purse is in the bedroom," I explained, slipping on my high heels.

"You're not going far." He gestured toward the door.

When we stepped out into the hallway, I offered a polite smile to the bodyguard who'd remained outside all this time, remembering how kind Damien had been to the security detail on Sanibel Island.

We started down the hall and I had sudden misgivings. Turning, I tried to retrace my steps, wanting to go back to let Damien know where I'd be.

Carter grabbed my hand and dragged me along with him. I'd been too sleepy to think straight. I should have at least brought my phone.

When we reached the elevator I asked, "Is this about my future with Damien?"

Carter punched the button. "Maybe."

"I should wait for him, then?"

"He's got enough to think about right now. Dad is relying on him."

I stepped into the elevator and turned to face him. "Of course."

I hoped my dad was doing okay. No doubt he'd try to persuade me to leave with him. That wasn't going to happen. No way was I leaving this hotel with my parents. It would hurt to tell them this, but I wanted to stay in America. I wanted to be able to at least see Damien, even if only occasionally. I couldn't bear the thought of not having him in my life. All this didn't mean I wouldn't support my dad, but that news story might not happen now. Not if I had my way.

The elevator doors slid closed.

Carter stood with his hands in his pockets. He stared at the carpet, seemingly distracted.

An ice-cold chill slithered up my spine.

I had learned the hard way that he could be crueler than the devil. We'd never gotten on. He'd always seen me as a spoilt princess and I'd always seen him as the irreverent youngest son who was full of bravado, completely devoid of compassion. He'd never held back his feelings towards me or my family. Seeing his courteous behavior now set off my internal alarm bells.

The elevator landed on the basement level and the doors slid open.

Two familiar bodyguards stood there looking in at us.

One of them swooped into the elevator, lifted me up and threw me over his shoulder.

My scream echoed around us.

The burly stranger carried me out and down a hallway, the other guard walking beside us.

I struggled to get free. "Put me down."

"You've been a bad girl, Pandora," said Carter. "My dad wants a word."

Upside down and feeling nauseous, I was hauled to the end of the corridor and then man-handled through the kitchen—they were sneaking me out.

Dread saturated my flesh and I was afraid I might faint. "Where's my dad?"

Carter's hand crashed down on my butt. "I have no fucking idea."

CHAPTER
FORTY-EIGHT

Pandora

I held my trembling hands in my lap, trying to remember that I wasn't the victim here—I'd made a plan and seen it through and I was prepared to suffer the consequences. Though for some reason regret lingered like a terrible dream.

Because everything was going wrong.

I'd been hauled out of the Fairmont Hotel and into the back of a town car and driven all the way here to Senator Godman's home. They had escorted me against my will into his office and I'd been shoved into the seat before his desk.

Then I'd been told to wait and they had left me alone.

My chest constricted at the thought that Damien would wake up and find me gone, knowing he would be hurt like hell. What would they tell him? How would he react?

I wanted more than anything to be back in bed beside him. 2:00 A.M. was too early in the morning to think straight.

An hour went by—I sat there fearing the moment when Senator Gregor Godman would walk in demanding answers. This man was set to rule the free world.

I had mixed emotions when it came to my future father-in-law. I admired his determination to take on important issues. But his forceful, controlling nature had always intimidated me. Nevertheless, I respected him.

His staff had removed the landline so there was no way I could call Damien. The guard outside the room refused to let me leave.

So here I sat, with nothing to look at but Godman's plush office. A stately leather chair sat on the other side of his antique desk, a row of impressive bookshelves behind it, displaying thick tomes and photos of the Senator with public figures. There was even a picture of him with my dad.

A widescreen TV hung on the wall, its volume turned down low. A newscaster was spouting political rhetoric on Salvatore Galante's *Real Nation*. The man stated that later today they'd be releasing an exclusive story on Brenan Bardot.

Oh, God.

If I wasn't allowed near a phone that story would run.

Threatening words spilled from the presenter's mouth, revealing that information pertaining to the Presidential candidate would shake the foundation of what had been a flawless campaign. They were going to run a story on Damien's dad first thing in the morning.

Galante had no idea I'd hacked into his BODI and transferred the entire collection of scandals into my own personal cloud. That man believed he was untouchable. He had no idea that two young women had the power to take him down.

Time will tell.

I needed my phone. I needed to call Galante.

I needed to kill both of those poisonous stories.

Did Senator Godman know what was going on?

He at least knew that I'd visited Galante's home. There was no other explanation for why my ass had been hauled in here, for why I was being sequestered away from Damien and my family.

But he and his men couldn't know everything.

The door suddenly flew open and Senator Godman walked into his office with a determined stride. Tall and intimidating, he threw me a discomforting glare. Carter followed him in, his snide smile hinting that shit was about to hit the fan and he would enjoy watching.

Theo Tamer hurried in after them and closed the office door. He threw me a reassuring glance, his expression a mixture of confusion and sadness.

"Call Damien," I pleaded with him.

His sharp nod told me he'd already done so, but a disapproving glare from the Senator warned me that he would be the one dealing with this situation—and me.

"We're going to ask you a few questions," Senator Godman began, dropping into his chair behind the desk. "As you can imagine, you chose a shit-awful time to do whatever it is you've done."

I swallowed hard. "Can I explain?"

"Go ahead." Godman leaned forward, his nostrils flaring with fury. "Explain what you were doing at Salvatore Galante's home last night."

"Were you following me?"

He ignored the question. "Galante's network is now stating they have information that threatens my reputation. Coincidence? If you can't be with Damien, you'll destroy me? Is that it?"

I squeezed my eyes shut, realizing how bad this looked.

"You don't deny it?" he asked.

Theo looked devastated. "What did you do?"

"I have to make a call."

"The fuck you do," snapped Carter. "Just tell us."

"You can only imagine how disappointed your father is," said Gregor. "We're going to try to walk back the damage you've done."

"Pandora, you need to tell us what Galante knows," said Theo.

The door burst open.

Damien appeared in the doorway. He was out of breath and looking disheveled, having been woken abruptly and brought here in a haze of confusion. He'd brought my purse. Goodness knows what they'd told him. Or what he believed.

My heart soared at seeing him, even under these circumstances. But the pain in his eyes as he looked at me, along with his disbelief, cut me deep. It hurt every cell in my body knowing that I was causing him agony.

"Pandora, come with me," said Damien. "We're leaving."

Carter glared at him. "Back off!"

Damien came closer. "Tell them you never went to Galante's."

Carter sneered. "Want to see the photos of her coming out of his house?"

"She was with me," snapped Damien.

"For how long?" Carter folded his arms. "You were her alibi from what time, exactly?"

Damien stared at me in confusion. "Say something, Pandora."

"It's not what you think." I rose to my feet.

"Sit down!" snapped Carter.

I crumpled in the seat.

Carter was staring at the TV monitor. "Want to tell us what they have on my father?" He pivoted to glare at me. "We hate surprises."

"Get him out of here," said the Senator, pointing at Damien.

Damien handed over my purse to Theo. "I'm not leaving."

With the snap of an order, Damien was dragged out of the room against his will by two of Godman's men. Agony ravaged my insides at seeing what this was doing to him. To him, this must have felt like being in the pit of hell...the ultimate betrayal.

After this was over, I'd explain everything to Damien, tell him how I'd done all of this for my father and for his. I just hoped that I would get the chance—and if I did, that he would believe me.

"I need to speak with Senator Godman alone," I said.

"Carter, get out," snapped the Senator. "Theo, I want you to stay."

The sneer Carter threw me sent shivers up my spine. I breathed a sigh of relief when he left the room.

I looked at Theo, and held out my hand for my purse. "I can stop the story from airing."

"How?" said Theo, handing me the purse.

I pulled out my phone. "Galante was going to run the story on the Senator even before I went to his house. It has nothing to do with what I did."

"What did you do?" asked Theo, shock glimmering in his eyes.

"Galante has no idea I was even there."

The Senator leaned back in his chair. "We're listening."

"They are now in my possession, sir." When the Senator didn't follow, I added. "Galante's secret files."

Comprehension flashed over his face.

With shaking hands, I fished out Galante's business card and dialed his number.

"Who are you calling?" asked Theo.

"Trust me." I gave him a thin smile. "I'm making this go away."

Theo shook his head. "Pandora, if you say one wrong thing…"

After a few rings, a woman's tired voice answered the line.

"Mrs. Galante," I said, "this is Pandora Bardot. I'm sorry to wake you at this hour, but this is an emergency. Your husband asked me to call him. Can you hand the phone to him, please? This is regarding his imminent news story. He's going to want to hear this."

Theo and the Senator swapped angry looks. I clutched my phone, afraid one of them might snatch it away at any second.

I tapped the speaker setting on my phone so they could hear what was about to transpire.

Galante's gruff voice came on the line. "What do you want?"

Swallowing hard, I said, "Mr. Galante, I need you to check the BODI. I believe you'll find it's not there. I have it. Your access has been removed. Your name has been added to the list of men who have 'damaging indiscretions.'"

Galante went quiet—perhaps he was trying to verify what I'd told him.

Theo looked horrified.

Covering the phone, I mouthed. "Not that kind of BODI."

"What the hell is going on?" Galante's voice came back on the line.

"Did you look?" I asked.

"Young lady—"

"Pull the story on Senator Godman." My eyes were fixed on the TV. "And don't run the story now, or ever, on my father, Brenan Bardot. Or I'll release the intel I have on you. I have proof of how you like to spend your Friday nights."

"You and I need to have a talk," said Galante, his voice strained.

"No…no, there'll be no negotiating," I said. "Pull the story. Both of them."

The phone went dead.

A sharp, burning pain like indigestion hurt my chest. I rubbed my solar plexus with a shaky hand to soothe the ache, nausea welling up with the thought I'd just dared to threaten the most powerful man in the news industry.

"What just happened?" Theo's focus was on the TV.

All three of us watched the screen.

Within minutes, the newscaster was pressing his finger to his ear as though listening to instructions coming from off-camera— the producers, probably. His back straightened in his chair as he addressed the camera, stating that the upcoming story due later today about the Presidential candidate was being pulled until sources could be verified.

Godman rubbed his face as though trying to release pent-up tension. Then his blue eyes refocused on me. "The BODI?"

"You knew about it, right?" I asked, unable to keep my surprise from showing.

The Senator threw a wary glare at Theo.

"I had time to review the names in the file." I shoved my phone back into my purse.

"Are we talking about that mythical collection of scandals?" asked Theo.

The Senator gave a reluctant nod.

Theo shot me an astonished look. "Don't mention anything else. I don't want the Senator involved on any level."

"I get that," I said.

"Is that why you were in Galante's home?" asked Theo.

"He'll never know I was there," I told him. "I would never betray your family, Mr. Godman."

Theo shot the Senator an uneasy glance. "I think this matter is tied up, then."

"Take her home," said Senator Godman.

Theo rested a hand on my shoulder. "Your father sent a car."

I stood up slowly, my legs feeling shaky. "I wish you all the luck in the world on Election Day, Senator."

"I appreciate that." It was as calculated an answer as I could expect from a Godman; though his eyes and expression softened, as though he were seeing me in a new light. "Stay out of trouble."

"You're welcome," I said, sounding cheeky. He deserved it.

In the quiet of night, I was escorted out of the Senator's home and led toward a car.

Once inside the sleek limo, which I recognized as one of my father's, I pulled on my seatbelt, my hands still trembling. This time, I'd stood up to the Senator and I'd spoken my mind. This time, I'd come through for me.

Theo joined me in the back of the limo. "What the hell just happened?"

"I diverted a disaster."

"I'm just trying to get my head around that."

"Last person on earth and all that, I imagine."

"You imagine right. Did you really break into Galante's home?"

"A friend let me in. We probably shouldn't talk about it."

"He probably has cameras."

"He does, and I wiped all the footage from that day." *Poof*, all evidence of Phoebe and I coming and going now erased from his security system. It had been easy to hack into from inside the house, using the last sixty seconds I had left after the files had transferred into my possession.

Theo looked astonished. "I can see what Damien sees in you."

"Finally."

He gave me a sly smile. "I'm going to need access to the BODI."

I rested my head back and stared at him.

"No more games, Pandora." He held out his palm. "Write the password down, please."

"This car's not taking me home, is it?"

He looked at me with an expression I'd never seen on his face before, and then he looked away. "The driver has your passport."

I took a deep breath. "Take care of Damien. Tell him I'll always love him."

He looked stunned. "You're not going to give us access to the files?"

The person who had the access held all the power. And I wasn't ready to give it up just yet. "There's a kill switch on it."

Theo stared at me. "Pandora!"

"I need you to do me a favor, Theo." I reached into my purse and handed him an address. "Her name's Phoebe Walden. She needs to leave the city. Find her a new home where she'll be safe."

"Who is she?"

"She helped me save the campaign, Mr. Tamer. Treat her well."

"Got it." He leaned over and whispered, "Will you tell me what Senator Godman did to put him on that list?"

"Goodbye, Mr. Tamer."

With an uneasy expression, he climbed out of the car and shut the door.

The driver maneuvered the limo out onto the thoroughfare. Peering out the window, I watched the darkness fall away as we drove through the city. I recognized the route that led toward the airport.

My time in Washington, D.C. was over.

I forgave my parents for doing this to me because I understood them. They didn't know what I'd done. In saving my father, I'd sacrificed my chance to stay.

What lesson had I learned from this experience? Even if someone has hurt you, even if someone has let you down, even if someone has tried to destroy your life beyond repair, it was a sure test of your character to do the right thing no matter what.

This was the true measure of a woman's strength.

CHAPTER
FORTY-NINE

Damien

"**O**ver there!" I pointed to the jet sitting on the runway.

Recognizing the Bardot logo stamped on the side of the private plane of a lion wearing a crown, I gestured so the driver would pull up beside it.

Theo had come through for us, telling me Pandora was being driven to the airport. He had told me everything. My old friend had procured this car and had all but shoved me inside it.

Theo's words to me: "Go get her."

The town car made it through airport security in record time. Being the son of a Senator came in handy at times like this when you were willing to break all the rules and people were willing to let you.

The metal stairs were about to be pulled away from the plane. Scrambling out of the car, I rushed toward them. "Wait!"

"You're on this flight?" a crew member asked as I hurried up the steps.

"Is Pandora Bardot on here?" Without waiting for an answer, I flew in, hurrying down the short aisle, stopping only when I reached the front passenger seat and saw her sitting in the cream chair.

Pandora blinked up at me in surprise.

"This is a small plane," I said, out of breath.

She waggled her eyebrows. "Usually, I prefer them much bigger."

This was the cheeky Pandora I'd fallen for.

"You didn't think I was just going to let you leave, did you?" I reached out to steady myself on the low ceiling. "Without saying goodbye?"

A fleeting expression of sadness showed on her face, and then she said, "Did you hear the good news about my dad?"

"It means our contract is back on. You're tied to me irrevocably."

She didn't smile. "Did they send you after me because of the access I have to the BODI?"

"What?" I peered down at her. "It's true? You actually went to Salvatore's house? What were you thinking?" She started to buckle her seatbelt. "No, don't get comfortable. You're not flying off to God knows where so I can't find you."

"Is there a choice?"

"Yes, there's a fucking choice." I moved closer. "Dad told me what you did for him. That somehow you prevented *Real Nation* from airing some ridiculous lies about him."

"I have no idea what you're talking about."

"That's good. That's discreet." Looking around me, I made sure we had privacy. "Was I on the list?"

"Yes." She looked at me wide-eyed. "You certainly were."

Shit.

That meant my future was compromised. Though somehow knowing Pandora was the only one who had access to the files was vaguely reassuring. It also meant she'd been exposed to what Galante had on me.

"In what capacity?" I asked, trying to bluff.

"Really want to know?"

"Who doesn't have an orgy on their bucket list?" It had sounded funnier in my head.

She rolled her eyes at me. "Seriously?"

"You're referring to the one at Vanguard?" I said softly. "I only watched."

"Of course, you did."

"That's what my BODI entry indicated, right?"

"And you took me to Vanguard, remember?"

"You begged me." I cringed as the memories flooded in of the debauchery we'd enjoyed.

"I deleted all evidence pertaining to you."

"Thank Christ."

She looked amused. "Unless you intend to make some new memories, you're all good."

"I think I'm done there."

"Well, you never know." She brightened. "Tell Madeline I deleted all the evidence Galante had on her, too. She's a kinky bitch. Though not half as kinky as you, apparently."

I grinned. "I had to come after you."

"To get me to hand over the BODI?"

"I don't give a crap about that." I exhaled sharply. "I promise I'll never bring up that database. It will keep you safe, I imagine. That's more than I could ask—for you to be okay, more than okay. For you to thrive and be happy."

She rewarded me with a beautiful smile. "I'm sure your father's going to win."

Right, there was still that monumental event occurring in two days that had haunted my nights for years. Yet here I was, trying to win my girl back as though this was all that mattered.

But that's truly how it felt.

I took a deep breath. "It was you, wasn't it? You put the Fairfield Project back on track."

"Helen and I had a lovely chat."

"Galante had something on her? You saw her name in the BODI?"

Her lips quirked. "She's a wild one."

"Helen?" I had trouble imagining it.

"Luckily, I was able to persuade her to see how the project would benefit all of those needy families."

Her words made me wonder if I'd ever know what Pandora had on Helen King.

"What's to stop Galante from releasing the names anyway?" Then I realized the truth. "You have something on him?"

"He had an interesting way of relaxing on Fridays."

Pure disgust showed on my face; she laughed at my reaction.

"Thank you for being here, Damien. It means everything to me that you wanted to say goodbye."

"Look, Pandora, if you want to leave Washington, I won't stop you. But I love you. "I've never met anyone who's as annoying as you—"

"Thank you, I think."

"No, listen. You're my first love, Bardot. I've never come close to feeling this way about anyone else." I pressed a hand to my chest to show my sincerity. "I love the fact that you've surprised everyone, that you showed the world how incredible you are, and proved you're a remarkable woman." I paused to take a breath. "Marry me, Pandora. Have my babies. Hell, let's do it all…let's aim to live in the White House one day, with you as my First Lady."

"That's a lot to take in," she whispered.

"I get that. Only with you I feel anything is possible. I know that all this time you've been imagining your life without me."

"Maybe at the beginning. When you were a prime asshole."

"I can accept that."

I tried to read her expression, afraid that maybe I had come on too strong, been too high-handed and heavy when she was clearly vulnerable. What kind of man insisted his own happiness was more important than someone else's?

Maybe letting go and giving her the freedom she had asked for was how I could prove my love.

I stepped back. "I'm going to get off the plane, give you the space you need to decide. After all you've done for me and my family, you've more than earned your 'get out of jail free card' from me."

"Damien."

"No, listen. Don't give me an answer now. Just join me back on the runway if you still want me. I'll wait. If your plane taxis off into the blue horizon, I'll take the hint. Because if you are happier without me that's what I want for you. I'll always love you and I *need* you to know that."

Turning to go, I breathed through my sudden panic that this was goodbye. Would I be strong enough to see this through?

Could I be that man?

On the way here, the plan to set her free had felt doable. But now, with her so close, my heart was shattering with the thought that I could be minutes away from losing her.

Placing Pandora's happiness above mine, I headed back down the aisle toward the exit, fearing what kind of man I'd be without her.

CHAPTER
FIFTY

Pandora

I wondered how Damien must be feeling.

With so much happening, it was enough to have his world spinning out of control.

Today, his family would gather with their friends and strategists and the campaign staff to find out if Senator Gregor Godman was to be the next President of the United States.

Gregor might be a bastard at times, but he had the courage to lead a country into a better future. And with Damien there to remind him of important social issues that were close to his heart, much good could be accomplished by this administration.

I hoped Damien would one day find a way to forgive his family for forcing us together, and then ripping us apart. Forgiveness was a slippery friend. One minute I felt like I'd evolved enough to move on, and then other times I remembered the misjustice and it wrenched my gut.

Time would heal the chasm of hurt. I held on to that thought, at least.

Now when I looked in the mirror, I saw myself differently. Not the young woman who'd once been jostled and nudged toward a certain man who would determine her future, but a woman I respected…the new *me*.

My father's scandal wasn't that much of a surprise, really. He'd had an affair decades ago. Maybe one day I'd talk to my mother about it. According to the notes in Galante's file, she knew. He'd hoped to use it against my dad to leverage him out of politics. All that devastating evidence was wiped from the BODI. Galante had underestimated the Bardots.

I finished applying my bright red lipstick and pushed up from the seat at the vanity table, turning to look at my reflection in the long mirror. The gold blouse and pencil skirt were chic enough for this evening's event. I was ready to face the world as a confident woman who knew what she wanted and knew how to get it.

Making my way downstairs to the sitting room, I came to the conclusion that I could live here permanently. I loved this house. Leaving it would be hard, but the security wasn't as effective as it could be. Drones could fly over the wall. I remembered the day Damien had told me that, my first time here.

I adored him in every way possible.

And there he was, standing before a mirror and working on his tie, weaving it into a neat Windsor knot.

Watching Damien from across the room, I now saw this once complicated man so differently. He was a man of integrity, willing to fight for all that was good, including *us*.

He hadn't noticed me yet. I cherished these stolen moments.

I saw his mouth forming the words of his speech as he practiced, clearly hoping he would have reason to deliver it tonight to the public if the election went their way.

I admired the handsome lines of his face, the dark suit that clung to his tall, toned body. The way his brow furrowed as his thought processes played out on his gorgeous features.

When I'd boarded my family's jet, I'd never expected to see Damien again. We'd both had our chance of escaping our arrangement.

I'd peered up at this man and realized how much I'd fallen for him. It had happened so quickly. I'd hardly recognized the fake fiancé I'd once hated. He'd become the man I now loved with all my heart.

Finally, Damien saw me standing in the doorway. "You look beautiful."

"You scrub up nicely yourself." I smirked.

His mouth curled at the edges. "I'm always up for a good scrubbing."

"Is something happening tonight? Remind me."

"Can't believe it. Years in the making."

"You're so calm."

"We did everything we could." He brightened. "We had you, our secret weapon."

"You know, *you're* his secret weapon in all this, Damien. The loyal son, willing to give everything up for your dad."

"I have my limits." He looked over at me. "Some things are too precious to lose."

I smiled. "They really are."

He sighed. "Ready to join the family?"

We strolled down the hallway and paused by the front door, as though rallying our courage to leave the house and go watch history unfold.

He glanced at his phone. "We'll soon hear about votes coming in from Florida."

"Exciting. How's everyone holding up?"

"As well as can be expected, considering the pressure."

"How about you?" I fiddled with his already neat tie. "You're the only one I care about."

"I'm glad you're with me."

"Now that you've tasted the edge of power, Damien Godman, are you craving it for yourself?"

"I fit the profile. Grumpy bastard with an egocentric personality."

"Yes, but with the right woman by your side to remind you of what's important."

He gave me a knowing look. "What's so important?"

"This—" Reaching behind my skirt, I unfastened the catch.

It fell to the floor, pooling around my feet, showing off my lacy thong and black stockings. I unbuttoned my blouse flirtatiously.

Before us was the door that would lead out to the waiting car. Behind us, the red door that led to his room of pleasure waited.

His jaw went slack as he took in my half-dressed state. "Well, you've got my vote."

"Want to lead the way?"

He moved toward me swiftly and shoved me back against the wall, cornering me there. "What you're inferring is that you want to make us late, Ms. Bardot. That you're willing to seduce me so that I forget how important today is."

"Well, yes. That's exactly what I'm doing."

He stepped back abruptly. "I will have to fuck you hard for this."

"As a punishment?"

"I will be showing you what happens to very bad girls who blow off elections."

"These things always take time. We have hours to go before the final decision."

"Indeed." He threaded his fingers through mine and pulled me along the hallway toward the red door. Together we descended the steps into his dungeon.

He paused in the center of the room, looking thoughtful. "I know I promised to never talk of it, but…"

"Go on."

"Maybe we should clear something up?"

Easing my blouse open, I said. "I'm listening."

"We should talk about the elephant in the room."

My gaze moved to his groin.

"Not that." He rolled his eyes.

"What then?"

"Pandora's fucking box?" He pressed his point with his hands sweeping through the air. "Pandora's Box!"

"I had thought about that, yes."

"What are you going to do with all that power?"

"Harness it." I paused, thinking. "I may delete it all. Haven't decided."

"Think of the careers you'll save. Your father is going to be the Foreign Secretary for the U.S."

"Your reputation was also my priority." I flashed him a cheeky look. "And your father's, too, I suppose."

"You're my everything. You know that, right?"

"Show me what I mean to you," I purred the words as I peeled off my blouse.

Damien was on me fast, nudging me backward toward the bed and shoving me onto it. Leaning low, he tugged at my panties, ripping them off and burying his head into my sex, causing me to moan as his mouth possessed a sacred part of me.

"You taste amazing," he said gruffly, moving up my body and lifting my arms so that he'd pinned me against the bed. "Pandora Godman...it's got quite a ring to it."

"Tell me you'll love me forever, Damien."

He squeezed his eyes shut for a beat. "I have a confession."

"Am I going to like it?"

"I married you the day I met you. You were distracted with the hem of your dress, and that glass of champagne you spilt on me, and the canapés you couldn't seem to get enough of—"

"Hey!"

"Then I brought in the marching band and we had a ceremony right there at your debutante ball, ten seconds after we met. You don't remember?"

"I thought you hated me back then."

"I knew then that if I gave my heart to you, I'd never get it back. It scared me."

"What changed?"

"You stole my heart anyway, Pandora. Like a burst of light that chased away my shadows. You broke down my defenses and proved love always wins."

He let my wrists go.

Leaning up, I pressed my mouth to his and kissed him leisurely, feeling his lips soften against mine. I cupped his face with affection. "Let's promise to always be there for each other. No matter what life throws at us."

"Think of what you and I can achieve together as equals, as

husband and wife. Best friends. Lovers. Soul mates. Give me the chance to prove it to you. To stand between you and the world and stop it from ever hurting you again—or at least try. I want to marry you."

"You've already asked me, remember?" I whispered.

"That was the old Pandora. I'm talking to Pandora 2. 0. The woman who altered the course of history."

"It's still a yes." I brushed my fingertips through his hair. "Let's make this world a better place."

"You already have," he whispered, as his lips crushed mine.

And sometimes, I mused, being a little late is still fashionably early.

Especially when making history.

ALSO FROM AUTHOR VANESSA FEWINGS

MAXIMUM DARE

PERVADE LONDON and PERVADE MONTEGO BAY

PERFUME GIRL

THE ENTHRALL SESSIONS:

ENTHRALL, ENTHRALL HER, ENTHRALL HIM,
CAMERON'S CONTROL, CAMERON'S CONTRACT,
RICHARD'S REIGN, ENTHRALL SECRETS, and
ENTHRALL CLIMAX

&

THE ICON TRILOGY from Harlequin:
THE CHASE, THE GAME, and THE PRIZE

vanessafewings.com

ABOUT THE AUTHOR

USA Today Bestselling Author Vanessa Fewings writes both contemporary romance and dark erotic suspense novels. She can be found on her Facebook Fan Page and in The Romance Lounge, Instagram, Twitter and Goodreads.

She enjoys connecting with fans all around the world.